B

Bluebeard's Room

Emma Cave

CORONET BOOKS
Hodder and Stoughton

First published in Great Britain in 1995
by Hodder and Stoughton

First published in paperback in 1995
by Hodder and Stoughton
A division of Hodder Headline PLC

A Coronet paperback

British Library Cataloguing in Publication Data

Cave, Emma
Bluebeard's Room
I. Title
823.914 [F]

ISBN 0-340-63250-X

Typeset by Avon Dataset Ltd, Bidford-on-Avon

Printed and bound in Great Britain by
Cox & Wyman, Reading, Berks

Hodder and Stoughton
A division of Hodder Headline PLC
338 Euston Road
London NW1 3BH

To Anne, with love

'For there is no friend like a sister'
Christina Rossetti

Acknowledgements

My thanks to the Imperial War Museum, London, the Museum of Tolerance, Los Angeles, the British Council Library, Nicosia, and to Sir M.G., I.V.S.E., P.C., G.H., I.K., and J.M.

Warmest gratitude to Shirley, Kyle, Philip, Bill and Margaret, Gill, the late Meric Dobson and, most especially, Camilla, for unfailing help and patience. Also to George.

This book, set in the summer of 1989,
is Volume One of the *Rooms* Chronicle

Part One

LUCY

One

In London, this summer was hot and humid. By early evening on the last Sunday in July, the sun was latent in a haze the colour of dirty linen. In this long Kensington street, the dull light matched the buff stucco of the houses: two facing terraces, each topped by a squat balustrade.

The street seemed narrower than it was because the houses were heavy: their square porches had thick pillars; their big front doors and double railings of iron spikes were painted black.

Traffic could be heard from neighbouring streets; here there were only parked cars. On the left pavement, two women were coming towards each other.

The one slouching down towards the Cromwell Road was not tall, though high heels raised her. She wore a short black skirt, and her bare legs were lean. A sleeveless black satin blouse, cut low, showed a corded neck hung with heavy gold chains. One bony hand – her nails were long and purple – gripped the strap of a snakeskin bag.

Actors in stage make-up look bizarre by daylight. This woman's face had that inordinate quality. Even her thicket of cochineal hair could not dim the maroon flush on her cheeks, the violet lids of eyes slightly darker than her yellow-brown skin, the thick vermilion grease that enlarged her mouth.

The other woman – taller, even in flat shoes – walked faster. She wore jeans, with her hands in the pockets of a loose khaki jacket, open over a plain white T-shirt. A blue, bolster-shaped weekend bag hung from her left shoulder.

In this hot summer, her fair skin was the colour of a pale-brown eggshell. She had grey eyes and a nose not too long for a face longer than oval: a serious face, lightened by her smile-shaped mouth. The mouth was charming; what was remarkable was her thick Rapunzel plait of champagne-coloured hair.

Both women had been walking in the centre of the pavement. They noticed each other simultaneously, four houses apart. The fair woman blinked; the dark one's look expressed an inherent acrimony.

At about three metres distance, the fair woman swerved slightly; the other did not diverge at all. The sight of purple-nailed fingers against snakeskin and a gust of bitter-sweet scent made the fair woman shrink, as from something scorching. Passing her, the dark woman said, 'What *you* grinning at, hey?'

'Me?' The fair woman hesitated, half turning her head, but the other moved on without a backward glance; now so did she, faster than before and frowning, her shoulders tensed as if to stop her looking back until she reached her destination near the top of the street: a house with an old well-kept Jaguar coupé parked outside. Seeing the car, she smiled. Now she allowed herself to glance back down the street: the dark woman was no longer in sight. She started down stone basement steps behind the double railing of black spikes.

The basement window was a large square of glass with two narrow slats open at the top. Behind was a closed venetian blind. At the bottom of the steps was a door, black like the front door above. She pressed a bell labelled 'Deyntree'; a thin high buzz sounded inside.

4

She waited, rang and waited. A minute passed. She glanced up at the parked Jaguar and frowned. She sighed. Her hand hovered near the bell, but she was turning back towards the steps when the venetian blind twitched. She called out, 'Rupert! It's me – Lucy.'

Behind the blind, a man exclaimed 'Lucy!', then called, 'Hang on.'

'Right.' She sat down on the third step, dumping her blue bag on the ground. Several minutes passed. Her glance lighted on a red and white cigarette packet below the railing. She went to pick it up and drop it into a black dustbin: the only object in the small glum basement area. She was replacing the dustbin lid when the door opened.

'What on earth are you doing, Lucy?' The man standing in the doorway, who wore a dark-blue towelling bathrobe, laughed.

She laughed too. 'You know how I hate litter. I was disposing of some. What were *you* doing, lurking behind that blind?'

' "Lurking", indeed! How sinister you make it sound. I just wanted to see who was there. I didn't think you'd be back from Yorkshire. Why didn't you telephone? I might have been out. As it was, I'd fallen asleep.'

'I should have telephoned, but there was a queue. I took a chance, and came straight from the station.'

'Anyway, it's amazing to see you, darling.'

Rupert's oldest friend, Francis Larch, sometimes said, 'Rupe has a typical Old Etonian glamour,' adding, 'although he didn't go to Eton.' Nowadays, Francis would also remark, 'Age simply *cannot* wither him.'

Even Lucy's mother – Rupert's enemy – admitted he looked young, but she added, to Lucy, 'He's old enough to be your father.'

'Twenty-two when I was born? Very young to be a father!'

5

'But perfectly *possible*. And his mouth's so petulant.'

'It's not petulant. It's sensitive.'

Lucy's hair was remarkable; so were Rupert's eyes. There is a plant called ceanothus with flowers of a derangingly seductive blue. Could blue be bluer . . . yet hasn't it a hint of slate? This question can nag someone who has glimpsed it till they return to check. (If they wait a week they may find only dusty leaves.) Rupert's eyes, with their ceanothus colour, and an added shine, had a similar effect: people glanced at them repeatedly.

In the course of his forties, Rupert's blond hair had faded rather than greyed; usually it was lighter than his skin. But today he was pale, and now Lucy said, 'Are you feeling ill? You look exhausted.'

'No. It's just the weather, and that Sunday feeling. *There's a time on Sunday when the nails of clenched fingers dent the palms.*'

'Is that a quotation?'

Rupert often quoted but now he said, 'No, I don't think so. I invented it. Come on in.' He held the door open, and she picked up her bag and went inside. Dropping the bag on the floor, she turned to him, but he stepped back. 'I must have a shower,' he said. 'I feel sweaty and revolting. It's so muggy today.'

'It was wonderful up on the moor.'

'*She dwelt among the untrodden ways.*'

'That "Lucy" poem of yours!'

'Not mine – Wordsworth's.'

'Yes. You're always quoting. You're just like my mother.'

'Heaven forbid.'

'Oh, Rupert!' It was a reproof but a half-hearted one. Lucy was sniffing now. 'What an awful smell,' she said. 'Is it air-freshener?'

'Mmm. I just puffed some round. It gets a bit stuffy down here.'

'Of course it does, in this horrible basement, with no proper windows, just those slats. And I'm sure it's damp. Basements always are. Mouldy. But nothing could be worse than that air-freshener.'

He laughed. 'Stop complaining. How about a drink?'

'No, not now, thanks. Have your shower. Then I'll tell you my news.'

'News?'

'After your shower.'

'All right, bossy.' He smiled as he crossed the large dim room, and went through a door at the far end, shutting it behind him. Lucy stood for a moment, frowning and sniffing.

This flat was rented furnished. A sofa and two armchairs had muddy Jacobean-patterned chintz covers. Small tables were dotted about, and an empty grate was surrounded by tiles the colour of turtle soup.

The large dining-table had become Rupert's desk – he never entertained at home – with angled lamp, computer, telephone, answering machine and fax. On a trolley in front of the sofa were a television and VCR. Two bookcases – one tall, the other long and low – held a varied collection of books, and on the low one, video cassettes were stacked. Personal possessions were few. On a small table by the sofa was a misty Lenare 'studio portrait' of Rupert's mother who had died when he was seventeen. Calm, beautiful, with a centre parting and a large, fair coil of hair, she wore a single string of pearls.

Lucy went over to the fireplace. On the way, she picked up and put down a video cassette that lay on top of the television; its cover showed a man in a dark suit firing a machine-gun. Lucy did not share Rupert's fondness for Mafia films which, he told her, had replaced an earlier taste for Westerns. 'But they're so violent,' she said, when he told her he found them relaxing. 'Bang – another baddie bites the dust,' he had answered, laughing, and she laughed too: she usually laughed when he did, and he laughed often. Shortly before he died, her father had told her that she must marry someone who made her laugh.

Now she stood looking at the picture that hung above the fireplace, as she usually did when she came to the flat. 'What is it?' she had asked on her first visit.

'It's a Blake. An original colour print. Quite valuable as he finished it himself, with pen and watercolour, like the one in the Tate gallery. It's called "The Good and Evil Angels".'

The Evil Angel filled two-thirds of the picture, on the left. He hovered in space, naked, with extended arms. His face was furrowed and ravaged; he seemed to stare, yet his raised lids revealed only sightless, unmarked marbles of flesh. He seemed to press forward, but his ankle was bound with a heavy fetter: bronze like the pointed flames that, darkening his flesh, rose behind him.

On the right – backed by the rising sun – The Good Angel, also naked, was poised above clouds: upright, though the force of the bronze flames blew back his hair. The Good Angel was pale, like the child in his arms that shrank in horror – surely it shrieked? – from blind stare, outstretched arms, seeking tongues of fire.

'That child *must* be safe,' Lucy said the first time she saw the picture. 'The Good Angel's holding it. The Evil Angel has that great chain on his foot. And yet one can't be sure.'

'No, one can't, can one? The Evil Angel is in command.'

'In command?'

'Of the picture, I mean. He dominates the picture. So one feels . . .'

'But that's a very heavy chain. And, after all, he's blind.' Lucy paused, then she said, 'They're angels, but they haven't any wings. I always thought of wings, as a child, when I prayed to my Guardian Angel. As a matter of fact, I still do.'

'Still pray to your Guardian Angel?'

'Yes. And think of great, soft, enfolding wings.'

'Enfolding wings . . .' That was the first time he put his arms round her. It was a week after they met, at a charity art auction. Lucy was there because she worked for the charity, Rupert because he enjoyed art sales.

Later she told Rupert she didn't know whether she liked the picture or not. He said, 'You must learn to love it for my sake. It's my most precious possession.'

'I'll try.' Today, after studying it, head on one side, for a minute or two, she went and lay down on the sofa, eyes closed, feet crossed at the ankle, hands clasped on her chest.

'You look so peaceful,' said Rupert. She opened her eyes. In khaki trousers and a cream silk polo-neck sweater – he was fond of polo necks – he was standing looking down at her. She smiled and stretched out her hands. He pulled her to her feet and they kissed.

It was she who drew away. She said, 'Don't you want to hear my news?'

'Of course I do.' Holding hands, they sat down, side by side, on the sofa.

'Mummy's come round at last,' she said.

'*Really*?'

'Yes – really. She's had a letter from that pet Monsignor of hers at the Metropolitan Tribunal, confirming that there's no religious obstacle. Those civil marriages don't count. And this weekend I convinced her that, as there's no problem with the Church, I'm determined to go ahead. She has to accept it. And I've told her she must stop talking about your age and never call you "Bluebeard" again.'

Rupert laughed.

'It's not funny,' Lucy said. 'It's awful. I mean, Bluebeard *murdered* his wives. Yours are perfectly all right.' She tilted her chin; the line of her jaw was beautifully clean. 'And we're going to Rivers next weekend.' ('Rivers' was the abbreviation members of Lucy's family used for Rivendale, their Yorkshire house.)

'I shall be terrified.'

'What nonsense! She'll have a chance to get to know you at last.'

'That's just what I'm afraid of.'

'Silly!' she exclaimed, but she was smiling.

He pulled her plait forward over her shoulder. Her hair was her one vanity. Her father had loved it, and her mother disliked it, saying that long hair was 'dowdy' or 'arty'. Today it was in a simple plait, an elastic band on the crown and another above the tassel at the end, but she did it in many different ways. Sometimes she coiled it; sometimes she wore it in a French pleat; at other times, she plaited the sides together and let the middle part hang down straight behind the braid. Rupert's special pleasure was to unplait it. She would shake her head and it would fall down in a silky cape that reached her thighs. He would bury his face in it and quote from Browning: '*Kissing her hair . . .*' He was fiddling with the elastic now, as he said, 'Can we actually name the day?'

She twitched the plait back over her shoulder. She said, 'Well, actually, I agreed we'd be engaged for six months. So that she can get to know you better. And it'll give you more time to decide if you really want to become a Catholic.'

'But I do.'

'I want you to be quite sure. It would be lovely to have a Nuptial Mass, but it's not necessary. Rupert, you must be really sure.'

'You're so sweet when you're serious.'

'It's a serious subject.' But she smiled. 'Anyway, we can put the engagement in *The Times* right away.'

'*The Times*?'

'Yes – and the *Telegraph*. A lot of Mummy's friends read the *Telegraph*.'

10

Rupert was frowning. 'Aren't I a bit ancient to be announcing my engagement in the papers? And doesn't it seem a bit absurd after . . . those other marriages?'

'No. This is a fresh start – and a real marriage. I agree it's a bit old-fashioned, but Mummy is old-fashioned. I think when it's in the paper, she'll really accept that it's a fact. I thought we could put it in this coming Friday – I'll organize it. That's the day we go to Rivers. When you go away on your trip on Monday, everything will be settled.'

'*Alles in Ordnung*.'

'What does that mean?'

'All in order.'

'Oh Rupert,' she said, 'do you think I'm bossy?'

His laugh was warm. 'Darling, of course I don't. You're just highly efficient. Blissy Lucy!'

'Blissy! I love that 1920s word of yours.'

'I actually acquired it in the late 1950s.'

Lucy – born in 1962 – shrugged as if the two decades were equally remote. Now they kissed again, at length. This time, when she pulled away, her cheeks were flushed and her pupils dilated. She said, 'Please don't let's get started . . . blissy Rupert.'

'Even now we're engaged?' But he leant back on the sofa, folding his hands behind his head. He gazed up at the central light-fitting: a wheel, from which rose fake candles topped with pointed bulbs. Lucy put a hand on his arm.

He turned to look at her. He smiled. He said, 'You must be the only twenty-seven-year-old virgin in England.'

'What nonsense!' She laughed.

'Apart from cripples.' She winced at the word and he changed it: ' . . . handicapped people. And nuns. My darling, can God really care whether you're a virgin or not?'

She said, 'If one believes in a religion, one ought to practise it. I would have thought you'd understand . . . after taking instruction.'

'I do really. It's just that now we've plighted our troth in earnest. Putting it in *The Times*.' They both laughed.

She said, 'We'd done that already. With my lovely ring.' She stretched out her left hand: two sapphire hearts were entwined and encircled with tiny flowers made of seed pearls and garnet chips, and with sprays of leaves that sparkled with minuscule diamonds.

'You really like it?'

'I love it. It's perfect. And it's so nice that it was your mother's.'

He said, 'And that I saved it for you . . . my little virgin.'

She said, 'A church wedding . . . the white dress – all that would be dishonest—'

'Darling, don't get upset. It's just that I find you irresistible.'

'I'm glad of that.' She smiled. Then she said, 'I thought we might go out.' She glanced at her cheap, efficient, digital watch. Rupert begged to buy her a prettier one, but she had refused: 'I like cheap watches. They work just as well, and it doesn't matter if you lose them.' Now she said, 'It's nearly seven. We could go to the Firenze and then have an early night. You do look tired you know – even though you slept this afternoon. Let's do that. Anyway, I'm famished.'

'That noble appetite! It's amazing you're so slim.'

'I'm not *thin*, though,' she said. 'Some people say you can't be too thin.'

'Not me. I loathe really thin women. They're all neurotic. Byron said the young ones were like dried butterflies and the old ones like spiders.'

'Ugh.' Lucy stood up. She glanced round the room. 'We'll have to start looking for somewhere to live,' she said.

'Yes. We'll have to buy something. I've been lazy.'

'Mmm. It's amazing you've borne this gloomy place so long. This awful basement.'

'Oh come on – it's not *that* bad.'

'I hate this part of London anyway. My mother had a terrible old aunt who lived just round the corner from here. Whenever we were in London we went to Sunday lunch with her, after Mass at the Oratory.'

'*I* think the Oratory's rather charming, though you don't like it.'

'No. It's so smart. I always meet friends of my mother's there. Don't let's buy anything round here. Anyway, it's fearfully expensive. We'll have to buy furniture, too.'

'It's a shame . . . when I think of all that stuff in Islington.'

'Did she have to keep all the furniture as well as the house? It's not even as if you'd had children. I could never be so . . .' She left the sentence unfinished.

'So grasping. Of course you couldn't, darling Lucy. But you're not Chris – thank God.' He shrugged. 'Oh well, I never much liked living in Islington – too yuppie.'

'Hampstead's the only part of London I know really well. I wish we could find something there.'

'Hampstead's fearfully expensive,' Rupert said.

'Mmm. But we might be lucky. When the Dumbles come back, I'll get Mag onto it.'

'The Dumbles! Such a ridiculous name – and rather ridiculous people.'

'Oh, but, Rupert, they've been so wonderful to me. I've been so happy staying with them.'

'I know, darling. I was only joking. You're so fiercely loyal. "Love me, love my Dumbles!" '

Lucy laughed. 'Oh, you don't have to *love* them. Apart from me – of course – the only person you have to love is Vee.'

'The famous Vee! I'll do my best. Is she fearfully aggressive?'

'No – why do you say that?'

'American women so often are.'

'That's just prejudice. Oh Rupert, you're bound to like her.

I'm longing for you to meet. She'll be coming over soon, when her tour's ended. Though there's some guy she's keen on. But she's definitely coming. *She* wants to meet *you* – after all, she's my best friend.'

'And not tough as old boots?'

'Anything but!' After a moment she repeated, 'Tough as old boots. Chris sounds rather like that, to me.'

'Oh she is – the archetypal yuppie. Callous, ambitious, ruthless . . . hard as nails. And, as you say, tough as old boots.'

After a moment Lucy said, 'It's odd, in a way, that you fell in love with someone like that.'

'She seemed so cool and capable. After the chaos of life with Barbara.'

'Well, I suppose she was.'

'Was what?'

'Cool and capable.'

'Cold and calculating's a better description. I thought she was calm. But actually she's very neurotic.'

'And thin?' Lucy smiled.

'Oh, *very* thin. And now on her way from dried butterfly to spider.'

He laughed, but Lucy's expression was thoughtful. She said, 'I'm sure she must have hurt you terribly.'

'You're so sweet.' He stood up. 'Shall we go now?'

'Yes.' By the door, she picked up her weekend bag.

He said, 'Why don't you leave that here? We'll fetch it after dinner, and I'll drive you home.'

'No. An early night, remember. I'll go by tube.'

He sighed. 'That baffling passion for public transport! And then you'll have to walk alone back to that empty house.'

'Yes – nice and peaceful.' She slung the bag over her shoulder.

'At least let me carry that thing.'

She shook her head. 'No, it's not a bit heavy.' He shrugged.

14

Then he opened the front door and stood back for her to go out ahead of him. In the area, as he locked the door she said, 'Vee may think your amazing manners are chauvinistic.'

'I guessed as much!'

'But I think they're nice. I was telling Mummy how you open doors and walk on the outside of the pavement and all that.'

'And she undoubtedly said it shows how ancient I am.'

Lucy blushed as she started up the steps. Then she said, 'Mummy loves good manners.'

'Admit she said that.'

Ignoring this Lucy said, 'I met such a weird woman on the way here. Out of the blue she asked me what I was *grinning* at. And I wasn't even smiling.'

'Weird indeed – and appallingly rude.' Then he said, 'It's the shape of your mouth. Like the smile on Greek statues. The archaic smile, it's called.'

They were on the pavement now, and Lucy gestured ahead. 'We passed just down the road here. She was strange-looking. Dark – perhaps she was Indian – but with orange-red hair. It must have been dyed. Dressed all in black with terribly thick make-up and horrible scent. Actually she was rather creepy. When I was a child we had a maid who used to frighten me with stories about someone called Winnie with the Long Green Hands. This woman reminded me of that – though of course her hands weren't green. They were brown. Very bony, with long purple nails.'

'She sounds gruesome,' Rupert said.

'Yes she was rather. Goodness, Jessie – that maid – used to frighten me. My father found out and made her leave. Mummy was annoyed because she was good at her work, but Daddy insisted and I was so relieved. She told me that when dogs barked for no reason it was because the Evil One was passing by.'

15

Rupert laughed. 'Why, I can hear a dog barking now.' And indeed, not too far away, a dog gave a series of deep barks. Rupert looked up and down the street. 'No sign of the devil!' he said.

Lucy said, 'I ought to laugh but I can't. At the time, it really terrified me.'

'Poor darling.' Rupert squeezed her hand. Then he said in a light tone, 'Perhaps Colonel Al will be at the Firenze tonight.'

Lucy laughed. 'Perhaps he will.'

Al Dente, who liked to be addressed as 'Colonel' but was actually a mafioso, was one of a range of characters invented by Rupert. There was Con Brio, feckless and garrulous, half Irish and half Italian. 'So of course,' Rupert would say, 'he's the ultimate con man.' There was Ludi Kraus, an earnest German. There was Sir Percy Flage who had an airy manner and a secretive French wife called Camou. Uttered by Rupert, these puns never failed to make Lucy giggle. Now he said, 'Perhaps the Flages will be there tonight. Camou really only likes French food, but pasta's smart at the moment, and you know what fashion-snobs the Frogs are.'

'You're full of prejudices.' But as she said it, she took his arm. They were a striking couple and anyone seeing them would have guessed they were in love.

Dink had travelled on the Underground from Gloucester Road. Now she slouched across the bus terminus outside Finsbury Park station. A beige man, reading the *News of the World* in a 19 bus without a driver, gave her a startled, avid glance as she passed.

She turned left under the railway bridge where 'Thatcher Out' was sprayed – bloody on the bricks – above an Emva Cream Sherry bottle and three Strongbow cans. Dink kicked a can. Its rattle towards the gutter was drowned by a sudden passing of a train overhead. In the hot greyness, this hot roar gave a momentary sense of thunder.

Today the greengrocer's window showed only some hairy roots, matted with earth. The butcher's trays were desolately white, though 'Cow heels! Pig tails' was chalked on a blackboard. Next door, straight tresses hung against the glass with a hand-lettered card, 'Human Hair – Special Price'; a poster for skin-bleach had faded to cream and grey. Passing it, Dink raised a hand to her cheek. In a TV shop, three lit screens showed the same picture of teams of men rolling in mud.

So far Dink had met no one. Now two people were coming towards her: black, elderly and dressed for church. The man – slightly the shorter – wore a dark suit and tie, the woman a navy-blue dress and matching hat of shiny straw.

Sighting Dink, they perceptibly flinched from the shock of her lounging walk, her garish hair and make up, her shining chains. Their bodies stiffened in righteousness.

Like a lion as it begins its charge, Dink accentuated the swing of flank and shoulder. Ignoring the man, she surveyed the woman: broad feet in broad shoes, legs solid from shoe to skirt-hem in stockings that looked dusty because they were lighter than her skin. Dink's steady gaze moved up – bored by every inch of the thick body – until it reached the large solemn face. Now, for an instant, Dink closed her eyes. Opening them again she gave a lion's yawn.

As earlier, in Kensington, she held her ground in the middle of the pavement. However this new opponent – unlike Lucy – did not budge; the woman even gave her grey plastic handbag a small combative swing. But then the man grasped her sleeve tugging her aside as if to draw her attention to the shop they were passing. Dink raised her eyebrows. It was a barricaded off-licence; the couple's teetotal aura was now reinforced by the woman's affronted look and an angry shrug which however did not quite free her from the man's hold. Dink, just as she passed them, flipped up the back of her skirt. She swung her buttocks – accentuated rather than covered by a strip of crimson lace – towards them. The man's jaw dropped, and the woman gasped. Dink, letting her skirt fall back into place, turned left into a side street called Tolland Road. Her good teeth, white and even, showed for a moment in a smile.

Just round the corner, a shop was open, and Dink went inside. Near the door, on a shelf under a rack of shiny magazines, a few Sunday papers still lay. Dink's eye was caught by a tabloid headline. She picked up the paper and, holding it close to her face, scanned the story on the front page before turning to its continuation inside. This failed to hold her interest; she dropped the disordered paper back on the shelf.

From the moment she came in, the middle-aged Indian behind the counter had watched her with recognition and dread. Now, as she turned towards him, he looked away. 'Twenty Marlboro,' she said. He took the cigarettes from a shelf behind him and put them on the rubber mat that lay between the till and a tinsel profusion of sweets and chocolate. Dink opened her snakeskin bag.

The back of the shop held two double-sided stands of groceries and, against the end wall, a large cold cabinet and freezer. It was a small supermarket: self-service, but when Dink said, 'Small milk,' the shopkeeper scarcely hesitated before he went to fetch it. Out darted Dink's bony, long-nailed hand to snatch a bar of chocolate and slide it into her open bag before he came back with a small carton of milk and put it on the mat next to the Marlboros. His glance went to a space where the chocolate had been but then shifted nervously to the till. After he had rung up the cigarettes and milk, he put them in a paper bag. 'Carrier,' Dink said, and he put the bag into a plastic carrier. She took it, paid and left. As she went out he shivered. There was sweat on his forehead and he wiped it with the back of his hand.

This shop was the only one in Tolland Road. Beyond it, on

both sides, were small terrace houses of sallow London brick. Their front gardens were tiny, but gates and fences reaffirmed the meagre privacy asserted by wan net at every window.

The terrace was followed on the side where Dink walked by a brutally red brick box of flats. A sign said that the building across the road was a church, but it looked like a hall of judgement. Its blackened stone bulk, fronted by pocked, scabbed columns, reared above a ponderous flight of steps. A slab was missing from the heavy cornice: this gap seemed to threaten that the whole building would topple forward.

Looking up can be as dreadful as looking down: the weight of a black sky or a menacing structure can evoke terror of being crushed, suffocated, buried. Dink, across the road, glanced away; outside the red flats a small girl stood staring at her. Dink puffed out her cheeks and squinted. The child turned and ran into the building; again Dink's teeth glinted white.

Next to the church was a builder's yard, its high walls topped by tangles of barbed wire. Dink took her Marlboros out of the carrier and a yellow throw-away lighter from her bag. Dropping wrappings on the ground and then lighting a cigarette she started to cross the road. On the other side a small car was approaching. The driver hooted but she took no notice. He shouted as he jerked to a halt within a metre of her but then, as she stepped onto the pavement, drove on.

A metal sign on the door of the builder's yard showed an Alsatian's head and the words 'Beware of the Dog', though someone with black paint had changed 'Dog' to 'God'. Dink banged on the sign; from inside came a sound that was half bark, half howl, then silence. Dink moved on.

The next house – identified as 63 by contorted metal numbers placed aslant on its brown-varnished door – stood on its own: three storeys of very yellow brick and a grey slate roof. It was narrow and ill-proportioned; the ground-floor bay window, placed too high, looked as if it had been added as an afterthought, like the unrailed front steps with their high uneven treads.

Although set back from the road, on a corner site, this house had no garden. From the builder's wall to the pavement on the other side and in front, all the ground was cemented. Only a small part of this bleak space was taken up by a neat Japanese car, an old Volkswagen, and three dustbins near the steps at the top of which two urns of mauve geraniums seemed only to accent the general dreariness. An elaborate pink satin festoon-blind in the bay window looked preposterous.

As Dink mounted the steps, she pulled a key ring – embellished with a gilt high-heeled shoe – from her bag. At the top, she ground out her cigarette in one of the urns.

By the door were the bells of the three tenants. The house had been bought long ago by a Turkish Cypriot. His first action had been to cement its garden. ('For convenience,' he always said, presumably meaning that it provided parking and needed no upkeep.) Then he converted the house into three flats, to let. Later, he had intended to sell them, but suddenly departed for Turkish-occupied northern Cyprus. Who owned the flats now was not clear, but the rents stayed low and were collected each month by a morose elderly woman who always made the sign against the evil eye before she rang Dink's bell.

Dink – her bell was labelled 'D. November' – lived on the ground floor. John Tessier, a classical flautist, rented the first floor, and Patricia Pringle, a social worker, the top one.

John Tessier was on exceptionally good terms with Dink; she had never been rude to him. He smiled and greeted her whenever they met. Often she only grunted; sometimes she returned his greeting; occasionally she smiled; once or twice they held conversations. With Patricia Pringle, Dink was at war.

'Trish', as her friends called her, had lived in the house for ten years. Although now in her mid-thirties, she cultivated a girlish, flowery look, and spoke in a soft voice.

Trish was concerned about the upkeep and appearance of the building. In addition to the urns – in summer, she regularly watered the geraniums with a miniature watering-can – she had provided a hall table and waste-paper basket, and she Hoovered the hall and stairs every Saturday. When Dink moved in, Trish had remarked to her at their first encounter that it was 'such a pity' about the cement outside.

'Bodies underneath,' Dink said.

'What?'

'Sure to be.' Laughing at Trish's expression, Dink had turned her back.

A week or two later, Trish had suggested that it was important to fasten the dustbin lids firmly; Dink's had been pushed off by plundering cats who had scattered debris. 'Well, clear it up,' Dink had replied.

Trish no longer spoke to her, but still wrote her little notes. The last of these – written only a few days ago – had pointed out that with a waste-paper basket in the hall, it was unnecessary to drop envelopes and junk mail on the floor. The note – like its predecessors – Dink had scrumpled and dropped in the hall.

This evening, as Dink slammed the front door behind her, the hall, long and narrow, was dim but not cool. Weak light came down from a window on the half-landing above.

A sound made Dink glance up. Trish, holding her watering-can, was coming down.

'Hey!' Dink exclaimed. 'Here comes Miss Pringle with her dolly can. What a lot of time she's got to waste! And writing her little pink love-notes. Do you fancy me – is that it?' She looked appraisingly at Trish. 'You might still find yourself some kind of man.' She made a thrusting gesture. 'He'd be more use to you than that watering-can.'

Trish stood on the stairs, blushing and trembling. Dink called out, 'You can stuff those little notes of yours. If you write me any more I'll do it for you. See?' As Dink unlocked the door of her flat, Trish was shaking so much that water spilled out of her can onto the stairs.

Inside Dink's flat, two doors opened off a tiny hall. She went into the room on the left. She kicked off her shoes; like her hands, her feet were long and bony. She tugged off her red wig; the hair beneath was thin but fuzzy, a slightly rusty brown. Immediately she seemed diminished and, in spite of her bright make-up, faded.

Dink put down her wig, her carrier and, after taking out cigarettes and lighter, her bag. The room was hot and stuffy. Lighting a cigarette, she padded over to the French window at the end of the room, opened it and stepped out onto a railed terrace big enough to hold two orange vinyl chairs, a cardboard box of empty bottles, a dead plant in a pot garnished with a drooping bow, and an empty saucer.

The small garden below was a mess of dried grass and weeds. However, against the end wall soared and spread a giant horse-chestnut. Once, in May, Dink had wandered onto her terrace when John Tessier, resting briefly from Mozart, was leaning out of the window overhead. Looking up, she called out, 'Toot-toot, toot-toot.'

'Does it disturb you?'

'Agh, I don't mind it. But it's funny *you* don't get sick of it.'

He laughed. 'It's my work.'

'Work can be helluva boring.'

'Not mine.'

'You're lucky, man.' She was smiling up at him, and he gestured towards the chestnut, thick with cones of blossom.

'Wonderful, isn't it?'

'That big old tree? Blocking the view. I hate it. I'd cut it down.'

'You're joking.'

22

'I'm not.' But she laughed. 'Us South Africans like to see what's coming. We go for the wide open spaces.'

'You're South African?'

'That's right.'

'I love your name. November! It's so romantic and unusual.'

'Romantic, hey?' She laughed. 'It's not unusual in Cape Town. But I don't mind it. My first name's shit, though – Dorcas. My father found it in the Bible. He was a *predikant*.'

'*Predikant*?'

'Clergyman, you'd say. Dutch Reformed. But nobody calls me Dorcas – they'd better not! People call me Dink.'

'Dink? That's unusual too.'

'It started when I was a kid. People said I was dinky – cute, you know. My parents called me Dorcas, but nobody else did. Dinky, then Dink! Nothing to do with "kinky".' She gave a loud laugh, and went back inside. Next time she saw John Tessier she only grunted.

Today she made the same face at the chestnut tree as she had made at the child down the road. Then she saw a ginger tom sitting on the right-hand wall, watching her. She picked up the saucer next to the dead plant and took it indoors where she filled it with milk from the new carton she had just bought, carried it out and put it down. She dropped her cigarette over the terrace rail: the patch of ground below was littered with cigarette ends.

Dink went inside again, past a dining-table of imitation teak, and four metal chairs with seats and kidney-shaped backs upholstered in orange plastic. In the middle of the table stood a vase of artificial gladioli, and on the wall behind it was a print of an orchid discarded on a flight of steps. Its colours, livid and jaundiced, contrasted with the pattern of orange and green triangles with which the room was papered. Opposite the dining-table was a kitchen area. Between this and the door to the hall, pastel plastic strips hung in the entrance to a passage leading to the bathroom. Facing this entrance was the black glass coffee-table on which Dink had dropped wig, bag and carrier. It stood on a shaggy orange rug in front of a black fake-leather sofa. Over the sofa hung an imitation oil of a small boy with ruffled hair. Two large tears rolled down his cheeks from eyes that exactly matched his blue open-necked shirt.

Dink put the milk carton in the refrigerator, and the bar of chocolate from her bag in a kitchen cupboard where there were several others; she was not fond of chocolate. She looked at her watch, and sighed. Then, carrying wig, shoes and bag, she went through into the room on the other side of the hall.

Though, like the living-room, medium-sized and square, this cream-painted room seemed quite differently proportioned because almost a third of it was taken up by a deep closet extending, on the left, from the wall by the door to the edge of the bay window. Near the window, a large mirror filled the part of the closet door that faced the bed.

This huge bed was covered with a pink satin counterpane. Three little cushions, two frilled and white, one pink and heart-shaped, nestled against the pillows. The shiny cream headboard was edged with gilt curlicues. Above it hung a large picture of four kittens, rampaging among roses. On either side a small, matching table with cabriole legs crouched like a pale, gilded spider; each table held a lamp with a pink satin shade, and on the one near the window was a white telephone. In addition to the pink festoon-blind, heavy pink velvet curtains – open now – hung from under a cream pelmet across the recess of the bay. Under the window, on a trolley angled towards the bed, were a television and VCR. To the right of the door, a dressing-table and stool completed the arachnoid gilt-and-cream suite. On the dressing-table were a large bottle of Dior's *Poison*, a gilt triple-mirror and the room's only ornament: a china bridal couple.

The bride's veil was worn off the face; her hair fell in dark ringlets to her shoulders. To the knee, her white dress fitted closely; there it slit, to reveal long slim legs and gold-sandalled feet. The dress swept round them in a train lined with a mass of pink ruffles. Like the bride, the groom had blue eyes and perfectly neat features, though his hair, arranged in blow-dried waves, was yellow. Over a white pleated shirt and red cummerbund, he wore a pale-grey dinner-jacket; its lapels, like his trousers, pointed shoes and bow-tie, were black. One of the bride's hands was tucked into the crook of his arm; from the other trailed the ribbons of a bouquet of white roses.

Now, although it was still daylight, Dink switched on a gilt-branched ceiling light. She crossed the room to close the pink velvet curtains. Then she took a key from the drawer of the bedside table near the window. She unlocked the closet door and slid it open.

In contrast to the pink-and-white bedroom, the inside of the closet was shockingly bright and crowded. On the left, facing outwards, were three crowded racks of clothes. Some glittered; others had the sheen of leather. A long white Victorian nightdress hung next to a military tunic, and what looked like a nun's habit was between sequinned red satin and short black crêpe with attached small white apron. From one hanger dangled a complicated leather harness, and from another a pair of handcuffs. Against the left wall were propped whips and canes.

Above the clothes-racks was a wide shelf. Wig-stands were crowded on the left; Dink now put her red wig on a vacant one: a head with a bald crown and featureless face. Most of the other stands were covered: by saucy schoolgirl pigtails, by the grizzled bun and straight parting of an old-fashioned schoolmistress, by a huge Afro, by the ringlets of a Southern Belle. There were also copies of old filmstars' styles: a red Rita Hayworth 'pageboy', a blonde Veronica Lake 'peekaboo-bang', a dark Audrey Hepburn 'urchin cut'. Next to the wigs, hats were stacked. Over a stetson was a boater with striped band and, above that, a maid's cap with streamers. Under a soldier's peaked cap, a black bowler rested on a wide-brimmed straw trimmed with artificial daisies. A rhinestone tiara encircled a top hat.

On the floor were various pairs of boots and shoes, mostly high-heeled, though there were some plain flat ones. A black surgical boot was next to a pair of mules with pink fluffy pompoms.

The closet stopped half a metre short of the ceiling. On the left it was topped with plywood, but the right section was open to admit air and some light, though much more came in through the mirror which, from inside, was transparent, giving a lavish view of the bed. Behind it were an armchair and a small chest-of-drawers on which stood a video camcorder. From the back of the closet Dink now dragged a folded framework of pale-blue wooden bars.

Half an hour later she was ready. The bed was entirely covered by a black rubber sheet; near the foot lay a pile of baby's towelling napkins. The bedside table nearer the door, draped with a white cloth, held baby powder, medicine bottles, a spoon, a baby's bottle full of milk, a large thermometer and a coiled rubber tube. The lamp from this table – moved to the dressing-table – now provided the only light in the room. On the floor, on another spread rubber sheet, stood the playpen Dink had pulled from the closet. In it lay a rattle and a teddy bear. A child's blue plastic chamber-pot, decorated with a duck in a sailor hat, stood on the floor near the playpen.

Dink had taken off her make-up, and her hair was quite covered by a nurse's cap. She wore a starched white apron over a grey dress with a stiff white collar and stout black shoes over grey stockings.

As the doorbell buzzed, she was locking the closet. She replaced the key in its drawer on her way to step behind the curtains into the bay where she could see the person standing on the doorstep. She re-entered the room and went into her small hall where she pressed the buzzer that opened the house door. Then she opened her own front door just a crack; when her caller appeared, she stood back to let him in. Shutting the door after him, she ushered him straight into the bedroom.

He was an elderly man in elderly clothes: a tweed jacket, grey flannel trousers, a tie printed with the insignia of some school or club. He had thin grey hair and a receding chin. He headed straight for the bed, sat down, took off his jacket, and lay back on the rubber sheet. 'Nanny,' he murmured. 'Nanny Thompson.' He closed his eyes.

'Yes, Nanny's here,' Dink said. 'Nanny will take care of you.' As she unfastened his tie, she looked down at him with the expression of one who performs a tedious, rather than distasteful, task, an expression tolerant though touched with contempt. Her face, without make-up, seemed shrunken, sallow against the white cap. On it, this look, from her narrowed eyes, was reptilian: a lizard's look, cold and ancient.

Francis Larch – fifty years old, small, lively, grey-haired and sharp-nosed – lived with his mother in a Gothic Revival house in North Oxford. At ten, that Sunday evening, he was sitting, though not working, in his study.

The study, with its Morris wallpaper, handsome mid-Victorian furniture, well-polished by Mrs Larch's daily 'treasure', and walls of books, was appropriate – though in a style not achieved by many of his colleagues – to Francis's work as a university lecturer in Latin. His mother's money supported the house, the study and their very comfortable, though not ostentatious, standard of living. Francis's father – handsome, charming, idle, feebly dishonest – had been Beatrice Larch's one weakness; she had come to regret it until his death, as a Japanese prisoner of war, redeemed him and relieved her.

27

Francis could not remember his father at all.

'Dear old Francis has everything he could want. Peace, comfort, not a worry in the world. Even a little bolt-hole in London. All he's had to give in exchange is his soul,' Rupert told Lucy before he introduced them.

'His soul?'

Rupert laughed. 'Don't look so startled, darling. I should have said "his freedom". Bea has grappled him to her with hoops of steel.'

'Hoops of steel?'

'Just a quotation. I meant that she's very possessive. A vampire. But quite a dear old vampire. Actually I don't think Francis minds . . . or hardly at all. He's habituated to his daily sessions with Countess Dracula. In fact he'd probably miss them if they stopped. She's very well educated and broad-minded, and they discuss absolutely everything together except Francis's sex-life, though of course she must know. The bolt-hole in London is where he takes his pick-ups.'

'He's gay?'

'Gay as can be. You don't disapprove?'

'Of course not.'

'No "of course" about it. The Church condemns active homosexuality.'

'But *I* don't have to, personally.' There was a moment's pause. Then she said, 'Does he pay these . . . pick-ups?'

'Oh yes, I'm sure. He likes them young and slightly dangerous. What's known as "rough trade".'

Lucy said, 'It's hard for me to understand sex with people one's got nothing in common with. It's not *serious*.'

Rupert laughed. 'It's serious sex.'

'Mmm. And the *paying* – I don't like that either. I mean, I can't imagine anyone I know that's heterosexual paying for sex. It's . . . sort of degrading.'

'So you disapprove of prostitutes?'

'Oh, not of them. They're victims.'

'Well, that's one way of looking at it. Some people see them quite differently. I was reading Aretino the other day and he describes the Roman prostitutes as witches, with boxes full of skulls, hair, ribs, teeth, dead men's eyes, the navels of little children, the soles of shoes and pieces of clothing from tombs. He even writes about them going to the graveyard themselves to fetch bits of rotten flesh to smuggle into their lovers' food . . . all this designed to make themselves more attractive.'

Lucy's expression was disgusted. 'Oh, Rupert – I don't believe a word of it. Who is this Aretino?'

'An Italian writer . . . in the sixteenth century.'

'You're teasing me again. I thought you meant *now*. Anyway, I'm sure those awful stories weren't true.'

The look Rupert wore now was certainly teasing. 'Perhaps they *were* true. If so, no wonder Pope Pius the Fifth drove all the prostitutes out of Rome to be massacred by bandits in the campagna.'

'Was that in the sixteenth century, too?'

'Yes. Not exactly a humane man. Nor was his successor, Gregory the Thirteenth . . . though he had an illegitimate son. He was the pope who had a commemorative medal struck to celebrate the St Bartholomew's Day massacre.'

But now Lucy smiled: 'I remember my father telling me about that medal. No one can ever surprise me with horrors from Church history. Daddy was always talking about them. It used to make Mummy furious, but I think he was quite right.'

'He always stayed a Catholic?'

'Oh yes – of course.'

After a moment, Rupert said, 'Goodness, we've wandered a long way from my friend Francis.'

'Yes,' Lucy said, and then, 'I'm looking forward to meeting him.'

The meeting – dinner at the Firenze – had been a success. 'He's nice, and very amusing,' was Lucy's comment to Rupert afterwards. Francis said later, 'She's charming – what beautiful hair! – and she's *good*, too. Far too good for you, Rupe.'

'Yes, I know.' They both laughed.

This evening in Oxford was still and balmy. The open study window let in a fragrance of night-scented stock. Mrs Larch, aided by a twice-weekly assistant, was a keen gardener. After cold – but delicious – Sunday supper, Francis had said he was going to work and his mother that she was going to read. Actually, she watched television, which she preferred to do unobserved, even by Francis, and he read a guide to gay nightlife in the United States – a country he had no plans to visit – between attempts to reach Rupert on the telephone. Each time, the answering machine replied, and Francis left no message. Now he tried again and, after only two rings, Rupert said, 'Hullo.'

With a smile of satisfaction, Francis leant back in his chair. (The chair, a present from his mother, was utterly comfortable. Although modern – the only modern piece in the room – it was so well designed that it looked quite at home with the old leather-bound books, the mahogany desk, the antique globe.) 'And where have you been, Rupe?' Francis asked.

'Oh hullo, Francis. I've been out to dinner with Lucy. Did you ring earlier? Why didn't you leave a message?'

'You know how I detest those machines.'

'All vain people do.'

'What *can* you mean, Rupe?'

'They can't bear the idea of leaving a message, and the other person not ringing back.'

Francis laughed. 'I assure you that's not *my* reason. I simply refuse to talk to a machine. You know how I distrust all machinery.' (This was true; Francis did not even drive a car.) 'Did you have a nice dinner?'

'Yes. Quiet. Lucy said I looked tired and ought to have an early night.'

'What a thoughtful girl.'

'As I've learnt, Francis, you must say "woman" nowadays, never "girl". "Girl" is undignified, diminishing.'

'Yet women seem to try harder than ever to look young.'

They laughed. Rupert said, 'Anyway, Francis, guess what? The old bag has caved in!'

' "Old bag?" I'm sure you're not meant to call *any* woman that! What are you talking about?'

'My future mother-in-law has given her consent. Lucy and I are officially engaged.'

'How wonderfully old-fashioned.' Francis giggled. 'Next you'll be telling me you're going to put the engagement in *The Times*.'

The sound Rupert made was between a sigh and a groan. 'As a matter of fact that's exactly what we *are* going to do. Put it in *The Times*, and the *Telegraph* too.' Now Rupert laughed. 'Aren't you going to congratulate me? On my first engagement?'

'Yes, I suppose it will be your first official one. Just as this will be your first marriage in church. What a bit of luck *that* is – though, of course, if people are important enough, the Romans will always manage to cook up an annulment.'

'You don't know Lucy, Francis. She really disapproves of that sort of thing. Special treatment for the rich and famous.'

'Well, the Rivens may not be rich, but they're certainly famous Catholics. So, if you'd married in church before, Lucy would have *renounced* you?'

'I think she would. She's a funny mixture. She believes in the dogma and the sacraments – marriage is a sacrament, of course – but not in all the "social teaching" as she calls it. She thinks priests should be allowed to marry, and even that women should be able to become priests. She abhors abortions, but

31

she thinks the ban on artificial contraception is absurd . . . and terrible for the Third World.'

'She's very serious, isn't she? Lucky for you she won't insist on having fifteen children.'

'She thinks three would be nice.'

'Three! I've always felt two were *more* than enough for you.'

'It could be different with Lucy. Anyway, she may change her mind.'

'It's surprising she's so modern. The Rivens are such *ancient* Catholics. There was even a martyr, wasn't there?'

'Yes, the Blessed Hugh. I made a joke about him spying for the Spanish. It's the only time I've seen Lucy really furious. I had to back down in a hurry. Anyway, I don't think it was true. He was just a fanatic. But Lucy admires him. Of course her mother is really one of the old school. Always harking back to the good old days before Vatican Two and longing for the Latin Mass.'

'That's forbidden now, isn't it?'

'No. Latin's not forbidden, though it's not used much. It's the Tridentine Mass that's prohibited.'

'Goodness, Rupe, you're amazingly *au fait* with it all.'

'Of course I am. You forget that I'm taking instruction.'

'No, I don't. How could I? Jessop the Jesuit is famous for converting intellectuals. Eminent poets, and so on. Rather a compliment his taking on *you*, Rupe!'

They both laughed. Rupert said, 'More a compliment to the Rivens, I think.'

'How do you find him?'

Rupert's tone was neutral: 'He's an intelligent man.'

'Of course, old Anglicans like me always think of Jesuits as very *devious* . . . they have a sort of sinister glamour.'

'Not Jessop. He's very plain, and he blinks a lot. Sometimes, when my mind wanders from what he's saying, I count the blinks.'

'Your mind wanders? I though you said he was intelligent.'

'Oh, he is. In *their* terms.'

After a moment's pause, Francis said, 'So you're not going to "turn" after all?'

'Oh yes, I am. It would make Lucy so happy.'

'Not if she knew how you really feel about it.'

'But she won't.'

'Oh Rupe, Rupe . . .' Francis made a clicking noise with his tongue.

Rupert said, 'I suppose that's the sound that's written as "tut-tut" in books.'

'I suppose it is . . . Rupe, you're quite impossible.'

'That's just what Lucy's mother feels. She's persuaded Lucy to wait six months before we get married. Of course she hopes Lucy will change her mind.'

'But she won't, will she?'

'Not a chance! It's Lucy who decided to put the engagement in the paper. To prove to her mother that she's quite determined.'

Francis said, 'Well, the announcement will certainly cause a stir in some households.'

'Such as?'

'Chris's, for instance.'

'Ah, Chris! She only hears the news on her wireless, when she's dressing. She never reads anything but typescripts and book reviews. A typical publisher.'

Francis laughed. 'But she's sure to find out.'

'Yes, I suppose so. Sarah may see it.'

'Does James still live with her?'

'Mummy's little soldier? I don't know.'

'He must be just about Lucy's age.'

'Mmm,' Rupert said.

'And the girl – Barbara's child – how old is she now?'

'Belinda? She must be – oh, twenty-two, I think.'

'Isn't Lucy curious about your children?'

'She was at first. Perhaps she still is a bit. But I explained how their mothers had turned them against me.'

'Mmm. You used to see Belinda when you were married to Chris.'

'Yes, I did a bit. But somehow now we've lost touch. Poor old Belinda. She certainly hasn't inherited Barbara's looks. Barbara won't see the announcement. She's strictly a *Guardian* reader. Plus the *Morning Star*, I expect – if it still exists.'

'She's still a Communist?'

'Actually I haven't the faintest idea.'

'When does the announcement go in?'

'This coming Friday – the fourth of August. We go up to Rivendale that evening, for the weekend. So that Ma Riven and I can get to know each other better. *Quelle horreur*!'

'Charm her, Rupe. Charm her. You can charm any woman!'

'Not Ma Riven.'

'What's her Christian name?'

'Teresa. But I'm sure she won't ask me to call her that.'

'I can't see why not. After all you must be practically the same age.'

'What a bitch you are, Francis!' But Rupert laughed. 'I'm sure she's ten years older than I am. And she can't stand me. Every time we've met it's been like bumping into an iceberg.'

'That *does* sound unpleasant.' Then Francis said, 'And how is Jeanne Duval going to react to your engagement?'

This nickname had been inspired by the poet Baudelaire's mixed-race mistress. ('But you mustn't say "mistress" anymore, Francis,' Rupert had recently warned. 'You must say "lover". "Mistress" is considered demeaning, though I can't think why, when it sounds so dominant and "lover" sounds so suppliant.') Today, after Francis spoke the name, Rupert sighed. Then he said, 'Well, she certainly won't read it in *The Times* or the *Telegraph*.'

'She *can* read, I suppose? Baudelaire tried and tried to teach *his* Jeanne, but it just wouldn't take.' Francis laughed.

Rupert, however, was evidently not in the mood for literary jokes. 'Of course she can read,' he said. 'But she doesn't read what some people call the "quality" newspapers.'

Francis, always happy to diverge down a pedantic byway, said, 'Yes, it makes such a *vulgar* adjective, doesn't it? "Quality" can *only* be a noun. Though nowadays, of course, no one knows the difference.' Getting no response to this, he quoted '*Bizarre déité, brune comme les nuits, au parfum mélangé de musc et de havane.* I'm sure your Jeanne is just like Baudelaire's. A strange goddess, dark as night, smelling of musk and cigar-smoke. I can just picture her even though you've never let us meet.'

'You'd have nothing in common.'

'Except our devotion to you. When are you going to tell her about your engagement?'

'Oh . . . soon.'

'I mean, I know that ever since you got involved with Lucy, you and Jeanne Duval have been just friends . . . well, haven't you?'

Rupert said, 'That's right.'

'And I presume you've stopped helping her financially. I know you earn quite a bit, but getting married's expensive. And that money you got from Chris can't last for ever.'

'Not from Chris, Francis. From the divorce settlement.'

'Yes, that's what I meant, of course.'

'I don't support Jeanne Duval. I told you – she works. Does a bit of modelling.'

'She sounds quite fascinating – the way you say she sometimes looks like a courtesan and at others modest as a violet – but isn't she getting on a bit, for modelling?'

'She's not forty yet. And she does other jobs.' Rupert's tone was irritable.

'Then *that's* all right,' Francis said in a soothing tone. 'And as you're just friends now, if she found out about Lucy, she wouldn't make scenes like the ones she made with Chris . . . would she?'

After a moment Rupert said, 'We were involved for a long time.'

'Oh, I know.'

'All in all, nearly twenty years.'

'So she *might* make a fuss?' When Rupert didn't answer, Francis said, 'Rupe, why don't you tell Lucy all about her.'

'Absolutely not.'

'But *why*? After all, Lucy's not a child. She's twenty-seven. And as it's all over, I'm sure she'd understand. She's kind.'

'Oh yes. More. As you said yourself, she's *good*.'

'I don't think I've ever heard *you* say that about anyone. Certainly not about any of your wives.'

'It didn't apply.'

'Well, not to Chris.' Francis laughed. 'Perhaps not to Barbara. But how about Sarah?'

'Sarah wasn't actually *bad*. But she wasn't good either. In fact she was awfully dull. I should never have married her, even though she was a Huscott-Fenn: it was really only because the vet's daughter's family was closing in on me. Her father and her four beefy brothers.'

'The vet's daughter – I'd forgotten her. She was stunning-looking. What was her name?'

'Valerie. Yes, she was stunning-looking, but quite impossible. I really had to elope with dreary old Sarah. No, Sarah wasn't *good* – like Lucy. Lucy's really quite extraordinary.'

'My dear Rupe, there are quite a lot of good people around, you know.'

'Really? Well, Lucy's the only one *I* know. And it fascinates me. I love contrasts.'

'How do you mean – contrasts?'

'Oh, I don't know. Anyway, Lucy's good, and she loves me.'

'Then she'd understand about Jeanne Duval.'

'Oh do stop *nagging*, Francis.' Then he said, 'I'm sorry. I know you're just trying to be helpful. We'll talk another time. I'll ring up when I get back from Rivendale.'

'I long to hear every detail.'

'You shall – I promise. The lowering skies, the moors, the crusader's tomb, the Riven ghost, wailing and clanking its chains.'

'There's a ghost?' Francis asked with interest.

Rupert laughed. 'Not that I know of. But, to misquote Voltaire, if it doesn't exist, we'll have to invent it. And of course I'll tell you all about Mummy, and Mummy's ADC – she's a Hungarian refugee – and Nanny and Rufus.'

'Who on earth is Rufus?'

'A dog, Francis. Lucy's dog. And you know how I detest dogs. Good night, Francis.'

'Good night, Rupe.' Smiling, Francis put down the receiver. A moment later his mother opened the door and peeped round it.

'Francis?' Mrs Larch had a large head – she was a large woman – and the way she peeped round the door and spoke her son's name was arch ('girlish' rather than 'womanly'). However when Francis said, 'Come in, Mother,' and she entered the room, any hint of absurdity vanished. Dressed in a black-and-white silk print – she always changed in the evening, even for Sunday supper – with her white hair rigidly set round her square face, she was a formidable figure.

Last thing every evening, she and Francis had a drink in the study; it was a ritual only prevented by absence or illness. Even when they came home late, they observed it, dissecting the performance after a concert or play and the company and conversation after a dinner party.

'Time for our nightcap,' Francis said now. Going over to a tray of bottles and glasses on a table by the window, he prepared the drinks: the only domestic task he ever performed. (Pouring drinks was admitted to be 'a man's job' by Mrs Larch.) She always had a whisky and soda, without ice – 'a dreadful American custom' – and Francis, who disliked spirits, drank a glass of port.

Mrs Larch sat in an armchair facing the desk and Francis, when he had put her drink on the little table next to her, returned to his own chair behind it. They always sat in this tutorial position, though it was hard to believe Francis the tutor.

'*A votre santé,*' Mrs Larch said, raising her glass. While she thought the expression 'Cheers!' common – she used the word 'common' without unease – this French equivalent escaped her censure.

'*Santé,*' Francis responded. Then he said, 'I was talking to Rupe on the telephone.'

'Oh really,' she said, though her appearance had been so felicitously timed that she was probably aware of the telephone conversation. 'How is the old scamp?' Her tone was affectionate. Always charming to Francis's friends – all men; she might have been less tolerant of women – she was particularly fond of Rupert whose life was a constant source of the enlivening though repetitive gossip which was such a bond between herself and her son.

Now Francis giggled. 'Old he may be, but he's getting engaged . . . in *The Times.*'

'Engaged! That does seem a little *outré* at his age and after three marriages. It's to this Lucy girl, of course?'

'Yes.'

'She's charming, you said.'

'Yes. Delightful.'

'But there was some problem with her mother?'

'Her mother has finally given in.'

'Ah, that's good. Possessive mothers are so tiresome. In any case, who asks for a parent's consent nowadays?'

'I think Lucy wants everyone to be happy. She's more than delightful – she's *good*.'

'I would never have expected that to appeal very much to Rupe.'

They both laughed, but then Francis said, 'Yet it does. He was just saying so. Rupert likes contrasts.'

'And the Vatican consents to the marriage?'

'Yes.'

'Such hypocrites! Just because she's a Riven, I suppose.' Mrs Larch – who, like Francis, was a practising Anglican – had a marked distrust of 'Rome'.

Francis said, 'That's not *quite* fair, Mother. There's some sense in their position: as the others were civil ceremonies, they weren't marriages in the sight of God. It's logical.'

'They've always been great logic-choppers. And Rupe's been taking instruction, you said . . . from a *Jesuit*?'

'Mmm. I think he's going to convert.'

' "*Pervert*," I always say. He isn't sincere, is he?'

Francis evaded the question. 'He's sincere about Lucy. He's really in love.' Then he frowned. 'But I can't help worrying about Jeanne Duval.'

'The beautiful octoroon? Don't tell me he's still carrying on with *her*!'

'Oh *no*!' Francis sounded shocked. 'I wasn't suggesting *that*.' He paused. 'You call her beautiful. But I don't know if she is, as I've never seen her. He's so secretive about her. Always has been.'

'I can't help wondering if he's ashamed of her. Of her colour.'

'Oh *no*!' Francis said again, then, 'Rupe's not a racist. In fact, at the beginning, their relationship was, well, in opposition to racism.'

'Yes of course. It was illegal, wasn't it? That dreadful apartheid!' At seventy-five, Mrs Larch prided herself on being modern: in sharing – verbally at any rate – Francis's hostility to racial discrimination. (With social distinctions, it was different: for Francis, too. His sexual partners attracted him partly because they came from a different class.)

'He had to flee the country . . . well almost. He brooded about her. But then he met Chris. He and Barbara were divorced by then. And they got married.'

'But Jeanne Duval followed him?'

'Yes. But she worked for years and years to manage it. Like someone in the Bible?'

'Jacob.'

'Ah yes. But for *more* than seven years. Eight I think. And she came over here and tracked him down.'

'That was why he and Chris got divorced.'

'Well, they were very unhappy anyway. I always thought it was a dreadful marriage, though it lasted so long.'

'But Jeanne Duval played a part? And he's been carrying on with her ever since? Until he met this Lucy?'

'Yes.'

'But now it's all over?'

'Yes. But he wants them to remain friends.'

'Has he told her about Lucy?'

'Not yet.'

'I wonder if he's afraid to. Men are such cowards. And she was very aggressive when he was married to Chris, wasn't she?'

'But it's over now.'

'Hmm. Has he told Lucy about her?'

'No.'

'Goodness me. So he's just letting things slide. *What* a scamp he is! And very foolish. If it's going in the paper Jeanne Duval could easily find out.'

'Rupe says she doesn't read that sort of paper.'

'But she could find out from someone else. And make a scene – naturally she'd be annoyed he hadn't told her. After knowing her all that time. No, he must tell her and tell Lucy, too. He must face up to it. He'll be able to bring them round. He's such a charmer. You must persuade him, Francis.'

'I've tried.'

'You must try again.'

'I'll see if I can pluck up the courage.'

' "Pluck up the courage" indeed! He's your best friend. Anyone would think you were talking about a complete stranger.'

A breath of wind moved the curtains. At that moment, abruptly, Francis stood up. 'I'll have to think about it. Time for beddy-byes now, I think.'

When he rose, his mother had frowned and glanced at her not-yet-quite-finished drink. But when she heard the nursery phrase she smiled, and drank the remains in one decisive swallow, and put the empty glass down on the little table next to her. Now she too rose – rather heavily – and, as Francis came round the desk, said, *'Nous verrons*. We shall see.' This expression – the French phrase always followed by its translation – was a favourite of hers.

'Yes, Mother. Undoubtedly we shall.' Francis sighed.

'You'll do whatever's best, I know.'

'Whatever that may be.' He sighed again. But then he put his arm round her solid shoulders and gave them a small squeeze. She clasped the hand that rested on her sleeve and in this rather awkward position they moved towards the door.

Dink's visitor had gone. As soon as she had closed and locked the door of the flat behind him, she went to the bay behind the velvet curtains. Darkness had quite fallen now, and it was by the light of a street lamp that she watched him carefully negotiate the unrailed front steps. He trudged across the cement and then turned right to wherever he had parked his car: Dink allowed none of her callers to park on the cement or even by the curb in front of the house. Those intrepid enough to ask why were told it might cause talk – something they themselves were anxious to avoid.

Now Dink stepped back into the bedroom. She flipped – automatically recounting – through the money in her left hand, then put it in the bedside-table drawer. Then she cleared away every trace of the scene she had set for her caller, folding up rubber sheets and playpen and putting them and the other paraphernalia away in the cupboard with her nurse's outfit.

Tonight she had not needed to change her underclothes; the ministrations this caller had required were conducted fully clad. Now she dropped her red-lace briefs and brassiere on the floor, and smiled and stretched in front of the two-way mirror, though no one was behind it to see her.

Naked, Dink was all assertion. Her body hair – never shaved – grew in dark springy tussocks. Her breasts, with dark-brown nipples and purple areolae, tilted upwards; so did her buttocks: muscular, but small and protrusive. This whole yellow-brown body, with its lean arms and jutting elbows, lean legs and long bony hands and feet, had a Jazz-Age look, as if, at any moment, it might break into a syncopated dance. It might jerk and jounce – head back, mouth open, a glint of eyes between almost closed lids – to a spasm of jactation from which, finally, it could only slump to the ground: empty flesh, discarded, dispossessed.

Looking in the mirror, Dink ran her hands down her sides. She examined her body as an art-expert might examine a picture. Then, picking up her discarded underclothes, she went through to the bathroom.

This, like the living-room and bedroom, was clean. A fluffy

pink bathmat and lavatory-seat cover almost matched the pink fittings. After dropping her underclothes into a gilt wicker laundry basket, Dink turned on the bath, adjusting the water, though the evening was so hot, to a very high temperature. She poured in bath oil; the ultra-sweet smell of lily-of-the-valley – very different from *Poison,* her chosen perfume – rose strongly in foam and in a cloud of steam. When the bath was two-thirds full, she tested the temperature. Then she turned off the taps, stepped in and – with one gasp, half shock, half pleasure, at the heat – slid down. A moment later, like a water predator, she was almost completely submerged. Only her features and the tips of her long toes showed above the surface which soon became as still as she was, though little bubbles in the foam burst with a continuous tiny susurration.

Slowly the water cooled, until she sat up with a sudden movement that was almost a shiver. Quickly she shampooed her hair and washed her body, scrubbing it with a loofah. She stepped out of the bath and rubbed her head and body with a big pink towel. She slathered a pink lotion over her body and smeared anti-wrinkle cream on her face and neck. Then, vigorously, she brushed her teeth.

She was naked when she went back into the bedroom. She took the little cushions from the bed and put them on the dressing-table stool. She folded the satin counterpane and put it on top of them.

The bed was made up with fresh white sheets and pillow-cases. From under the pillow on the window side, she took a pair of plain white cotton pyjamas, which she put on. Then she got into bed.

She sighed just once before, from the drawer in the bedside table, she took a Barbara Cartland novel, and began to read. Ten minutes later – the bedside light still on – the book dropped from her hand. Her damp hair, like a drowned person's, left a wet patch on the pillow. Dink's sleep looked so deep and dreamless that a casual observer might have thought her dead.

It was dark when Lucy emerged from Hampstead Underground. Changing from the Piccadilly line at Leicester Square, she had waited half an hour for an Edgware train on the Northern line.

While they were finishing their dinner at the Firenze Rupert had again raised the subject of her journey: 'Do let me drive you home.'

Lucy had looked at her watch. 'No – it's not late. You're tired. And the station's so near – nearer than the car. Much quicker and easier.'

'I simply don't believe you.' Rupert smiled. 'On that Northern line? It's notorious. Endless delays, filthy old trains like cattle-trucks, and long waits in tunnels.'

'It's not that bad. Though the trains do stop for ages between stations sometimes.'

'And you see on every face the mental emptiness deepen
Leaving only the growing terror of nothing to think about.'

Lucy said, 'It's the waste of time that annoys *me*, specially when I'm in a hurry. Anyway, I've lots to think about.' She tossed her head, and her plait swung.

'Darling, I wasn't talking about you. It's a poem of T. S. Eliot's. That's what he said about those stops between stations.'

'Oh – quoting!' She added, 'It didn't *sound* like poetry.'

Now they both laughed. But then Rupert said, 'Quoting's a vice. I must give it up. It's old-fashioned.'

'*That* isn't a vice.'

'Yes, it is – a social vice. Nobody quotes any more.' He sighed. 'Crosswords used to be full of quotations. Now they're just dreary little word-games.'

'I'm hopeless at crosswords. Mummy loves them. Perhaps you'll be able to do the crossword together at Rivers.'

'Mmm. Are you sure you won't let me drive you home?'

'Quite sure.'

This conversation might have been thought to confirm Rupert's earlier remark about Lucy's 'passion for public transport'. In fact – as she had admitted only to her friend Vee – there was a different reason for her inexorable use of the Underground. 'It's a challenge,' she had told Vee. 'A sort of challenge from London. When I first lived here I really felt intimidated. By the crowds and the noise and the odd-looking people and the feeling that nobody cared, that if you fainted' (here Lucy laughed) '– though of course I don't faint – they'd just step over you. All that seemed sort of summed up in the Underground. Going down out of the daylight into another world. Yet at the same time it was – oh, I don't know – the heart of London beating down there. So I felt I must face up to it.'

'You're crazy,' Vee had said. 'Of course it's not as bad as the subway in New York. But you should have a car of your own. Your office said they'd give you one, didn't they?'

'Yes, but we've got better things to do with our money. Anyway, it's cheaper and easier to take taxis when I need to. I hate driving in London. All the traffic jams, and never anywhere to park. One's freer without. To live the real life of the city.'

'Perhaps you should be living in Brixton instead of Hampstead.'

Vee had laughed as she said this, but Lucy had blushed; she blushed easily. 'Perhaps I should. But I love it in Hampstead. And it's economical – staying with the Dumbles. Anyway, there are quite a lot of burglaries in Hampstead. There've even been some muggings.'

'I'm glad about that, if it makes you feel good,' Vee had said, straight-faced. Then they'd simultaneously burst into one of those uncontrollable fits of laughter which most often occur between people who have known each other since their schooldays.

For Lucy, with her quick stride, the walk from Hampstead station took less than quarter of an hour. Now, as she turned into the road where the Dumbles lived, her keys were already in her hand, so that she would not have to pause on the doorstep of the empty house and extract them from the zipped inner pocket of her jacket. Soon after her arrival in London she had attended a short police course on avoiding robbery and attack. Although superficial in comparison to the self-defence training Vee had done in Los Angeles, it had provided sensible pointers to safety. It had also stressed the importance of never looking lost, helpless or vague; these were instructions Lucy did not find it hard to follow.

The Dumbles' road was circular, with a communal garden in the middle, in addition to the houses' own front and back gardens. Bernard Dumble – a lover of paradox; he was a great admirer of G. K. Chesterton – liked to describe it – and often did – as a round square. The large, detached red-brick houses had been built at the turn of the century. They looked alike, though they had been designed to differ. Some of them incorporated decorative stonework; some had wooden, some wrought-iron balconies and porches; there was a variety of Gothic doors, chimneys and windows; other windows had leaded panes; there were one or two Dutch gables. Classical features, however, were absent: the desired effect was rustic with a touch of quaintness. Another favourite paradox of Bernard Dumble's was *'rus in urbe'*; for those ignorant of Latin he would kindly add, 'country in the town'.

The original owners of the houses had been prosperous Edwardian professional men. They were pleased by the presence among them of a well-known – though controversial – painter, Arthur Elwyn. Mag (short for Mary Magdalene) Dumble was Arthur Elwyn's only child, and had inherited the freehold from him; all the other houses in the street were now owned by the very rich. New residents went in for carriage

lamps, topiary and shiny white front doors. Only the Dumbles'
house, with its herbaceous garden, faded green front door and
slightly flaking cream-painted woodwork, retained the rustic
effect originally intended. However the road still kept a near-
rural quiet and, at night, a near-rural dimness. Street lamps of
an old-world design were set far apart, lighting small circles
of road and pavement.

Although lights were on in most of the houses, the curtains
were closed. This innovation was regretted by Mag Dumble:
'No one round here ever used to close their downstairs curtains.
They didn't mind people seeing them reading or writing or
playing the piano.'

Bernard had replied, 'I doubt if our new neighbours engage
in any such activities.' His eyes twinkled, and he added, with
the glee he always showed when uttering a new colloquialism,
'They're probably all watching "video nasties".'

'Or just television,' Lucy's tone was slightly wistful. There
was no television at Rivendale, and the Dumbles' old black-
and-white set was in the 'playroom'. This room, with its huge
north-facing window – it had been Arthur Elwyn's studio –
was seldom used now that all the children (except Perpetua
who had almost decided to become a nun) had left home; its
atmosphere was bleak. Besides, the set flickered.

Mag had groaned. 'They'll probably all have those space-
ships in their gardens soon.' She referred to the recent
appearance of a satellite dish outside a house three doors away.
'We really ought to think of moving. The neighbourhood is
going down so dreadfully.' Then she added, 'But I mustn't be
snobbish.'

Tonight, as usual, the Dumbles' front curtains were open.
Normally the mullioned front window would have revealed
the huge sitting-room, well lit and probably crowded: a
gathering near the fireplace vigorously discussing something
important over coffee or red – never white – wine, a young

couple talking seriously on the window-seat, a former monk accompanying his own singing of Gilbert and Sullivan on the old upright piano. Tonight, however, the house was quite dark. Three days ago Bernard and Mag had left for their customary month in France as voluntary helpers at a children's holiday-camp funded by a Catholic charity, and this year Perpetua had gone too. They always pressed Lucy to come: 'It's so rewarding . . . a wonderful atmosphere,' Mag would say, and Lucy, fiddling with the end of her plait, would answer, 'I wish I could get away, but it's impossible. Next year, perhaps.' She usually took her holidays a week at a time, often at Rivendale, though once she had visited Vee in California for three weeks.

Now she went quickly up the path and the steps to the rustic porch. She unlocked the oak door and, as she closed it behind her, turned on the hall light. Dumping her bag on the floor, she fastened the cylinder lock and a heavy black bolt. Then she turned right into the sitting-room, crossed to the window and drew the curtains before she returned to the door and switched on the centre light.

The room was cleaner and much tidier than usual. Before she left for the weekend, Lucy had taken advantage of the Dumbles' absence and the annual holiday of Mrs O'Leary, the twice-weekly charwoman, to give the kitchen and sitting-room a vigorous cleaning. Mrs O'Leary, a thin, exhausted woman, was not efficient, but Mag sympathized with her problems: her husband drank; two of her five surviving children – three had died – were mentally handicapped and another was in prison. 'Such faith – in spite of all her troubles,' Mag would say to Lucy.

Tonight the clean, tidy room looked lifeless. The unencumbered furniture was noticeably shabby and the green curtains unevenly faded.

In winter, there was always a log fire in the enormous fireplace; this was the only house in the street without central heating. Lucy did not mind: there was no central heating at Rivendale; she found the sitting-room fire and the Aga in the kitchen quite adequate; and she hardly ever lit the gas-fire in her bedroom. However, on different occasions, both Vee and Rupert had described the house as 'freezing'. In summer, the fire was replaced by dried grasses in a large copper vase. Tonight this had a depressing aspect, even though Lucy had shaken the dust out of the grasses and polished the vase.

Large reproductions of famous paintings always look ill-at-ease in private houses; the mixture here of religious scenes and Dutch interiors was no exception. Over the fireplace hung the Sistine Madonna. 'I don't like it much – too wishy-washy,' Lucy – always tentative about Art – had confided to Rupert; she had looked pleasantly surprised when he agreed. There were no Arthur Elwyns in this room or, apart from two small drawings in a corridor, anywhere else in the house.

Elwyn was one of those often successful painters who combine technical brilliance with a style neither dully conventional nor alarmingly innovatory. The Elwyn 'manner', notably individual, had retained both popularity and respect in the forty years since his death. His early paintings, though they included some landscapes and portraits, were chiefly nudes; many depicted the sullen model, Consuelo, whom he lived with for many years. When he eventually left her, she killed herself, and he, aged sixty, became a Catholic, married a fragile Irish girl of nineteen, started to paint religious subjects in modern dress and – at sixty-two – fathered Mary Magdalene.

Seven years later, his wife died of tuberculosis, and Mag was sent to a convent boarding-school where she was far happier than at home in the holidays: her father now drank heavily, and was bad-tempered. She was eighteen when he died, and she immediately married Bernard Dumble, fresh from the seminary where he had unsuccessfully tested a call to the priesthood.

49

She never said so, but it was evident that Mag had disliked her father and still disliked his pictures. She found the early ones 'worldly' and the religious ones repellent. While Mag spoke reverently of Old Masters and hung reproductions of them on her walls, her personal vision of 'Our Lord' and 'Our Lady' was probably closer to the pictures and statues in religious repositories or the small Holy Pictures (called 'HPs') inscribed by old schoolfriends which, transferred from her old Tridentine missal, now crammed her new one. Since Catholic as well as secular critics admired her father's paintings, she had no need to feel ashamed of them, but she never grieved when – as quite often happened – she had to sell one. In any case, it would be already on loan to an art gallery: 'to save insurance', as she would explain.

Mag often described the Dumbles' carefree life as a gift from God; if so, His intermediary had been Arthur Elwyn. Bernard's family business – a religious publishing company for which he had worked since testing his vocation – was modestly prosperous thanks to the acumen of his elder brother (Bernard's own contribution as a director was minimal, though he enjoyed taking theologians out to lunch) but it could not have sustained the family's 'happy-go-lucky' but by no means inexpensive way of life. All their six children had been privately educated at the best Catholic schools, and they entertained generously, with plentiful food and what Bernard called 'honest' wine. Although, now that the children were grown up, Mag sometimes talked of selling the large Hampstead house, such a decision was always postponed: it was a place for their family to gather; they had so many visitors; they often had people to stay – apart from Lucy, their dear 'paying-guest'.

Indeed it was quite exceptional for the house to have a single occupant, as it did tonight. Now Lucy went to the kitchen where she dealt with the Aga. Then she turned off all the downstairs lights except the one in the hall which, in common with many other people, she believed to be a burglar-deterrent. She picked up her bag and started to go upstairs. She had reached the first landing when the telephone rang.

It was in the hall, with one extension in the kitchen where everyone ate at a vast table and where Mag spent much of her time. Dropping her bag, Lucy bounded down two steps at a time, ignoring the banisters; she picked up the receiver just after the third ring.

'Hullo?'

'Lucy – hi!'

'Oh, Vee!'

'I called you last night when I got back from the tour. But no one answered and I was so beat that I didn't try again. I fell asleep and just wakened an hour ago.'

Lucy said, 'I've just got in. I went home for the weekend, and when I got back Rupert and I went out to dinner.'

'So that romance is *still* on?'

'Of course it is.' Lucy laughed. 'This weekend I convinced Mummy that I was going ahead.'

'That's the spirit.'

'We're putting the engagement in the paper this week.'

'When are you getting married?'

'I told Mummy we'd wait six months.'

'So she's still manipulating you.'

'No, she's not. I just told you—'

'Forget it. And it's all okay with the Holy Roman Empire?'

'Yes. All settled. And you'll be my bridesmaid.'

' "Matron of Honour", I think they call it. Don't forget I've been married, too.'

Lucy laughed. 'I do forget. It lasted such a short time.'

'Yeah.' Vee sighed. 'I think it's over with this new guy, too.'

'The musician?'

'Mmm. He's so moody and he smokes such a lot of dope. I don't expect Rupert does that.'

'Oh no. He doesn't even drink much. I've never seen him drunk.'

'I'm just dying to meet him.'

'I know you'll like each other. I was saying so to him this evening.'

'And what did he say?'

'He said he'd do his best.'

Vee laughed. 'Tell him I really appreciate that!'

Lucy laughed too. 'He calls you "the famous Vee".'

'That's me!'

Lucy said, 'Oh Vee, I'm so happy.'

'That's wonderful. I'm so thrilled that you've met the right guy at last. I'm planning to come over very soon.'

'Oh do. As soon as possible. You can stay here with me.'

'And all those Dumbles?'

'No – they're away till the end of August.'

'In that case, I'm almost on my way.'

'Oh Vee, you're not fair to them.'

'You're right. I know I'm not. I just find the Dumble brand of Catholicism a bit oppressive.'

'Actually Rupert does too.'

'Well, that makes another bond between us – as well as you, I mean. But you did say he's thinking of becoming a Catholic?'

'Yes, I think he's going to.'

'But not a fanatic? A Dumble Catholic?'

'Oh no,' Lucy said, and then, 'After all you don't think *I'm* a fanatic, do you?'

'You're different. How long did you say the Dumbles will be gone?'

'Till the end of August.'

'I'm sure I can get over before that.'

'Terrific! Oh, just one thing. The day after Rupert and I get back from Rivers, he goes abroad on a business trip. That's from the seventh of August till the fifteenth.'

'I'll remember. I just have to sort myself out first. This tour was a killer – and the assistant tour manager's always directly in the line of fire. Let alone all the hassle with this guy, Rick. And he's in LA now. He thinks he's in love with me.'

'But you're not in love with him?'

'He's a great guitarist.' At this they burst out laughing again.

Lucy said, 'Vee, your telephone bill!'

'Oh, that's okay. I'll call you again soon. Meanwhile, take care.'

'You too,' Lucy said. Then, 'Rupert says "Take care" is a ridiculous expression, and that you should only use it if someone's in danger.'

'It just means "Take care of yourself".'

'That's what I told him. And he said, "Then why not say 'Take care of yourself'." He's fussy about words. Like Mummy.'

'Well, that'll be something for them to talk about. Words. And perhaps you can all play Scrabble.'

Lucy said, '*I* suggested they could do the crossword together.' Vee laughed. So did Lucy, but only for a moment. Then she said, 'Seriously, Vee – he's wonderful.'

'I believe you. Bye.'

'Goodbye.' Lucy was smiling as she put down the receiver. She went up, collecting her bag on the first-floor landing, to her bedroom on the second floor. At once she crossed it to put on the bedside light. She disliked overhead lighting, a nicety to which the Dumbles were immune.

Lucy's room was clean and tidy. There was a watercolour of moorland over a small desk, and a photograph of her father on the bedside table. Another photograph – of her red setter, Rufus – was on the dressing-table with jars of cosmetics and a bottle of her favourite scent, *Fleurs d'Orlane*.

'Your room smells different from the rest of the house,'

Mag had said one evening recently. She sometimes dropped in for a 'little chat' with Lucy, last thing.

'Different? How?'

'More worldly. It's your posh scent, and all those cosmetics, I suppose.'

'Not so very many,' Lucy said, looking up from her book. (Nowadays, she always tried to read for a short time before going to sleep; she was working her way through various novels that Rupert admired.)

'Did I tell you I read this article by a famous dermatologist?'

'Yes, you told me.'

Mag ignored this. '*He* said all you need is Vaseline. I've been using it ever since.' Mag's skin was healthy-looking but weatherbeaten. However, like many mothers of large families who have not had to worry about money, she looked rather younger than her fifty-eight years.

'You're probably right,' Lucy said. 'Isn't it a bit sticky, though?' She made an involuntary grimace.

'No, no. Perfectly pleasant.' Mag opened a jar and sniffed the contents. 'I'm sure *this* costs a fortune,' she said. She peered at the label: ' "Restores the hydratic balance",' she read aloud, derisively.

'It *feels* nice,' Lucy said.

'Hunh!' Mag put the jar down with its lid askew. 'You should try Vaseline.'

'Mmm,' Lucy said. She had not done so. Tonight, as usual, when she had put on her cotton nightdress and brushed her teeth, she used the 'worldly-smelling' creams.

'Worldly' was a favourite word of Mag's. She had produced it a year ago, after the first time Lucy brought Rupert to the house: 'Rather worldly, isn't he?'

'Worldly? You mean because he makes jokes?' But Lucy was not smiling, and her tone was cool.

Mag looked startled. 'Lucy, what on earth's the matter?

54

Jokes? No, I meant his looks . . . his manner.'

'He's sophisticated,' Lucy said. Then she added, 'My mother's much more worldly than Rupert is.'

'Your mother? What can you mean? Teresa's a very devout Catholic.'

'Catholics can be worldly. Lots of my mother's friends are. Even some priests are. Like Father Jessop.'

'Father Jessop?' Mag gave a nervous laugh. 'Are you keen on this Rupert, Lucy?'

'I haven't known him long. Longer than you have, though.'

'You're quite right, dear. I haven't had a chance to get to know him.'

When Lucy repeated this conversation to Rupert, he said, 'It's no use. *Never the twain shall meet.*'

'You mean you won't meet Mag again?'

'Oh, of course I'll *meet* her. I meant that we'll never get on. Not *really.*'

'Perhaps you're right. Oh dear! She's been so good to me.'

'I'm not criticizing her. I'm sure she's perfectly splendid.'

'Mmm.'

A few weeks later Lucy said to Mag, 'Have you read Evelyn Waugh?'

'*Brideshead Revisited*? Oh yes. There's a beautiful death scene.'

'Rupert's very keen on Evelyn Waugh. But it was *Decline and Fall* he lent me. Now, that's what *I* call worldly.'

'Waugh was a convert. Perhaps he wrote it before he was received into the Church.'

Next day Lucy said, 'You were right, Mag. Waugh wrote *Decline and Fall* before he converted. I'll try the *Brideshead* one.'

But when she had finished that, she said to Rupert, 'I didn't like it.'

'Terribly sentimental, isn't it?'

She didn't answer directly. 'I thought it was so depressing. Being Catholic made them all so miserable. It's not meant to do that.'

'Darling Lucy.'

Now Lucy unfastened her plait. She shook her head and down came the hair which Rupert had called, at various times, 'your magic cloak', 'your Pre-Raphaelite dream', 'your golden tent', 'your silken involucre'. ('Silken *what*?' she had asked.) It sparked and shimmered as she brushed it. ('When we're married,' Rupert had said, 'I shall always brush your hair.')

Now she went out onto her balcony: a rustic wooden appendage to the back of the house, with plump struts like fat legs. The night was warm. The evening haze had gone and the moon was out. Lucy leant on the wooden rail. Beyond the fence of the bushy back garden was a triangular patch of heath with a road on either side of it. Beyond the road on Lucy's right was Hampstead village; beyond the one on her left was the main body of the heath. The little portion directly ahead of her was edged with a few trees and a cluster of bushes. As on other warm nights Lucy absorbed peace and air for a few minutes before going back inside.

Lucy's bed was made up with her own blue-and-white-striped sheets. The Dumbles' sheets were all old, and often Mag did not bother to sort them into matching pairs. Lucy secretly took her washing to the launderette: the Dumbles' old washing-machine did not get things very clean. She had her own iron and ironing-board in her cupboard; Mag seldom ironed. A story had once been current that the Dumbles kept a room full of clothes; in the morning each member of the family would pull out an armful and put it on. Their appearance was not wholly incompatible with this legend.

One evening shortly before she left for France, Mag had popped in while Lucy was brushing her hair. Hesitantly, Lucy had asked, 'What do you and Bernard do about your prayers?

At night, I mean. Do you kneel down?'

'Oh yes. One on each side of the bed. We always have. Why?'

'Oh, I don't know . . . it's a private sort of thing.'

'Private?'

'I don't mean in church. But one's own prayers . . . at night.'

Mag had laughed. 'Well, we don't pray *aloud*.'

'No. I see.'

However now, alone, after kneeling down and making the sign of the cross, Lucy did pray aloud. She said the Our Father, the Hail Mary, the Glory Be. Then came her list: the people she prayed for. Over the years some names had been dropped and others added, but nowadays her prayers always ended in the same way: 'God bless Daddy, and deliver him from Purgatory if he's still there. God bless Vee and help her to be happy. God bless Rupert and make him a Catholic, but only if it is Your will. God bless Mummy, and please make me love her.'

When she was in bed, with the light out, she murmured, as she always did, 'Guardian Angel, watch over me.'

Two

'She look'd as if she sat by Eden's door,
And grieved for those who could return no more.

'She was a Catholic, too, sincere, austere,
As far as her own gentle heart allow'd
And deem'd that fallen worship far more dear
Perhaps because 'twas fallen: her sires were proud
Of deeds and days when they had fill'd the ear
Of nations, and had never bent or bow'd
To novel power; and as she was the last,
She held their old faith and old feelings fast.

'She gazed upon a world she scarcely knew,
As seeking not to know it; silent, lone,
As grows a flower, thus quietly she grew,
And kept her heart serene within its zone.
There was awe in the homage which she drew;
Her spirit seem'd as seated on a throne
Apart from the surrounding world, and strong
In its own strength – most strange in one so young.'

'When we met last night, I knew there was something you
reminded me of – but what was it? Driving off, I suddenly
remembered, and as soon as I reached home, hurried to the
bookshelf, and found my Byron, and his best poem . . . *Don
Juan*.

'Sure enough – there you were. It was a pleasure to
recognize you again so soon. But how much I hope you'll
let me see you "in the flesh" again almost as quickly. I'll
telephone during the week. Perhaps we could have dinner?
                              'Yours,
                        'Rupert Deyntree'

This was the letter, marked 'Personal', that Lucy received at
her office two days after her first meeting with Rupert at the
charity art sale. No one had ever sent her a poem before, and
she re-read it numerous times before their first dinner at the
Firenze. Over a year later, she still sometimes took it from its
place in the back of her father's copy of the Jerusalem New
Testament.

'Of course you're more Catholic than any of us,' Mag Dumble
had once said to Lucy.

'I wish you wouldn't say that. No one's "more" Catholic
than someone else. Either you're a Catholic or you aren't.
Anyway, it would be impossible to be more Catholic than you
are, Mag.'

Indeed Mag's religion rioted through her life like the lantana
plant, illegal in some countries because it takes over whole
tracts of land. There was a picture of the Sacred Heart in her
bedroom above a stoup of Holy Water, frequently refilled from
a gallon jar, blessed by a cardinal. A rosary, said to be of olive
wood from the Garden of Gethsemane – and blessed by Pius
the Twelfth – hung from her bedpost. In the kitchen, over the
sink, hung a framed poem about how even a housewife could

humbly follow the example of 'Perpetua, Felicitas and all the strong and steadfast saints whose names are mentioned in the Mass'. The paper under the glass was yellowed, and the poem itself was outdated. Perpetua (after whom one of Mag's daughters was named) and Felicitas – saints who, like St George, had possibly never existed – were not mentioned in the new Mass.

But Mag said, 'Oh Lucy, I'm sure all that history must make a difference.' She began to sing, *'Faith of our Fathers, living still, we will be true to thee till death.'*

Mag's contralto was fruity, with a marked vibrato. 'An *embarrassing* voice, I always thought at school,' Lucy's mother had once commented. 'There was a sort of quiver in it that made one cringe. And she had such a *soulful* look when she was singing. Rather like a dog. Though of course dogs don't sing – thank goodness.' Teresa had sighed before adding, 'And they always gave her solos.'

'Oh, I think she sings quite well,' had been Lucy's reply. 'In tune, anyway.' She always felt impelled to protect people from her mother's little darts. All the same the word 'embarrassing' was not inaccurate: Teresa's darts were not only sharp, but well aimed. As Mag warbled, Lucy blushed and, turning away, fiddled with the end of her plait.

Mag sang on: *'Our fathers, chained in prisons dark, were still in heart and conscience free. How sweet would be their children's fate if they like them could die for thee.'*

Lucy said, 'My father couldn't stand that hymn.'

'Couldn't he?' Mag sounded astonished. 'I would have expected it to mean a lot to him. With the Blessed Hugh and so on.'

'He said "sweet" was a stupid word for being tortured, hanged and disembowelled.'

'Oh! Well, perhaps "noble" might be better, but it wouldn't scan. "Great," do you think? But that sounds so slangy nowadays – "You look great," and so on. What about "fine"?'

But Lucy did not have to answer: the telephone rang. Mag, at once absorbed in arrangements for the church bazaar, was distracted from the history of the Rivens, a subject which Lucy had told Vee she usually remembered in terms of the conflict between two incompatible people: her parents.

Lucy's grandfather, Hugh, had not been one of the combative Rivens. He had wanted to live the quiet life of a Catholic country gentleman, but this plan was interrupted by the First World War. In the Coldstream, he was awarded the DSO, and twice mentioned in dispatches. At the very end of the war, he was badly wounded. Fragments of shrapnel left in his body would pain him and make him irritable all his life. However, soon after the war, he met Louise Upperley: young, pretty and – though the word had not yet been invented – sexy. Later it would be rumoured that a liaison with the family chauffeur had prompted her parents to marry her off so quickly to Hugh Riven: nervy, far from rich and a Roman Catholic. (All the same, the Rivens were an ancient family and with no history of madness; unlike other Catholic families, they had never married their cousins.)

Louise converted with apparent enthusiasm; Hugh said she was a natural Catholic. In fact, she converted so easily because one religion meant no more to her than another.

They were married in 1920. A year later, Lucy's father, Edward, was born. In 1922, Louise ran away with a handsome American she had met on a visit to London. Abandoning Catholicism – as well as Hugh and Edward – she obtained a divorce in the United States, and remarried in a civil ceremony.

Of course, as a Catholic, Hugh could not remarry. He read, shot, supervised the estate, practised his religion, and became increasingly reclusive and sombre. In the circumstances, it was surprising how cheerful the motherless Edward managed to be. When he was told at fourteen – in his first year at Downside, the family school – that his mother, whom he could not remember, had been killed in a motor accident, he showed no grief; grief could hardly have been expected. At this time he started to dine with his father in the school holidays. After the meal, he would have a single glass of port, but his father would usually have several while he discoursed on various subjects: trench warfare, family history and books, but never his marriage.

Edward, like his father, was a reader. He was clever. From Downside, he went to Oxford. He had read History for a year when the Second World War broke out and he joined his father's regiment, the Coldstream. Like his father, he was brave. He was awarded the Military Cross for saving the lives of three of his men at extreme personal risk. In 1945, aged twenty-four, he was gallant, devout, thoughtful but still cheerful: a lieutenant in the 6th Independent Guards Tank Brigade, which was moving eastwards through Germany to reach the river Elbe before the Russians. The brigade was encamped near Celle, a town on the main road from Hanover to Hamburg, when, in April 1945, his life changed.

British troops had reached Bergen-Belsen only a few days earlier. Edward was in one of the first parties of officers stationed in the neighbourhood who were brought to see the camp.

He wrote to his father:

'An imposing barracks and a wood hid the camp. There was just this small road through the trees leading to it.

'When we got there, ambulances were coming and going. We couldn't make out why the stretchers were all empty till we discovered that it was impossible to distinguish between a stretcher with just blankets on it and one which held an incredibly emaciated body.

'All the inmates were in huts meant to hold about thirty people, but the Nazis had crowded over a thousand into each. In one hut we saw the living (if an ability to talk and eat can be termed "living"), the dying – those who would die in the next few hours – and the dead, all lying packed together.

'We'd roped in local Burgomasters to clean the compounds outside the huts where accumulated excreta and rotting flesh had lain, but the state of the place was still appalling – there were still dead bodies outside most of the huts. The SS guards who were captured when we took the place are doing the job of corpse lifting and burying. Some objected, apparently, that it was "against the rules" to make them do this work – I gather that our troops gave them a very rough time. We heard that the women SS were even worse than the men.

'We saw the incinerator where the bodies were burnt. We heard that the camp doctor injected corpses and *live people* with creosote and petrol to see what effect burning would have on them. He would also often go into a hut, saying "Far too many here", and loose off his revolver. According to prisoners, children were clubbed to death before being burnt; older people were put in alive. Precautions against escape were watch towers, etc., though how the Germans imagined that these people with thighs the size of my wrist could escape I don't know.

'The camp was the most appalling sight I have ever seen or ever will see. This could have happened to us if the Germans had captured our island. It brought home to me so much more clearly what we have been and still are fighting against, and it made me sure that the lives of many friends lost have been worth while.'

Edward remembered the visit for other things which he left

out of the letter: the smell of rotting flesh that was everywhere, the steady drip of excrement from one tier of bunks to another in the huts, a hand that clutched at him from a bunk where the living and the dead were indistinguishable. He left out the way the skin of naked bodies glistened like thin yellow rubber stretched over the bones. He left out the mass grave to which German guards were wheeling bodies in handcarts from a lorry, and tipping them into a pit while a British soldier kept a tally of the number. Edward had gone to the edge and looked down at the mass of bones, flesh and rags. The bodies were small, like children's; most of the heads were shaved, yet thick blond hair grew round one staring mask.

Normal things seemed alien. The bark of the birch trees planted round the compound shone, and their leaves were a young, bright green. The pine forest round the camp had a delicious smell of resin, and nearby Lüneburg Heath was the same mixture of colours as the moors round Rivendale. Bach had visited Lüneburg town, with its carved stone buildings, because it had the most beautiful organ in Europe. High on one of the cathedral walls was the English coat of arms: the coat of arms of the House of Hanover.

Edward prayed constantly at this time. But he shouted and groaned in his sleep, and his spontaneity seemed to have dried up, his cheerfulness to have been drained from him.

When he came home, someone said to Hugh, 'Not quite his old self – Edward'; Hugh answered, 'Give the boy time.' When he asked Edward if he were going back to Oxford, Edward said, 'I suppose so.' Before the war, he had thought he might become a don if he achieved the First his tutor expected. Now the prospect no longer attracted him, and Oxford had lost its charm. He made no friends: the boys fresh from school seemed callow, and other 'demobbed' undergraduates unbearably hearty.

He changed from History to Law. Perhaps he might practise

as a barrister on the Northern circuit. Law soon bored him – it seemed to have little to do with justice, which interested him – but he persevered. He ate his dinners in the Middle Temple. It was in the summer before he was admitted to the Bar that he met Teresa de Rawley in London, at a dinner party to which he had gone reluctantly: she was seated next to him.

She was beautiful: dark-haired, pale-faced, with huge brown eyes. She was intelligent. She was nineteen and very fresh. All this enchanted him. And she thought him handsome and 'smooth', a word she and her friends applied to attractive older men. (Edward, nearly thirty, was definitely an older man.) She was party-loving but also a very pious Catholic, and she was captivated by Edward's family history. 'Riven?' she said when they were introduced. 'Like the martyr – the Blessed Hugh?' (Hugh Riven, with several other English martyrs, had recently been beatified.)

Teresa found out all she could about the Rivens. She filled her head with medieval knights and crusaders and the two Riven martyrs. (Peter Riven, who had been hanged after the Pilgrimage of Grace, had also died for his religion.) It was romantic, too, that the Rivens were one of those rare Catholic families with a direct descent in the male line and that they still lived in the ancient place that shared their name. (Their house – like a few far grander houses – was not 'Hall', 'House' or 'Manor' but simply 'Rivendale'.)

By Teresa's family's standards, the Rivens were poor – Hugh Riven now let his shooting – but they still owned an estate, farmed by tenants, and their house contained treasures, and also holy relics. The de Rawleys were very devout Catholics. When Teresa's father, Lord Federham, proudly told Hugh that the family had been received into the Church three years before Cardinal Newman – England's most famous Victorian convert – Hugh smiled and nodded politely; he was determined to be amiable to the de Rawleys.

He was worried by Edward's gloomy moods and his unenthusiastic approach to the career he had chosen at the Bar. Fond though Hugh himself was of reading, he felt that Edward spent too much time in the library at Rivendale. Surely this beautiful girl would revitalize him? And – best of all her qualities – she was a devout Catholic: what had happened to Hugh could never happen to Edward.

Rivendale was spring-cleaned for the de Rawley's visit. Extra staff were brought in. Hugh's own charm – grown rusty – was polished up and brought out to shine. On a tour of the house, the guests were shown the priest's hole in the attic; the Blessed Hugh's shirt – frayed and yellowed, but still with a faint brown stain of Edmund Campion's blood – was taken from its wrappings, and his famous letter was examined in the library. Later the party walked to the barn where the stone crusader had lain since the destruction of the chapel. The de Rawleys were more than awed; they were overwhelmed.

Six months later, Edward and Teresa were married in London: Teresa's choice; Edward would have preferred a country wedding. The Nuptial Mass was at Teresa's favourite church: the Brompton Oratory, which the Rivens considered vulgarly ornate and un-English. The reception was held at the Dorchester, a hotel Hugh and Edward thought 'nouveau'. But a wedding is the bride's affair. It was a fine day, and everyone was happy.

They spent their honeymoon in Rome: Teresa's dream; she had never been there. All the de Rawleys loved Rome and, since becoming Catholics, had visited it whenever possible. (Shortly after their reception into the Church, the wife of the convert had exclaimed in St Peter's, 'How wonderful that this glorious building is now *ours*!') Edward had been to the city briefly as a boy, with his father, on their way to Florence. Rivens had never cared for Rome.

Teresa's family had wanted to arrange an audience with the Pope, but Edward had said, 'Not on our honeymoon, darling,' and she had acquiesced. (If she had pressed the point, he would have agreed: he was in love.)

The Spring was sunny; the old-fashioned hotel was comfortable; the food – at a time when English meals were meagre and dismal – was delicious. They both liked walking. Five days after their arrival, Edward – guidebook in hand – pointed to the stone church in the Piazza del Gesu: 'That's the Jesuit church.'

'Shall we go in?'

'No, don't let's. It might be unlucky.'

'Unlucky?' Although the day was warm, there was a wind blowing through the piazza. Teresa smoothed her hair.

Edward said, 'I remember this square. It's the windiest one in Rome. My father told me a story about it. He said the Devil and the wind were once walking together, and the Devil said, "This is a bit chilly for me. But there's a place here where I always get a warm welcome." And he went into the Jesuit church.' Edward laughed again.

'Oh, *Edward*!' Teresa said.

'Don't look so horrified, darling. It's only a joke. Our family can't stand Jesuits. We're famous for it.'

'But what about Blessed Edmund Campion?'

'Oh, he was all right – the exception that proves the rule.'

Teresa looked blank. After a moment she said, 'I've got several relations who are Jesuits.'

'I know, darling. It's not your fault.'

'*Fault*?' But then, as he was laughing, she laughed too. 'You're impossible,' she said. She added, 'I suppose being a Riven entitles you to make wicked jokes.'

'Absolutely.'

Next afternoon, they were going to Benediction at St Peter's, a special occasion, celebrating the Beatification of a Breton priest. Teresa had visited a cousin of her mother's, the Reverend Mother of a convent, who had given them tickets, and in St Peter's they sat on one of the grandstands under the dome. They could see everything from the west door to the altar. There were thousands of people below, and all the chandeliers glittered. Teresa gazed down the golden-vaulted nave to the plaited columns of Bernini's baldachino, then up to the riot of gilt angels and gilt clouds above the altar. She gave a deep happy sigh, then glanced at Edward. 'You're very pale,' she whispered.

'I'm quite all right. Just a bit hot.'

The church was fiercely hot as well as dizzyingly bright. Now the Pope was carried in on a red chair. 'How holy he looks,' Teresa murmured. As he blessed the congregation, the church was filled with shouts of 'Viva il Papa,' and then with loud clapping. The Pope's hand was upraised in Edward and Teresa's direction, and simultaneously they made the sign of the cross.

There was much choral singing – followed by clapping – in the Benediction service. 'Wonderful, wasn't it? Wonderful!' Teresa said when they were walking back to the hotel. Then she added, 'Though I was quite surprised when they all clapped as if it were a concert.'

'A dreadful concert,' Edward said. 'That nauseating version of Mozart's *Ave Verum*. As for the rest of the music, it was worse than banal. And the singing was pretty poor. Perhaps the Pope should bring back the *castrati*.'

'The what?'

'Oh, nothing.'

She said, 'I don't know much about music.'

They were passing a pavement café. 'Aren't you thirsty?' he asked.

'Yes, awfully.'

He smiled. 'Let's have a drink then.'

69

While they were waiting for his vermouth and her lemonade she said, 'You didn't like it, did you?'

'Nonsense. It was most impressive. Apart from the music.'

'Seeing the Holy Father was wonderful.'

'Yes.'

They smiled at each other, but something had changed. It had happened the night before.

Sexually, it had been their most successful night so far. Until now, like many men of his generation and class, Edward had bought sex from prostitutes. He had done so in London before the war, in France during it and since the war, several times in London and once or twice in Darlington. He always felt guilt and disgust afterwards, and had dreamed of an affair with a glamorous older woman, like the affairs he had read about in French novels. (Just such a woman had pressed his foot under the table at a dinner party soon after the war, but he had believed it was an accident and moved his foot away.) Now on his honeymoon he was very conscious of Teresa's purity and saw her passivity as virtue and delicacy. He had been distressed by her pain on losing her virginity and had apologized for it.

However, on the night before they went to St Peter's, she had shown signs of pleasure, and had nestled close to him after the act. 'Sweet one,' he had said, 'is it getting better for you?'

'Oh yes,' she said.

'Really?' He was eager to believe her.

'Oh yes.' She stroked his hair.

'I love you so much,' he said. Soon they fell asleep. He had woken two hours later from one of his dreams.

Her hand was on his arm. 'Edward,' she was saying. 'Darling, what's the matter? You were shouting and shaking.' She took her handkerchief from under the pillow and wiped his forehead. 'You're perspiring. Your pyjamas are soaked.'

'Yes. I'm sorry. I get these nightmares sometimes. It's to do with the war.'

He had not talked to her about Belsen. He had not wanted to upset her. But his father had mentioned it to her one day when they were walking in the dale. 'It upset him a lot, you know.'

Now she said, 'Your father told me. That you'd been to that place. Belsen. Is that what you dream about?'

'Yes.'

'It must have been awful.'

'Worse than awful. It was far worse. Evil. Absolute evil.'

She stroked his arm. Her expression was concerned; her brown eyes were hazy with sympathy. 'Poor darling Edward,' she said. 'You must try to forget it.'

'I don't think I'll ever be able to do that.'

'Oh but you must.' Then she said, 'And after all, they were only Jews, weren't they?'

He started up into a sitting position. She said, 'What's the matter?' He stood up. She said, 'Where are you going?'

'Oh, just to the bathroom, to change my sweaty pyjamas.' He went over to the chest of drawers and took out a clean pair. In the bathroom, he ran a bath and lay in it for a long time. She was asleep when he came back.

'You're very quiet this morning,' she said to him towards the end of breakfast. 'Is anything wrong?' Perhaps she had forgotten his dream or perhaps she thought it would be embarrassing for him to remember it.

'No,' he said, and then, 'Oh, by the way, there were all sorts of people in that camp. Russian prisoners of war, German Communists, Greeks, a wonderful Dutchman who'd been in the Resistance in Holland. Even a couple of English people. I'm sure there must have been Catholics, too – there were some Polish officers. But you were right – most of the prisoners were Jews.'

Her look was puzzled. 'Oh,' she said, and then, 'Catholics? Really? How terrible.'

They had finished breakfast. He said, 'Well, what shall we go and look at this morning?'

Of course, at the time of his visit to Belsen, Edward had not known who the prisoners were. He found out later: since the war, he had read everything he could find about the camps, because he needed to understand how they could have happened.

He read about the rise of Hitler; he learnt what post-war politicians – especially in the United States – would try to hide: that the only people who had really fought it were the Communists. Hundreds of thousands of Communists, gypsies and homosexuals had died in the camps, as well as six million Jews.

Edward was anti-Communist because of the atheism and terror of Stalin's Russia; he was ignorant of homosexuality, which he had been taught was a terrible sin. He had seen an occasional gypsy caravan, and heard that gypsies told fortunes. It was the figure 'six million' and the words 'the Final Solution' that sank into his mind where they encountered the anti-Jewish remarks he had heard all his life from members of his Church and his class. The history of Christian anti-Semitism was the particular darkness into which he descended. He, whose own family had been persecuted for their religion, now found he had to yield to a stronger claim.

St Augustine had declared them outcasts. Wherever Christianity became the state religion, anti-Semitism became active. Crusaders were among the first to massacre whole Jewish communities. Later, the Inquisition institutionalized the torture and murder of Jews. Pogroms became everyday occurrences.

Edward grew aware that Protestants, though often anti-

Semitic, had never persecuted Jews as Catholics had. At first thinking of persecution of Jews as 'Christian', he came to see it as 'Catholic'. Surely his Church, shamed by its terrible history, should have stood out with special strength against Hitler's extermination campaign?

It had not done so. On orders from the Vatican, the German Catholic Church came to terms with Hitler. It endorsed his foreign policy and ignored the concentration camps. Belated papal criticism of Nazi policy made no mention of anti-Semitism, and the Vatican did not intervene when the Germans took a thousand Jews from Rome to be gassed.

Sickened by this knowledge and by the eager collaboration in Jewish extermination of occupied Catholic countries – especially Poland but also Croatia, Hungary, Vichy France – Edward sought consolation in patriotism. Belsen had given him passionate faith in the rightness of the Allied cause: Belsen had represented what they were fighting against. Then he discovered the facts of Britain's refusal – like that of the United States – to take substantial numbers of Jewish refugees. He learnt that the existence of the camps had been well known to the British government in the 1930s, and that the Foreign Office and the BBC had deliberately suppressed information about them: many memoranda in high places dismissed Jewish 'hysteria'. And when, in the winter of 1942, all the facts about Auschwitz and other Polish camps had been documented, and Jewish organizations had pressed for access routes and gas chambers to be destroyed, their requests were ignored, though nearby targets were precision-bombed. Now Edward began to doubt that Britain had engaged in a crusade against Nazism, against Fascism; perhaps it had only been conducting a traditional war over territorial power. And if it had been occupied, what would have been his country's attitude to the fate of its Jewish citizens? He could not answer this.

For the Rivens, both their Church and their country had

always been objects of devotion; for Edward now, both seemed dark with stains of blood and shame.

Teresa had seemed to be becoming more sexually responsive on the night when she woke Edward from his dream. Now, in a new atmosphere, she became passive again. He still desired her, though in a more detached way than before.

During the rest of their honeymoon, they saw a lot of art, though few of Edward's favourite painters were well represented in Rome. However there were numerous works by Teresa's favourite: Raphael. 'You don't like him?' she asked, seeing Edward's indifferent expression.

He shrugged. 'Not particularly.'

'Who *do* you like?'

'They're mostly in Florence and Padua . . . Piero della Francesca . . . Giotto.'

'But everyone looks alike in their pictures.'

'Perhaps that's what makes them spiritual rather than sentimental.' He laughed. 'Raphael slept with every woman he met, and his great ambition was to be a cardinal. If he hadn't died, they would have made him one.' He paused. 'One day I shall go to Ravenna and Torcello to see the Byzantine mosaics. I love Byzantine art. It's so pure and secret. You'd say all the faces are alike – and it's quite true. But they have *hesychia*.'

'What's that?'

'It's a Greek word. For quietude. For serenity.'

Teresa said, 'Byzantine's Greek Orthodox, isn't it? Not Catholic?'

'Mmm.'

When they first met, he had asked her how her name was spelt. 'Oh, without an aitch,' she said. 'I'm called after Saint Teresa of Avila, not St Thérèse of Lisieux.'

'Ah!' Edward's tone was approving. 'The great Teresa.'

Now, in Rome, in front of Bernini's sculpture of her

namesake, Teresa said, 'I don't like it. She's too swoony.'

'Ecstatic. Perhaps you *should* have been named after the little Thérèse.'

'Why?'

'Cooler.'

'Oh. But she was so middle-class.'

'Ah!'

As their train drew out of the station, he said, 'I don't really like Rome.'

'Why?'

'It's so triumphant.'

She did not ask him what he meant, but opened the copy of *Vogue* she had bought for the journey.

There were letters waiting for them on the table in the hall. 'Someone's written to me as Mrs Teresa Riven instead of the Hon. Mrs Edward Riven. What an ignoramus!'

'Mmm.'

She would be astonished when in the 1951 election he voted Labour: 'How *can* you? These awful taxes. Daddy's being ruined.' Her father was rather rich.

'Oh well, he can console himself with St Augustine: "Business is in itself an evil." Or St Jerome: "A merchant can seldom, if ever, please God." '

'Daddy isn't a merchant. And I prefer sermons on Sunday – from a priest.'

'Priests seldom preach about Christ's utter contempt for wealth.'

'We're not exactly paupers ourselves.'

'No.' He sighed.

It was a cold war in which they drew constantly further apart, meeting for brief skirmishes. They continued to have sexual relations because they wanted children, but from the time of Edward's father's death in 1955 – he died of cancer, despondent that Edward had no heir – they moved into separate rooms. Edward would visit hers once or twice a week. 'You remind me of the Blessed Margaret Clitheroe,' he said once.

'What do you mean?'

'She accepted her martyrdom even when she was crushed beneath a heavy oaken door.'

'That's blasphemous.'

'No. Just a rather irreverent joke.'

'I don't think it's funny.'

'Nor do I, really.'

Still there was no child. The estate was prospering. Teresa, who had her family's business sense, took an interest in its management. Edward gradually stopped even pretending to practise at the Bar and spent most of his time in the library. Teresa paid frequent visits to family and friends in London. In 1956, Eva, a Hungarian refugee, joined the household. In her forties, a reactionary Catholic, devoted to Teresa and politely hostile to Edward, she was of practical help in running the house, but added to its tensions.

It was in 1960 that Teresa first suggested that they should make a pilgrimage to Walsingham to pray for a child. 'Next year perhaps,' he said. That year he went to Germany, to Bergen-Belsen. Inside the gate, overpowered, he knelt down to pray. A young girl, passing, gave him an astonished glance. She was heading for the Museum. After a few minutes Edward followed her and found her crying. 'I don't believe it,' she said to him.

She was Australian; her parents had emigrated after the war. They had prospered, but had both been killed in a motor accident the year before. On this trip to Europe, she had decided to visit the place where she was born: in a camp, they had said. 'I thought they meant a holiday camp.' She was sobbing. 'I had no idea at all. Why didn't they tell me?'

'I expect they wanted to spare you because they loved you,' he said.

They talked for some time. When they parted she said, 'You're very kind.'

Teresa would not have agreed. But next year he went with her on the pilgrimage to Walsingham. It was a cold day, with drizzling rain. They covered the last half mile on their knees: Teresa's stockings were torn and her knees were bleeding. A man and a woman were standing by the gate, holding placards inscribed, 'No Popery' and 'The Lord forbids Idolatry'. After they had prayed by the ruins, Edward said, 'I'm glad we came.' For several days a rare warmth persisted between them. Lucy was born nine months later. They had both expected a boy, to be called Hugh.

'I'd like to call her Lucy,' Edward said. He was sitting by her bed. The baby had been born at Rivendale.

'Why Lucy?'

He smiled, 'Because she'll be the light of our lives.'

'I'd thought of Mary. Because of Our Lady of Walsingham.'

'Lucy Mary.'

'All right. There's a St Lucy, isn't there?'

'Yes. I looked her up. She had beautiful eyes. A pagan nobleman wanted to marry her, but she'd sworn perpetual virginity. So she tore her eyes out and gave them to her suitor, saying, "Now let me live to God." Later her eyes were miraculously restored, but the rejected nobleman denounced her as a Christian, and she was martyred. In art she always carries a palm branch and usually a plate holding two eyes.'

'I don't like the eyes on the plate much. Is she blind in the pictures?'

'No. Remember, her eyes were miraculously restored.'

'Mmm. Lucy Mary. All right. Oh Edward, I so wanted a boy.'

'It's still possible.'

'Thanks to Our Lady.'

He picked up her hand and kissed it. She smiled.

Edward had a special reason for the name he had chosen for his daughter. He hoped that a longed-for new light was going to penetrate the dark corners of his religion. For this was 1962, the year of 'Vatican Two'.

The Council satisfied some of his expectations. Above all, Edward rejoiced in the acknowledgement that the Church's persecution of the Jews had been evil. He also delighted in the fresh emphasis placed on the New Testament: the Bible had been almost a forbidden book to Catholics of his generation. And, detesting the Church's long association with right-wing regimes and causes, he responded whole-heartedly to one Cardinal's impassioned cry: 'This is the Church of the Poor!'

To Teresa, on the other hand, Vatican Two brought anxiety and depression. She disliked the new '*rapprochement* with heretics', as she called it. 'They killed your ancestors,' she said to Edward.

'*They* did? What nonsense! Politicians did.'

'I can't understand you, Edward. And they've taken away our lovely Latin Mass.'

'Oh, it was all very well for *us*. I know Latin, and you followed the translation in your missal. But thousands of Catholics had no idea what was going on.'

'Of course they knew.'

'No, they didn't. They waited for bells to ring to tell them what to do. Meanwhile they said their rosaries. I once talked to an old Irish woman . . . she had absolutely no idea—'

'Oh well, the *Irish*!'

'The Irish have suffered for their Faith more than any of us. That old woman was holy.'

'You admit that? Even though she couldn't follow the Latin?'

Eva – as upset as Teresa by Vatican Two – smirked. Edward said, 'Oh really, Teresa.'

'And all that *shaking hands*,' Teresa said.

'It's like the kiss of peace of the Early Christians.'

'Well, I suppose I should be thankful I don't have to *kiss* all those people.'

At Mass, Teresa's cool, almost limp little handshake contrasted with Edward's eager grasp. Vatican Two had renewed his spiritual life; it had petrified Teresa's.

Eva – who had a horror of 'heretics' – always supported Teresa. But when Teresa's 'old school chum', Mag, met at an Old Girls' Reunion at their convent, came to stay, she put herself in the position of a good-humoured referee, as at some sporting event. Curiously, this lightened the atmosphere. Teresa patronized Mag – who at school had a 'crush' on her – quite fondly; Edward liked her though he sometimes tired of her reverence for his ancestors.

Before inviting her, Teresa, referring to Mag's husband, said, 'I shall ask her without that dull little man.'

'Will she come?'

'Oh yes . . . to *Rivendale*.'

Teresa was right. Indeed, Mag appreciated what she called 'this little break from household cares'. She added, 'You're so thoughtful, Teresa.'

'You must come again,' Teresa said, and Edward warmly agreed. Only Eva, feeling displaced from her position in Teresa's life, looked sour during Mag's visits.

Teresa's initial regret that her child was a girl – calmed by Edward's kindness at the baby's birth and by the hope of another child – hardened as time passed. For a further twelve years she would try to conceive. They undertook another pilgrimage to Walsingham in 1966, but no pregnancy followed. When she suggested a third, two years later, he refused: 'Really, Teresa, you're so superstitious. You remind me of the lady who, when she kissed the corpse of your namesake, bit off a toe so that she could take home a holy relic.'

'Sometimes you're quite disgusting, Edward. Going to

Walsingham worked the first time.'

'Well, it didn't the second time. Perhaps God doesn't want us to have any more children. Let's stop bothering Him.'

'Christ said, "Ask and you shall receive." '

'There's nothing to stop you *asking.*'

Wanting 'an heir' was something he could not reconcile with his approach to his religion. He said, 'She may be the last in name, but she's not necessarily the last. She'll probably marry and have children.'

'But they won't be Rivens,' Teresa said.

'It's odd that you mind that more than I do.' He minded less because he loved Lucy more; Teresa resented her being a girl. And Lucy, reciprocally, loved him more than she loved her cool, critical mother.

'When I was small,' she once told Vee, 'I thought they were just disagreeing, though somehow it always made me uneasy. But gradually I couldn't help realizing that underneath was . . . well, a sort of hostility.'

The Riven family motto was *'Certum est'* ('It is certain'). Edward liked to believe that this derived from an early Church Father's comment on Christianity: *'Certum est quia impossibile est'* ('It is certain because it is impossible'). Despite its impeccable source, Teresa did not care for this derivation. 'For God, all things are possible,' she said.

'That's just the point. Can't you see?'

Teresa said, 'Well, *I* think *"Certum est"* just refers to our Catholic faith.'

'Of course you can think what you please.' Hearing the bored patience of her father's tone, Lucy saw her mother's lips tighten.

A genealogist had suggested that the Rivens were descended from a Norman knight called de Rives. 'But there's a gap of three generations in his calculations,' Edward said. 'Apart from the different name. I'm not at all keen on those Norman bullies.

I like to think of our famous fairness – there's that fifteenth-century reference to us as "Fair but Few" – and our equally well-known obstinacy as Anglo-Saxon.'

'Well, we know all about the obstinacy,' Teresa said with her hard little laugh, 'but I can't think why you want to be descended from people who painted themselves blue and lived in caves.'

'I think you're confusing the Anglo-Saxons with the Ancient Britons, Teresa . . . a mere gap of ten centuries.'

Lucy observed her mother's angry blush.

She told Vee of another occasion when she and her parents had taken Mag to see the crusader's tomb.

'Everyone loves the crusader,' Teresa said. It was true. The effect of the stone tomb in the empty, dusty barn to which it had been taken after the chapel was burnt down was powerful: at once awesome and touching. The sides of the tomb were darkened by the flames that had destroyed the chapel. On top, the crusader lay in his mail coat with his shield over his chest and his sword at his side. His face was stern and calm. His legs were crossed at the ankle. This, as Edward told Mag, showed that he had been on one crusade. If he had been on two, his legs would have been crossed at the knee, and if on three, at the thigh. His little dog lay at his feet. (The first time Lucy saw the tomb, as a small child, she had exclaimed, 'Oh, I love the little doggy!' 'Dog, not doggy,' Teresa, who thought pet names, nicknames and abbreviations 'common', had reproved her.)

To Mag, Teresa had quoted, '*A very parfit gentil knight.*'

'Oh, *yes*!' Mag's voice was breathy.

'Absolute nonsense, of course,' said Edward. 'He was a looter and a mercenary. Almost all those crusaders were utter thugs. The first crusade wasn't so bad. But the others were really just expeditions for plunder. *Parfit gentil knight* indeed! His brother who fought for England at Crécy and Poitiers

81

deserved a monument far more than Geoffrey did.'

'You always try to tarnish beautiful things, Edward,' Teresa said.

Mag broke in: 'I think your crusader's simply super! And, gosh, what a lot of history you know, Edward.' She had chattered all the way home ignoring Edward and Teresa's grim silence.

Yet once, when Edward and Lucy, on a walk, had gone into the barn alone, Lucy had seen affection in the way her father ran his hand over the knight's mailed head.

Nothing could alter Teresa's romantic devotion to the Middle Ages and to her idea of 'chivalry'.

'Chivalry!' exclaimed Edward. 'The Black Prince is called a model of chivalry. Yet he massacred the whole population of Limoges – men, women and babes in arms – and was still longing for revenge against his enemies on his deathbed. The Church said all those warriors were like ravening wolves – you should remember that, Teresa. Or are you thinking of tournaments? *They* came into being because the nobles were so crazed about fighting that, when there was no war, they had to find a substitute. What a stupid business – not even funny, unlike that tournament your ancestor the convert arranged, when it poured with rain and he fell off his horse.' Edward's laugh was hearty.

He often made jokes about Teresa's family, especially the third Baron Federham who, in 1844, had become a Catholic and whom Edward always referred to as 'the convert'.

'I can't think why you mock *him*,' Teresa said. 'It was he who brought us back to the Faith.'

'Yes – but really he was a pretty hilarious character. All that medieval nonsense. Adding the "de" to "Rawley", and that ridiculous tournament. I can just imagine him, immobilized by his armour, crashing to the ground from his horse, and having to be helped off the field, covered in mud.' Edward laughed. 'But washing tramps' feet – that was best of all – I hear they came from all over the country for the free meal and alms they got afterwards.'

'I don't see what's so funny about trying to follow Our Lord's example,' Teresa said. 'And I still think the Middle Ages were beautiful. Courtly love – a knight's devotion to his lady . . .' Her face softened as she said this.

'Courtly love? Affairs with married women, you mean. Adultery's the word you're looking for. Of course, in those days, love and marriage seldom coincided. Marriage was a matter of property and succession. So men turned to married women. Like Edward the Second – now he was a fine example of courtly love! He became obsessed with the Countess of Salisbury, and sent her husband off to Brittany. When she turned him down, he raped her, and left her fainting and "bleeding from the mouth and nose and other parts" as the chronicler put it. When her husband came back from France, she told him what had happened, and he thought of his former great friendship with the King, and decided he couldn't live in England any longer. He got rid of all his lands – though he made sure his wife would have her dowry – and went to the court, where he told the King that he had thrown him in the dung. Then he left the country. It was a great scandal. Everyone blamed the King.'

'Well, if everyone blamed him, it can't always have been like that – courtly love,' Teresa said. Then she asked, 'Did Salisbury take his wife with him?'

'No. She'd been dishonoured.'

'I think that's horrible and unfair.'

'*Unfair*! Sometimes you sound like a schoolgirl, Teresa.'

Lucy was sitting on the terrace outside the library when this conversation took place. Her father would not have talked of rape and adultery if he had known she was there. Now her mother came out of the library onto the terrace. She did not notice Lucy, but Lucy saw that, as she went down the steps into the garden, she – like the Countess of Salisbury – was crying.

'I felt sorry for her. I wanted to run after her,' Lucy told Vee years later. 'But I knew she'd freeze me off.'

'I'll bet!' Vee laughed, but then she sighed. 'It must have been awful for you – your parents arguing all the time. Didn't they *ever* agree?'

Lucy hesitated. Then she smiled. 'Well, they both hated Henry the Eighth. I do too – it's hard not to. What a brute! Cruel, vengeful, greedy, cunning, sex-crazed. A liar, a thief and a murderer.'

'Not the ideal founder for a new Church, I guess.'

'Daddy always said Henry wasn't really interested in religion – only in getting his own way and stealing Church property. And when people protested, he killed them. Like he killed Peter Riven for taking part in the Pilgrimage of Grace. All the pilgrims wanted was for spiritual things to stay in the care of Rome, and when they made their case to the King's Council, they were given a written free pardon. But of course Henry reneged on it. He had them rounded up as rebels and hanged in chains. Two hundred of them, including Peter.'

'I can see why you all hate Henry. But what did your parents feel about "Bloody Mary" – as the nuns never let us call her.'

'My mother felt the same as the nuns, but my father said it was better to kill for politics, as Protestants like Henry and Elizabeth did, than for religion, like Mary. He said *that* was really unChristian. And my mother said, "So you call Mary, who restored the Faith, worse than Elizabeth who murdered the Blessed Hugh?" '

'What did your father say to that?'

'Oh, he began talking about the Papal Bull of 1570 – the worst year in English Catholic history, he called it. The Pope declared Queen Elizabeth a bastard and didn't only excommunicate her but everyone who obeyed her laws. My father said the Pope was a "vile fanatic". "Edward!" – my mother turned pale, she really did. "Vile fanatic," my father repeated. "Plotting to put a Spaniard on the throne!" He said the Pope had forced patriotic Catholics like us to choose between our religion and our Queen. Until the Bull, Elizabeth hadn't executed any Catholics for their Faith, but after it – everything changed. Hundreds of Catholics were tortured and executed, and thousands more imprisoned and ruined by the huge fines they had to pay if they didn't attend Protestant services.' Lucy paused. Then she said, 'That was when it got really difficult to be a Catholic. You had to be really brave – and even braver to be a Catholic priest, like Edmund Campion.

'Everyone thought Campion was going to have a brilliant future. His patron was the Earl of Leicester – Hugh Riven's patron, too – though Hugh wasn't a cleric, like Campion. Hugh was a courtier – the only one in our family history. A wonderful dancer – Queen Elizabeth was very keen on dancing – and a wit. At court, he'd given up practising his religion – although he was Peter Riven's nephew.'

'Perhaps his uncle's fate put him off,' Vee said.

'Perhaps. Campion hesitated before he gave up his career, but finally he made his choice. He went to France, and then to Rome where he became a Jesuit. Jesuits were a new order, founded by a Spaniard, and lots of English people believed they were agents of Spain. My father said some of them were – but not Campion. Anyway, in the year Campion came back to England, a new act was passed making it High Treason to be reconciled to Rome. For just hearing Mass, the penalty was a year in prison and an enormous fine. Yet Catholics gave Campion a terrific welcome as he travelled through England – he was in disguise – saying Mass and bringing them the sacraments.' Lucy paused again. 'You see, Vee, they were starving for spiritual food.'

Vee raised her eyebrows, but said nothing. Lucy went on. 'Campion was arrested – betrayed by a spy – after a year, and brought to London. His arms were tied behind his back, and his feet under his horse. He wore a placard saying, "Campion, the Seditious Jesuit." They took him through a yelling crowd to the Tower, where they left him for four days in a hole at the end of the torture chamber – it was so small that he couldn't either stand up or lie down. Then they brought him – you can imagine how filthy he was – straight into the presence of the Queen and Leicester. Hugh Riven was in attendance.

'The Queen asked Campion if he acknowledged her as a lawful sovereign, and he told her that he did. They said the past few years would be forgotten and a great future would be open to him again if he publicly gave up his Faith and entered the Protestant ministry, but he said he couldn't. They told him that all that was wrong with him was that he was a Papist, and he said, "Which is my greatest glory." So they sent him back to the Tower where they racked him for two days. After that they offered him pardon and liberty if he would just appear in a Protestant church. He refused.'

'Crazy!' Vee exclaimed.

'Things were different then.' Lucy's tone was remote, almost stern. 'They tortured him more before they decided to bring him and two other priests to trial. Then they had to postpone the trial because the racking had dislocated his limbs so badly that he couldn't move at all. When they finally held it – Hugh was there – Campion still couldn't lift his arm. When he had to testify, the other two priests raised it for him. Campion said, "Our religion, and our religion only, is our crime," and absolutely no evidence was brought to disprove that. Just the same, they were all sentenced to death as traitors.

'They were executed in December. It had been raining for days. They were dragged on hurdles, behind horses, through the mud from the Tower to Tyburn – that's where Marble Arch is now. There was a huge crowd. Just by the scaffold, a group of courtiers – Hugh was one of them – were having a scientific discussion when Campion, all muddy, was untied from the hurdle and put on the cart under the scaffold with a noose round his neck. The crowd was making a terrific noise, and only the people – like Hugh – who were very near could hear Campion say that he was completely innocent of treason. One of the courtiers shouted that it was too late to deny what had been proved, and Campion said, "If you esteem my religion treason, then am I guilty." He prayed for the Queen, and another courtier shouted, "What Queen do you pray for?" Campion answered, "For Elizabeth, your queen and mine." Then the cart was driven away. Campion was lucky. They let him hang till he was unconscious or dead before they cut him down and quartered him. When they flung his entrails into the cauldron of boiling water that was waiting, blood splashed on the sleeve of Hugh's shirt.'

'Ugh,' exclaimed Vee. 'Horrible!' but Lucy didn't seem to hear her.

'A week later, Hugh went home to Yorkshire to visit his family. Then he went to France. He left the shirt splashed with Campion's blood at Rivendale, with a letter to his brother. They're still there. The writing of the letter's hard to read, so Daddy made a copy for me. I keep it in my missal.'

Hugh Riven had written:

'Since the trial and martyrdom of Father Campion, my conscience has become settled that our old Romish religion is the most true Catholic Church. Indeed, when his blood splashed upon my sleeve then knew I that unless I am a true member thereof I cannot be saved. Yet is reconciliation with it High Treason by Act of Parliament. Which odious name of traitor I do wholly detest, and that our house and name be this falsely attainted. You know that I will never plot against Her Majesty nor, whatever may betide, serve the King of Spain or any of his agents so long as he is enemy to our Queen. Neither shall I be guilty of any conspiracy against Her Majesty's person. I am and will be as good a subject for allegiance to Her Majesty as any is in England, and this thou knowest full well. Yet must I save my soul.'

Lucy told Vee how, when he left England, Hugh had gone to the English College for priests at Douai in France. 'He didn't become a Jesuit, like Campion. He was suspicious of the plots so many of them were involved in. He became a secular priest and then returned to England. Eighteen months later, they arrested him in London while he was saying Mass. He was taken to the house of a terrible man called Richard Topcliffe.

'I used to have nightmares about Topcliffe as a child. I used to be afraid I'd meet his ghost in the passages at Rivers. Silly, as he'd never been there. But I was more frightened of Topcliffe even than of Winnie with the Long Green Hands. I imagined him as pale, with a twisted face – he sort of symbolized Evil to me.

'He was a persecutor of Catholics – that was his *job*, though he was called "one of Her Majesty's servants". Well, he was, in his personal torture chamber at his house. Apparently people were getting upset by how much the rack was used at the Tower. Topcliffe wrote letters to the Queen, describing the tortures.

'Topcliffe hung Hugh by his hands from stanchions in the wall. His toes brushed the ground, and the weight of his body stretched him – just like a rack. As he hung there, Topcliffe asked him to confess to treason and name his accomplices. "I cannot and I will not," Hugh said. He prayed until he fainted. Servants held his body up till he started praying again, then they let go. That happened eight or nine times in one day.

'He was kept at Topcliffe's house for three months, and tortured over and over again. Over and over again, he repeated that all he'd done was carry out the work of a priest. When at last he was tried, that was all they raised against him. But he was sentenced to death for High Treason.

'He was dragged to Tyburn on a freezing February day, wearing only a shirt. He had to stand on the cart, with the noose round his neck, for nearly two hours while Topcliffe hectored him to recant and confess treason. Hugh said, "I die for religion, not for treason."

'At last Topcliffe shouted, "Away with the traitor," and the cart was pulled away. But at once Topcliffe ordered that he should be cut down. Someone who was there said, "When the tormentor was pulling out his bowels, Father Riven was alive, and gave a very great groan." '

'It's disgusting,' Vee said. 'It's horrible. How could your parents have let you hear that stuff, as a child? No wonder you had nightmares!'

'No – you're wrong,' Lucy said. 'I'm glad they told me, in spite of the nightmares. Anyway, all children have nightmares. It made me so proud that Hugh was so brave and wonderful. I still feel that because of what he did and how he died, God will never let us lose our Faith. I'm sure *both* my parents would agree with that. After all we've been Catholics ever since. He was our highest point.'

'How do you mean?'

'After him, it was really just – holding on. We lost a lot, paying those huge recusancy fines. And when we backed Charles the First, and Cromwell won, all our estates were confiscated. That was when a band of Puritans destroyed our chapel. They hacked the carvings and mutilated a crucifix before they burnt the whole place down. All that was left was the crusader on his scorched tomb. We got the estate back at the Restoration, but nothing else – Charles the Second was always desperately short of cash. After that, we lived very quietly. My father used to point out that my mother's family, the Rawleys – they weren't de Rawley yet – made their money and got their title under the Georges. "Four coarse, dull kings who could hardly speak English," he said. "Their one popular asset was that they weren't Catholics." '

'But you weren't being persecuted any more, by then,' Vee said.

'Well, not *persecuted*. But we weren't allowed to take part in public life or to go to university or into the army. The Mass was still illegal. We called it "Prayers" and celebrated it behind locked doors. We paid double land-tax. There were even restrictions on Catholics inheriting land, but we managed to get round those, and one Riven married a great heiress. It was his son who built a great classical mansion behind our old house. He collected pictures and statues and was interested in science and new ideas. He even corresponded with Voltaire. When the new house and all his collection were destroyed by fire, his wife, who was very pious – rather like my mother – thought it was a Divine judgement on him. We've lived in the old house ever since.

'Lots of Catholics who'd been heroic under the Tudors, drifted into the Church of England in the eighteenth century because life was so frustrating. We held on – but we wanted to be accepted as patriotic English people. We worked for Catholic Relief. We used to quarrel with other Catholics who were closer to Rome. We'd always suspected Jesuits – we wanted an English kind of Catholicism, and thought the Pope should keep quiet about everything except dogma. But after Catholic Emancipation, we even got involved in a quarrel about that. My great-great-grandfather studied theology in Munich under a famous Catholic scholar and dreamed of uniting Liberalism and Catholicism against unbelief and against Tories – "people like your family," my father told my mother. Oh, I think they had their worst arguments of all about my great-great-grandfather, who went to Vatican One in 1870. Just as my father said that 1570 was the worst year for English Catholics, he said that 1870 was the worst year for *all* Catholics.'

'Why?' asked Vee. 'What happened then?'

'What happened then? Papal Infallibility! My great-great-grandfather thought its acceptance was a scandal. Fewer than half the Council agreed to it, and a lot of them were coerced by threats. After the dogma was announced he left Rome for ever. He hated the place, and he thought a Jesuit was trying to poison him. When my father said that, my mother said, "What outrageous nonsense!" "You think so?" my father said in a sarcastic voice. Then my mother said, "Sometimes you don't talk like a Catholic at all." '

'What did your father say then?'

'Oh, he made a sort of speech.' Lucy paused. 'Perhaps he made too many speeches – but I always agreed with what he said. I did that time. He said that since the reign of Henry the Eighth, our family had been martyred and persecuted, and then discriminated against and isolated from English life, and yet we'd always remained Catholics. He said that my great-great-grandfather was a Catholic and that so was his son – my father's grandfather – who battled for the movement called Modernism, which tried to harmonize Catholicism with science and modern thought. But the Pope condemned Modernism and when my father's grandfather invited a priest who'd been excommunicated for his Modernist views to stay with us, the local bishop refused him Holy Communion in the diocese unless he sent the priest away and publicly abjured Modernism. He refused, and often travelled long distances to receive Communion. "That sustained him," my father said, "and so, I like to think, did our family's history, including its tradition of independent thought. He was a Catholic, just as I am, for better or worse, though since Vatican Two, things seem to be getting better." '

'What did your mother say to that?'

'Oh – yet again – she left the room.'

From the time Lucy was nine, her mother had pressed for her to be sent as a boarder to her own old convent school. Edward refused to consider it: 'She's too young.'

'Nanny certainly can't teach her. I'm always correcting Lucy's grammar and that Yorkshire accent she's picked up.' Teresa was not fond of Nanny, a forthright local woman to whom Lucy was devoted and whom Edward liked. Teresa would complain that Edward had dismissed an efficient maid 'just because she told Lucy fairy stories' yet kept on Nanny long after she was needed.

'Nanny's useful in all sorts of ways. We can teach Lucy ourselves,' Edward said.

'She ought to meet other children of her own class.'

However, it was not till Lucy was twelve – with a good knowledge of French, from Eva, English from her mother, and Latin and History from her father (also a less proficient teacher of Geography, Maths and Science) – that she was sent away to school. By this time Edward realized that she would appreciate more Maths and Science than she could acquire at home and that learning English from her mother was putting her off the subject; she read less and less for pleasure.

Edward went with Teresa and Lucy to the interview at the convent, housed in a large country house in Surrey. In an argument beforehand with Teresa, he had said, 'I don't want Lucy to be soaked in shame.'

'What do you mean?' she flushed.

'Oh, all that stuff I've gathered from you and Mag: never being naked even when you were alone and not wearing shorts for tennis and going down to the river to bathe in your overcoats.'

'I'm sure all that's changed.' She added, 'You don't want her to be modest?'

'That's not what I said.' He repeated, 'I don't want her to be soaked in shame.'

Teresa looked away. Over the years her distaste for sex had turned to a disgust that extended beyond the act itself; seeing a couple kissing, she would involuntarily turn away. It was in the year that Lucy went to school that Edward and Teresa's sex-life ended one night when he heard her teeth grinding and became conscious of her fists clenched at her sides. He moved away. 'Do you offer it up?' he asked.

'I don't know what you mean.' She turned from him.

He was standing by the bed. He said, 'Teresa, I'll trouble you no more. Never again.' He saw her body become limp with relief, but she said nothing. He went back to his own room. He kept his word.

At the convent many things had changed since Teresa's day. The obsession with preventing 'special friendships' had gone: girls could walk in pairs and in the fifth form even shared study-bedrooms. In the dormitories there were no more cubicles with curtains which had to be closed while dressing or undressing, though these functions were still performed draped in a dressing-gown: what had been called 'immodesty' in this regard had been renamed 'vulgarity'. Intense *surveillance* – spying (part of the order's French inheritance) – was no longer practised: the girls' desks were not regularly searched or their correspondence read.

All the nuns were now known as 'Sisters'. (In Teresa's day the upper-class nuns who taught and supervised had been called 'Mothers' and only the working-class ones who did the manual labour had been 'Sisters'.) Since the reforms of Vatican Two, several of Teresa's favourite 'Mothers' had left the convent. A few of those who remained still wore the fifteenth-century habit with its long black skirt and cape, starched white pie-frill and black veil, but the rest had changed to what Teresa described as 'District nurse – dowdy skirt, blouse and cardigan.

So *charmless*!' ('Are nuns meant to be charming?' Edward asked.)

Since Vatican Two, the number of vocations had decreased: a different type of person was being attracted to conventual life, one with a desire to help others materially as well as spiritually. (The convent's novice house had been moved to an industrial town.)

There were many more lay teachers now and much more emphasis on 'careers'. There was a male science teacher – science had not really been taught at all in Teresa's day – and the Bursar was a retired army officer. However, when Lucy arrived at the convent there were still thirty nuns. (By the time she left there would be only twenty and a few years later the school, though still Catholic, would be transferred to lay management.)

Religious observances had altered too. 'Doctrine' had become 'Religious Education'. Attendance at daily Mass was voluntary. In Teresa's day 'second rising' – the term still used in Lucy's time for the extra half hour in bed when Mass was not attended – had been allowed only on Saturday. 'It was a real treat!' Teresa said. ('Should missing Mass be a treat?' asked Edward.) Sunday Mass, prayers at the morning assembly and evening prayers were still held. But the abolition of Benediction and of the daily rosary in May – 'Our Lady's month' – distressed Teresa, and she cried when she heard that the procession was no longer held on the eighth of December – Feast of the Immaculate Conception – when each girl dropped a lily into a basket in front of the statue in the chapel, saying, 'Oh Mary, I give you the lily of my heart. Be thou its guardian for ever.'

What had not changed was an emphasis on quiet and order which Lucy found appealing. She also enjoyed the international character of the school, though she became involved in political arguments with girls whose families supported the dictatorships still existing in Spain and Portugal. But now Lucy's left-wing views, instilled by her father, were considered an eccentricity not the crime they would have been in her mother's day. She was liked by most teachers and girls, though some of the older nuns did not care for the remote manner she adopted when they gushed over not only her Riven ancestry but the more obvious grandeur of her mother's family. However, the only great friend she made was Vee.

Vee was American. She was not a Catholic. Although her Jewish mother had converted to Christianity, when she married Vee's Episcopalian father, Vee, at this time, always declared she was Jewish. She would not allow anyone to call her by her Christian name, Veronica, but insisted on being called Vee. Her parents were separated. Her father had brought her to England, a country which she constantly announced that she hated. She was on the brink of being expelled from the convent when Lucy arrived there.

Their friendship – the instant bond they formed – changed things. Lucy gave her a sense of safety she had never known before. She gave Lucy a sense of adventure, and tempered her seriousness. With Vee, Lucy became more light-hearted.

When they were both thirteen, Vee came to stay at Rivendale. At lunch on her first day, she announced, 'I'm Jewish.'

'Really?' said Edward. 'I'm very interested in Judaism.'

'I'm no expert,' Vee said hastily. 'But my mother was Jewish, and it descends in the female line.'

'Why are you at a convent then?'

'Oh, my parents are separated.' After a moment she added, 'My father thinks convent girls have beautiful manners. I'm the exception that proves the rule.'

Edward laughed. 'What nonsense! Your manners are charming.' When she left, he said to Lucy, 'You must ask her again. I liked her very much.'

Teresa said, 'What a strange friend for you to make, Lucy. An American and a Jewess. Not that she looks very Jewish. More like . . . oh, there was a little fawn in some ghastly cartoon by that awful American – Walter something.'

Lucy was often able to follow her mother's thought processes. '*Bambi*, you mean? Oh Mummy, I'm sure Walt Disney's name wasn't Walter.'

'*Walt* – ugh! He couldn't have been christened *that*, surely?' Teresa laughed. 'Though of course he probably wasn't christened at all. Probably another Jew. *Bambi* – yes, that was it. Big eyes and *vulgarly* long lashes.'

Lucy always winced at her mother's anti-Semitism, usually aimed at Edward: a counter-attack to his criticisms of the Church.

'So *Jewish*-looking,' Teresa once said, looking at a photograph in the newspaper.

Edward looked at it over her shoulder. 'Christ probably looked rather like that. I'm sure he wasn't tall and pale, with light-brown hair and blue eyes. Probably he and all the apostles were small and dark with hooked noses and black eyes. Religious painters used to make only Judas look Jewish – so idiotic!'

When Lucy and Vee met again at school, Vee said, 'Your father's great.' Then she added, cautiously, 'Your mother rather frightens me.'

'Frightens *you*? No one frightens *you*. She sometimes frightens *me*.' Disloyally, Lucy joined Vee in a burst of therapeutic laughter. But a moment later she said, 'I think Daddy's getting ill. It worries me terribly.'

Cancer, which would kill Edward, was making its first assault on him. He went to hospital, returned, went to hospital a year later, came home again. When Lucy was fifteen, for a whole year the disease seemed defeated. When it came back, his face had a yellow look.

He had always gone to Mass in the local town once or twice a week. Now he went daily, but taken by the gardener, because driving tired him. In the holidays Lucy went too. At St Cuthbert's, the ugly red-brick church, they sometimes formed the whole congregation, especially on winter mornings. During term, Lucy started going to daily Mass to pray for her father.

In Yorkshire, Teresa went to Mass only on Sundays and Holy Days of Obligation. With her distaste for the new liturgy – and the dislike she had always felt for the ugly little church – she preferred her private devotions: the rosary and various well-worn books of spiritual solace. When in London, however, she often went to weekday Mass at the Brompton Oratory, and always to the High Mass there on Sunday; afterwards, on the steps, she met old friends, smart and beautifully made-up, as she was, from Knightsbridge and Belgravia. Lucy hated these occasions. In her mid-teens, though not fat, she was solid; with these friends of her mother's she became stolid, too. She would not seem stolid at all when, back at Rivendale, lit with joy, she rushed to her father.

Edward was now almost exclusively preoccupied with religion. He belonged to a society dedicated to dialogue between Christians and Jews, and after 1975, when the Jesuits declared that henceforward their mission was to be a commitment to the service of the poor and the pursuit, throughout the world, of faith and justice, he abandoned the centuries-old Riven prejudice against them. Jesuits came to stay at Rivendale, and Teresa was horrified by discussions of liberation theology.

Lucy would often find her father reading the New Testament of the Jerusalem Bible. 'Much as I admire the Jews,' he told her, 'the Old Testament makes me shudder. Like Islam, it inculcates revenge, and the renunciation of revenge is the unique beauty of Christianity.' Teresa – an old-fashioned Catholic – never read the Bible.

On Edward's desk were many volumes of new theology; the drawers were packed with theological correspondence. Just as his great-grandfather had been influenced by an advanced German theologian, so Edward was now by the ecumenical Swiss theologian, Hans Kung. Indeed he read Kung's book, *On Being a Christian*, almost as often as his New Testament, and would quote from it to Lucy.

'Kung says the Protestants are too Biblical, the Orthodox too traditional, and we Catholics too authoritarian. Isn't that brilliant?'

'What does he mean – too Biblical?'

'Leaving no room for our mysteries, our sacraments – the links between God and us, between heaven and earth. That's what makes Protestantism seem so flat to us, and their churches so lifeless – no sanctuary lamp, no candles, no holy water, no Stations of the Cross.'

'Gloomy,' said Lucy. 'Empty.'

'Yes, we feel that. But what's more important – most important – in Kung is his picture of Christ. Infinite forgiveness, prohibition of judging, inward freedom from possessions. Christ was involved with irreligious and immoral people. He enjoyed the world. He relished eating and drinking. Yet, as Kung says, he has always remained "an uncompromising outsider". Remember that, Lucy: *an uncompromising outsider*.'

The winter of 1980 was the coldest in Yorkshire for thirty years. Edward was depressed by his illness, by a callous new mood in English politics, and also by the appointment of the new Pope, John Paul the Second. 'A Pole – they're all fanatics!' he exclaimed, and his fears were confirmed when one of John Paul's first acts was to strip Kung – whom he had never met and whose books he had not read – of his Catholic university post, pronouncing him no longer qualified to teach Catholic doctrine, and forbidding him to write or publish.

'Galileo all over again!' said Edward. 'And they still haven't

98

admitted they were wrong about *him*.'

When Lucy went back to school for the Spring term, her father knew he was dying; she did not. After their goodbye kiss, he said, 'Don't be too serious, my darling. Don't brood – I've always brooded too much. Laugh with your friend, Vee, and marry someone you can laugh with. Someone who enjoys life. Someone who can make you happy.' He paused. 'Lucy, your mother and I made a bad start. But it was mostly my fault. I found her intolerant. She was very young – and I was intolerant of her. Lately I've told her how sorry I am, but I think it's hard for her to forgive me.'

Indeed Lucy had seen no change in her mother's cold, dutiful manner, and had noticed how Teresa hated her religious discussions with her father. 'He's ill. He doesn't know what he's saying,' she had told Lucy, after she heard him talking to her about 'that heretic, Kung'. Teresa, instantly sensing his sympathy for reactionaries, thought the new Pope was wonderful.

Edward died, at home, three weeks after Lucy went back to school. Her mother did not summon her till after he was dead. She came home for the funeral. She recognized her mother's lack of grief; it contrasted with her own misery.

After the funeral, Lucy went into the library. The first thing she saw was that the piles of books and papers were gone from Edward's desk: it was empty, except for the Jerusalem New Testament. She opened the drawers of the desk, one by one; they were empty, too.

She was standing by the desk, staring at it, when Nanny came in. They embraced: 'It was a beautiful death, Lucy. He had the Last Sacraments. He looked so peaceful.'

'If only I'd been here. But Nanny, what's happened to all his books, his papers?'

Nanny shook her head, with a hesitant look.

'Where *are* they?'

In this household, there had always been a division: Edward, Lucy and Nanny on one side, Teresa and Eva on the other. Now Nanny said, 'Promise you won't talk about it.'

'About what?'

'Promise now, Lucy. This should be a house of peace. I won't say a word if you don't promise.'

'All right, I promise.'

'Your father died in the middle of the day, Lucy. And just before dark I heard them moving about downstairs – your mother and Miss Eva. I looked over the banister. They were carrying things out to the stable yard. They made two or three journeys. So I went to the blue bedroom and looked out of the window, and your mother was lighting a fire.'

'A fire?'

'Yes. In the middle of the yard. They'd piled all his books and papers there, and that Miss Eva fetched a can of petrol from the garage and poured a bit on. And then your mother set light to it – oh, it was quite safe! Miss Eva was standing by with a hose, in case of accidents. You could see it was all planned. And the flames rose up – it was just dark then – and you should have seen their faces. Oh I don't know, somehow – the fire and all – it made me think of old tales of witches.' Nanny made the sign of the cross. 'And they burned it all to ashes. You go out there. You'll see the dark stain on the cobbles. Like those marks on the old crusader's tomb.'

Lucy said, 'I'll never forgive her.'

'Now that's no way to talk. Your father wouldn't have liked that.'

'No. But he wouldn't have liked her burning all his things. He would have wanted me to have them.'

'Well, that's as maybe. But I know he wouldn't have wanted you to be so unChristian. Just before he died, it was, he took her hand and kissed it, and said something. But her face didn't move a muscle. Oh, well . . .'

'I hate her.'

'Now, Lucy . . .'

'I'm sorry, Nanny. I didn't mean that. And I won't say anything.' When they left the room, Lucy took her father's New Testament with her.

Back at school, alone with Vee, she cried. Vee put her arms round her: 'Oh Lucy, I'm so sorry.'

Lucy told Vee about the bonfire. 'It reminded Nanny of witches.'

'Sounds more like an *auto-da-fé* to me. Mrs Torquemada and her assistant.' In future, Vee would often refer to Lucy's mother as 'Mrs T'.

'You shouldn't call her that,' Lucy would say, and Vee would reply, 'T's short for Teresa.' It became a familiar joke, but the relationship between Lucy and her mother did not improve. Now they had many arguments. When Lucy had trained as a fund-raiser, and took a job with a famine-relief organization, her mother said, 'Why not a *Catholic* charity?'

'I don't want to meet only Catholics. Goodness knows, staying with the Dumbles, I'll meet plenty.'

'Perhaps not suitable ones. I hope you're going to see something of the de Rawley side.' This would lead to more arguments; Lucy cared for none of her mother's relations.

'Surely you want to marry a Catholic,' her mother said.

'Oh, yes.' But time passed.

'Are you never going to get married?'

'Yes, I expect so.' Then she met Rupert.

'Even though you are the last of the Rivens, I'd always believed you'd make sure there would be Catholics at Rivendale.' ('The last of the Rivens' was a favourite phrase of Teresa's, and Vee joked about it: 'Sounds like the final volume in the Rivendale Saga.')

'But there will be. Our children will be Catholics. And I think Rupert's going to become one.'

'Bluebeard's conversion!'

'Please don't call him that.' She added, 'After all, your family were converts.'

Teresa said, 'If only you'd been a boy.'

'I can't help my gender.'

'Your sex, you mean.'

'We call it gender nowadays.'

'You girls are all so ridiculous.'

'I'm not a girl. I'm a woman.'

'What's wrong with the word "girl"?'

'It's patronizing. You wouldn't call Rupert a "boy".'

Teresa's look was triumphant. 'No, I certainly wouldn't!'

Lucy took her religion seriously. She went to Mass every Sunday and sometimes on weekdays. She regularly confessed and took communion. She read her father's New Testament and the copy she had bought of Kung's *On Being a Christian*. These were all reasons why every night, after her prayers for the people she was fond of, she prayed to be able to love her mother.

Three

On Friday the fourth of August, Rupert Deyntree's first wife, Sarah, and their son, James, were having breakfast in the kitchen of their Suffolk cottage. Breakfast was the only meal they ate in the kitchen. This was one of a jumble of rules Sarah clung to: James never questioned them because it made her nervous.

This was Sarah's second successive presence at breakfast. On the previous eight days she had stayed in her room. Yesterday she had rejected James's suggestion that she should telephone Mrs Brigg, the cleaner who, once or twice a month, fitted Sarah into her schedule, at a higher rate than she charged her regulars. 'Next week, James,' Sarah had said. 'I just can't face her today. I'm a bit tired.' But by the evening she was exhausted, having cleaned the house herself with dogged, if not very efficient zeal.

The kitchen, though quite clean, was drab. Chris, Rupert's third wife, would have considered its uncoordinated 'appliances' – as she, though not Sarah, would have called them – almost as antique as its oak beams, but Sarah never thought of replacing them. Although the oven temperature was unreliable, the refrigerator had a noisy rattle and needed frequent defrosting, and the electric kettle boiled slowly and loudly – because it was old and also thick with scale – Sarah accepted these defects. She was rather proud that machines were mysterious to her. (James had twice shown her how to change an electric plug, but she forgot immediately, and he continued to do all such tasks.)

The vinyl tiles on the floor were old, too: once black and white but now dark-grey and cream. The blue checked curtains and tablecloth had also dimmed, like the blue flowers on Sarah's limp cotton dress.

The faded tiles, the washed-out curtains and cloth, the limp dress matched, rather than suited, Sarah, for she herself had a limp, faded look. Her hair, once brown, was patchily grey. Her eyes, though she herself would have called them 'blue' – the description on her outdated passport, issued when passports still recorded eye-colour – were now greyish. Her complexion, formerly pink and white, had a mauve tinge. She was thin, but her body looked slack, and her stomach sagged.

Small neat features like hers, pretty in youth, can get lost in the debris of middle age; Sarah's had. Her pouches and creases were noticeable, especially the two deep lines that ran from her nose past the corners of her mouth to the sides of her – never prominent – chin, which now merged with her loose neck. No one meeting her would have believed that she was the same age as her former husband, Rupert.

She was drinking her second cup of coffee quickly, in contrast to the way she ate her thin slice of white toast (unlike James, she preferred white bread and white eggs). She would break off a fragment, dab it with butter and marmalade, then nibble it. She had taught James to do this, but when away from home, which was seldom, he would spread a whole slice and then cut it in half. Anyway, for breakfast, he ate not toast but muesli.

Yesterday Sarah had filled a big glass jar with muesli

mixture. She believed eggs and bacon were the proper breakfast for a man, but James did not eat meat, limited his consumption of eggs, and in any case preferred muesli. Sarah had mixed oats with finely chopped dried apricot and apple, whole hazelnuts and sultanas, very little bran and a sprinkling of sesame seed. For the past week, James had been eating ready-mixed muesli from a packet. Now, swallowing his first mouthful of Sarah's mixture, he looked pensive.

Sometimes in the past, when he had said her mixture was superior to the commercial brands, she had expressed guilt at not having made it for a week or two. Yet, when he made no comment on a fresh batch, she could be hurt. He looked up from his *Guardian* at the same moment as she looked up from her *Telegraph*.

His eyes were a clear pale blue: Sarah's original colour perhaps, and certainly quite different from Rupert's deep slate-tinged shade. James resembled his father, like the line-and-wash sketch for a portrait. If they had stood side by side – something unlikely to happen – Rupert, though slim and fit, would have looked heavier, and of course older, but more handsome. Only their smiles, eager and charming, were identical.

'Chicken-food all right?' This was Sarah's term for muesli.

'Oh, brilliant!' He nodded with vigour.

'Really? Because if it's no different from the packet stuff, there's not really much point — '

'Yours is *much* nicer.' He hesitated. 'But if it's too much trouble . . .' He left the sentence unfinished.

'Oh no, darling.' She smiled, then returned to her paper. She needed glasses but would not wear them, and held the paper close to her face. There was an oven burn on her arm: a slight swelling round a red scar. (Sarah's injuries healed slowly and often turned septic.) She was reading the social page, her favourite section of the newspaper.

Yesterday she had collected a week's copies of the paper from her bedroom floor – some dishevelled, some untouched – and crammed them into the dustbin. Today she had returned to a routine of reading part of the paper at breakfast; she would finish it in the afternoon, doing the quick crossword but saving the other for James's return.

Now, with a sharp clink that made him look up, she put down her coffee cup, then clutched the edges of the paper in both hands. She stared at James over the top, but not as if she saw him.

'Mum! Is something wrong?' When she didn't answer, but went on staring at – or through – him, he said, louder, 'What is it?'

Her eyes focused. 'Your father,' she said.

'What about him?' The pitch of James's voice had risen. He lowered it for his next question: 'What's he done?' Now he sounded calm, but his spoon scraped on his pottery cereal-bowl. (He had given six of these bowls – brown, with creamy swirls – to his mother: an error of judgement; though she received them effusively, he noticed from the draining-board that when she ate alone, she always used her old bone china.)

'He's engaged,' Sarah said.

'He's *what*?' Involuntarily James laughed. He said, 'You can't mean he's engaged to be married.'

'That's exactly what I do mean. It's here, in the paper.' She jabbed at the page with her forefinger.

'To whom?' James asked.

'You can be so pedantic, darling. A typical academic!' (Her attitude to his occupation varied.) 'Anyone else would say "Who to?" ' But her hands, holding the paper, trembled. She read aloud, "To Lucy Mary, daughter of the late Edward Riven and of the Hon. Mrs Riven of Rivendale, Yorkshire." ' She paused, then added in a drawl, 'Goodness me! He's actually involved with a lady this time. Quite a change from his Jewish

106

tart and then that common little business-woman.'

James closed his eyes and lips for a moment. In moments of stress his mother reverted to prejudices inculcated by her upbringing and – he believed – his father. ('Green' himself, with a leftish tinge, he always pictured Rupert as virulently right-wing.)

'But I've heard of the family,' Sarah was saying. 'I'm sure I have. They're Roman Catholics. Very old ones. The kind that intermarry and go batty.'

James said, 'She must be batty if she's marrying him.'

'But how can she be marrying him at all? Catholics don't believe in divorce, and he's been divorced three times.'

James said, 'He's never been married in church, has he? But – goodness! – he's a bit old to be "getting engaged", isn't he?'

Sarah said, 'I wonder how old *she* is. It's obvious from the announcement that she hasn't been married before. A pious old spinster?'

James laughed. 'That doesn't sound *his* cup of tea.'

'Unless, of course, she's got *money*.' Sarah's stress on the word was vicious, and James sighed. Whatever his feelings about his father, he always tried to keep cool when the subject arose with his mother. 'Though,' she went on now, 'I always thought those old Catholics were as poor as church mice. Struggling to send their dozens of sons to Downside, even at reduced rates.' Putting down the paper, she started to twist a lock of grey hair between thumb and forefinger. 'If she's not rich, she must be attractive. And if she's attractive and not married, I suppose she's young.'

'Mum, you're out of date.' James's tone was light. 'Attractive women don't all marry young these days. Lots of them don't want to marry at all.'

'Oh, that's the "Women's Lib" line, I know. I expect that's Sue's line, isn't it? Though whether she really believes it is quite another matter.' Sarah disliked Sue, a young woman James took out often, but now she gave him the placatory smile that meant she felt she might have gone too far. 'Riven,' she said again. 'The Hon. Mrs Riven. She must be in Debrett, but I don't know her maiden name so it would be difficult to track her down. The Rivens are probably in Burke's Landed Gentry, but I've only got Debrett.'

'Can I see that paper?' He held out his hand, and Sarah passed it over. He read the announcement. 'Just Rupert Deyntree. No parents for him. Not even an address.'

'Not *grand* enough, I suppose.'

'Rivendale,' James said. 'Can't you just picture it, up on the moors? Black skies, howling winds.' (This imaginary scene resembled the one his father had created for Francis.)

'*Wuthering Heights*,' Sarah said and smiled faintly.

'Or *Cold Comfort Farm*,' James suggested, encouraged.

But the smile had faded. 'Oh, I'm quite sure they're not *that* poor.' She twisted her lock of hair again. 'If only we had a copy of Burke.'

'There might be one in our reference section. I could check.'

'Burke at Redbrick?' 'Redbrick' was Sarah's generic term for all universities except Oxford and Cambridge, and her specific one for the university – actually made of cement, glass and metal – where James lectured and was writing his Ph.D. on a neglected – with good reason, some said – Suffolk poet of the early nineteenth century.

'Our reference section's very comprehensive.'

'Anyway, you'd forget.'

'No, I wouldn't.'

'You forgot that book on Jane Austen I asked you to borrow for me.'

'I didn't. I told you – it was out.'

'Mmm.' Then she said brightly, 'Why don't I go into town and look it up in the public library? I know they've got a copy.

And it's Friday. There's a bus at ten and one back at half past three.'

James said, 'You'd have an awful lot of time to fill in.'

'An awful lot?' Her tone was still bright. 'Just a few hours. And you're always saying I should get out more.'

'But you were so tired yesterday. Don't you think you should take it easy today? And have a little rest this afternoon?'

'Anyone would think I was an invalid.' Now her tone was petulant. There was a moment's silence.

James said, 'Why bother to look up these people? You know thinking about my father upsets you. Why get involved?'

'Involved! How ridiculous you are. I just want to know a bit more about these Rivens and who the mother of this Lucy is. A bit of light detective work. Like Philip Marlowe.' She laughed. At Oxford in her day it had been fashionable to enjoy Raymond Chandler and she still thought his sombre books 'great fun', though a recent suggestion by James that he was a serious writer had seemed to her absurd.

James said, 'I could take you to town tomorrow. I would today but I've arranged to meet an American research student for lunch.'

'Oh, I noticed you hadn't made up your funny little snack.' James had finally persuaded her to let him organize a packed lunch of wholewheat bread, cheese and salad for himself each morning after his run and shower. (The run she called 'trendy', a word she had acquired in the 1960s, and she always bathed, never using the shower he had installed. 'Showers are for *hot* climates,' she would explain.)

'So why not leave it till tomorrow?' he said.

She leant across the table. She stretched out her arm – on it the red burn looked like a torture mark – and put a hand on his sleeve. 'You say that thinking about your father upsets me.' Her voice, low and intense, sounded stagy. 'Do you know what *really* upsets me?'

Looking down at his empty plate, he said nothing.

'Do you?' she repeated. 'Please answer me, James. Do you?' She tugged at his sleeve.

He started to pull away, but controlled the movement. 'No,' he said. 'I don't.'

'Well you should.' Now her tone was normal and she took her hand away. 'What really upsets me is to feel that you're worrying about me. Nothing's more likely to make me nervous than *that*. I'm perfectly all right. Don't you believe me?'

'Yes,' he said. 'Oh yes, I do.' Under the tablecloth, he crossed his thumbs: a childish superstition, meant to nullify a lie.

'Then that's all right.' She smiled. 'I'll enjoy my little trip. I'll go to the library and then I'll do a bit of shopping. You won't have to do any for me today.'

Unusually for this part of Suffolk where most cottages were owned by Londoners who brought their own provisions with them, Sarah and James's village had a shop, run by a retired schoolmaster, known as 'the gentleman grocer'. (Although he made only a small profit, the job, as he said, kept him active.) Unfortunately Sarah had quarrelled with him; James had not, and had an arrangement with him to continue daily newspaper deliveries. (A local schoolboy on a bicycle distributed them for him.) Sarah ignored the existence of their arrangement – she would have missed her *Telegraph* badly – and James paid the bill. However, though he and the grocer always greeted each other cordially, James felt he could not continue to use the shop regularly, after the quarrel; anyway, it was much more expensive than the supermarket near the university where he did most of the household shopping.

Now James said, 'Must go. Or I'll hardly get any work done before I have to meet this guy.'

'Work, work work. You should take some "hols".'

"Hols" was a joky expression, but Sarah found it difficult

to understand his going on with his research during the vacation. Indeed, in August, there were few people in the library. Sue, who was a sociologist, was off to Greece next week. She'd suggested they go together, but he had refused, for several reasons.

'Goodbye, Mum.' He kissed her cheek.

As he reached the door, she said, 'James!' He turned. 'Promise you aren't cross with me.'

'Of course not.'

'Promise.'

'I promise.' Then he said, 'I wish you'd promise *me* something.'

'What?' Suddenly her expression was suspicious: the look of an animal peering round before it leaves its burrow.

His shoulders sagged. He said, 'Oh . . . nothing . . . I've forgotten what I was going to say.'

'Silly-billy!' Her smile was relieved.

'You remember I'm going to be late tonight.'

'Late?'

'Yes, it's my FOE meeting – Friends of the Earth,' he added, because she always forgot, or appeared to. 'And then Sue and I are going for a snack.'

'A snack!' she said. 'Why don't you give the poor little thing a decent dinner?' (Both Sarah and Sue referred to each other as 'poor'.) Sarah added, 'I'm sure she's anorexic.'

'Nonsense,' James said. 'Sue eats like a horse.' (This was accurate in one sense; Sue was a vegan.)

A moment or two later, briefcase in hand, he was outside, breathing the sunny air – though the huge Suffolk sky would probably cloud over later; it usually did in August.

His Fiat was parked on the edge of the village green. He hurried down the brick path between flowers and shrubs. (Gardening was his passion.) An arching spray of purple buddleia caught at his arm, and a smell of crushed pennyroyal rose from the path. He inhaled deeply. By the gate he pulled off the head of a sprig of lavender and rubbed it between his fingers. As he opened the little gate, he turned. As usual – on those mornings when she came down to breakfast – Sarah stood at the kitchen window. She waved, and he waved back.

It was half past ten when James returned that evening. There had been showers earlier; as he opened the gate, a smell of damp earth was mixed with scents of honeysuckle and tobacco plant. Now the sky was cloudless and thick with stars. He stood still for more than a minute before going up the path.

Lights were on behind drawn curtains in the sitting-room and dining-room, and upstairs in Sarah's bedroom over the sitting-room. The kitchen and James's room above it were in darkness. 'Let it be all right,' James said aloud before he opened the front door. He glanced into the sitting-room on his left; a table lamp was lit. There were some pretty pieces of early Victorian furniture and a filled bookcase, but the room had a disused look which included the books: Sarah's 'Eng Lit' from Oxford and old hardcover novels with faded spines.

James put down his briefcase and turned right from the tiny hall – just room for coat hooks and a mirror – into the dining-room with its long oak table. (He and Sarah ate facing each other in the middle.) This room, too, was empty. 'Mum,' he called. There was silence. Perhaps Sarah had gone to bed, though usually she stayed up until he came home. 'Mum,' he called again.

Now there were movements upstairs. Then, high and bright, her voice called, 'Coming!' He closed his eyes for a moment, then took a step towards the sideboard with its pewter candlesticks. But now the top step of the narrow stairs – encased in beams and plaster – next to the door to the kitchen creaked, and he moved away and waited, his hands resting on the carved back of one of the dining-room chairs.

She stopped to avoid the overhead beam and negotiated the deep bottom step with care. She was wearing the green-and-white shirtwaist dress she often put on for outings; there was a brown stain on the front of the skirt. She was smoking a cigarette; her eyes were bright and her cheeks pink. James gripped the chair-back.

'Darling!' she said – high, bright – and then, 'Did you have lots of fun?'

'The meeting was fine,' he said.

'And you had something to eat afterwards?'

'Yes. A salad.'

'A salad! No wonder you look so glum. Though I know salads have improved since I was young. I suppose you went to that vegetarian place?'

'Yes.'

'And *Sue* – how's *Sue*? Was she wearing that funny little woolly hat of hers with the bobble on top?' Although Sarah had only seen this hat once, she often referred to it; unbecoming, it gave Sue's face a gnomish look.

'It's summer,' James said. 'You don't wear woolly hats in August.'

'*I* never wear woolly hats!' She laughed. Then she said, 'I was only joking. You do agree that it's a funny hat, though, don't you?' He said nothing, and she went on, 'Oh darling, you can be awfully priggish sometimes. I'm not criticizing Sue. She's a *splendid* person. So full of causes – stopping people hunting and smoking and so on.' Ash from her own cigarette dropped to the floor; it was hardly more than a stub now and she tossed it out of the window at the foot of the stairs: red sparks curved in the air. 'Like a nightcap?' she asked, with a gesture towards the drinks cupboard in the sideboard.

'No thanks,' James said. 'I think I'll go straight to bed.'

Leaning against the frame of the stairs, she blocked his way. 'Oh,' she said, 'but I *must* tell you all about my trip to town

113

and what I found out. The Rivens *are* in Burke. They're terribly, terribly ancient – *long* before Agincourt. And the mother's from a very grand family – the de Rawleys, you know?' She paused, and James, who detested pedigrees, shook his head. (Sarah often told him that he was an inverted snob.) 'I wonder if they're Catholics, too. But this Lucy! Guess how old she is. You won't *believe* it.'

'How old?' he asked, his attention captured.

'Twenty-seven!' She raised her hands, palms towards him, in a stage gesture of astonishment.

James said, 'Goodness – the same age as me.'

'Yes,' she said. 'Can you *believe* it?' A tendency to drawl and to stress words heavily was exaggerated this evening, and she gestured constantly as she talked. 'And she's an only child. So perhaps this *Rivendale* belongs to her.' Stretching out her arms to James, she said, 'Someone must *warn* her.'

James – beyond the table, behind the chair – was out of reach, but he stepped back. 'What do you mean?' he said.

'Why, that she mustn't marry him on any account. Poor girl!'

James said, 'She's quite old enough to make up her own mind.' Sarah, gesticulating, opened her mouth. He said violently, 'It's nothing to do with us. Nothing!'

'Sometimes I just don't understand you, James. That poor girl!' Tears rose in Sarah's eyes.

'Oh, please don't upset yourself. Though I suppose it's too late to say that now. Too late to say anything.'

'What *can* you mean?' Up went her chin, showing the ragged neck.

'I must go to bed.' He moved fast now. At the foot of the stairs he put his hands on her shoulders, not roughly but with enough firmness to shift her so that he could pass. He pounded up the stairs, disregarding her high call – 'James!' – and went into his room, shut the door and locked it. He did not switch on the light but went straight to his bed and dropped down on

114

it. He put his arms round the pillows and buried his face in them. He gave three deep, dry, gulping sobs.

'It' had begun again: the rite, the cycle, the bout; something which could not be halted but must run its course.

The interval had never been so short before: only three days since she had emerged from the last bout. Might the bout (some people said 'binge' but that sounded so cheerful) – unrelieved by spells of normality – itself become, endlessly – until death – the norm?

In the past she had often been sober for months, once for almost a year during which James's sense of dread had gradually dissipated. When, inexplicably, she drank again, the shock, as he had told Sue, was devastating. 'And that was ten years ago. Since then, worse and worse. All my hopes dying – and all her virtues.'

Sue gave a little laugh. 'Virtues?'

'Her courage, for instance.'

'Courage? Life hasn't exactly been a struggle for her. She's got enough money and that lovely old cottage.'

'You're so hard sometimes.'

'Just realistic.'

'She hasn't got that much money. Anyway money doesn't solve every problem.'

'But what problems has she? None, as far as I can see. She's got an incredibly devoted son.' Sue's tone was faintly derogatory.

'There was the divorce.'

'That was more than twenty years ago. Anyway, you say she was well rid of him.'

'Yes. All the same, divorce meant more in those days.'

'Why didn't she get a job?'

'At first she was looking after me. Later she should have. But what?'

'She could have taught. After all she went to Oxford.'

'Only for two years. Then she ran away with my father.'

'She could have taken a teacher-training course.'

'She hates the idea of teaching. It wouldn't suit her. And then there was that awful car crash.'

'When she killed a man?'

'It was an accident. He was a down-and-out. They thought he was drunk.'

'Perhaps *she* was drunk.'

'No one's ever suggested that. She broke two ribs and was concussed. At first she couldn't remember what had happened.'

'Well, that fits. And later she did remember, and she's full of guilt.'

'That's pure speculation. It just made her afraid of driving. She's never driven since.'

'Well that's fortunate. The way she is now.'

'Yes.' James sighed.

'She should see a therapist.'

'Mum thinks psychotherapy's strictly for nutcases and Americans. I don't think it's a universal panacea myself.'

'It might help her to straighten out.'

'Straighten out! You're so protective about animals but so tough on people. It's lucky you're an academic sociologist, not a social worker. Your cases would have a hard time.' Sue reddened. 'Don't be cross,' he said. 'I was only joking.' He smiled his father's charming smile.

After a moment she smiled back. (Sarah had once described Sue's teeth as 'untidy'.) She said, 'I'm not cross.' She paused. 'At least she should see another doctor.'

'I agree. *She* doesn't. And that one you found wasn't very helpful. Please let's talk about something else.'

'You started it. You always do.'

'I know, and then I can't bear it.'

She shook her head. She loved him; he did not love her.

She often irritated him, and her freckled face and rather childish body were not really to his taste. Their 'affair' – as his mother would have called it; he and Sue called it a 'relationship' – should not have started; now he could not end it. He liked her and – more important – did not want to hurt her: it was ironic that she considered his unwillingness to hurt Sarah a weakness.

He had often suggested to Sarah that she should see a doctor. Sober and on the mend, she would say, 'What nonsense. I'm perfectly all right.' Drunk, she raged, wept or mounted her high horse, which he hated most of all. ('I am a *lady*, you know,' she would declare, slurring and staggering.) It was only at the end of a bout, when she stopped drinking because she felt too ill to go on, that she was sometimes amenable, prepared to discuss her condition. ('I do have a problem, I suppose.') At this stage she had several times agreed to see a doctor, only to change her mind a day or two later when she felt better.

She had only once – at his urging – maintained the resolve. He had taken her to see a doctor in London. (She would not consider a local one.) Sue found him; he was connected with the National Council on Alcoholism.

In the waiting-room, Sarah was pale and shaky. James squeezed her hand. He accompanied her into the consulting-room; she had refused to come unless he promised to do so.

The doctor was middle-aged and urbane. He suggested an expensive clinic. When she rejected the suggestion, saying 'I'm sure I can do it on my own,' he adopted a common-sensical tone and gave her advice that delighted her. He recommended that she should shun spirits and drink in moderation: a glass of sherry before dinner, and perhaps a glass of wine with it, or a glass of beer. On social occasions she should have one or two glasses of sherry or wine. Her limit must be half a bottle of wine a day.

Sarah stuck to this programme for ten days. Then she raised her consumption of wine from half to a whole bottle of wine.

Within a month she was drinking spirits and sank into one of her worst bouts.

She would never agree to see another doctor. ('I've seen one.') Two years ago James, without telling her, had seen a younger, blunter man, who said, 'Of course the National Council on Alcoholism is largely funded by the drink industry. Anyway, I can't agree with its approach. No alcoholic can drink in moderation.' He laughed. 'There's a famous piece of research on seven alcoholics who became moderate drinkers. Unfortunately all of them are dead now.'

'You're sure my mother is an . . . alcoholic?'

'How can I be sure? I haven't seen her. But she sounds like one. Don't look so downcast. It's a disease. People can recover from it.'

'But she could never drink again?'

'In my view, she would have to abstain completely.'

'She couldn't do it.'

'Other alcoholics have. More advanced ones – it's a progressive disease. Has she thought of trying AA?'

'Alcoholics Anonymous?'

'Yes. They help a lot of people. Is she religious?'

'Not at all.' (Sarah had retained an agnosticism acquired at Oxford. Unlike their politics, it was something she and James shared.)

'Pity. It helps. But AA has worked for non-believers, though it talks about "a Higher Power".'

James smiled. 'Higher than what?'

'Higher than oneself.' The doctor shrugged. 'I've got some pamphlets.' He rummaged in a drawer. 'Here they are. I wish I could be more helpful. If she came in herself . . .'

'She won't.'

'Pity. An alcoholic's death is not a happy one.'

This sentence – perhaps a sentence in two senses – and the remark about alcoholism being a progressive disease stayed with James to haunt him. He looked through the pamphlets. There were mentions of 'a Higher Power' but the word 'God' also occurred frequently, and he found this as uncongenial as he felt sure Sarah would. One of the pamphlets however – it was called 'Is AA for you?' – impressed him. It consisted of twelve questions about drinking. At the end it said, 'Did you answer YES four or more times? If so you are probably in trouble with alcohol.' It seemed likely that Sarah would have had to answer 'Yes' to all twelve.

Although he could not imagine the pamphlets being acceptable to Sarah, he took them home. When she was weak after her next bout, he said, 'Why don't you try AA?'

'*AA*?' Her tone was shocked. Then, ill though she was, she made a joke: 'You must mean the Automobile Association. But I don't drive any longer.'

'You know I mean Alcoholics Anonymous,' he said.

'James – how preposterous!' Her veined eyes were too bleary to flash. 'You can't be serious. Go to revivalist meetings with a lot of tramps?'

'It might not be like that.'

'It would. And then I suppose I'd have to "bare my soul" to them.'

'I'm sure you wouldn't.'

'Someone would be sure to see me there.'

'The people who go are alcoholics.'

'I can just imagine how *they* talk their heads off. Anyway there might be other people there. Journalists . . .'

'They have closed meetings – for alcoholics only.'

'A journalist could easily *pretend* to be an alcoholic.'

'But why?'

'Oh, to get horror stories about life in the gutter. Anyway, if only alcoholics go, it would mean I thought I was one. "On Skid Row" as the Americans say.'

'Those are the alcoholics who *don't* go.'

'I'm not an alcoholic,' she said. 'Of any kind.' She put her hands to her head, pressing her fingers against her temples; it was evident her headache was dreadful. 'Perhaps I've got a bit of a problem. But I'll get over it.'

'You've tried so often, Mum.'

'Oh well, never say die!' But this sounded dreary rather than gallant.

'Mum, do something for me.'

'I won't go to one of those meetings.'

'Not that.' He sighed. 'Just have a look at these pamphlets.'

With a shrug she took them from him, but she never referred to them afterwards; nor did he. The bouts continued as before, except that each seemed worse than its predecessor. Certainly they occurred more often.

Anything could trigger them. Today it could have been the announcement of Rupert's engagement, but it could just as well have been a piece of good news or a blocked drain. Tomorrow she would be at breakfast, flushed and garrulous. In the afternoon she would probably sleep off the morning's drinks, and wake to prepare dinner; sometimes she dropped or burnt the food. While they ate she would be garrulous again; she would drink, but not openly: that was her rule. She would keep leaving the room 'to fetch something' and go to her hidden bottle.

James's halted movement towards the sideboard this evening had been to check what was now – without checking – certain. In the drinks cupboard would be three new, unopened bottles – whisky, gin, sherry – replacing the ones she had consumed at the end of her last bout. She insisted on the presence of these bottles. He had suggested that they should not keep drink at home. She would not consider it: 'How awful! What if someone dropped in and we had nothing to drink in the house? So uncivilized!'

'I could always nip out and get a bottle,' he said. It would have been so cruel to remind her that no one ever did drop in, and he had stopped inviting people, except Sue. Two years ago, Sarah had persuaded him against his will to have four friends – plus Sue – to dinner. The food had been appalling. After a rambling monologue throughout the meal, Sarah had passed out in her chair.

Another of her rationalizations for the stock in the sideboard cupboard was that he might want a drink himself.

Although he would have a pint in a pub or a glass or two of wine in a restaurant, James never drank at home. 'I never would,' he said.

'You *might*.' She turned away. Her tone had been obstinate and also wistful: his drinking would have sanctioned hers.

Today, as well as replenishing the cupboard, she would have bought other drinks, now concealed in her room. When these ran out in a day or two, she would probably still be well enough to make an expedition on the bus to replace them while he was at work. Only when she became too drunk – too ill – for this, would she start on the bottles in the sideboard; as she emptied them she would fill them up with water. (She always bought drinks bottled in dark glass.) By the time they held water only, she would be wrecked in her room. This would be the time when she would say piteously, 'James, get me some beer. Please.'

Sue told him he shouldn't do it, but he always did. How could he refuse when she was in such torment? Besides, the request was a good sign. It was the signal of the end of the bout: beer, for Sarah, was solely a hangover remedy; she never drank it at any other time and always said that she disliked the taste of it. James would go to the pub or, if it was closed, the gentleman grocer's. He looked away as he made his purchase, fearing a glance of complicity. He was aware that everyone 'knew'. Indeed Sarah had been almost blind drunk when she quarrelled with the grocer.

He would bring her the first beer – she always had two – in a big glass, not filled to the brim; her hands would be shaking so much that she might spill it in the bed. (For the same reason, she would always hold out both hands for the glass.)

Later she would say, 'Thank you,' and then, 'I'm sorry.'

'That's all right.'

But of course it was all wrong, all muddled: her shame and defiance, his pity and anger. 'I love her,' he would say to Sue when she told him he should move out. There was still love – on both sides – but her obsession and his desperation – both constantly growing – left less and less room for it.

'If you walked out, she might face up to things,' Sue said.

'She might die.'

'On the other hand, she just might pull herself together.'

'I'm not prepared to take the chance. She's been deserted once . . . and look what it did to her.'

'I'd say she did it to herself. But you think *he* did it, don't you. Your father. You really hate him, don't you?'

'I hardly ever think about him.'

Tonight, James had been lying prone on his bed for about half an hour when he heard his mother try the door handle. Then she called, 'James.' When he did not answer, she called out, like a drunken oracle, 'Someone must warn that girl.' But he kept silent and after a few moments she went along the passage to her room.

It was Saturday morning. Belinda Deyntree had come from Willesden Green tube station. The noise and ugliness of the High Road made her flinch, but the suburban quiet that succeeded them after a ten-minute walk pleased her no better. She scowled at the solid semi-detached houses, some of which, as well as numbers, had names – 'Chatsworth', 'Kowloon', 'Jofred' – on little swinging signs.

'How can you go on living here?' Belinda would say to her

mother, and Barbara would answer, 'I don't think it's so bad.'
Michel would say, 'You know why. To take care of your
grandmother.'

Belinda hated Michel, her mother's lover, even more than
she hated Willesden. She had escaped them both. Belinda was
buying a flat in what she called Islington but was actually –
though only just – Hackney: anyway, the area was 'coming
up' rapidly. The flat was on the top floor of a late-Victorian
house in a long street leading off the Essex Road. The street
was now almost completely middle-class, but at its far end
two tower blocks – signifying working-class territory – loomed.

On the other side of the Essex Road lay Canonbury: to
Belinda utterly desirable and impossibly expensive. But
between was the Marquess Estate, another working-class
enclave over which a police helicopter sometimes hovered.

'If only,' Belinda had said to her friend, Debbie, 'they could
pull down all those council flats, how great it would be. They
could build new Georgian houses like those ones in St Paul's
Road. Marquess Estate indeed! It's a nest of criminals. They
snatch bags from cars when people are filling up at that garage
on the corner of my street. Though at least,' she added, 'the
Marquess Estate is low-rise. Not like those two horrors at the
other end. I always hope they'll become unsafe like some of
those other tower blocks, and have to be demolished. Boom!'
Belinda's gesture, unusually exuberant, conjured up explosion,
dust, then utter stillness.

She would not have made these remarks to her mother and
Michel: prevented not by delicacy but by the sheer boredom
of what would have followed. Michel would have asked what
would happen to the flats' occupants. Belinda would have
replied that they could be rehoused in another area. Barbara
would have said something about the Group Areas Act in South
Africa.

Now Belinda stumped – she had a long body and rather

short legs – towards her mother's awful house in Willesden; it was dowdy and suburban, almost as bad as working-class.

When they came back from South Africa, Barbara and Belinda had moved into the upstairs flat in Willesden. When Barbara's father died, he left the house to Barbara whom he trusted to look after her mother who was quite determined to stay in the flat downstairs. As she grew up, Belinda said how much she disliked the place: 'You should sell this house and move somewhere else.'

'Your Gran would hate that. She's lived here ever since she married,' Barbara said.

'Will you move somewhere else when she dies?'

'I hope that won't be for ages,' Barbara said.

Belinda ignored this. She said, 'It's probably worth quite a bit – the two flats. You could move somewhere nicer – it would have to be smaller, of course . . . in a decent area.'

'Move to somewhere in yuppie-land?' Michel's laugh was sarcastic.

Barbara said, 'I don't mind this place. I'm really quite fond of it.'

'You must be joking!' said Belinda.

'We're used to it.' Barbara smiled at Michel. 'Imagine having to move all our stuff!'

'You could get rid of most of it.' Belinda's glance round the room was contemptuous.

Now, in August, there were roses, mostly salmon and flame, in the front gardens. The flowering cherries – ornamental, unfruiting – whose blossom the residents commented on unceasingly in Spring, were now thickly leafed, but not thickly enough for the one in the Korn garden to screen Belinda from the window by which her grandmother, almost chair-ridden, sat all day, watching television, but at the same time keeping an eye on everyone who passed. Belinda now tacked across the road; past the house, she re-crossed, to approach from beyond the porch which would conceal her from her grandmother.

Unlike other gates in the street, this one was open: neither Barbara nor Michel ever bothered to shut it. The garden was not as tidy as those on either side of it, though Michel mowed the lawn and weeded when old Mrs Korn complained. All the same, a few weeds poked up at the edges of the cement drive to the garage where Michel's old Morris was kept in winter: now, as always in summer, it was parked in the street outside.

The entrance to the upstairs flat was by a side door with a circle of nubbly glass in its upper section. Belinda paused here to run a hand over her hair: well cut, but perhaps too short to flatter her face with its low forehead and large features. This Saturday morning she wore trousers and top; the top, like her expensive running-shoes, identified its smart designer. These trademarks were appropriate, for Belinda believed in advertising; she was an assistant account executive in an advertising agency.

Now she raised her hand – she was shorter than she would have liked – to press the doorbell, which buzzed like a fretful wasp. (Mrs Korn's bell, at the front door, chimed the first seven notes of 'Home Sweet Home'.)

They were expecting her: she had telephoned. The door was probably unlocked. But she always rang the bell, ever since the time she had come upstairs unannounced and found them making love.

Michel's voice called, 'I'll go.' Firm footsteps came quickly down the stairs. Belinda took a step back.

'The door wasn't locked,' Michel said, and then asked, 'Been jogging?' with a glance at Belinda's shoes.

'It's called running now. I see you're collecting antiques.' Belinda gestured towards the faded Che Guevara T-shirt Michel was wearing with jeans and old moccasins.

Michel and Belinda always exchanged remarks which an

insensitive listener might have mistaken for friendly banter. Michel, who had narrow hips and long legs, led the way upstairs now, with Belinda trotting after.

'Barbara will be thrilled to see you,' Michel said. 'You haven't been here for ages.' Belinda said nothing.

The beige stair-carpet was worn and faded, like the cream paint on the walls. At the top of the stairs, on a large trunk covered with an 'ethnic' cloth, was a stack of leaflets tied with string. The passage to the living-room was lined with bookcases of different shapes and sizes, all packed untidily with books and pamphlets. As she passed the open door of Barbara and Michel's room, Belinda looked away from the unmade double bed.

Above one of the bookcases was a yellowed poster of Karl Marx. 'Why don't you get rid of that, now you've packed in the commie business?' Belinda had asked on her last visit.

'Altered perspectives don't mean one has to sweep one's whole past life under the carpet,' Barbara said, and Michel added, 'Marx will never be totally irrelevant.'

Barbara said, 'I sometimes think the trouble wasn't with Marxism. It was with people. We couldn't live up to communism. We just weren't good enough for it.'

'Communism's discredited, it's exploded, it's rot.' Belinda's voice rose as she said this. 'I suppose your feminism's better. But that's out of date too, now. Women have plenty of opportunities.' Belinda was a keen admirer of the Prime Minister, Margaret Thatcher, whom Barbara called 'that evil woman' or sometimes 'the milk-snatcher' in reference to a long-ago time when, as Secretary for Education, her first action had been to abolish schoolchildren's free milk. Nowadays, Barbara – a primary-school teacher – said that children were getting rickets for the first time since the 1930s.

'Victims!' Belinda had exclaimed. 'You're always on about victims.' She had picked up a leaflet lying on the table.

'Prostitutes' rights – ugh. What do you want to bother with *that* for?' She repeated, 'Ugh,' then added, 'Selling themselves!'

'Lots of women sell themselves,' Barbara said. 'But sometimes they don't even get paid for it. We don't only campaign for prostitutes, you know. We campaign for women at home to get wages for sex and housework.'

'Wages for sex! How disgusting!' Although Belinda's two experiences of sex had been unfortunate, she believed it should be marvellous for women as well as for men.

'Sometimes I think my mother and Michel are mad,' Belinda had confided to her friend, Debbie.

Debbie's answering giggle was cheering. 'They do sound a bit weird,' she had agreed. 'All that women's lib.' She added, 'Michel must be a very unusual man.'

'Yeah. Very unusual,' Belinda said.

Now Michel, entering the living-room, said, 'Here's the prodigal daughter, love.'

As Belinda came in, Barbara, who had been writing at the old – not antique – gate-legged table, took off her glasses and bounded up like some large animal. 'Darling!' (This was one of the few words she had retained from her Deyntree days.) Her impulsive movement knocked a little pile of pamphlets to the floor, and Michel at once hunkered down to collect them. 'Darling,' Barbara repeated, this time to Michel; Belinda frowned, but only for a moment: Barbara looked so genuinely delighted to see her. All the same, when Barbara hugged her, she stiffened and tilted her head away from the familiar smell of Indian fabric – a smell that survives innumerable washings – and of warm flesh and hair. She kissed the air near her mother's cheek.

'My mother's a bit plump,' Belinda had told Debbie, 'but she's tall.' She added, with pride, 'She used to be a model.'

It was true that Barbara's height saved her from being fat, but even if it had not, Belinda could probably not have brought

127

herself to describe her mother by a word she considered totally derogatory and which haunted her own life. Many official sins – pride, covetousness, lust, greed (when practised by a thin person) – did not shock her; fat did. Barbara's full hips and breasts, even more than her wild untinted hair and unmade-up face, were shameful, and the offence was aggravated by the huge eyes, the regular features, the white, even teeth, the soft apricot skin. Some people admired Barbara's naturalness, saw her as harvest goddess of grape and grain but, to Belinda, her looks, like her kaftans, were those of an out-of-style 'earth mother'. How could Barbara look like this, when she had once been a glamorous model? Photographs proving this always made Belinda sigh. For though the clothes – white leather mini-skirts, mesh stockings and high boots – were quaint, her mother looked beautiful in them, and ultra-slim.

'Do sit down, darling.' Barbara waved towards a shabby armchair, but noticing that a large cat – head bowed, paws folded as if in prayer – was ensconced there, she pulled out one of four unmatching chairs at the table. Belinda brushed a hand over its seat – her trousers were white – and sat down.

'Coffee?' Barbara asked.

'All right.'

'I'll make it,' Michel said, leaving the room.

Barbara's gaze now rested fondly on Belinda's face which she always said was attractive and interesting. Belinda disagreed, and was gradually accumulating the money for a 'nose job' at a Harley Street clinic. She did not mention this to Barbara who had never sympathized with Belinda's complaints about her nose: 'It's got character, darling.' This was true, and sometimes, when happy, Belinda looked handsome: but this word, applied to herself, filled Belinda with hostility. It was a word appropriate to men; what Belinda wanted to be was 'pretty'. Sketching the ideal nose had been a habit of hers for years: in telephone directories, in school exercise-books, in the margins of the notes she took at office meetings. The ideal nose was small, straight and absolutely un-Jewish. It was very like the nose of her father's third wife, Chris.

It was not because Barbara and Michel would think the nose job frivolous and unnecessary that she did not mention it to them, but because – though doing so had made her angry and resentful – she had borrowed the deposit on her flat from Michel. The nose job would postpone repayment, which was embarrassing, though Michel had said, 'Forget it till you're better off. You will be. And we don't need it.' This was true: despite specializing in 'causes', the firm of solicitors in which Michel was a partner was prosperous. But Belinda disliked being in debt to Michel.

Now, sitting at the table, facing Barbara, Belinda said, 'Heard the news?' (She never called her mother 'Mum' or 'Mummy', and ignored suggestions – old-fashionedly 'progressive' – that she should call her by her first name.)

'What news?'

'About Daddy.'

Barbara raised her eyebrows – she always did – at this use of an affectionate – and upper-class – diminutive for the father of whom Belinda had seen so little. ' "Daddy"?' she said. 'No, what's "Daddy" been doing?'

'He's engaged.' There was an odd note of triumph in Belinda's voice. 'Engaged to be married. Someone in my office saw it in *The Times* yesterday.'

At the mention of 'that Wapping rag' – as she called any newspaper owned by a tycoon whom she referred to as 'that fascist union-basher' – Barbara grimaced automatically. Then she said. 'What? *Engaged*? In the paper?'

Belinda, scanning her mother's face, saw no expression but amused incredulity. She opened her floppy Italian bag, and took out a wallet. From behind several credit cards – Barbara frequently announced that she would never own any card but a cheque card – Belinda took out a newspaper cutting. Barbara put on the 'granny' glasses which Belinda often said made her look like a superannuated hippie. (Belinda, also short-sighted, wore contact lenses, though she hated putting them in and taking them out, and they often made her eyes ache.)

Barbara read the cutting. 'How ridiculous,' she said.

'What do you mean – "ridiculous"?' Belinda's tone was hostile.

'Surely you understand the word "ridiculous"?' Barbara's tone was unusually sharp. 'And it is ridiculous – "getting engaged" at his age and after all those marriages.'

'Three,' Belinda said.

'Surely that's enough? And to put it in the newspaper – so pretentious!'

'You just say that because it's conventional.' Nowadays Barbara and Michel were the only people to whom Belinda defended her father.

At this moment, Michel came back into the room with a tin tray on which were three mugs of coffee and a plate of 'brownies', an American recipe which Barbara had adopted despite her political implacability towards the United States. Undomesticated in most respects, she enjoyed cooking and loved baking. 'My Jewish-mother streak,' she would say: a phrase that made Belinda wince. When Barbara baked, the flat was filled with a smell which to Belinda as a child had been the smell of happiness. Later she had come to dislike it, both because of changed feelings towards her mother and because it signalled temptation to abandon one of her numerous diets.

The coffee was ready to drink: Michel's with milk and no sugar, Barbara's with both and Belinda's with neither. Belinda refused a brownie. 'Oh darling,' Barbara said. 'Not dieting *again*?' But then she turned to Michel and held out the cutting. 'Have a look at this!'

Michel read it and exclaimed, 'The fucker!'

Barbara laughed and said, 'A very accurate description!' Belinda flinched.

Now Michel frowned. 'Someone ought to warn the wretched woman.'

'Victims, victims, victims,' Belinda said. 'I know you specialize in them. But why should this Lucy be one?'

'With his record it seems a reasonable assumption,' Michel said, and then, 'He seems to have moved back into the posh classes, doncher know. The Hon. Mrs Riven, bai Jove!' Belinda, who hated imitations of upper-class accents, scowled.

'I wonder if she's rich,' Barbara said.

'I don't see why you have to suggest that,' said Belinda. 'He didn't marry *you* for your money.'

'But we can't be sure about wife one and wife three, can we?' Michel said. 'Your mother's surpassing beauty compelled him to change his habits. I just hope this Lucy knows what she's doing.' Screwing up the cutting, Michel tossed it into an already full waste-paper basket.

'That's mine!' Belinda's voice was shrill. She stood up, and went to retrieve the cutting. Sitting down again, she smoothed it out carefully before replacing it in her wallet.

'Sorry,' Michel said. 'I didn't know you'd want it,' adding to Barbara, in a joky tone, 'She's got a father fixation. She even keeps cuttings of his engagements.'

But Barbara had suddenly become remote. She sighed, resting her elbows on the table and her chin in her cupped hands.

Immediately sensitive to this mood change, Michel said, 'What's the matter, love?'

Now Barbara leant back in her chair, gazing up at the dusty Japanese paper lampshade that hung from the ceiling. 'I wonder how old this Lucy is. He's probably cradle-snatching by now. Each wife's younger than the last. I was four years younger than Sarah and Chris was six years younger than me.'

Michel said, 'All these middle-aged men go for young women.'

'Bimbos!' said Belinda. 'But bimbos marry old men for their money. Daddy's not old and he's not rich.'

'That varies I should think,' Michel said. 'I expect his spying sometimes pays.'

'Spying!' Belinda exclaimed. 'Daddy's not a spy. He's a business investigator.' She looked at her watch. 'I'll have to go soon.'

'Go?' said Barbara. 'But darling, you've only just come. I hoped you'd stay for lunch. I've got a meeting this afternoon, but not till four. At the bookshop. We could have travelled to the Angel together.' Some of Barbara's feminist activities involved meetings at a women's bookshop in Islington. Belinda grimaced every time she passed it. On the one occasion she had been inside, with Barbara, its atmosphere had repelled her.

Michel said, 'I could take you both in the car.'

Belinda said, 'Sorry, I've got a lunch date.'

Barbara said, 'And you came all this way for such a short visit! Oh well, it's wonderful to see you anyway.'

Michel said, 'She came to tell you about that fucker's engagement.'

Belinda and Barbara spoke simultaneously:

'I wish you wouldn't call him that.'

'I'm sure that's not the only reason she came.'

Michel said, 'I know our Lindy's little ways.'

'My name's Belinda.'

Barbara, at this open show of hostility, glanced nervously from one to the other.

Belinda stood up. 'I have to go now. Or I'll be late for lunch.'

'Who are you meeting?' Barbara asked in a tone so studiedly casual that Michel smiled.

'My friend, Debbie,' Belinda said. 'We're going shopping afterwards, in Oxford Street.'

'Ah!' Nowadays Barbara only shopped for food. She particularly disliked buying clothes; most of hers came secondhand from charity shops, though she occasionally indulged in a new ethnic garment, like the kaftan she was wearing now. She said, 'When I was young, all the West End shops closed on Saturday afternoon.'

'Things have improved since then,' Belinda said.

Michel said, 'I wonder if the shop assistants would agree.'

'They get other days off,' Belinda said impatiently. 'Far more than they did then, I expect.'

Barbara said, 'When are we going to meet this Debbie of yours?'

'She's not *mine*.' A silence fell. Then Belinda said, 'I'll bring her round some time.'

'For a meal.'

'Yeah.'

Barbara said, 'Are you going to pop in and see Gran on your way out?'

'Too late. Next time.'

'She'll be upset. I'm sure she must have seen you arrive.'

'No. I crossed the road so that she wouldn't.'

'Oh.' After a moment Barbara added, 'She's very fond of you, you know. Family means so much to her, and you and I are all she's got.'

The air was thick with strong, confused emotions. 'See you later,' Belinda said. Waving – and avoiding a parting embrace – she moved quickly to the door, hurried along the passage and ran down the stairs.

Barbara wandered over to the window. 'See you later,' she repeated. 'That always used to mean the same day.'

'Not any more,' Michel said. 'Now it could mean in five years' time.'

'American,' Barbara said. Michel joined her at the window, putting an arm round her, and Barbara rested her head on Michel's shoulder. They watched Belinda cross the road and set off briskly on the opposite pavement: short legs and long body, short hair and large head. 'Poor darling,' Barbara murmured.

'She's as tough as old boots,' Michel said, though not harshly; the squeeze that went with the words was gentle.

'I don't think she's tough really.'

'Oh yes she is.' Michel laughed. 'It's in the blood. She's inherited it from Rupert the wrecker.'

'You know environment's far more important than heredity,' Barbara said reprovingly. 'Anyway half her blood's mine.'

Michel ignored this. 'The wrecker!' she repeated. 'Like one of those old Cornishmen who lured ships onto the rocks and then plundered them. Only, in Deyntree's case, the ships are women.'

'Mmm. I can't help thinking of that wretched Lucy Riven. But perhaps she's as bad as he is.'

'Impossible.'

Barbara laughed. She sat down at the table, and began to nibble another brownie: her third. She said, 'I wonder when Belinda will bring that friend of hers round.'

Michel hesitated, then said, 'I don't think she will.'

'But why?' Barbara said.

'Because of us.'

Barbara's expression became set; her voice rose. 'Oh nonsense! That's nonsense. One thing you must admit – Belinda's thoroughly modern.'

'Mmm,' said Michel.

'You're quite wrong,' Barbara went on. 'She might mind the place being a bit untidy . . . and all the political stuff, perhaps. But not about us.'

Michel shrugged. In a resigned tone she said, 'Oh well, you know her better than I do.'

'Yes. After all, she *is* my daughter.'

'Yes. Of course.'

'Yes.' For Barbara could not, would not recognize what had gone wrong between her and Belinda, and Belinda knew but would not say. She joked to Debbie about the untidy flat and the 'causes', but she never revealed that her mother's lover was a woman.

'Why do you spell your name like that?' Belinda once asked Michel. 'Surely it should have two ls and an e at the end?'

'My family spell it like that. But I prefer this spelling. I think it suits me better.'

Belinda looked away. She always avoided eye contact with Michel, just as she tried to avoid looking at the area between Michel's neck and waist: the area of Michel's small firm breasts.

It was after the death of Barbara's father, when Belinda was fifteen, that Michel moved out of the spare room to share Barbara's room and bed. (Mrs Korn was too lame and asthmatic ever to climb the steep stairs to the upper flat.)

Both Barbara's parents were sexually naïve, and had not suspected the nature of Barbara's relationship with her 'lawyer flatmate'. However if they had known the two women shared a bed, even they would have recognized the truth, and would never have understood or accepted it.

Barbara excused her parents because of their age. However she expected her daughter – brought up hearing talk of gay rights, pride and power – to react to her relationship with Michel just as if it were a relationship with a man. She was mistaken.

Barbara attributed Belinda's hostility to Michel to possessiveness. At the beginning this had been true. Belinda had felt Michel to be a competitor for Barbara's attention and affection, wished she would stop staying with them, and resented any criticism from her. When Michel moved into Barbara's room, the revelation had been overwhelming. Even

135

Barbara could see Belinda was 'surprised' and had said, 'Of course you've known for years that women can love each other just as men and women do. So I thought you understood about me and Michel. Anyway, from now on – except as far as poor old Gran's concerned – it can be honest and open. So much better for all of us.'

It was not better for Belinda whose dislike of Michel at once became hatred, and who felt an immediate physical and mental aversion to Barbara, whom, until then, she had loved devotedly. She avoided her mother's hugs and kisses; soon all Barbara's ideas, tastes and opinions seemed to her contemptible. This was the time when Barbara began to allow herself to criticize Rupert, and Belinda always defended him. A new Belinda had been born: Belinda 'the yuppie' as Michel started to call her. This Belinda wanted to be upper-class, rich and 'absolutely English' which meant 'not at all a Jew'.

She had always shrunk from her grandmother: not only from the smell of old age – musty and dusty – but from her foreign accent, her Yiddish expressions, the 'funny' food she cooked in her – ridiculously – kosher kitchen. 'Yuck!' Belinda would exclaim at the thought of Mrs Korn's moist gefilte fish and kisses. She also disliked the surname Barbara had resumed after her divorce.

'Why,' she had asked years ago, aged ten, 'did you change a lovely name like Deyntree?'

'Because it's not my name any more,' Barbara said. 'And Korn is. What's wrong with "Korn", anyway?' She gave Belinda a searching look.

It was with a shrill laugh that Belinda evaded the unasked question behind that look. 'It's corny,' she said. 'Korn's corny.' She ran out of the room.

Jewish law said Jewishness descended through the woman: a good reason for Belinda's determination not to be Jewish. After her mother 'came out' about Michel, she even considered becoming a Christian: 'That would show her!' she muttered to herself. But she soon realized that Barbara – an atheist who ate bacon and had loved two Gentiles – would not be hurt but merely puzzled by such a conversion. 'Do you really believe all that?' she would ask, and Belinda did not believe it.

There was perhaps another reason for her not converting. Belinda was a constant dodger of all books, films, television programmes and articles about the Holocaust. But once, when she and Debbie were discussing various nationalities, she had said, 'Oh, I could never marry a *German*.'

'Really? Why not?'

'Oh, I don't know.' Then she laughed and said, 'Some hang-up about Hitler and all that, I suppose. The Nazis.'

Debbie said, 'But that was all ages ago. Ages before we were even born.'

'Yes.' But in Mrs Korn's room were photographs – brownish-yellow now – of her father, mother, brother and two sisters. Only she had escaped, by marrying Ben Korn. They had all been gassed in the Buchenwald concentration camp.

Debbie said, 'I don't mind Germans.'

Belinda said, 'Perhaps I've seen too many old movies.'

'But you always turn them off when they're about Nazis.'

'I hate all that,' Belinda said.

'Mmm. It's a bit yucky.'

Debbie was wonderfully free from hang-ups: Belinda relished their friendship. However, this Saturday, she was not meeting Debbie, to lunch and shop. She had – as she often did – lied to her mother. Today she was lunching with her father's third wife, Chris Deyntree.

Ever since what had happened in February 1988 – eighteen months ago, now, but still daily in her thoughts, recurrently in her nightmares – Chris Deyntree had experienced fits of trembling.

When she was with other people, she would, at the first slight tremor, clasp her hands, close her eyes, and focus all the power of her will. Within two or three seconds, this proved effective . . . or had so far. (Might it fail on some future occasion?)

When alone – perhaps not under enough pressure to summon up the necessary resources – she found it harder to restore equilibrium. This morning, because of her father's telephone call, had been difficult. She needed to pause several times while she assembled lunch for Belinda, her former stepdaughter.

'Assembled' was the right word, as the food came from Marks and Spencer's chill cabinets. Chris served these meals – ready just to heat or to eat cold – to all guests except very important ones who, if they recognized the food's provenance, might feel she had not taken enough trouble. On such occasions, she hired a cordon bleu who left just before the guests were due. When complimented, she would say 'All homemade', which was true, though Chris was always prepared to lie in a good cause.

She was capable of all domestic tasks, but two young women from a firm of professional cleaners – no 'grubby old char' for Chris – came weekly to do the house from top to bottom, and a neighbour's son tidied the garden every Sunday morning. Her washing-machine, dryer, and dishwasher were the best available. Chris herself ironed – quickly and perfectly – once a week, with resentment, remembering her dead, despised mother's ceaseless, pointless domestic preoccupations. Even with servants, she had always been fussing about the house; TV was her only recreation, and she never watched that without knitting.

Although she did not cook, Chris's kitchen was lined with modern equipment, all black and white: she hated the thought that modern high-tech kitchens would ever go out of fashion; style was her goddess. She particularly disliked stripped pine furniture, hanging plants and red quarry-tiles. The floor of this large room – kitchen in front, dining-room behind – was tiled in spotless white.

The estate agent's term, 'garden room' – often applied to a dark basement – was exact in this case. A sliding glass door, covered now by a white exterior metal blind, took up most of the dining-room wall and led straight to the garden. The big front window, above the double sink between two working-surfaces, revealed more of the street outside than of the white-painted wall of a small area, protected by iron bars also painted white. This window, too, had an exterior metal blind, not closed this morning.

There was a container of gazpacho and another of seafood pasta for lunch. (Chris was one of those who believe that a 'two-portion' container holds enough for two women, though not for a woman and a man.) Afterwards there would be fruit. Chilling in the splendid refrigerator – a gadget in the door dropped ice into your glass – were San Pellegrino – Perrier which Chris used to drink had become too common – and California Chardonnay.

During the week Chris never drank alcohol at lunch. Earlier generations of publishing editors in the 1960s and 1970s had enjoyed very liquid lunches, even when not entertaining authors or other business connections; they often spent a couple of hours in a wine bar, drinking and chatting with office friends. Although the chat was usually about publishing and sometimes produced good ideas, it would not have appealed to Chris, and had no place in the mood of the 1980s or the views of the conglomerates which had taken over most British publishing houses.

Of course if Chris were entertaining an author, they would lunch at a good restaurant. (Although the lunch went on her expense account, Chris matched the restaurant's 'goodness' to the author's importance.) At such lunches Chris would ply her guest with wine while drinking mineral water herself, though many of her authors – health-conscious and business-minded – drank only mineral water themselves. Those. who seemed glad to polish off a whole bottle were mostly old-fashioned types with artistic pretensions. There were few of these on Chris's list; most of her authors were strictly commercial.

The books with which Chris had made her name were novels of sex, shopping and success. Once described in *Private Eye* as 'Queen of Crap', Chris had risen parallel with these books. In the 1980s, 'everyone' was reading them and almost 'everyone' was writing them: journalists, actresses, and tycoons' wives chronicled consumer goods, mergers and sexual techniques involving goldfish, pearls and electric toothbrushes.

In shops, these books were hard to tell apart: every cover showed the close-up of a dewy-skinned, flint-eyed young woman under a title in raised gold lettering. (Research had proved that such lettering sold extra copies.) The similarity continued within. But some books, helped by expensive promotion – given to those for which much money had been advanced and which were written by glamorous, promotable authors – succeeded more than others. Chris had a knack of predicting these winners, and she felt absolutely at home in the genre. Like its heroines she was intensely ambitious and loved expensive things; she found the gadgety sex as acceptably impersonal as the machines in her kitchen.

Sometimes she wondered if – as with her kitchen – the fashion might change. (It was almost as hard to imagine as that her heroine, Margaret Thatcher, might go out of office.) Worse still, might printed fiction itself go out of style, wholly replaced by video- and audio-cassettes? Surely it would last another couple of decades while she advanced her career, sniffing – with her commercial nose – changes of fashion ahead of colleagues and rivals? (These terms were, as those concerned were aware, synonymous for Chris. She was not popular; when she married Rupert, the office joke had been that 'Daddy bought him for her.')

Chris was not pretty: possibly she did not want to be; it was a word she spoke in a disparaging tone. Her features were small: successfully in the case of her nose but not of her mouth and eyes. She had always been thin. Recently, with no appetite – though she forced herself to eat and took vitamins – she had become scraggy: half way, perhaps, between Byron's dried butterflies and his spiders. However her face, like that of some actresses, could be transformed by make-up; she completely renewed hers every midday and, if she were seeing people, in the evening. Instead of contact lenses, she wore designer spectacles with patterned frames, and her thin, pale-brown hair was strikingly cut and streaked. Her clothes were chosen not for charm but for smartness or, as she called it, style.

Chris glanced at her watch. The time was just after twelve: Belinda was due at half past. Chris's life was governed by rules, but now she broke the one that forbade drinking alone (apart from one small single-malt whisky when she came home from work). She went to the refrigerator, took out the Chardonnay, uncorked it, and poured herself a glass. She took a sip as she sat down at the breakfast counter, and observed, through the front window, most of a woman and the whole of a pram and a small child, holding the woman's hand, looking up and, as Chris would have said, 'gabbling'. Chris took a gulp.

This morning she had been to the health club for her workout. Until eighteen months ago, Tuesday, Thursday and Saturday were the days when she ran; now they were the days when she drove to the club. On Tuesday and Thursday she reached it when it opened, at seven; on Saturday, she got there at eight. Today, at nine-fifteen, she was home, and just emerging from her 'power shower' – she liked the term; power in any context appealed to her – when the telephone rang. She wrapped herself in a towel and went through into her bedroom. (The bathroom and the ground-floor cloakroom were the only rooms in the house without telephones.)

She picked up the receiver, but said nothing.

'Chrissie?' It was her father, the only person who still called her by that name. His Yorkshire accent was strong: from ten years with Rupert, Chris had acquired a speech that was unfashionably upper-class. (People in her office imitated it behind her back. 'Frafly, frafly,' one secretary would say to another; both would giggle: all secretaries detested Chris.)

'Why, hullo, Dad! Nice surprise.' They were devoted, but seldom expressed it: Chris liked to be cool, and Jack Puttock to think of himself as a taciturn Yorkshireman.

Chris rarely went home, and her father hardly ever visited London. When he did, he stayed at the Hilton in Park Lane: at first because he did not like staying in the same house as his daughter's husband, and now – with a murmuring heart – because of the steep stairs. In any case he had never liked the old-fashioned Islington villa and, when Chris and Rupert parted, had suggested that she should sell it and buy a 'smart modern place'. But Chris, under Rupert's tuition, had learnt that, in London, 'smart' and 'modern' were very far from synonymous. Even though he knew it was worth a fortune – that had been proved when it was valued for Rupert to receive a half share in terms of the divorce settlement – her father was astonished that she should want to live in a 'semi'. He also asked if it did not upset her to go on living 'where you spent all those years with that bastard.' Chris had laughed and answered, 'D'you think I'd let him turn me out of my own house? It's mine, I like it, and I'm going to stick to it.' Her father admired this toughness, inherited, he believed, from him (he also believed their 'nerves of steel' were combined with 'hearts of gold'). Chris's brother, Tom, who would 'one day'

142

take over the thriving business Jack had built, who was married to a pretty, sensible wife and had three healthy children, who was satisfactory in every way, was not half as dear to Jack Puttock as his little Chrissie who had conquered the decadent south. She liked the semi: she must keep it, and good riddance to 'that bastard'.

There was only one shadow: that she didn't marry again. 'You're still in your prime, Chrissie. Not forty yet, but getting there, lass, even though you don't show it. If you want kids, you'll have to start soon.' Chris never told him that not having children was one thing on which she and Rupert had agreed. She would say, 'I don't want to make another mistake.' He would concur: 'Better wait for the real Mr Right. Not another *Deyntree*.' He spoke the name with hate, but was too old-fashioned to wonder why she didn't resume her maiden name after the divorce.

'Chris Deyntree!' If anyone queried her keeping the surname, she explained she was known by it to everyone in the publishing world; she had made it her own. She never said that she hated the name Christine (Chrissie) Puttock: so flat, grey, *northern*, it was everything Chris had set out to escape. To get away from it, she would have had to marry *someone*: anyway, she had been brought up to believe that a husband was an essential trophy. Well, she'd gained the trophy and a delightful name; so why should she remarry? Of course, more and more women now lived, unmarried, with 'partners', but what point had that with all the hassle of living with a man, and no prestige?

This morning, after their brief greetings, Jack Puttock said at once, 'Heard the news about that bastard?'

'No.' She did not have to ask whom he meant. She gave a short laugh: 'Not dead, is he?'

'Afraid not.' At this they both laughed. 'He's engaged to be married.'

'Engaged?'

'It was in the *Telegraph*. Of course the *Post*'s my paper, but old Bob Farley – the doctor, you know – showed it to me at the club. He said, "Isn't that the fellow your Chrissie was married to?" '

'Who is she, Dad?' Chris broke in.

'You'd never guess in a thousand years.'

'Well then, *tell* me.'

'He's marrying a Riven of Rivendale.'

'I don't believe it.' A faint trace of the north surfaced in Chris's speech; nowadays this hardly ever happened.

'It's true. She's the daughter, the heiress – though I don't know that there's much to inherit. She's called Lucy. Bob tells me she's about twenty-seven. He's a Roman himself, and he was their doctor before he retired. Now you know I'm no snob – that bastard's posh talk never impressed *me* – but they're a really old family. Real Yorkshire people. And famous for sticking to their religion – whatever you think of it, you can't help respecting that. And now their lass is going to marry *him*. I said to Bob: "Seeing they're such Catholics, how can she marry a divorced man?" But Bob says if he's not been married in church before, it may be all right. Remember how keen I was for you to have a proper church wedding up here? Well, if you had, he couldn't have done this.'

Chris had been wholly determined to avoid a Methodist wedding in the ugly church she had last entered at nineteen, for her mother's funeral. A 'C of E' wedding in a cathedral, or even a village church, would have been different though, even then, embarrassing relations would have been present. Now she said, 'Hunh!'

'Old Bob says she's a lovely lass. Good-looking, with beautiful fair hair. Nice-mannered – not a bit stuck up. Works for some charity in London.'

Chris's look as she listened to this was as cold as the tone in which she now said, 'Sounds too good to be true.'

'Too good for him – that's for sure.'

'Mmm.' Then Chris said, 'As a matter of fact, I'm having Belinda to lunch today.'

'His girl? So you still keep up with her?'

'Mmm. Actually, I'm a bit sorry for her.' Chris sounded defensive.

'You're too soft-hearted, Chrissie.' His tone was fond. Then he said, 'Perhaps she'll be able to tell you a bit more about this marriage.'

'I doubt it. Since he and I split up, she's hardly seen him.' Chris's hand, holding the receiver, had started to shake. She steadied her voice as she said, 'Dad, I must go now. I was in the shower when you rang. I'll phone you tomorrow evening, though, as usual. Can't miss our Sunday chat.'

'Well, I always like to hear your voice,' her father said. He added – in what was, for him, a strangely hesitant tone – 'You're not upset, are you, Chrissie?'

'Upset? Good heavens, no. I'm just surprised.'

'I should think her family must be upset – even if he does turn.'

'Turn?'

'Turn Roman. Bob thought he'd be likely to do that if he's marrying a Riven.'

'*Rupert*?' Chris gave an abrupt laugh. 'He's an atheist.'

'People can change, you know, Chrissie. Or seem to – if it's to their advantage.'

'Must go now, Dad. I'll ring. Bye.'

'Goodbye, Chrissie.'

She put down the receiver carefully. The telephone stood on her bedside table. Next to it was a jar of face cream: she picked this up and threw it across the room. It hit the white wall and dropped to the cream fitted-carpet. It left a mark on the wall, but did not break. Chris looked wildly round as if for something that would break. But then she clenched her fists and pounded the air with them. 'Fucker, bloody fucker. Fucker, fucker.' She first shouted the word, then gasped it again and again till it became a series of grunts. 'Unh, unh, unh,' she panted at last. A listener might have supposed her to be in the throes of orgasm, but that was something Chris had never experienced.

She had pretended for a long time. When the deception ended, it was a relief that Rupert stopped 'doing it to her' but it was also an insult: men were meant to want women; they were meant to want her. If only he had been one of the men other women complained about who 'got it over' in a few minutes, she might have borne it always; Rupert wasn't like that. But it was seven years before one night, after a particularly exhausting day at the office, she had groaned, 'Oh, why can't you leave me alone?'

'By all means,' he said, and then, 'Do you think I haven't known all along . . . well, almost? For the first few months I gave you the benefit of the doubt. But – in spite of all that writhing and moaning – you couldn't go on deceiving an old hand like me. Chris, you're frigid.'

'Frigid? I'm not frigid.' Chris sounded shrill.

'Yes you are. Unconquerably frigid. It must be some boring childhood trauma. Goodness knows I've tried hard enough to thaw you out.'

'Well, all that's enough to put anyone off. All that messing about. Treating me like a whore.'

'By a whore I presume you mean a woman who likes sex? Well I promise not to bother you any more.' He kept his word, but another three years passed before their divorce.

This morning she sat on her bed until the panting stopped. Then the trembling started. But she regained control. She even read fifty pages of a lust-and-loot typescript – there was a sex scene but, as far as she was concerned, it could have been a

146

description of tuning up an engine – before she assembled lunch.

Sitting at the breakfast counter, she had just finished her glass of wine when she heard the front gate creak. She went to the window: Belinda – ten minutes early – was coming up the path to the front steps.

Chris moved quickly: as the doorbell rang, she went first to the sliding doors to the garden. She turned a knob, and the metal blind outside started to rise – revealing the small lawn and its neat surround of perennials – as she left the room. She ran up the stairs. In the hall she hurried towards the front door, not yet to admit Belinda, but to press the buttons that turned off the alarms on the ground and the upper floor before her tread set off blaring noise and flashing lights outside. Then she went to the back of the hall, and raised the blind outside the glass door that led to steps down to the garden. Last, in the double drawing-room, she raised the blind on the back window.

Every garden-facing window in the house, including those of the bathroom and spare room on the upper floor – unapproachable, the security man had assured her, except by someone descending from the roof on a rope (she had shuddered involuntarily) – had its metal blind, except the ground-floor cloakroom with its tiny porthole. In front, only the kitchen had a blind; the front window of the drawing-room had those heavy wooden shutters that fasten with a metal bar. In any case, it – like the front windows upstairs – had metal fastenings which prevented it being opened more than two inches. In addition, little red sensors glowed in the corners of every room and passage, sensitive to any vibration, and ready to trigger the alarm when it was set. (Even a cat's movements could have activated them; fortunately, Chris was not a pet-lover.)

When Chris went out, she set the alarms on all floors. At night she set them on the two lower floors. (Upstairs, by her bed, was a 'panic button'.) Spending more than a short time on any floor, she set the alarms on the other two.

The system was an expensive one: the security firm guaranteed arrival within a few minutes of the alarm – connected to their premises – unless it was turned off at once and they received a telephone call that it had been set off by mistake.

Now Chris went to the front door, which had a double mortice lock as well as a Yale, a chain and a peephole. Even though Chris had seen Belinda from the kitchen window, she automatically checked through the peephole before unfastening the chain and unlocking the door.

Eighteen months ago, the house had been more vulnerable. She and Rupert had bought a simple alarm system, activated, when set, if a door or window were opened. It was not connected to a security firm's premises, and depended, when they were out, on 'neighbourhood watch'. After the divorce, Chris had the key number of the alarm changed; she set it when she went out and at night she set it on the two lower floors. However, she – correctly – believed that professional burglars prefer to enter a house in the occupants' absence; she was not fearful or imaginative ('morbid' was the word she would have used). The front door had a peephole and chain, but Chris never fastened the chain. In February 1988, everything changed.

It was half past eight in the evening. Chris had eaten her Marks and Spencer lasagne and radicchio salad, with a wholewheat roll. In those days she had a good appetite and, though careful what she ate, enjoyed her food. After the main course she had a treat: a small lemon sorbet. When she had cleared up, she was ready to go upstairs to her bedroom, to read and to watch the large television that stood at the foot of her large bed. Since Rupert moved out, she had become very fond of this bed.

Although the old mattress had been in good condition, she had ordered a new one when he left, and also bought a lot of pretty new sheets and nightdresses. (She never slept naked.) No one but Chris saw these things: she had bought them for her own pleasure. Sometimes she would pose in front of the huge bathroom mirror in one of the nightdresses or in other delicate items of lingerie. Occasionally she would kiss the reflection of her lips, her mouth lingering on the cool glass of the mirror till it clouded, but she never went further.

In bed she read and 'viewed', propped up on a heap of pillows. When she pushed these aside – she slept with only one pillow because she had read somewhere that more encouraged a double chin – she usually fell asleep quickly and slept far better than she had done during her marriage.

On that particular evening, she was coming up the stairs from the kitchen, carrying a mug of decaffeinated coffee, when the doorbell rang. Putting the mug down on the hall table, where her handbag lay, next to a telephone, she went to the front door and looked through the peephole. It was a cold night, and the woman who stood outside was huddled in an overcoat; from under a headscarf emerged a blonde fringe above large dark-rimmed glasses. Chris looked through the peephole, the woman shivered. Chris turned the Yale lock, and opened the door.

At once the woman began to speak. 'I'm so terribly sorry. I'm quite lost.' The accent was exaggeratedly upper class. Chris opened the door a little further. 'Could you possibly tell me the way to Highbury station?'

'Yes, it's about ten minutes' walk. I'll show you.' Chris stepped forward to point the way, but the woman did not step back. Chris hesitated. The woman's glasses were tinted: odd in this weather and at night. Suddenly she gave Chris a backward push into the hall, and moved in herself, slamming the door. Gloved hands came from behind Chris, and a pad was pressed over her nose and mouth. Stinging, reeking, it choked and then submerged her.

When she regained consciousness, the pad had gone, but she was gagged and blindfolded. She was naked, lying on the carpeted floor, her hands tied behind her back; a man was raping her. There was a whirring sound. She kicked out and the woman's voice said, 'Don't struggle. You'll get hurt.' No one spoke after that. Under the gag, Chris whimpered; there were gasps and grunts from the man; once the woman laughed. Chris was face up, face down, on her side; four hands moved her and moved over her. There was an implement. All the time, there was the whirring sound, and the overpowering smell of a cheap sickly aftershave. Finally, the choking pad came down again . . .

She felt sick; she became aware that, though she was still gagged and blindfolded, her hands were untied. Hesitantly she raised them – they shook – to fumble off the blindfold and gag.

She was on the drawing-room carpet between the two facing sofas; the coffee table had been pushed back near the fireplace. Saliva dribbled from her mouth; there was a trickle of her blood on the carpet. She throbbed inside; her pubic hair was sticky. 'Ugh.' Her thighs were tender where bruises would develop later.

Some of her clothes were on one sofa, the rest on the floor. The gag in her hand was a cheap scarf, folded round cotton wool, and the blindfold was the same. Holding onto the sofa, she stood up, and stared round. Nothing seemed to have been moved except the coffee table.

This was the moment to ring the police. But Chris did not go to the telephone. She staggered into the hall where her handbag lay next to the mug of cold, filmy coffee. She opened the bag. Her wallet and credit cards were still there. She went to the door, double-locked it, and fastened the chain. She set the alarm behind the door for the two lower floors, and the buzzer sounded for two minutes. She was on the stairs when it stopped: a few moments later, the alarm went off, blaring from the outside wall of the house where a red light would also be flashing.

She tottered down to the alarm to press the buttons, which was difficult because her hand shook so much. Silence fell. Then the telephone on the hall table rang. After several rings, she picked up the receiver.

'Chris?' It was a familiar voice: her next-door neighbour's. 'It's May Denholm.'

'Oh yes.'

'I heard the alarm. I just wanted to check that all's well.'

'Oh yes. Sorry to have disturbed you. I must have left a window open. I'll have a look. Thanks so much.'

'Not at all. Bye.'

'Goodbye.' Chris put down the receiver. She went into the drawing-room, and lifted the side of one of the closed curtains of the garden window. It was open a few inches; the catch of the sash had been forced.

She closed the window, went back into the hall, and set the alarm again; she stood on the bottom step of the stairs until the buzzer was silent. Nothing happened, so no doors or windows on the two lower floors were now open, and if they were opened the alarm would go off.

Chris went up the stairs very slowly, holding the banister. Upstairs, she went into the bathroom, pulled the blind and ran a hot bath. When she bathed – she usually showered – she always added scented oil to the water; tonight, instead, she poured in Dettol. She soaked in the very hot water, soaping herself again and again. At last, when her fingertips were creased from immersion, she hauled herself out, put on the white towelling robe that hung on the back of the bathroom door and which she hardly ever wore, and went into her bedroom where she drew the curtains before she turned on the light. (None of the windows in the house had net curtains; Rupert had taught her they were common.)

Most of her nightdresses were flimsy, but tonight she put on a heavy, genuine Victorian one Rupert had given her three or four years after their marriage. (She had disliked and never worn it because it was second-hand; she had also suspected Rupert would incorporate it in some sexual charade.) Under it she put on a pair of the plain white briefs she wore for tennis. Then she got into bed, with all her pillows round her and the lights on, and cried. She stayed awake, crying on and off, until five, when she dozed. She woke at seven, showered, and got ready for work.

That day she set in motion the procedures that would turn her house into a fortress. Until this was accomplished – with Chris at the helm, it took only two weeks – she never went into the basement in the evening. (It must have been while she was having supper down there, with the alarms all off, that the drawing-room window had been forced open.) Coming home, she would reset the alarm for the two lower floors and go straight upstairs. During this period – practical as always – she ate her main meal – though she had lost her appetite – at lunch, and brought home fruit and a sandwich which she ate upstairs. At this time she turned the central heating up several degrees and kept it on all night because she shivered so much.

Once the house was fully armoured with its new defences, she resumed her old routines, except that she bought pyjamas to wear instead of nightdresses and, instead of running, went to the health club. Chris was 'in control' (a favourite phrase of hers), apart from the trembling; she was determined to control that, in time.

She told no one. She did not tell the police, with their intrusive questions and scepticism (she herself had always been sceptical about rape, believing that – except in wars – it only happened to 'victim types'). She did not tell her doctor: her period arrived ten days after the rape; her bruises and scratches healed; she never thought about AIDS which she was privately convinced affected only homosexuals and drug addicts. She did not tell a friend: she had none; the only person she ever invited to the house alone was Belinda whom she thought of not as a friend but as a protégée.

Chris opened the door. 'Hullo, Belinda.'

'Oh hullo, Chris.' Belinda had an eager puppyish look. 'How are you?'

'Fine.' This was Chris's automatic response to queries about her health. Once when she was in bed with flu and a high temperature, and her boss telephoned to ask how she was, she had croaked the word. (Her mother, when people asked how she was, had told them.) Chris said now, 'Let's go downstairs. We might sit in the garden.'

'Brilliant!' said Belinda; this was her favourite term of approval. As they passed, she glanced into the drawing-room: 'My ideal room,' as she had once told Chris. Its huge white sofas and pale carpet were immaculate; glossy new magazines were arranged on the coffee table and the bookcase was full of new-looking hardcover books in shiny jackets. There were two large green pot plants. A black-and-white still life – a framed poster for a photographic exhibition – hung over the sofa facing the front window and a steel-framed mirror over the fireplace. Chris did not care for pictures or rugs. She had been delighted when Rupert took away 'The Good and Evil Angels'.

On the stairs, Chris said, 'Have you heard about your father?'

'Oh, you've heard too.' Belinda's voice held the disappointment of one foiled in a desire to break dramatic news. 'Someone in my office showed it to me in *The Times*. I've got the cutting with me.'

'Oh.' Downstairs, Chris unlocked the sliding door. On a

small, paved area between the house and the lawn wrought-iron chairs stood round a marble-topped table. 'Let's have a drink.' She brought out the Chardonnay and two clean glasses. When they had taken their first sips, she said, 'Let me see.'

'What? Oh, the announcement.' Belinda extracted the cutting from her wallet. 'I'm afraid it's a bit crushed,' she said. 'Michel threw it in the waste-paper basket.'

'Really?' Chris's slim pale hand with its large solitaire diamond ring, transparent fingers and long pale nails came out for the cutting with an incongruous avidity. When she had read it, she went on looking at it for a moment or two before handing it back, saying, 'You've been to see your mother?'

'Yes.'

Chris was the only person Belinda had told about her mother and Michel. Chris had looked shocked, and Belinda had been comforted by this response. Surely she herself could be shocked if Chris – so modern and sophisticated – was? And Chris had added, 'It must have been difficult for you.' 'Yes.' Then Chris said, 'Still is perhaps?' 'Yes, a bit.'

That had been soon after Rupert and Chris's divorce. (Belinda would never have told *him* about her mother and Michel.) Chris and Belinda continued to see each other. Possibly Rupert had underestimated Chris's liking for Belinda. ('It's why most people give to charity,' he once said. 'Makes you feel good. Or perhaps you're actually flattered by that doggy devotion?')

Now Chris said, 'Was your mother upset?'

'Not upset exactly. Indignant. Worried for the Lucy person.'

'Goodness,' Chris said. 'How very disinterested!' (Rupert had branded the difference between 'disinterested' and 'uninterested' on Chris's consciousness. She had even – apologizing for pedantry – pointed it out to one of her authors; normally she did not bother to correct their solecisms: only crude errors.)

'They – my mother and Michel – thought someone ought to warn her.'

'How dramatic. I'm sure Lucy's quite able to take care of herself.'

'You *know* her?'

Chris laughed. 'Lucy Riven? They're neighbours of ours in Yorkshire. I'm not sure that I've seen her since she was a child – I spend so little time up there. But I believe she's quite nice looking. Full of good works – they're Catholics, you know. A very old family. She's twenty-seven.'

'Wow! Only five years older than me!'

'Why, yes. I suppose so.'

Belinda enjoyed her lunch and, according to the new doctrine, it wasn't fattening: a small quantity of pasta was no more fattening than a steak and better for you. It was, appropriately, the decade of the high fibre diet: many uptight yuppies suffered from constipation.

Belinda's relationship with food was tormented. 'If only I were anorexic,' she had once said to her mother. 'Belinda, how can you say that!' Barbara sounded horrified, and added, 'Anorexia kills people.' (Her own rejection of dieting was related not only to a love of food but to an abhorrence of her early career as a model.) 'Better dead than fat,' Belinda had muttered, but she found diets so hard to follow that there was actually no danger of her starving.

Today, when she and Chris had eaten their raspberries and low-fat yoghurt, she said, 'I haven't heard from Daddy in ages.'

'Perhaps you should get in touch. Why not ring up and congratulate him?' Chris said.

After a moment Belinda said, 'Do you think I should?'

Chris was looking preoccupied. 'Should what?'

'Phone him.'

Chris shrugged. 'Up to you.' Then she said, 'Coffee?'

The offer sounded half-hearted, and when Belinda said,

'I don't think so,' was not repeated.

A silence followed. Belinda broke it by saying, 'I ought to go now.'

'Must you really?' Chris stood up. 'You must come again soon.'

'Yes.' As Belinda stood up, she looked crestfallen, glancing at her watch. The time was only just after two. She said, 'I have to go to the launderette.'

'Awful for you. You must get a washing machine as soon as possible.'

'Nowhere to hang anything, one needs a drier, too, and they're so expensive. I'll wait a bit.'

'But the launderette! All those fat women and creepy old men and screaming children.'

'Mmm.'

As Chris saw her out, she called after her, 'Shut the gate,' and Belinda closed the creaking gate. Chris locked the door and fastened the chain. Then she closed the metal blind at the back of the drawing-room and, although it was so early, fastened the shutters in front. She went downstairs, cleared up, putting glasses and crockery in the dish washer, after she had closed the door to the garden and its blind. Then she closed the front blind and went upstairs. Back in the hall, she set the alarms for the two lower floors before going up to her room. She lay on her bed, reading a typescript, but often breaking off to stare up at the ceiling.

Belinda, especially when she was lonely, didn't mind going to the launderette. But as she walked home from Chris's she looked downcast, though she usually enjoyed the walk through pretty Canonbury. She crossed the Essex Road. There was a newsagent in her own street, just round the corner. She passed it, but then turned back and went in to buy two Mars bars. She unwrapped one as soon as she was inside the house, and had finished it by the time she reached the top floor. As soon as she was in her own flat she started on the second.

The weekend was almost over, though its atmosphere persisted while Eva drove them to the station. Eva – housekeeper, chauffeur, sometimes cook – was still Teresa's worshipper, invariably sharing her attitudes. As she drove off, Lucy and Rupert simultaneously sighed and exchanged glances, then laughed, though Lucy's laugh was rueful.

On Friday at King's Cross Rupert had wanted them to travel first-class, but Lucy resolved that they should get cheap weekend returns (and to pay for her own ticket). Their compartment had been packed and noisy.

This Sunday afternoon at Darlington, the train was less full. Rupert bundled the luggage – his leather suitcase and Lucy's blue bag – onto the rack, and they took window seats; Lucy's, at Rupert's insistence, faced the engine.

He sprawled on the seat. 'I shall repel all boarders,' he said.

'It may fill up, though this train's never as crowded as the two later ones.' Then she said, 'Admit it. That telephone call you made last night wasn't anything to do with having to get back to London early, was it?'

Her hand – small and neat, with its pretty ring and short nails – was resting on the table between them. Now he covered it with his own: large and well-shaped. He stared straight into her eyes. (A woman had once compared this experience to 'having a long drink of blue.') He said, 'I didn't make a call at all. By yesterday evening I just knew I couldn't stick it out beyond lunch today.'

'You hated it,' Lucy said. There was pain in her voice. 'You hated Rivers.'

'Darling. What absolute nonsense. I liked the place all right. The only problem was that it didn't like me.'

' "It?" '

'The inhabitants I mean, of course. No, don't look sad.' He

squeezed her hand. 'I'm perfectly cheerful now.'

Lucy smiled only faintly. 'That's because you've escaped,' she said.

'Darling Lucy, you must admit it's a bit oppressive when everyone disapproves of one: your mother . . . that ghastly old Eva.'

'Oh Rupert, Eva's had a sad life – and I don't know what Mummy would do without her.'

'I've never felt such a general atmosphere of suspicion. As if I were going to steal the silver. Actually those ancient heavy knives and forks *were* rather tempting.'

Lucy laughed with him now. 'Oh, how ridiculous you are!' After a moment she said, 'Eva doesn't really like anyone but Mummy. And Mummy . . . I know she's difficult. Not warm.'

'Warm? She's an iceberg.'

'Oh . . .'

'And what about Nanny, your famous ally – when she came up from the village. So grim. I knew at once she couldn't stand me.'

'Oh, I'm sure that's not true. But' – Lucy laughed – 'I think she's always had a picture of the kind of person she wanted me to marry. A young Catholic duke.'

'Not many of them around. Perhaps a few foreigners.'

'Oh Nanny wouldn't like *that*. Nor would I – any kind of duke, I mean. I can't stand grandeur. Some of Mummy's relations are rather that way. One of the things I love about Rivers is that it's so simple.'

'Simple? That great hall with the banners and suits of armour.'

'But no gold. Or paintings on the ceilings.' After a moment's pause, Lucy said, 'When you saw that engraving of the new building – the eighteenth century one that was burnt down – I had the feeling you liked it better.'

'Better?'

'Better than our house – the old one.'

'Nonsense. I've always admired Georgian architecture, of course. But I think Rivers is wonderful, truly. That huge chimney . . . the stone . . . the panelling in that amazing library. And the relics, of course. Marvellous . . .'

'Really?'

'Really.'

After a moment Lucy said, 'I know Nanny will love you when she gets to know you.'

'And Rufus – will *he* come to love me? Barking and growling whenever he saw me . . .'

It was a fast train, and now it was rocking slightly, swaying from side to side; they gazed at each other. Lucy looked away. Then she said, 'They'll all come to love you just like I do.'

'Not *just* as you do, I hope – old Eva with that horrid wart.'

'You're dreadful.' Then she said, 'I think Rufus was jealous – he's always been specially fond of me.'

'Well, I suppose I should honour him for that. A bit smelly, isn't he?'

'He's *old*.'

'Yes. Poor old Rufus.'

'Are you sure you wouldn't like Rivers to be grander?' she asked a little later.

'No, it's perfect. A bit dark, perhaps – those mullioned windows. And quite cold – even in August.'

'You see – you would have liked the Georgian house better.'

'No. Honestly. I really admire that . . . simplicity.'

'Me too. Like the catacombs.'

'The catacombs?'

'So simple . . . and pure.'

'Full of bones.'

'I just imagine the early Christians there.'

'Escaping from the lions?'

'No, from the Romans. So old and tired and worldly.'

'Just like me.'

'Oh Rupert, what nonsense! They were horrible. So cruel and perverted. So debauched.'

'What a splendid word!'

'My father used it – about the Romans.'

'I suspect your mother thinks *I'm* debauched.'

'I'm sure she doesn't.' Lucy sounded indignant.

'That name she gave me – Bluebeard.'

'She only meant you'd been married so often.'

'But Bluebeard murdered his wives. Kept a room full of corpses. Dreadful secrets. "That Bluebeard chamber of his mind into which no eye but his own must look." '

'Is that last bit a quotation?'

'Yes, but heaven knows where it comes from.'

Lucy said, 'I'm sure Mummy wasn't thinking of all that.'

Rupert laughed. 'No, I'm sure she wasn't. She just compares me unfavourably to some *preux chevalier* like Nanny's young duke.'

Lucy said, 'They'll all come round. When they see how happy you make me.'

'Even Rufus?' They both laughed. Then he said, 'Your mother must have been very beautiful when she was young.'

'Yes.'

'But not as beautiful as you.'

'That's just not true.'

'With your wonderful hair,' he said. He stretched out his hand and gave her plait a little tug.

'Mummy's never really liked my hair. She thinks long hair's dowdy. She wanted it cut. But my father said no. And after he died, I wouldn't give in.'

'Thank goodness. I wonder what your father would have thought of me.'

'Oh, he would have liked you so much.' Lucy spoke with certainty. 'He told me I should marry someone I could laugh

160

with. That was practically the last thing he said to me. He wanted me to be happy.'

'He thought you weren't?'

'No, I think he was thinking about himself and my mother. They weren't happy, really' she said as they drew into York station. Then, 'After this the country changes.'

'And you're changing the subject.'

'Yes. Did you like the moors?'

'Such a strange light up there. And the heath such extraordinary colours. Rufus was skulking round as if you needed a guard dog. And that grouse starting up right under our feet. Bang-bang.' He imitated the action of someone firing a shotgun into the air.

'Do you *like* shooting? I specially brought you up before it started. They'll be banging away next weekend. Our shooting's let, you know.'

'I haven't shot since I was in Kenya. Before I went up to Oxford.'

'I believe my great-grandfather shot. My grandfather couldn't stand it after he came back from the First War, and my father hated it, too. He would have liked to leave the birds alone. But my mother said it was absurd not to let it.'

They had kept their table to themselves at York. At Doncaster quite a lot of people got in, but Rupert's stare intimidated prospective occupants of the seats next to them, and others were available. At Peterborough however, the compartment filled up. A middle-aged woman sat firmly down next to Lucy and the small boy with her next to Rupert, who shifted with a sigh. The woman conversed with Lucy for the rest of the journey; Rupert did not join in.

As they got out at King's Cross, Lucy said, 'You look depressed.'

They were standing on the platform. He said, 'I am a bit – everyone at Rivendale disliked me so much.' Then he said,

'Darling, will you do something for me?'

'Of course.' They stood still, ignoring the people passing.

'I'd so much like to spend the evening with you.'

'Go out to dinner?'

'No, come with you to Hampstead. We'll take a taxi to my flat – please don't start talking about the Underground – and I'll drive you home. And we can be peaceful – sit in the garden perhaps. If we get hungry, though I don't think I shall, after all that Yorkshire pudding and apple tart, we can have scrambled eggs.'

She said, 'Do you really think it's a good idea?'

'The scrambled eggs, you mean? Too much cholesterol?'

She laughed. 'No, of course not. I meant you coming back.'

He said, 'I promise not to seduce you.'

She blushed. She said, 'It wasn't that. I was thinking I ought to wash my hair, and it takes such ages to dry.'

'Ah. But couldn't you leave it till tomorrow? When I've gone. For over a week, remember?'

'Yes, I know. All right.'

Later, when they were on the Dumbles' sofa, it was a long time before she broke away; she murmured, 'You promised.'

'Yes, I know.'

She sat up. 'I must telephone.'

'But who, why?' He had the same dazed look as she did.

Lucy stood up. 'Mummy. I usually telephone her when I've been up for the weekend. By the way, you'll write, won't you? She'll expect it.'

'Yes, of course,' he said.

Lucy went into the hall. Rupert had undone her hair, and it hung round her thighs, thick, blonde and silky. She dialled Rivendale, and her mother answered.

'Mummy, it's me. I wanted to thank you for the weekend. Rupert says he'll be writing.'

Teresa said, 'Are you at his flat?'

'No. I'm at home in Hampstead. Oh, really!' Then, low but angry – there was desperation in her voice – she spoke fast: 'Why, why don't you like him? You don't like anyone I care about. You don't like Vee, who's my best friend, and now you don't like Rupert.'

Her mother's tone was cool: 'We aren't obliged to *like* everyone, Lucy. Surely you remember learning that as a child.'

'But this is the man I'm going to marry. I love him.'

'Yes, I know all about that.'

'Then you should try to like him. You and Eva and Nanny and Rufus were all perfectly horrible.'

'Horrible? Don't be absurd. Everyone was entirely courteous. And you can hardly blame poor old Rufus for his instincts. Animals have very keen instincts. And though I've never cared for Nanny, as you know, it's natural that she should be sad that he's so old and not a Catholic.'

'Old! He's not *old*, and he's going to become a Catholic.'

'I can only hope he's sincere.' Teresa sounded as if she thought this improbable.

Lucy said, 'You should *pray* to like him.'

'To St Jude?' asked Teresa. 'He's the patron of hopeless causes.'

'You're *cruel*.'

'Lucy, please don't speak like that. It's foolish as well as impertinent. You want me to approve of a man whose origins are obscure—'

'It wouldn't matter to me if they were – but they aren't. His father farmed in Kenya after he retired from the army, and his mother was a Canon's daughter.'

'Anyway, they were divorced. Quite a family tradition, it seems. And I've heard rumours that his father had an unsavoury reputation.'

'I'm not interested in the gossip of your snobbish chums.'

'Snobbish? It's not a question of snobbery. Quite apart from his parents, what about *his* reputation? He has been through a form of marriage with three women, he has two grown-up children whom apparently he never sees, and he is engaged in some mysterious, perhaps shady form of business.'

'Mysterious! Shady! He's a financial investigator.'

'A sort of detective.'

'No, he investigates business opportunities abroad. For investors.'

'It sounds very vague.'

'You just don't understand about business.'

'And you do?'

'Mummy, I'm a trained manager and fund-raiser.'

'But hardly an expert on foreign investments. Lucy, this conversation is quite pointless. By the way, before we ring off, I must just tell you that a woman rang up. She said she knew you and wanted your telephone number. To congratulate you on your engagement. She didn't give her name. She sounded . . . well, middle-aged. An educated voice. So I gave her the number.'

'Because she had a posh accent?'

'Lucy – what an appalling word. *Posh* indeed!'

'Everyone uses it.'

'I'm sure they do. It's very *common*.'

Lucy was silent. Then she said, 'Oh please, Mummy, try to like Rupert.'

Teresa said, 'Lucy, you're spoilt. Your father spoiled you. Unfortunately I couldn't prevent that. Nanny spoiled you—'

'And you got rid of her as soon as Daddy died.'

'You certainly didn't need a nanny any longer. And, as I say, I never cared for her. Or the way she spoiled you. You expect to have everything your own way. And when you don't get it, you sulk.'

'That's not fair. I'm not sulking.'

'You sound as if you are. And meanwhile poor Mag's

telephone bill is going to be astronomical.'

'I always pay my share.'

'Good night, Lucy. God bless you.' Before Lucy could answer, her mother rang off.

'Oh!' she exclaimed, and then, 'So hateful!' She stood quite still by the telephone for several seconds, before suddenly, quickly, going to the living-room door, which she had closed when she went to telephone. She opened it. Rupert, on the sofa, was – improbably – paging through the parish magazine. He looked up and smiled, but she stared at him intensely for a moment, before returning him a brilliant smile. She said, 'Wait just two minutes.'

'*Another* telephone call?' But he smiled.

'No. Just wait two minutes,' she repeated. Then she turned and ran upstairs. But it was ten minutes before – from the first-floor landing – she called, 'Rupert!'

He came into the hall. She stood on the landing, leaning forward, elbows on the banister, chin cupped in her palms. Then she straightened. Her hair was all round her, nearly to her knees, but under it she was quite naked. She held out her arms.

Chris's telephone was ringing. In her study, she picked up the receiver, and when she heard her father's voice said, 'Oh, hullo, Dad. I was going to phone you.'

'Yes I know. But I've just heard some gossip, and I know how you enjoy that.' Actually it was he who enjoyed relaying local titbits, but he liked to believe he was indulging her when he did so.

'So, come on. Tell me.' There was affection in her voice.

'Well I just popped into the club this evening for a drink before supper, and I saw old Bob again. He's always there – to get away from that awful wife, I suppose.' Chris laughed, and he went on, 'Well, Bob told me that at St Cuthbert's this morning, he met the whole Rivendale party – including that bastard!'

'So Rupert's actually become a Roman Catholic!' Chris's tone was incredulous.

'That's what I thought. But Bob says that isn't necessarily so. He didn't take their Holy Communion though all the others did. And after the service – the Mass – Bob had quite a long talk with the Riven lass. She was so sweet and friendly, he said, though he hasn't been her doctor for years. She'd left home before he retired, you know. "And I'm never ill," she said to him. Then he asked her what she was doing in London, and she told him she had this job with "Feed the Children". "You've got your own flat, I expect," said Bob – he's a real old nosey-parker. But she said no, she lived with a family in Hampstead, the Dumbles. Bob seemed to know all about them. They're well-known Catholic publishers, he said. Have you ever heard of them?'

'Vaguely,' Chris said.

'Anyway, Bob says she's a lovely lass, and he thought that bastard was a very good-looking fellow. "Even if he is a few years older," says Bob. So I say, "How old's she, then?" "Must be twenty-six or -seven," Bob says. And then *I* say, "He's twenty years older, and more." Bob could hardly believe it. Well, I said no more, because, for Bob, the Rivens can do no wrong. He said she and that bastard made a handsome couple.'

At this last piece of information, Chris gripped the receiver tightly. Then she said, 'Well, I hope they'll be as happy as they deserve.' She laughed.

'I'd say she deserves a lot better than him, from what I hear of her. Really, I quite pity the lass.'

'She sounds a real prig to me,' Chris said. 'With her do-gooder job, and dragging Rupert off to church. I wonder how long he'll go along with that.' Chris's laugh was so hard that her father's chuckle in response was half-hearted.

He changed the subject: 'How's *your* weekend been, Chrissie? Still not got a new fellow?'

Chris ignored this second question. 'I've been working,' she said. 'Apart from seeing Belinda, like I told you yesterday.'

'She hasn't met the bride-to-be, I suppose.'

'Not a chance. She never sees him. I suggested she should ring up and congratulate him, but I doubt if she will. He's a dreadful father.' She added, 'I'm lucky to have you.'

'And so am I lucky, lass. Well, I'll say goodbye now. Don't work too hard – though I suppose it's no use saying that.'

'It's you that should be easing up a bit, Dad.'

'I'll die in harness.' This was a favourite saying of Jack Puttock's, unappreciated by his son.

When they had rung off, Chris stared out of the window at the houses opposite. It was half past seven and just getting dark. She drew the curtains, and switched on the light. This little study next to her bedroom held a desk and office chair, a small word-processor, her fax, and a filing-cabinet, which she now unlocked. Here she kept all her financial and personal records, meticulously; among the files was one relating to her divorce. She had not taken it out recently. Now, she did so. As she opened it on the desk, her whole body tensed. She put one hand to her head as if it throbbed; her breathing quickened; her hands trembled as she went through the papers to find the private detective's report which she had commissioned despite its irrelevance to modern matrimonial law.

Before 1973, a wife had no obligation to support a divorced husband, whatever their respective financial positions. But since the Matrimonial Causes Act of 1973, courts had been empowered to make financial orders against a wife in favour of a husband, and the Matrimonial Family Proceedings Act of 1984 had – in Chris's view – worsened the situation still further. Nowadays, both parties approached the court in an absolutely equal position with regard to financial provision. The length of the marriage was taken into account, and Chris and Rupert had been married so long – ten years – that all Chris's assets had been taken into account, even a trust her father had set up for her. Rupert had obtained half the investments made with her capital, on his advice, and half the value of the house: a wedding present from her father. She could hardly believe it when an eminent London lawyer made the situation clear to her; she was incredulous when he also informed her that the law no longer apportioned blame in reaching its settlements. 'But he's been unfaithful to me. I'm sure of it,' she said, and the lawyer replied, 'I'm afraid that makes no difference, Mrs Deyntree.' Yet she had hired the detective: not for legal reasons, but because she was obsessed with finding out. Well, she had found out a lot. Now, to confirm certain details, she went through the report once more.

Although she slept so badly, Chris, with her hatred of dependence, seldom allowed herself a sleeping-pill, but tonight she took one.

Both Francis and his mother eagerly awaited Rupert's Sunday telephone call that evening: he for a first-hand account of Rivendale and its occupants and she for his subsequent vivid re-creation of it. However Rupert did not telephone. Francis tried his number at ten, and again at half-past ten, just before he and his mother had their nightcap. On both occasions he rang off when answered by the intolerable machine. 'Goodness knows where Rupe can be. He's off to the Middle East early tomorrow for a week,' he said to his mother.

'Deserting his new affianced?' Mrs Larch smiled. She might have made some reference to Rupert's lovable scampishness, but Francis was frowning.

'It's a business trip,' he said almost curtly, and then, 'You know, I worry about that woman.'

'Lucy Riven?'

'Well, yes, in a way. But I meant the other one.'

'Jeanne Duval?'

'Yes. You remember we were talking last Sunday about how she behaved with Chris. If she found out about the engagement, she might start all that business with telephone calls and packets and so on with Lucy. Behaving like a witch.' He picked up a book that was open in front of him on his desk. 'It made me think of that old poem, "The Witch's Ballad", about how a witch loses the love of the Devil.'

'Surely you're not comparing poor Rupe to the Devil?'

'Of course not. It was the witch I was thinking of.' He read aloud:

> *I saw, I saw that winsome smile,*
> *The mouth that did my heart beguile,*
> *And spoke the great Word over me,*
> *In the land beyond the sea.*
>
> *I call'd his name, I called aloud,*
> *Alas! I called on him aloud;*
> *And then he fill'd his hand with straw,*
> *And threw it towards me in the air . . .*
>
> *My lusty strength, my power was gone;*
> *Power was gone, and all was gone.*
> *He will not let me love him more!'*

'That witch sounds sad,' Mrs Larch said.

'Yes – sad about losing her lover. But witches can be vengeful, too, you know. Rupe really must sort it out.'

'Perhaps that's what he's doing this evening.'

'Oh, I hope so.' Then he said, 'I thought I might take Lucy out to lunch while he's away.'

'Surely *you* don't think of telling her?'

'Oh absolutely not. Behind Rupe's back? My oldest friend! No – I thought it might cheer her up a bit. I've got a meeting in London on Wednesday evening, so I'll spend the night at the flat. But if Lucy's free for lunch . . .'

'Good idea!' As usual, Mrs Larch made no enquiry about Francis's London meeting. She said, 'Of course, I long to hear more about Lucy – "Fairfax Rochester's girl-bride," you know.' This reference to Jane Eyre made them both laugh.

Dink's inflexible rule forbade penetration – she catered to other needs, and had often described herself as 'more an actress than anything else' – but tonight's caller was probably the least demanding of all her regular visitors: she did not have to touch him at all.

He was a middle-aged Turk. Before he arrived, she would spread one of her rubber sheets on the floor and put on a simple black dress – on other occasions it formed part of a maid's uniform – and a scarf he had given her which was hemmed with little gilt coins.

He brought the chicken with him in a covered cage. He sat in a chair and watched her. She had to hold the squawking, fluttering bird for several minutes, while he prepared himself for orgasm. Then, at a nod from him, she would break the chicken's neck with a broom-handle in the way his dead half-sister used to when he was a poor peasant boy. As he came, he would call out, 'Fatima, Fatima!'

Sometimes he left at once. On other evenings he liked to talk: about his beautiful house in Ealing and his – much younger – English wife and their two children. 'Both very fair, like her,' he would say proudly; he himself was almost as dark as Dink.

On his first visit he had taken the dead chicken away with him. On his second, she asked him what he did with it: 'Do you take it home to your wife?'

He had laughed. 'My wife couldn't clean a chicken to save her life. She buys them oven-ready from the supermarket.' There was a mixture of pride and contempt in his voice. 'No, I dump it in some garbage bin.'

'Can I have it?'

'Sure. You can clean a chicken?'

'Oh yes. I was well brought-up. I can do all sorts of things.'

Tonight, before he left, he spoke of some property deal in which he had outwitted an Englishman. She pretended to listen. After he had paid her and gone, she put the chicken in the fridge. She was smiling. The Turk paid well, came twice a month – phoning first – and was no trouble at all.

Lucy was unused to sharing a bed. 'Hot!' she murmured, waking in the middle of the night. Then she became conscious of Rupert leaning over her, looking down at her and fingering a strand of her hair.

She said, 'Mmm,' and then, 'Oh!' and then, 'I never expected it to be like *that*.'

'Darling one,' he said. 'Like what?'

'Well, you know, in the new movies, there's sort of a bit of rolling about and then press-ups.'

'Lucy!' He laughed. Then he said, 'Very amateur.'

This word made her frown but only for a second. Then she smiled.

He had spent so much time, taken so much care, paid so much attention to the crooks of her arms, the soles of her feet, the backs of her knees, before he even touched her breasts. And all the time there were the kisses. He dissolved her in a series of acute pleasures before there was pain, a pause and then something different: exquisite, unfamiliar pleasure – the pain forgotten – before they slept.

'You're mine,' he said now.

'Yes, and you're mine, too.'

He said, 'Darling, I have to go soon. I have to catch my plane in the morning, and there are things I have to do. But I can hardly bear to leave you. I don't know how I'll get through the next week.'

'Nor me.' But, still deep in a luxurious bliss, she seemed scarcely to take in the fact of his departure. Then she said, 'How *can* it be a sin?'

'A sin? Darling, we'll be married soon. We're pledged.'

'I meant to wait,' she said.

'Are you sorry?'

'I don't know.'

'Oh, darling Lucy . . .'

'No, no I'm not sorry. Not now.'

Four

During the hours she spent at the office of 'Feed the Children', just off Oxford Street, Lucy was usually fully concentrated. Even Rupert had learnt to telephone her there only when it was necessary, and then to be brief, confining himself to practical arrangements. She gave herself to work as she did to everything that mattered to her: as she had given herself to Rupert last night. 'Lucy is whole-hearted in all her endeavours,' one of her school reports had said.

This Monday morning, however, her concentration was not as intense as usual. Occasionally she gazed into space with a dreamy look. Once she had to ask her assistant to repeat what she had just said.

It was half way through the morning when, answering the telephone with her usual, 'Lucy Riven speaking,' she was answered by a male voice, saying, 'Lucy, how business-like you sound! Quite intimidating. This is Francis Larch. Remember me?'

Her laugh was friendly. 'Oh, hullo, Francis. Of course I remember you.'

'Do you know if Rupe got off safely? He said he'd telephone me last night. I tried his number, but there was only that infernal

173

machine which I refuse to speak to.'

Lucy said, 'We got back late . . . from Yorkshire.'

'Ah, you had a good weekend?'

'Oh yes. Wonderful,' Lucy said. She added, 'Rupert will have left by now.'

'Yes, I expect so. What I really rang up about was to ask you to lunch.'

'Today?' Lucy said, and then, 'I don't usually have lunch. I just gobble a sandwich in the office.' (This was perhaps the only habit Lucy shared with Chris Deyntree; Chris however would have said 'nibble' rather than 'gobble'.)

'Oh, not *today*.' Francis, punctilious about social arrangements, sounded shocked. 'I thought Wednesday, if that suited you. Do make an exception for me, Lucy. I want to get to know you better. After all Rupert's my oldest friend. I expect you're missing him.'

'Oh *yes*.'

'Then let me try to cheer you up . . . on Wednesday. It would be nice to try, though I probably shan't succeed.'

Lucy said, 'Oh . . . well, that sounds lovely. Just let me look in my diary. Wednesday the ninth. Yes, that would be fine.'

'Splendid! Where do you work?'

'North of Oxford Street. Quite near Baker Street.'

'Can't think of anywhere one can eat *there*. Soho, perhaps?'

Lucy said, 'As a matter of fact there are several quite nice little restaurants just near my office. In James Street – almost opposite Bond Street tube.'

'Ah, near the Wallace Collection?'

'I think I've seen the name . . .'

'One of my favourite galleries. In Manchester Square. Gorgeous French furniture and some beautiful Bonington watercolours. A lot of rather boring armour, but one can avoid that. Perhaps I should take you there instead of giving you lunch.'

'Oh . . . why not?' Lucy's tone was unnaturally bright.

Francis laughed. 'How polite you are! But I shouldn't dream of dragging you round a museum in your lunch hour. Do you know the names of any of those little restaurants?'

'There's quite a nice Italian one, but I can't remember . . . Why don't we meet on the corner of James Street and Oxford Street? Outside the Body Shop.'

'The *Body* Shop! Such a wonderful name. It sounds like a necrophile's paradise I always think.' Then he continued, hastily, 'What time would suit you? Does one o'clock sound all right?'

'Fine,' Lucy said.

Soon after they rang off, a colleague of Lucy's came into the room. 'What's a necrophile?' she asked him.

'Er . . . someone who makes love to corpses.'

'Oh! *Do* people?'

'I believe so – but not from personal experience.' They both laughed.

Usually Lucy's day passed quickly, but today she kept looking at her watch and – most unusually – she left the office at exactly half past five. Oxford Street was hot and noisy; the trains were hot and crowded. In Hampstead she wandered home at a much slower pace than usual, pausing in Holly Walk at the Chalybeate Well, where Rupert had recently declaimed the inscription:

> '*Drink Traveller and with Strength renewed*
> *Let a kind thought be given*
> *To Her who has thy thirst subdued*
> *Then render Thanks to Heaven.*'

Lucy now glanced at the official notice announcing that the water was unfit for drinking. She and Rupert had laughed, and now she smiled.

When she reached home, she went straight upstairs and ran a tepid bath into which she poured some extravagant Chanel Bath Milk Rupert had given her. 'It reminded me of Cleopatra,' he said, 'bathing in asses' milk. Do you think this is asses' milk?'

'I hope not,' Lucy said. She had taken the cap off. 'Mmm,' she said, sniffing. 'It smells marvellous. I'm sure it isn't.'

Now in the scented, slightly clouded water, she raised an arm, a foot, to study. Then she submerged all her loose hair, and shampooed and rinsed it, before washing her body. Afterwards she had a total rinse under the shower, her hair, darker now, dripping all round her. The telephone rang.

'Oh, *damn*!' Bundling her hair in a towel, she ran naked down to the hall. Rupert had said he would ring as soon as possible. Her tone was eager as she said, 'Hullo,' but it was a woman with a crisp voice who answered.

'Is that Mrs Dumble?'

'No, I'm afraid she's away.'

'Oh.' There was a pause. Then the woman said, 'When will she be back?'

'Not till the end of the month.'

'Who's speaking, please?'

'My name's Lucy Riven. Can I take a message?'

'No, that's all right. I'll phone next month.' The caller rang off.

Lucy went upstairs and towelled and combed her hair. She put on shorts and a T-shirt, and went downstairs to eat some biscuits and cheese. There were eggs – she and Rupert had forgotten about food the night before – but she could not be bothered to cook, just as she had not bothered to shop on her way home. She did a little desultory gardening and some watering with a can. (After fine weather the use of hosepipes was prohibited, in the English way.) Then the telephone rang, and she rushed indoors to answer it in the kitchen. 'Hullo?'

'Is that Lucy Riven?' This woman's voice was different: loud, with a blurred sound.

'Yes.'

'I have telephoned to warn you.'

'To *warn* me?'

'Yes. Against Rupert Deyntree. You must give him up. He will bring you nothing but sorrow. Be warned.'

The tone of these utterances was reminiscent of the witches in *Macbeth*, which Lucy had hated at school though Rupert said it was his favourite Shakespeare play. 'My father loved Shakespeare,' she said to Rupert. 'He used to madden my mother by saying he could never have happened without the Reformation.'

'He was absolutely right.'

'There was this line he used to say: "We all owe God a death." '

'Hotspur.'

'Oh. My father thought it was gallant.'

'Yes – gallant and reckless,' Rupert said.

Now Lucy said to the woman on the telephone, 'Who *are* you?'

'That is totally irr-rr-relevant.'

'You're drunk.'

'Drunk? How dare you! I telephoned to help you . . . out of *conshern*. He's killed three wives already.'

Lucy rang off. She went to the door that led from the kitchen to the garden. It was almost dark. She shut the door. She was locking up downstairs when the telephone rang again. This time after picking up the receiver, she said nothing.

'Lucy Riven, is that you? It's very rude to ring off when someone is speaking to you . . . espeshully when they have your . . . besht intereshts . . .' Lucy rang off again. This time she left the receiver off the hook for several minutes, while she finished locking up. She replaced it before going upstairs to dry her hair with the hand-drier.

That evening, at the end of her prayers, she said, 'I didn't mean to sin. Oh please forgive me.'

After supper that evening, Michel said to Barbara, 'I may be a bit late. You know how these women's group legal meetings can extend themselves. There's always so much . . .' She left the sentence unfinished.

Barbara, sprawled on the sofa in an old kaftan, torn under one arm, looked up from her book and the cat she was stroking: 'That's all right, love. Bye.'

'Bye,' Michel said. As she ran down the stairs, she whistled *Finch' han dal vino* from *Don Giovanni*.

'You're very lively today, Michel,' someone in her office had said that morning. 'Anyone would think it was Spring instead of this stifling weather.' It was true that Michel was filled with a restless euphoria. On and off, now, as she drove, she continued to whistle.

Reaching her destination, she zoomed into the large parking space next to it, got out and locked the car. Then she sprang up the front steps. After a glance at the labels with tenants' names on them, she rang the top bell. A moment later, a muffled voice asked, 'Who's there?'

'It's Michel.'

'Oh, come in.' A buzzer was pressed; when Michel pushed the door, it opened, and she was confronted by a short, bald man who gasped and gave her a glance of what looked like terror, before he dodged round her and hurried down the steps. Michel raised her eyebrows. The door clicked shut behind her. She crossed the hall and ran up the stairs. All her movements this evening were as quick as if she were pursuing, or pursued.

On the top floor, Trish was waiting at the door of her flat. On earlier occasions when they had met – at the courts or at a consultation in an office – Trish had always conveyed a hint of flowers: in a scarf or blouse, in a whiff of *eau de toilette*. Tonight she seemed all floral: her dress, her sweet scent, even the headband round her soft, wavy hair and the pastel tints of her make-up.

'Hullo there!' It was with a hint of boyish swagger that Michel followed her into the flat, which she had not visited before, and over which Laura Ashley – goddess of flowers – hovered: hers were the green and blue wallpaper, the loose covers and cushions. A trailing plant in a macramé basket hung at the window and little bowls of *pot-pourri* were dotted here and there. 'Hope it was all right for me to park in that space outside?' Michel said.

'Oh, yes. That's all it's good for. So depressing. I rent this flat. I'm looking for a place to buy, but with property values the way they are . . .'

'And the flat's so pretty.'

'Do sit down.' Trish gestured to the sofa, and Michel sat down, leaning back and stretching out her long legs in their blue jeans and cowboy boots. She ran a hand over her well-cut hair. Trish said, 'What would you like to drink?'

'It's so hot,' Michel said. 'Do you have a beer?'

'Yes. I don't like it myself, but I keep it for friends.'

Trish went out, and Michel looked round the very clean, tidy room. There were two Redouté rose prints on the flowered walls, and several photographs stood on a bookcase: all of women, alone or in groups. Next to the *pot-pourri* on the coffee table was an anthology called *A Book of Beauty*; sighting it, Michel made a slight grimace. All that this living-room had in common with Michel and Barbara's was cats: here a shelf of china ones, there large, furry and often moulting. A cushion shaped like a cat lay on one of Trish's flowery armchairs, and a large ceramic one served as a door stop.

'You're fond of cats, I see,' Michel said as Trish came back with the drinks.

'Oh yes. Don't you love my pussy cats?'

'I've got three at home.'

'Three *real* ones? I always feel it's so difficult in London . . .'

'Mmm.' Michel took a long drink of lager and Trish a sip of her white wine and soda. 'Peaceful here,' Michel said.

'Yes it *is* quiet. Of course the neighbourhood isn't exactly *desirable*.'

If Belinda had said this – as she well might have – Michel's response would have been a caustic remark or at least a sardonic look. Now her face expressed nothing as she said, 'Well, Willesden, where I live, isn't exactly glamorous.'

'Willesden? I'd have expected you to live in Islington . . . or Camden perhaps.'

'No. I live with a friend. We take care of her mother who lives in the flat downstairs.'

'Oh I see. How . . . nice.'

'Yes. Barbara and I have been together for twelve years.' Michel was studying Trish keenly.

'What a long time!' A sparkle now enlivened Trish's face. Perhaps she was one of those people who are stimulated by competition and like to damage an existing relationship: often reasons for young girls' affairs with boring married men.

'You've never been married?' Michel asked.

'Oh no.' Trish's reaction to this question was prudish.

'Barbara – my partner – was married, a long time ago. In fact she has a grown-up daughter.'

'She's much older than you, then?'

'Just a few years.'

Flute notes rose in the pause that followed this. Trish said, 'A flautist lives downstairs. He's a professional. Mostly he practises while I'm at work. It's amazing that the woman on the ground floor doesn't make scenes about it. She's a terrible creature.'

Michel laughed. 'I saw her window-blind. And an odd name by the door. November. Is that hers?'

'Yes. It's Cape Coloured, apparently. So she told John Tessier – that's the flautist. She and I don't speak. She's been outrageously rude to me. Outrageously!' Trish paused. Then she said, 'I often wonder if she's some kind of prostitute. You've no idea how appalling she looks sometimes. Wigs and leather mini-skirts and layers of make-up. Though at other times she looks quite ordinary. Anyway, a lot of *men* come to see her.'

Michel laughed.

'No, I mean really a lot. Very different types, and at the most extraordinary times. They often have a furtive sort of look, glancing from side to side, you know. And none of them park near the house, though I'm sure some of them must have cars.'

'Well, I must say, a man I passed going out as I came in just now looked frightened.'

'Was he tall and fair?'

'No. Short and fat.' Michel laughed again.

'I was watering my ivy a bit earlier this evening' – Trish gestured to the macramé basket – 'when I saw a tall fair man arrive. I've seen him before. I wonder if they were there together.'

'*Orgies*, do you suppose?'

'You keep laughing – but honestly she's quite creepy. I don't know about orgies. I don't hear a lot of noise. Though of course there's a floor between her and me, thank goodness. Another drink?' Trish got up from her chair and came over to the sofa.

'No, I don't think so,' Michel said, but Trish didn't move, and after a moment, Michel raised a hand and touched her arm. Immediately Trish sank down on the sofa. They kissed. Then Trish nestled up with a little sigh, resting her head on

Michel's shoulder. After a moment or two, she raised her face to look up into Michel's.

'Is anything the matter?' Trish asked. 'You're frowning.'

'No.' Then, after a moment, Michel said, 'You're a lovely woman.'

'No I'm not. I'm just a silly little girl.' As Trish raised her face for another kiss, she closed her eyes, and did not see Michel flinch. But then Michel put her hands on Trish's shoulders, and moved her back. 'You're a lovely . . . girl, but Trish, dear, this just won't do. I realize that . . . well . . . I have to be faithful to Barbara.' The shock on Trish's face was changing to anger; Michel added, 'You're so sweet, so pretty, so tempting – oh, please understand.'

It was the word 'tempting' that seemed to soften Trish. After a moment she said, 'Why did you come here, then?'

'Oh, I fully intended . . . you were so tempting. But . . .'

Trish stood up with a brave smile. She said, 'But we can still be friends.'

Michel's glance around the room was desperate but, rising, she said, 'Of course. Though I suppose we oughtn't to meet too often. Certainly not alone.' Suddenly Michel was at ease again; the racy look that accompanied her last phrase, showed it.

Trish was no longer upset. She said, 'I might have to consult you professionally if that woman downstairs gets any worse. A lawyer's letter might cool her down.'

'On the other hand, it might heat her up. I must go now. Out of temptation's way.' Incurably flirtatious, Michel ran her forefinger from the base of Trish's throat to the tip of her chin; Barbara often did this to her cats. 'We're sure to bump into each other again,' she said, at the door.

Trish followed her. 'I'll see you out,' she said.

'Oh, please don't bother.' But Trish came down to the first landing. Behind his door, John Tessier played a phrase, then repeated it as, clearly visible from this landing, the door of the ground-floor flat opened and a man came out. He closed the door; as he turned Michel glimpsed his whole face and then had a slightly longer view of his profile. She craned forward as he headed towards the front door.

As he went out, Trish said, 'That was the fair-haired man,' and then, 'Why, what's the matter?' For Michel, frowning, was standing dead still.

She said, 'I thought he was someone I knew.'

'*Really*?'

'But only for a moment. I was wrong.' Michel ran down the last flight of steps, blew a kiss: 'Bye.'

'Bye.'. Trish looked despondent as Michel hurried to the front door.

On the doorstep, Michel glanced up and down the road but could see no one. She glanced again at the 'D. November' nameplate, and then, on her way to her car, at the festoon blind filling the bay window.

'Whew!' Dink was hot. She sat on the disordered bed. It was pulled away from the wall to leave room for a man to hang by his hands from two heavy stanchions normally concealed by kittens and roses.

Dink's black leather briefs lay on the floor, but she still wore her black leather waistcoat and leather-look bra, her tiny black leather mini-skirt and high boots over black stockings fastened – midway between skirt and boots – by black suspenders attached to a small belt.

Dink lolled; she did not look sullen; she looked dreamy. Slowly she took off her sleek black wig and her leather things and then still without haste, rehung the kitten picture and pushed the bed back against the wall. She picked up a whip that lay on the floor and a pair of handcuffs, discarded on the dressing-table, and put them and the clothes and wig away in the cupboard; she closed its mirrored door on them and on the chair and on the – now inactive – camcorder on the table.

Dink was sweaty, but she did not shower. The sheets on the bed were stained and tousled but she did not change or smooth them. She sank back into the bed, into its smell of sex. She smiled, as a woman does remembering a lover.

All the way home, Michel looked preoccupied, though she drove in her usual macho style, with as many gear changes as possible.

When she came into the living-room, Barbara said, 'You're early.'

'Yes.' Head up, she met Barbara's eyes full on. She said, 'We cancelled the meeting. Hardly anyone turned up. It's really no use arranging anything in August. So many people are away. Like some coffee?'

'Mmm. And there are a few brownies left. Bring the tin.'

'Right.' Michel smiled but, as she left the room, she did not move as lightly as she had earlier and she did not whistle the aria from *Don Giovanni*.

At half past ten that evening Francis and his mother came home from a concert. Although Mrs Larch did not listen to music, she enjoyed accompanying her son to events. As they entered the house, the telephone was ringing; Francis hurried into his study to answer it. 'Hullo,' he said, slightly breathless. Francis had a tendency to asthma.

'Francis, it's me.'

'Oh Rupe, I thought you'd gone on your travels. Lucy said you'd left early this morning.'

'Lucy?'

'Yes, I rang her up today.'

'But why?'

'To ask her to lunch on Wednesday.'

184

'Oh?'

'Don't sound so amazed. I want to get to know her better. And I thought I might cheer her up a bit in your absence. Anyway, it's all arranged.'

'Mmm.'

'Sound more gruntled.'

Rupert laughed. Then he said, 'Well, for heaven's sake, don't tell her I rang you this evening. She thinks I did leave this morning. But . . . it was postponed – and as I had a lot to do, I didn't tell her.'

'Oh, I see. Well Rupe – how was Rivendale? You must tell *all*, but just hold on a minute.' He put the receiver down, and went back into the hall. 'It's Rupe, mother. I'll just have a little chat with him. I won't be long.' Smiling and nodding she headed for the drawing-room. Back in the study, Francis sat down at his desk and picked up the receiver: 'I'm agog,' he said.

'Rivendale!' Rupert exclaimed. 'I really can't call it "Rivers" as they do. It sounds much too friendly. It's icy – even in August. It's big, but not grand. It's ancient and terribly grim: all stone. Darling Lucy says it reminds her of the catacombs, and I agree, but we don't mean the same thing. She thinks it has a wondrous simplicity and I think it's like a gloomy old tomb. With an actual holy relic: the shirt of the Blessed Hugh, stained with the blood of Blessed Edmund Campion . . . though it could be brown ink. Oh dear! – there's an engraving of the really gorgeous classical building put up by some Riven who married an heiress in the eighteenth century. But he was a freethinker and my future mother-in-law implies that when his new building burnt down it was a judgement on him. Perhaps it was a judgement on *me*! You know, Lucy half guessed that I preferred it when I enthused over the engraving, but I denied it hotly. She would have been so upset. She loves the place. Oh, but Francis, far worse than

the place – the people. Teresa, drawling away gimlet-eyed –
needless to say she didn't ask me to call her "Teresa", and I
felt she longed to call me "Mr Deyntree". Then there was a
hideous old Hungarian refugee who's Teresa's slave and
glowered steadily. And I had to meet Nanny, who lives in the
village – she practically crossed herself every time she looked
at me. Oh yes, and there was a terrible Baskerville hound that
bayed incessantly.'

Francis was laughing. 'Really?'

'Well, actually it was a red setter. Anyway, it detested me.
Hung around Lucy, growling whenever I approached her.'

'That must have rather cramped your style. You've never
liked dogs, have you?'

'No, I've always sympathized with Evelyn Waugh – he
detested them. I wonder if they hated him back. Never – even
after Saudi Arabia – have I been more thrilled to be back in
London.'

'Didn't you tell me Lucy thought of living at Rivendale
one day?'

'She once said she had some idea of turning it into a hospice.
But fortunately – from that point of view, anyway – Teresa is
fighting fit. I'm sure she'll live for years. And she and Lucy
could never live together. I don't think they like each other.'

'*Really?*'

'Lucy's so full of *bonté* that she'd never admit it. But Mrs
T treats her very coldly. Mrs T for Torquemada – that's what
Lucy's American friend, Vee, calls her, though Lucy doesn't
really approve. But she laughed when she told me. Well, that's
something the famous Vee and I have in common. I hope we'll
get on well.'

'But not *too* well, Rupe.'

'Really, what an outrageous suggestion! But oh Francis,
those moors. They really quite gave me the creeps. There's
such an awful light up there. Remorseless, somehow.

Inescapable. And yet one can't see where one is – there's this thick heather everywhere. Rather gaudy, though it must be worse when there's no colour at all. A pheasant jumped up under my feet. The shooting'll start next week. It's let. Lucy hates hunting and shooting and all that. Darling Lucy, she's so sweet. Well, Francis, I must ring off. I really do have to leave early tomorrow, and I'm quite exhausted. Give Lucy a good lunch and tell her what a wonderful chap I am. Right?'

'Right.'

'But not a word about my still being in London tonight.'

'Not a word.'

After ringing off, Francis went into the hall and called, 'Mother.' The television in the drawing-room was switched off, and Mrs Larch joined him in the study saying, 'Now you must tell me all about Rivendale.' There was much shared laughter as he did so.

On Wednesday morning at eleven, when Dink, in a cotton dressing-gown, padded barefoot into the hall, the house was quiet. Trish was at work, and no flute music came from John Tessier's flat. Yawning, Dink went to the hall table to see if any post had come for her. There was one letter, with a first-class stamp: 'D. November' and the address were typed. Ripping the envelope open, she went back into her flat, to the bedroom where a cup of coffee waited on the bedside table. She flopped down on the bed, took a single sheet of paper from the envelope, and unfolded it.

It was a photocopy. At the top was an enlargement of the newspaper announcement of Rupert and Lucy's engagement. Lucy's name was circled in red ballpoint, and from it a red arrow pointed down to two enlarged entries from the London telephone directory. One was that of 'Feed the Children'; the other was the Dumbles' address and telephone number in Hampstead, though their name had been omitted.

Dink's lips moved as she read what was on the paper. She read it twice. Now she made a sound somewhere between a howl and a wail. It was not loud; its lowness added to its desolate quality. Then, dropping the sheet of paper on the bed, she started to pace up and down the room. On the fourth of these journeys, her glance settled on the china ornament of bride and groom. Darting to the dressing-table she grabbed it, and hurled it at the wardrobe mirror; the mirror did not crack, but the figure shattered into fragments. After the crash, Dink stood quite still for several moments. Then she flung herself onto the bed, seized a pillow and buried her face in it. Her shoulders shook violently and she made incoherent sounds. When at last she rolled over and lay supine for a moment, as if exhausted, her face was contorted with rage and grief, tears still rushed from her eyes, but gradually her sobs subsided. She pulled at a handful of sheet and wiped her face with it.

Then she picked up the piece of paper and re-read it.

Francis, with his thin grey hair, rather plump figure and lined face, looked out of place outside the Body Shop. It was hard to believe that he and Rupert were the same age. At the Italian restaurant, he said, 'Inside, don't you think? I'm sure it's cooler. Anyway I always think it's ridiculous eating out of doors in England.'

Lucy nodded and smiled, but she gave a single wistful backward glance at the cheerful little tables under the pavement awning as they went into the dark restaurant. Lucy was fond of eating out of doors, something seldom possible in Yorkshire; her childhood had not included picnics.

Usually she did not drink at lunch; perhaps shyness was part of the reason why today she joined Francis in a bottle of Frascati; besides, the pale liquid in its moisture-clouded bottle looked tempting. 'You often come to London?' she asked politely.

'Oh, fairly often. I have this tiny *pied à terre* in Bloomsbury, well Holborn, really.' Lucy, perhaps remembering Rupert's remark about the 'bugger-hutch', fiddled with her plait. 'And I'm meant to go to a meeting this evening. Very depressing – especially in this weather. I may play truant and go to the theatre. Do you like the theatre?'

'Fairly,' Lucy said.

'And Rupe's great passion – the opera?'

'I don't really know much about it.' Lucy's tone was hesitant. Then she laughed. 'I've been put off by how fashionable it is.'

Francis laughed too. 'How *much* I agree with you. Nowadays people go just because it's the thing. All these yuppies gazing glassily ahead, proud of how expensive it is but waiting for it to end. I shall never forget when I went to *Parsifal* with Rupe and Chris. She said she simply loved opera, though I felt a bit sceptical, especially as it was Wagner – I'm not too keen on him myself, though Rupert adores him.'

'Yes, he told me. I don't really know Wagner. My father hated him.'

'Ah – anyway, I could feel Chris between us, taut as a bow-string. To stop herself sagging or yawning. Her face was quite stiff. "Marvellous," she said afterwards, and it sounded quite heartfelt, because of course what she found marvellous was that it was over . . . at last. Poor Chris! The leitmotivs, in Wagner are what keep me going.'

Lucy said, 'You must have known them all.' He looked at her blankly. 'All three,' she said. 'Sarah, Barbara, Chris.'

For a moment Francis looked taken aback. Then he said, 'Ah! *Dear dead women, with such hair, too.*'

'*What?*'

'Sorry. I've got this dreadful habit of quoting.'

'Rupert does it too. But what did you mean – "dead women"?'

'Not a thing. It just came into my head. Browning, you know. *Dear dead women, with such hair, too – what's become of all the gold Used to hang and brush their bosoms? I feel chilly and grown old.* Quite inappropriate, even the hair. Sarah's was rather mousy, as far as I remember. Barbara's was all right, I think. Dark. Chris had hers cut very short. I always thought it must have cost a lot, but it didn't really suit her. No, their hair was nothing to write home about. Not like *yours*, Lucy. Now yours really would have bowled Browning over . . . and Dickens too. They both had a thing about hair.'

Lucy said, 'It was just so extraordinary – you talking about dead women. You see I had this telephone call, on Monday night. From a woman. She was drunk, I'm sure. Anyway she was saying how Rupert had killed three wives.'

'But how awful. And what nonsense!'

'Exactly! I rang off, and then she telephoned again, and I left the receiver off the hook for a bit. She didn't ring again. Last night I went to an early film with a friend from my office. I don't know if she tried again.'

'Quite extraordinary.'

'You've no idea who it could have been? Someone from *Rupert's past*?' She stressed the words in a way that made them sound joky. Then she said, 'Actually I wondered if it was one of them – the wives, I mean.'

'Oh, surely not? Sarah and Barbara were over such a long time ago. And I can't imagine Chris drunk and raving.'

'What was Sarah like?'

'Oh, rather ordinary. Not right for Rupe, at all. They were both so young – an undergraduate elopement.'

'And Barbara?'

'I hardly met her – they went rushing off to South Africa. She was certainly very beautiful in those days.'

'I feel you . . . don't like Chris much?'

'Your instinct's absolutely right. I think it was quite amazing

Rupe stayed with her so long. Cold, heartless, ruthless. But I admit I may be biased. She couldn't see the point of me at all, and was *very* offhand with my mother when they met. Almost rude.' Francis's tone was indignant.

'And the children? James and Belinda? It's so awful that they won't see him.'

'Well . . . you know, when a child's brought up entirely by the mother . . . I'm sure they've both been indoctrinated against poor old Rupe.'

'It's such a shame,' Lucy said. 'For them as well as for him. My father was so wonderful. I can't imagine . . . just having a mother.' She sighed. 'Anyway, I don't ask Rupert too much about that. I feel it must be so painful for him.'

Francis finished his wine and refilled his glass after Lucy refused more. He had eaten as much as he wanted of his saltimbocca, and Lucy had polished off a large plate of lasagne. He picked up the menu. 'How about some zabaglione?' he said. 'Or there's something called tiramisu?'

'That's lovely – tiramisu. But I couldn't eat anything else. Just coffee.'

'An espresso?'

'No. Cappuccino, please.'

Francis gave the order. When the waiter had gone, he said. 'Rupert's my oldest and best friend.'

'And you're his, I know.'

'He's a wonderful chap. My mother's very fond of him too. She always calls him "that lovable scamp".'

'Scamp?' Lucy said.

'Oh, it's not a criticism,' Francis said hastily. 'She just means he's led a rather unsettled life. Until now. Anyway, she's longing to meet you. When Rupe gets back, perhaps you could both come down to Oxford one weekend. If that wouldn't be too dull?'

'It would be lovely.'

191

'Splendid. My mother hardly ever comes to London nowadays. She thinks it's awful.'

'So does mine,' said Lucy. 'Even though she sticks to Knightsbridge and stays at the Basil and goes to the Oratory. But she's given up Harrods. She says it's vulgar now. And she's always complaining because they closed the bank. Apparently there was a huge banking hall with leather armchairs, where the scent is now, and you could meet your friends there as well as cashing cheques.'

'I remember it well,' Francis said, and then, 'Rupert gets back next week, doesn't he?'

'Yes. On Tuesday, if everything goes according to plan. Whatever "plan" is.' She laughed. 'He's always so discreet about these business affairs of his. Anyway, business isn't really my thing, although I'm a fund raiser.'

'I'm sure everyone wants to give you their money,' Francis said.

Lucy laughed. 'How I wish that was true.'

'Rupert's very lucky to have you. Very lucky indeed.' Then he said, 'I hope you don't get any more of those horrid telephone calls.'

'I hope not, too. It's a bit nasty getting weird calls when one's all alone in a big house.'

'I thought you stayed with friends.'

'I do, but they're away.'

'Oh dear. If you get any more calls, you should ring the police.'

'Yes, perhaps I should.' She looked at her watch. 'I really ought to rush back to work now,' she said.

'You go ahead. I'll settle things here, and then wander round the corner to the Wallace Collection. You really must go there one day, even if only to see the Boningtons. Now, promise.'

'I'll try,' Lucy said. 'But I never make promises unless I'm absolutely certain I'll keep them.'

He watched her quick walk and swinging plait as she left the restaurant. He sighed, wiping a hand across his forehead.

Soon after she got back to her office that afternoon, Lucy's telephone rang. When she picked up the receiver, there was silence. 'Lucy Riven here,' she said. The silence continued. 'Hullo,' she said, 'Hullo?' There was a click and then the dialling tone. She jiggled the receiver rest.

'Yes?' said Becky, at the switchboard.

'Did you put a call through to me just then?'

'Yes. A woman asked for you.'

'Oh, we must have been cut off. She'll probably ring back.'

The woman did not, but Rupert telephoned to Hampstead that evening. She told him she had seen Francis but did not mention the drunk woman's telephone call. Most of their conversation consisted of words of love and re-statements of how much they missed each other. Lucy was smiling when they said goodbye.

All next day – Thursday – she was cheerful. She worked late that day and did not reach home till past eight. As she came up the path, the telephone was ringing in the hall. Opening the door, she switched on the light. Pushing the door shut behind her, she dashed – almost oblivious of something that seemed to squelch beneath her foot – to the telephone: 'Hullo.'

'Lucy Riven, is that you?' It was the same voice Lucy had heard on Monday, but much more slurred, almost as dragged out as a tape played too slow. 'Did you lishen . . . lishen to wha' I tole you. Rupert Deyntree is dangerous.'

'You must stop telephoning like this,' Lucy said. 'Whoever you are. Or I shall call the police.'

'Poleesh? Po-o-leesh? You talking ashif it's me thash dangrush . . . ish *him*. Carn you unnershan?' The woman began to sob, but then suddenly the voice was cut off.

A male voice said, 'Hullo. Who is that, please?'

'Who are *you*?' Lucy said.

'My name's James Deyntree.'

'Oh! Rupert's son?'

'I'm afraid so. Are you Lucy Riven?'

'Yes, I am.'

'I thought so. My mother told me the other day that she'd telephoned you, and I begged her not to do it again. She said she wouldn't. But I've just got in and heard her. Were you saying something about the police?'

'Yes I was. And I still am.'

'Please don't do it. I'm sure I can persuade her. She's . . . fallen asleep now. But when she wakes, I'll really make the situation clear to her.'

'I hope you'll be able to. I'm sick of weird telephone calls. Your mother's persecuting me.'

'Yes. I'm really sorry. I'll do my very best. It's difficult . . . when she's . . . not herself. I'm sorry.'

'Well, it's not your fault.' After a moment Lucy went on, 'Actually I'm glad to know who it was. It's a relief. It was the mystery that was really getting me down. Quite creepy.' Then she said, 'I was talking about you only yesterday.'

'About *me*?'

'Yes. About Rupert's children. Saying how sad it was he never saw them.'

'And what did *he* say to that, I wonder.'

'*He*? Oh, I wasn't talking to your father. I was talking to a friend of his.'

'Has he got friends? How surprising.'

'Now please don't criticize Rupert. Anyway, I really should ring off now. And do control your mother. Or I shall ring the police.'

'Sorry. I was rude. Forgive me. And I'd really like to explain to you about my mother. Couldn't we meet?'

'Well, Rupert's away at the moment. But when he gets back—'

'Oh, I couldn't meet him. Just you.'

'I'm sure you're quite mistaken about him.'

'Well, tell me how – when we meet. I come up to London sometimes. I have to look something up in the British Library next week. I thought of Wednesday. Do you work?'

'Yes, of course I do.'

'I thought you might be a lady of leisure.'

'Well, I'm not.'

'Where do you work?'

'Doesn't your mother know?'

'I'm sure she doesn't. She rang up your . . . house in the country, in Yorkshire to get this number. Made up some story. Like Philip Marlowe, she said.'

'Like *who*?' But Lucy didn't wait for an answer. She said, 'Oh *that* was her, was it. My mother said someone had rung.'

'I expect that was her. You still haven't told me where you work.'

'I work for "Feed the Children". Just off Oxford Street.'

'Well, that's quite handy for the British Museum. We could have lunch.'

'I don't go out for lunch. Too busy.'

'Well, how about a drink after work. There's a pub just opposite the Museum. As a matter of fact, it's called the Museum Tavern. It's crowded at lunch, but not in the evening.'

'Just for a drink?' Lucy said.

'Yes. How about six o'clock?'

'How shall I recognize you?'

'People say I look very like my father,' he said.

'Oh. And I've got a long plait of hair. And I'm quite tall.'

'It'll be easy,' he said. 'Wednesday then. At six.'

'All right.' But as she rang off, Lucy frowned. She had sat down in the hall chair while they talked. Now something made her look down at her feet, at her low-heeled white shoes, and she saw that the toe of the right one was stained red, and there was a splash of red on her ankle. She examined this foot with a puzzled look, and then her eyes followed the little track of red that led to the front door, There, under the big letter slit, lay something that was squelched and bloody. Slowly she stood up; slowly she approached. It was a small plastic bag, fastened with an elastic band, but she had squashed it underfoot: blood and unidentifiable fragments of soft dark matter – animal innards? – had burst from it. As Lucy looked down, a smell of blood and corruption ascended; with a reflex gesture, she pressed her hands over her mouth and nose. Now she turned, and headed for the telephone, and dialled the first five digits of Vee's number in Los Angeles. But then she put down the receiver and just stood, clutching her plait like a lifeline, until she straightened and let go of it; up went her chin. Now began the hateful business of clearing the mess: scraping it into a large plastic carrier – into which she later also put the rag she used to mop up the blood – and then knotting the carrier and dumping it in the dustbin. Afterwards she cleaned her shoes, and went upstairs to have a bath.

Later, in her nightdress, she went out onto the balcony: here, outside, there was always some sense of nature, even if dilute, diffused in comparison to what she loved at Rivendale. Tonight the air was soft, almost balmy; pale light seemed poured into the small cup of heath among the bushes. But the bushes looked different tonight. Usually, between the clumps they formed, was a gap, but tonight something occupied this space. Absolutely still, it could – almost – have been mistaken for a small tree. Lucy blinked. Then – as earlier she had pressed her hands over mouth and nose – she pressed her fingers against her closed eyes. She leant against the rail to peer forward: now, between the clumps of bushes, was the accustomed empty space. What – if not imagined – had seemed a tree, must instead have been a silent watcher, now merged with the bushes or concealed behind them or . . . quite vanished. Lucy went inside, locking the door to the balcony, then locking herself into her own room. Tonight, she prayed, 'Oh, help me, help me. I'm frightened. Deliver me from evil,' and, in bed, 'Guardian angel, please, please watch over me.' But she kept the light on all night, and slept badly. She was dozing in early daylight when she heard the telephone ringing. She ran downstairs. It was Rupert.

'Darling. Expect me when you see me on Tuesday. I'll come to Hampstead.'

'Oh . . .'

'Darling, are you all right? You sound a little odd.'

'Oh no – I was asleep . . .'

'Oh, I'm sorry.'

'No, no.'

'And you had to career down all those stairs. Why won't you let me give you a mobile phone? You're such a puritan.'

'Perhaps I'll reconsider.' She produced a small laugh.

'You will? Amazing!'

'No, I won't.' The laugh was stronger this time.

'Darling Lucy, I adore you.'

'I love you too.'

The conversation with Rupert seemed to brace her. All the same, walking to the tube, she kept glancing behind her, and in the office two people told her she looked tired. She was. Normally an untroubled sleeper, any dislocation of her customary eight hours tended to affect her; last night's circumstances had been peculiarly unsettling. She worked hard all morning, but at noon, she went out: to the Jesuit church in Farm Street, where she rang the bell for a priest to hear her confession.

'I have committed fornication.'

'How many times?'

'Only once. I'm engaged to be married – but I know it's still a mortal sin.'

'Anything else?'

'Not that I can remember now. Oh yes – I've been angry. With my mother.'

'Have you a firm purpose of amendment?'

'Yes. Yes, I have.'

'For your penance say one Our Father and three Hail Marys. Now say an act of contrition while I give you absolution.'

After she had said the prayers and lit a candle for Rupert and dipped her hand in the Holy Water stoup – frowning when she found it empty but still making the sign of the cross – she looked more cheerful. 'Absolution,' she had once said to Vee, 'gives you such a wonderful feeling of freedom.'

Vee had laughed: 'Freedom to sin again.'

'No, no. That's not it at all.' Lucy sounded indignant. 'Freedom from guilt. Freedom to start again and do better. I don't know how you manage without it.'

'I have my therapist.'

They had both laughed; then Lucy said, 'She can't forgive you.'

'But any old priest can?'

'Not the priest – God. No one would ever believe you'd been educated in a convent.'

'I never listened to that stuff,' Vee said, but at once she added, 'Don't look so worried. I'm only teasing. I know it's right for you – it's just not right for me.'

By the end of that afternoon, Lucy was exhausted; she left the office punctually at half past five. Oxford Street was crowded with tourists and with released office workers in the Friday rush. The Underground was packed, and a delay made the crowd on the platform even thicker. When at last the train came, one or two passengers forced their way off, and then Lucy was pressed forward. Suddenly her hair seemed caught and her head tugged back, just as her foot touched the train floor. The crush behind her was too dense for her to free herself or even to turn. Then she was released; her head jerked upright. As she was borne into the train, she managed to raise a hand to the back of her head.

Part Two

VEE

One

West, scrupulously embalmed, lay the green corpse of Beverley Hills; to the east, red anger and black despair fermented. Vee lived between.

From the small stretch of Sunset Boulevard called Sunset Strip – where young people, casual but costly-looking (much had been invested in their bodies, their teeth, hair, skin and clothes), strolled into appropriate restaurants – this street rose; it was very steep. At the top was stony scrub, still frequented by coyotes; deep underground lay the San Andreas fault.

Vee's three-storey building – a tufted palm outside was taller – was painted dusty pink. Her middle-floor apartment was white, flecked with light by restless leaves: trees – home to birds and grey squirrels – separated the building from an azure house next door. In the living-room, with its blond parquet and pale furniture, beautiful Amerindian rugs and artefacts gave colour: stone, sand, straw, rust – like memories of harvests and sacrifices. In her bedroom, over her big, fresh-looking bed, hung a framed Hopper print of a gas station on a lonely road, a quintessence of America, like the music she listened to constantly: jazz, new young singers distilling confused emotions, and the curious country blend of desolation and determination to survive.

This morning Vee had just showered after a visit to the gym. Her firm muscles looked piquant in comparison to her light build and fawn's face. When the telephone rang, she answered, wrapped in a huge towel, in the bedroom. She picked up the receiver, and waited in silence as women who live alone in cities do.

'Vee?'

'Yes. Lucy!' Then, as heavy, gasping sobs came down the line, she said, urgently, 'Lucy, what's wrong?'

'My hair.' There were more sobs. Then Lucy said, 'Sorry. But someone cut it off. Just now, on the Underground.' She started to cry again.

'What? Your wonderful braid?'

'Yes. I can see my hair in the mirror now. It's all ragged. There are pieces hanging down in front and the back's . . . hacked. Oh Vee, Rupert loved my plait so much . . . my hair.'

'I can't believe this. Who did it?'

'I don't know.' As she talked, Lucy's sobs gradually diminished: 'It was as I was getting on the train, coming home from work. Just before the doors closed. I think the person who did it must have stayed on the platform. I felt this great tug. The train was so packed that I couldn't turn. I didn't realize what had happened at first. But then there was hair flopping in my eyes and my head felt so strange. I put up my hand. And then I realized. It was such a shock. I must have looked odd – quite an elderly man offered me his seat, and I took it. But when I got out at Hampstead, I started running . . . ridiculous. But I just ran all the way back to this empty house. And Rupert's away. Somewhere in the Middle East. Vee, I had to ring you.'

'Of course you did. Have you told the police yet?'

'The police. No really, I don't think . . . Vee, such awful things have been happening. Telephone calls, and someone watching me – I'm almost sure – and a bag of blood . . .'

'*What*? But you must go to the police at once.'

'What could *they* do? Blundering around . . .'

'Oh, Lucy. Really! Anyhow, I'm coming – right away. Today. I've been meaning to get it together. But I've been beat. The tour was so exhausting.'

'And what about . . . your musician?'

'That ended yesterday. He was stoned. We had a fight. It's fate, Lucy. I was meant to come. Now I'll just check with the airlines and call you back.'

She did so, ten minutes later, with the flight number. 'Leaves here 20.45. Arrives Heathrow tomorrow. 15.05.'

'Five past three. Saturday afternoon. I'll meet you.'

'You mean you've got wheels at last?'

'A car? No, I'll come on the Underground.'

'Oh no, Lucy. After what's just happened?'

'I mustn't develop a tube phobia. It's like falling off a horse.'

'What *do* you mean?'

'You have to get on again right away. Anyway, I *want* to meet you. Oh, Vee, you're the most wonderful person.'

'What about Rupert?'

'He's wonderful too.' Lucy's tone changed: 'Oh Vee, he's going to be so terribly upset. About my hair.'

'He'll get over it. It'll grow. Anyway, we'll get you an amazing new style. The Dumbles are away – yes?'

'Till the end of the month.'

'So I can stay with you.'

'Of course.'

'What are you going to do tonight? Why don't you go to a hotel?'

For the first time, Lucy laughed. 'A hotel? Vee, don't be ridiculous. I'll be all right here. After all, what can happen to me now?'

'Lucy!'

'Really I'll be all right. And the thought of seeing you tomorrow's so wonderful.'

'And I can stay a bit – I don't have to be back here till the last week in September. When's Rupert back?'

'On Tuesday.'

'Oh, I'm so looking forward to meeting him.' Then she said, 'I wonder who the bastard was that did this to you.'

'You think it was a man?'

'Of course.'

'I don't know. The telephone calls weren't. But I'll tell you all about that when I see you.'

Before they rang off, Vee asked, 'What's the weather like? Snowy? Or just rain pelting down?'

Lucy laughed for the second time. 'No. Hot and sunny.'

'Well, *that* won't last.' Vee's hostility to the English climate was implacable.

As Vee pushed her trolley up the ramp at Heathrow, her eyes passed over Lucy who, usually bareheaded, now wore a scarf over her head. But Lucy saw Vee and her big Haliburton – a tough metal suitcase that shone like silver – at once. She waved, and Vee recognized her and quickened her pace. They met and hugged: one of those warm embraces rare in both their families and discouraged in even the 'modernized' convent.

The train was crowded with tourists and their luggage. But Vee insisted they should get a taxi from King's Cross. 'Change to the Northern line with this suitcase and this carrier of wine? Forget it! And what about at the other end?' In the taxi she asked Lucy to take off her scarf. With the short jagged hair – even the longest strands only reached half way down her neck – Lucy's face looked longer. Vee said, 'I know this really great hairdresser. His name's Douglas. We can call him – I've got his number in my book. He's a great cutter.'

'*Cutter*?'

'Yes, it's got to be cut, shaped. I'll call him first thing on Monday. See if he can fit you in then.'

'But I've got to go to work.'

'Take the day off. Haven't I flown all the way from LA to be with you? Anyway you don't want to go to the office with your hair like that.'

'No.' Lucy replaced the scarf. 'I expect this Douglas is awfully expensive.'

'I'll treat you. As an engagement present. Let's see the ring. Oh, it's pretty. Just right for you. He's got good taste.'

'It belonged to his mother. He says he's been saving it till he met me.'

'That's nice.'

'But I can't let you pay for the hairdresser.'

'Oh yes you can. Lucy, you can be so generous, and yet you're so uptight about spending anything on yourself.'

'It's the way I was brought up.'

'Yeah, I know. Holy poverty . . .'

'You have to admit it's a beautiful idea.'

'No, I don't – and I won't.' They had arrived at the Dumbles'. 'And now I'm going to pay for the taxi. And later I'm going to take you out to eat.'

As she opened the front door and Vee dumped her suitcase and other impedimenta in the hall, Lucy said, 'Oh Vee, this really is so wonderful. I did feel . . . rather tense last night. But I prayed a bit, and it was all right really.'

'You look tired.'

'Well, I didn't sleep a *lot*.'

'You will tonight. I've brought some great wine from the Napa Valley. Best in the world. And then we'll go out and have a huge curry like we always do on my first night.'

'Yes. I'd bought cold stuff. But we can have that tomorrow. Rupert doesn't like curry much.'

'Tragic! All the more reason for us to pig out while he's away.'

'Pig out!' Lucy laughed. Neither she nor Vee had ever tasted a real curry – at the convent, there was a pale brown dish with apple and raisins in it – till together in London they discovered a mutual enthusiasm for its tawny, spicy satisfactions in restaurants with red flock wallpaper.

Drinking the light, delicious white wine before they went out, Vee listened while Lucy told her everything that had happened.

Vee said, 'You don't think that this drunken Sarah could be responsible for it all.'

'No. I really don't. She was trying to warn me . . . poor twisted woman.'

'Of course the hair . . . could have been a stranger. Some hair fetishist. You really should tell the police. He may have been doing the same to other women.'

'Let's wait till Rupert gets back.'

'And the blood?'

'Children perhaps?'

'Round *here*? And it's not Hallowe'en.'

'The person on the heath could have been just a loiterer.'

'You only saw him once.'

'I haven't been going onto the balcony at night the way I used to.'

'I don't wonder. You didn't see a face?'

'No. But I felt . . . it . . . was staring at me.'

Vee said, lightly, 'A Hampstead poet – gazing?'

'Poets can't afford Hampstead nowadays.'

'The ghost of John Keats?'

'Not so friendly.' Suddenly Lucy shivered. 'Don't let's talk about ghosts and creepy things. We had this maid I told you about who used to terrify me with them.'

'I remember.' Vee laughed. 'Winnie with the Long Green Hands.'

'Oh *don't*.' Then she said, 'Oh Vee, aren't I cowardly?'

'I think you're very brave. Staying here alone last night after what happened!'

'I prayed to my Guardian Angel.'

'You still do that?' Without waiting for an answer, Vee asked, 'When did you say the Dumbles would be back?'

'The Bank Holiday weekend. Somewhere round the twenty-seventh.'

'And when Rupert gets back on Tuesday, I won't be cramping your style – staying here?'

'Oh no. Not a bit.'

Vee said, 'Don't tell me you still aren't . . .?' With a reticence she would have shown to no one but Lucy she left the sentence unfinished.

The reticence was justified for Lucy blushed before she said, 'Sleeping with him? I did . . . for the first time. Last Sunday. The sixth of August. It's engraved on my mind, like my birthday. But I'm not going to again. Until we're married.'

Vee said, 'You didn't like it? It often gets better.'

'Oh, I *did* like it. It was wonderful . . . overwhelming. But Vee, it's *wrong*.'

After a moment Vee said, 'You're crazy! You have great sex the very first time' – she looked and sounded astonished at this revelation – 'and then . . . and then, you *pack it in*?'

'Till we're married. Vee, please don't go on about it. I went to confession on Monday, and I got absolution. I couldn't do that on false pretences. Without a firm purpose of amendment.'

After a little pause, Vee said, 'What will Rupert feel about that?'

'I'm sure he'll understand. He's always known I meant to wait.' She hesitated. Then she went on. 'What makes it worse is that I did it for the wrong reasons. We'd come back from Rivers. Everyone had been awful to him.'

'Especially Mrs Torquemada, no doubt.'

209

'Eva was dreadful, too. And Nanny wasn't nice. Even Rufus . . .'

'Old Rufo?' Vee and Rufus had been friends since his puppyhood. 'Rufo didn't like him either? Poor guy!' Vee laughed.

'Rufus was jealous, I think. Anyway, we came back here from the station . . . Rupert and I. He was a bit depressed. I wanted to be . . . close to him. But we were getting too close. I rang Mummy.'

Vee giggled. 'To ask her advice?'

Lucy laughed too. 'No, of course not.' Then she looked serious again. 'For some kind of moral support. Strength. But she was . . .well . . . horrible. No other word, really. And I felt this great rush of defiance. Sort of like a tidal wave.'

'And it carried you away?'

'Well . . . yes.'

'But you're going to stop?'

Lucy smiled. She said, 'Rupert will understand. He's going to become a Catholic. And he's so sweet. You don't know him.'

'Roll on Tuesday.'

'Yes . . . but oh, Vee, he's got – he had – such a thing about my hair.'

'He loves you. He'll get over that.'

'Yes. Oh I'm sure you're right but I can't help brooding on it. And Vee – I know it's vain – but I liked it too. My hair.'

'Dear Lucy.' Vee, sitting next to her on the sofa, squeezed her hand. 'We all did.'

'Except Mummy. She'll probably be pleased. She always said it was "dowdy" and "arty".'

'Oh, how I hate that woman.'

'Oh no, Vee. Not hate her. Though you don't have to like her.' Lucy smiled, but then said, 'I'm being horrible . . . Let's change the subject. There's something else that's worrying

me. Meeting this James on Wednesday. He doesn't like Rupert.
He doesn't know him, you see. His mother's always kept him
away. And I don't know how Rupert will feel about our
meeting. Anyway I don't really want to tell Rupert about the
calls from Sarah. He'd be so angry. Oh, I'll tell him about all
the other things. But I think that would be just stirring up
trouble. And I'm not prepared to listen to this James running
Rupert down – I'm sure he'll try to. I'd cancel the meeting,
but I don't know how to get hold of him. I don't know where
he and his mother live.'

'He lives with his mother? How old is this guy?'

'Oh . . . about our age.'

'Wow, how weird. Rupert's son . . . our age.'

'You sound like my mother.'

'Sorry.' They both laughed. Then Vee said, 'I could go
instead – to meet him.'

'And pretend to be me?'

'Don't be ridiculous. No, I'll make some excuse . . . tell
him you didn't know how to let him know. You won't have to
say anything about it to Rupert. Or tell lies. I know how you
hate doing that.'

'Yes, I do . . . Would you really? And find out if his mother's
connected with these other things. I don't think so but I gather
she's really brainwashed him about Rupert. Francis implied
that, too.'

'Francis?'

'Oh, didn't I tell you about him? Francis Larch. Rupert's
best friend. Lectures in Latin at Oxford.'

'Does anyone still learn Latin?'

'Seems they do at Oxford. He's very nice. He took me out
to lunch the other day, and was really sweet. Wants me to
meet his mother.'

'Wow! Is he keen to marry you, too?'

'Goodness, no. He's gay.'

'Rupert's not homophobe?'

'No, not a bit.' Lucy laughed. 'Why should he be?'

'So many older guys are. Sorry, I didn't mean to sound like Mrs T again.'

'You never could.' Indeed, trust and affection were powerful between them, seemed impregnable: in their looks, their words, their ease with each other.

After the wine, the huge curry, and with Vee in the next room, Lucy slept well. So did Vee, still dozing when Lucy returned from Mass next morning.

Lucy was a church-hopper, seeking the particular atmosphere she found most congenial as far away as Notting Hill and the Servite church in the Fulham Road where Filipino nurses dropped in after the night shift. The Brompton Oratory was the one church she avoided. Today she went to the tiny Hampstead church which only opened on Sunday.

They spent most of the day in the garden, talking: not, today, about Lucy's horrible experiences but of their lives in general which, in Lucy's case, involved many references to Rupert: his charm, his eyes, his intelligence, his humour and imagination – she told Vee about Colonel Al Dente and the others, and Vee laughed – and his quotations.

'You really love this guy,' Vee said at one point, a little wistfully.

'Oh yes, Vee. So very much.'

'And he loves you. Oh Lucy, I'm so happy for you.'

First thing on Monday morning, Vee rang Douglas the hairdresser who washed, cut and dried hair in his flat in a street off the Fulham Road. He said he could fit Lucy in at eleven, and she telephoned her office to say she would not be there till the afternoon.

As they got onto a train – after twenty minutes wait – Vee

212

said, 'I'm thinking of hiring a car while I'm here.'

'Oh, Vee, but driving in London's so awful.'

'Couldn't be much worse than this.' Vee said, looking round the grubby coach with its listless occupants.

'Well, at least it's not the rush hour.' Lucy flinched as she said this.

They changed trains, and got out at South Kensington station and walked down the Fulham Road to Elm Park Gardens.

The hairdresser – a young man – looked horrified when Lucy took off her scarf. He said, 'Looks as if someone's been at it with a pair of shears.'

'It was an accident,' Lucy said, just as she had told Vee she was going to. 'Even though it is a lie,' she had added, and then, 'Of course, as far as *I*'m concerned, it was. *I* didn't do it.'

'That's what Father Cullinan at school used to call casuistry,' Vee replied with a laugh. For a moment Lucy looked dejected but then shrugged and laughed too.

Douglas had to cut her hair shorter than she wanted. 'Keep it as long as you can,' she told him.

'But I have to get the ends even,' he said, and when it was dry, it was beautifully shaped but came just to the line of her jaw.

As they walked back to the Fulham Road, Lucy said, 'My face looks bigger and longer.'

'Oh, nonsense.'

'It *does*,' Lucy said passionately.

'Who cares – with those great big grey eyes?'

'They aren't so very big.'

'And that smiley mouth of yours.'

Lucy looked happier. She said, 'Rupert says it's like the archaic smile on Greek statues.' They had reached the Fulham Road now, and she gestured opposite to where Cranley Gardens led up the Gloucester Road. 'His flat's quite near here,' she said. 'Up past Gloucester Road station.'

'Oh, shall we go there now?' Vee said. 'I'd like to see it.'

'Goodness no. It's horrible. Well, not horrible exactly. But it's a basement, and I hate all basements. He rents it furnished. There's nothing to see. Oh, books and videos and stuff. But nothing really interesting. Except his Blake picture, I suppose. "The Good and Evil Angels". Anyway, I haven't got a key.'

'You haven't?'

'No, why should I? As I say, I don't like the flat. And he keeps a spare key with an old lady on the ground floor. Though that's not ideal. Once we locked ourselves out and he had to get the spare from her. She kept him talking for ages. A bit dotty, I think, and in a wheelchair. Poor thing, she must be lonely.' Lucy looked at her watch. 'Just after twelve. Let's have a sandwich and some coffee, and then I should go to work.' She took her headscarf out of her bag and started to put it on.

Vee said, 'Don't wear that. Your hair looks really good.'

Lucy put the scarf away, but she said, with a little sigh, 'Oh, I feel as if I'd got a missing limb.'

Back in Hampstead that evening she said, 'Everyone in the office was really nice about my hair, but I could see they didn't like it.'

'You didn't tell them what happened?'

'No. I just said I'd been to the hairdresser for a change. Well, *that* was true. But I think they thought I was mad.'

'You'd rather they thought you were crazy than felt sorry for you?'

'Well . . . yes.'

'You're no Riven!' Vee laughed.

'What on earth do you mean?'

'Oh I don't know . . . martyrs . . . victims.'

'Oh Vee, sometimes you say such . . . extraordinary things. Martyrs aren't victims. People don't pity them. They revere

214

them. Though, in a way, you've got a point. Losing my hair's really such a small thing. I ought to be braver about it . . . I ought to offer it up.'

Vee said nothing. There was a moment's empty silence before Lucy said, 'Let's have a glass of your lovely wine.'

Next day Lucy came back punctually from work. Uncharacteristically she had bought food from Marks and Spencer. As she explained to Vee, she was not quite sure what time Rupert would arrive and felt too tense to cook. Vee, who constantly bought take-aways, said, 'You don't have to make excuses. You're such a puritan.'

Lucy laughed. 'So gloomy and joyless? Do you mean that?'

'No, I don't.' Vee laughed too. 'Anyway you certainly don't look like one.'

Lucy was wearing more make-up than usual and more *Fleurs d'Orlane*. She had put on a blue dress that Rupert liked, and was drinking a glass of wine. She and Vee were sitting at the kitchen table. There was Mozart on the radio. From time to time Lucy raised a hand to tug at her hair as if this would make it longer, but now she shook her head vigorously, as if to clear it, and said, 'Oh, everything will be all right, I know. Oh, Vee, I'm so thrilled you're here, and that you and Rupert are going to meet. The two people I love most in the world – yes, that's really true.' She stood up and came round the table. Vee stood too. Impulsively they hugged.

The music had drowned the opening of the front door, the footsteps in the passage. 'Caught *in flagrante*!' Rupert exclaimed in the doorway. He laughed. Vee, who had her back to the door, turned. Lucy dashed blindly towards him. It was Vee who saw his look change. As Lucy almost flung herself against him, he exclaimed, 'Oh Lucy, what have you done to yourself?' Rage and horror were in his voice.

Lucy started to cry, her head on his chest, as his eyes –

cyanotic, slaty – locked with Vee's.

Vee stood in the doorway of the Museum Tavern, looking round. It was not crowded. A thin young man, alone at a table under the window, glanced, then gazed, then, with an embarrassed expression, looked away. She approached the table.

He stood up now. He said, 'I'm sorry. You said your hair—'

She broke in: 'I'm not Lucy. But I'm her friend. I'll explain. Can we sit down?'

He smiled. 'Of course. But let me get you a drink.'

She glanced at his mug of bitter. 'I can't stand that flat stuff. Can I have a glass of white wine?'

'Of course.' Then he said, 'You're American?'

'Yes. My name's Vee Westwood.'

'And I'm James Deyntree.'

'Yes.' Sitting down, she watched him as he fetched her drink. When he came back with it, she said, 'You're like your father – but better-looking.'

He said stiffly, 'I can't believe that, I'm afraid. Of course I'm younger.'

When she laughed, he smiled. She said, 'Some people might think he's more handsome, but *I* don't.'

'You know him well?'

'No. I only met him for the first time yesterday. Let me tell you what's been going on. Lucy and I were at school together. We were best friends and still are. We're always in touch though she lives here and I live in LA. Once, when I was in trouble, Lucy came to be with me. And I came here on Saturday to be with her because awful things had been happening, and she was terribly upset.'

He said, 'Not by my mother's telephone calls?'

'No – far worse things than that. Someone dropped a bag of blood through her letter-box, and she felt someone watching her. And then her hair was cut off. She had this plait that she mentioned to you. It was wonderful. When she undid it, this pale blonde hair came right down below her knees. And in the subway on Friday, in one of those awful jammed trains, someone cut it off.' Vee paused. Then she said, 'Could your mother—'

He broke in. 'Oh no. Not in a thousand years. Anyway she was in Suffolk, where we live. I *know* that. Believe me.'

'I do – really. Lucy didn't think it was her. But, you've no idea how special Lucy's hair was. She had it tidied up – nicely shaped – on Monday. It looks fine. But afterwards she said she felt as if she had a missing limb. And it's true in a way – as if a part of her had gone. Anyhow, apparently your father was wild about her hair – he was away when this happened; he only got back yesterday. We were in Hampstead, where she stays – Lucy and I – and Lucy'd just said something so nice to me, and we were hugging. And the radio was playing and we didn't hear him arrive. And he bursts into the kitchen and says, "Caught *in flagrante*!" Oh, I know it was meant to be a joke, but somehow it sounded sort of dirty to me, and obnoxious. And then he saw Lucy's hair, and his whole face changed – he looked so angry, and . . . well, disgusted . . . And he said in this horrible voice, "Lucy, what have you *done* to yourself?" And she ran to him and started crying. And he and I just looked at each other, over her head. And it was war.'

'*War*?' James said.

'Yes. Like . . . a declaration of war. I felt it, and I'm sure he did too.'

'Extraordinary.'

'Yes.' There was a moment's pause. Then Vee said, 'He's got these really weird dark blue eyes. Yours aren't like that – I'm glad to say.'

James laughed. 'My mother wouldn't agree with you. She says they're the only thing she really wishes I'd inherited from him.'

'Lucy thinks they're great, too.' Vee smiled. 'But I like yours better. They're more natural.'

'Natural?' He laughed. 'Why, my mother says his eyes are like deep blue flowers.'

'Well?' Vee said. 'That's not natural. People's eyes aren't meant to be like flowers.' Then she said, 'You know, when I first saw you here, I saw a likeness to him. But now I've quite lost it. I think you look completely different.'

'I'm glad.'

'Mmm. That's one reason Lucy didn't want to meet you today. She said you'd put him down. And she wouldn't have allowed that. She's so loyal.' Vee paused. 'And she's so in love with him.' She paused again, then added, 'And I can't stand him.'

'That makes two of us.'

'But you don't know him, do you?'

'I know he ruined my mother's life. As far as she's concerned – I don't know anything about his other wives – what she said on the telephone was true. In a way he did kill her. She'd never have drunk as she does . . .' He left the sentence unfinished.

'She's an alcoholic?'

His look was uneasy. 'Well . . . yes.'

'Don't be ashamed. It's a disease. I've found out a lot about it. My mother was an alcoholic.'

'Really – she's cured?' His face lightened.

'She's dead.'

'Oh, I'm sorry.'

'But not from drink. She was recovering. After years and years of drinking. James, I could blame my father and his horrible woman for that. But no one makes someone else an alcoholic. In the last resort they do it to themselves. Has your mother had treatment?'

'Not really.'

'Has she tried AA?'

'She wouldn't dream of it.'

'Pity. That's what helped my mother when all the doctors and clinics had failed. Perhaps I could talk to her about it. Since my mother died I've been to a lot of meetings, read a lot of their stuff.'

'I . . . er . . . really don't know . . .'

'Don't go all British on me.'

He laughed. 'Am I doing that? *She*'s pretty British. Go on about your friend Lucy. Has she been to the police?'

'No. I wanted her to. Though she's not at all a snob, she's got this upper-class thing of running her own affairs. And she said she wanted to talk to Rupert about it. Of course we all talked about it last night. Lucy told him about everything but your mother's telephone calls.'

'That was kind. What did he say about telling the police?'

'He seemed to be against it. Said he'd think about it, that he was exhausted. He'd been away on his business trip.'

'Spying, I suppose.'

'*Spying*?'

'My mother always said he was in Intelligence.'

'Oh surely not. He's some kind of investment consultant. Specializing in the Middle East.'

'Perfect cover.'

'Oh, I don't *believe* this. Anyway, last night, he may have been tired but *I* thought he was in an awful mood. About Lucy's hair. Those eyes of his were sort of blue-black – the way the sky sometimes gets before a storm. He hardly ate a thing, though he drank a bit – but he wasn't drunk. And then – terribly early: it was only about nine – he said he was so tired he had to go home. Lucy was upset, I could see, but she told him to go and get a good night's sleep, and as soon as he'd gone, she started asking me if I didn't think he was wonderful. Well, what could I say? I said he was great-looking and that I was looking forward to seeing more of him. Anyhow, this morning, he called her before she went to work and she told me he said he didn't mind a bit about her hair and that he was sorry he'd been "a bit boorish" last night. She was radiant. And he said he wanted to take us both out to dinner tonight at this Italian place they often go to. I'm meeting them there.' She sighed. 'I wish I didn't have to go.'

'So do I,' he said. 'You could have had dinner with me.'

She said, 'I'd rather do that.' Then she said, 'But in a way I want to see more of him. Perhaps I was wrong last night.' After a moment she went on, 'You know, I'd really like to talk with your mother. Not about AA – I don't mean that . . . though if it came up, I could. But about *him*. Lucy doesn't seem to want to find out about his past. Look how she avoided meeting you tonight. But *I*'d like to find out, for her sake.'

He said, 'I don't see why it couldn't be arranged.'

'But I can't tell Lucy. She'd be furious. I shan't even tell her you and I might see each other again.'

'*Might*?' he said. 'You mean *must*.'

She smiled. She flushed: a faint dusky rose.

He said, 'Oh, I'm so glad you're not Lucy Riven.'

Rupert was exuberant at the dinner at the Firenze that followed Vee's meeting with James at the Museum Tavern. His high spirits were almost manic. He was assiduously attentive to both women, entirely eager that they should enjoy themselves. Such spirits, such charm were hard to resist. Vee laughed and chattered, yet when Rupert's glance caught hers, she looked away: this happened several times. Avoiding eye-contact, someone had told her, was a sign of hostility. Just before the evening ended she focused on what she had called his "weird" eyes. Next time she saw James, she would say, 'I made the effort – and then he wasn't there. He was miles away. In some other place. But he kept on laughing and talking and offering us more coffee.'

After dinner, he drove them back to Hampstead. This time it was Lucy who said she was tired, and he said he was still jet-lagged. After he had driven off and they had gone inside, Lucy asked Vee about the meeting with James.

'Oh, it was all right,' Vee said, and then, 'His mother couldn't have had anything to do with the blood, or your hair.'

'I thought not. What was he like?'

Vee shrugged. Then she said, 'He doesn't like Rupert.'

'It's sad,' Lucy said. 'Perhaps one day . . .' She left the sentence unfinished. She said, 'Rupert and I agree we shouldn't go to the police, unless something else happens. He says he has a feeling it won't. And you know, so do I.'

Vee said, 'Mmm.'

'You don't agree?'

Vee shrugged. 'It's not up to me.'

Vee had taken James's telephone number, and called him on Sunday morning, when Lucy and Rupert were at Mass at Farm Street. He answered the telephone. 'Hi,' she said. 'It's Vee.'

'Yes,' he said, and then, 'When are we going to meet again?'

'Soon. Perhaps I could drive down to you?'

He said, 'Let's meet by ourselves once more. In London. How about tomorrow?'

'Tomorrow?'

'Yes, tomorrow.'

'Well, okay.'

They lunched at a pavement café on Hampstead High Street, and then walked on the Heath. 'Lucy's so loyal,' Vee said. She sighed.

'But you're loyal too. Coming here right away as soon as you knew she was in trouble.'

'She did the same for me. But I wasn't thinking of that. I was thinking of the way she's fallen in love with Rupert. Other people have admired her – mostly earnest Catholic guys – but she's never really fallen for anyone till now. And now it's total and she trusts him completely. She's "trusting" just as much as "loyal". She's given him her love, so she's given him all her trust, too. If it had been me, I'd have wanted to find out more about his past – especially those three marriages. But she's just accepted everything he's told her – and I don't think it's much – about your mother and the second and the third – the commie and the yuppie as he calls them. I think she feels it would be disloyal to do anything else. And intrusive. Oh, she's so reserved, and she expects everyone else to be the same.'

'Even you?'

'Perhaps I'm an exception. But she never asks me really personal questions. That would be prying. And perhaps I am prying – trying to find out more about Rupert – but you know I really feel I have to.'

He laughed. 'You're setting up as a private eye. That's why you wanted to see me again . . . so that I'll introduce you to my mother.'

'I really want to meet her. But apart from that – actually I'm really pleased to see you.'

'You are? Me too.' James's face sometimes looked too fine-drawn; lit, it was transformed.

Vee evidently thought so. She said, 'You're so good-looking.' She added, 'As I said before – far better-looking than him. You know those weird eyes of his are almost like something out of science fiction.'

James laughed. 'The man who fell to earth.'

'Or a fallen angel. Lucy believes in angels.' Vee laughed: 'Of course she doesn't believe Rupert's one. But she *almost* adores him. I simply couldn't tell her how I feel about him. I've never believed anything could spoil our friendship . . . but well, that just might.'

'Then, in a way, isn't it a bit reckless of you to do this private-eye stuff?'

'Yes, but I just can't bear the thought of him making her miserable – you say he made your mother miserable. She's so in love. But perhaps it's just a sexual obsession. That's certainly part of it. I'd never have expected Lucy—' She broke off. Then she said, 'It could also be connected with her thing about her father – his being so old would fit in with that. She really doted on her father. I wish she'd talk some of these things through in therapy.'

'*You*'ve been in "therapy"?' James put the word in inverted commas.

'Sure. Don't look so shocked. Typically British. But I needed help after my mother died and my marriage broke up.'

'You've been married?'

'Only for six months. It was a big mistake.'

'Your therapist – was he—'

'She.'

'Was *she* a Freudian or a Jungian or what?'

'I don't know. A friend recommended her. You're laughing. Why should it matter, as long as she helped?'

'Oh quite.'

'Oh quite! You really are too British. Lucy's just the same about therapy. Oh, she doesn't say so, but I can see she thinks it's . . . well, undignified. Is that what you feel?'

'Perhaps just a bit.'

'I thought so.' They both laughed. Then she said, 'Are you dating anyone?'

'Dating!' Then he said, 'There's a woman I've been seeing a bit of.'

'What does *that* mean?' Vee laughed.

'Well,' he said, 'we're really just friends.'

'Just good friends?' She laughed again.

'Actually,' he said, 'I think that's exactly it. Yes, it really is.' There was surprise in his tone. 'I like her. But we don't really click in any other way. She's on holiday in Greece. She wanted me to go too. I said I couldn't leave my mother for so long. That was true. But I think I didn't want to go anyway . . . with her.' He added, 'Though she's a very nice person.'

'What does your mother think of her?'

'She can't bear her.'

'She'll probably hate me, too – if you let us meet.'

He said, 'I'm just afraid that, if I fix something up, she'll be drunk.'

'If she is, she is. You don't have to worry about my reactions. Remember, my mother was an alcoholic, too.' Then she said, 'I wish you could meet your father. I'd really like to have your impressions of him.'

'No thanks.'

She said, 'I'd have thought you'd be . . . well, curious.'

'I hate him so. I blame him. When you suggest it, I feel horror.'

Vee said, 'I'm not keen on *my* father, but it's not as bad as that.'

'I suppose I've built him up into some kind of ogre.'

'Don't you feel you ought to cut him down to size?'

'You're probably right.' With a visible effort, he smiled. 'Perhaps *I* should go into therapy.'

'Perhaps you should.'

'To find out what? Why I detest my father? I *know* why. Because he abandoned us.'

Vee wailed, 'Oh – don't use that word.'

He took her hand. She left it in his. He said, 'We don't know much about each other, do we?'

'There's time,' she said after a moment. Then she looked at her watch. She said, 'It's only half past two. Lucy won't be back for another four hours. Why don't we go to . . . where I'm staying.'

Two

In Vee's room – once Catherine Mary Dumble's – they lay close together: the bed was a narrow one. But in this closeness and the heat, they were both smiling faintly, as if hearing music in their heads. Their lips were slightly parted; their eyes were half closed. They breathed slowly, deeply.

In an earlier time, he would have lit a cigarette, then put it between her lips before lighting another for himself: this ritual can be observed in old black-and-white films. Now, instead, James looked round the room. Facing the bed – above which hung the Madonna of the Rocks – a square patch of wall was darker than the rest, and a picture stood, face to the wall, on the floor below it. 'What's that picture?' James asked. 'And why's its face to the wall?' He laughed. 'Is it obscene?'

'No,' Vee said. 'I put it there.' She sighed. Then she said, 'It's a picture of Veronica's handkerchief.'

'I'm not sure what that is.'

'It's a cloth kept at St Peter's which Saint Veronica is meant to have used to wipe the face of Christ on his way to Calvary, and on which his features have remained imprinted till today.'

'Goodness! Vee – you're not a Catholic, are you?'

'Absolutely not. And the thing's a fake, of course. Like

225

Veronica herself – she probably never existed. That was my name – Veronica – till I changed it to Vee.'

'Actually changed it?'

'Yes. Legally. As soon as I could. In California.'

'I don't think it's such a bad name.'

'I hate it. My father's horrible girlfriend chose it for me. Maureen. She had a picture of Veronica's handkerchief in her bedroom – just like the one here. That's why I put its face to the wall. I couldn't bear to look at it.'

James kissed her neck. He said, 'It sounds as if you didn't like her much.'

'I can't joke about it. I hated her. I'm sure I would still, if I ever saw her. She's married to my father now. I never see either of them. But I don't hate him like I hate her.'

'Tell me.'

'Oh, it's a long story.'

'But I want to know. I want to know all about you.'

'You may not like it.' She turned away from him. He kissed her shoulder.

'Please,' he said.

'I have to go back a bit. Family history. You'll be bored out of your mind.'

'I won't.'

'Well . . . my father's family has got a lot of money. The Westwoods. My great-great-grandfather came to New York from England. That's all I know about his origins. I'm sure they were poor – otherwise the family would have dug them up and boasted about them.'

'You don't like the family?'

'No, they're all snobs and obsessed with money. My great-great-grandfather made a fortune and they've gone on the same way – the women marrying money and the men making it. Except my father. He doesn't make money – he spends it. But not enough to be dangerous. He's not the black sheep of the family – he's the grey one. They can put up with him. He drinks a bit but he's not an alcoholic. He's above average at sports but not exceptional. He reads. Not good stuff but not trash. Travel books and so on. People say he's good-looking – he's not *bad*-looking. He's nothing. I used to wonder why he married my mother. I think it was . . . like a trophy. She was a showgirl. Feathers and fishnet. Coming down flights of stairs – can you believe it? I would have thought all that was old-fashioned even then.

'She was Jewish. At school I used to say *I* was Jewish, but really I don't know what I am. Her family never wanted her to go on the stage, and when she said she was going to marry a Gentile, they cut her off. Her father said the prayers for the dead – and from then on, she was dead to them. I didn't know that till she told me – just a few years ago. That's when I stopped saying I was Jewish – I thought it was so horrible. So did she, of course. When her father did that, she converted to Christianity. My father's family are Episcopalian – sort of like the Church of England – and my parents got married in an Episcopal church. Well, the family weren't pleased about the marriage, being snobs and anti-Semitic, but when she converted they made the best of things. I expect they were pleased her family had cut her off – no embarrassing Jewish relations. But they never made her feel really at home with them. Then she got pregnant. I don't think my father was pleased. I've thought about it a lot. I think he just wanted his showgirl as a showpiece, and I don't think she was really his type at all.'

'How do you mean?'

'Sort of blonde and lazy and smiling – I've seen pictures. Maureen was just the opposite. Like steel. Sharp as a needle. Good-looking I suppose. Black hair and dead white skin and greeny eyes. Ugh!' Vee gave a sudden shiver.

James said, 'Is this upsetting you too much?'

'No, no. Actually, it's great to talk. I always hold back a bit with Lucy. She's sort of . . . oh I don't know . . . innocent. It was just the thought of Maureen that suddenly made me shiver. My father started this big affair with her when my mother was pregnant. And it's gone on ever since. Heaven knows what hold she's got over him. He's a weak person. Anyway, do you know it was Maureen who suggested to my father that I should be called Veronica? After her favourite saint. Apparently she had a "special devotion" to Saint Veronica. Don't you think that's nasty – her choosing my name?'

'Really bad taste,' he said.

'There's British understatement at its best. Stiff upper lip, you know.' Turning, she ran a finger along his lips. He kissed it. She said, 'Bad taste! I'd call it sick. Anyhow, my father said to my mother when I was born, "How about Veronica?" She hadn't any objection. So that's what I was christened. And soon after I was born, my father's sister – her name's Lois – told my mother all about my father's affair with Maureen. I think the family hoped my mother would be able to break it up. They'd got used to her, and they didn't take to Maureen at all. I think they thought Irish was as bad as Jewish, and that she was common: "A common little Irish typist." And Catholic, too. Well, my father never liked society girls – you can say that for him.'

James broke the silence by saying, 'Hmm? Go on.'

'Oh well, my mother didn't even try to break it up. She just started to drink – really drink. My father got a separation within eighteen months. Not a divorce. Maureen wouldn't have wanted that.'

'Why not?'

'Why not? Because she was a Catholic. One of those Catholics who confess the same sin to a different priest each week, then gabble the penance, take communion on Sunday, and sin again that night. And I bet she left contraception to my father – she'd have felt more guilty about that than adultery

228

because all Christians forbid adultery but only "the Church" forbids contraception. As for marrying a divorced man – she'd have burned in eternal fire for that. So a separation suited her perfectly. It made sure my father couldn't marry anyone else. And Maureen probably felt my mother would die of drink quite soon. She had access to me – my mother – till I was three, but then she came to visit me one day absolutely paralytic. Do you know, I can remember it, I'm sure. Her big face swaying to and fro and the smell of gin – I still can't stand that smell – and then her falling, falling – right down a flight of stairs. And I screamed – I remember screaming. After that I didn't see her again. For twenty years.'

'Poor Vee.'

'Yeah – poor old Vee.' But then she saw his sympathetic look. She said, 'You really are sweet. But aren't you getting sick of this soap scenario?'

'Don't be like that.'

'Oh, well. We moved to England. Dad and Maureen and me. And some nanny – there was a whole string of them. We had two adjoining apartments – one for Dad and me and the nanny, and the other for Maureen. It was an awful block, right near the Dorchester – grand but sort of poky. I loathe that bit of London.'

'Why did they move to London?'

'To get away from their families, I think. His couldn't stand Maureen. And hers were so religious – two of her brothers were priests – and always telling her she was heading for damnation.

'Sometimes Maureen would be sickly sweet to me. Like when she told me how she'd chosen my name and about Veronica's handkerchief. That's when I said I didn't want to be called Veronica any more, and that everyone had to call me Vee. I was set on it – d'you know even my father called me Vee after a bit. Maureen was the only person who went on

calling me Veronica. Of course she wanted me to turn Catholic
– Dad was on my side about that. But he let me go to these
convents. First a day school in London. Convent of the
Assumption – I used to call it Convent of the Ass. And then
when I was ten, this boarding school. I tried to persuade my
father not to send me, but he was under Maureen's thumb, and
he had this idea that convent girls have good manners.

'Well, in a way, I was glad to get away from them. I hated
Maureen so much I was starting to hate my father, too. He was
so useless. They led this stupid life, playing bridge and going
to the races, and she talked all the time. I don't think he listened
to half of what she said. I'll never understand why he stayed
with her.' Vee gave a violent wriggle.

James stoked her dark, downy hair. He said, 'You liked the
convent?'

'Not *liked*. I was so anti-Catholic because of Maureen, and
I started telling everyone I was Jewish – Maureen was always
making anti-Semitic remarks. And I used to argue in the
Doctrine classes. I was getting angrier and angrier – I think I
would have been expelled. But then Lucy came, when we were
both twelve. And – just like that – we were friends. I'd never
had a friend before, and nor had she. It was like magic. She
calmed me down and I sort of livened her up. She was very
serious even then. I taught her to make jokes . . . and she made
me work a bit. Till she came I was only interested in music.
But after that I started to like Math. I found my mind was
quite sort of . . . quick.'

'So's the way you move. Like a little deer.'

'Oh, don't mention Bambi – please. Like Lucy's dreadful
mother. She used to talk about *Walter* Disney.' Vee giggled.

'And your mother? What about her?'

'Oh James, it gets so dark.' She raised her face. They kissed.
When they lay still again, she rested her head under his chin.

He said, 'Would you rather not talk about it?'

'No. I want to. Well, as soon as I left school I wanted to go back to the States. I was sure I hated England – everything about it except Lucy. My Dad wanted me to take this secretarial course first, and Lucy persuaded me. She was living here, in this house, training as a fund raiser. And I shared an apartment with two other girls – it was okay. I think my father was still thinking of shorthand and manual typewriters, you know. But I took to computers right away – I really enjoyed the course. And then I headed for New York. I was keen to take a bite out of the Big Apple. But I hated it. The crowds and the climate and the tension – I'm tense enough already. And my father's relatives – they were a real pain. I only saw them because I wanted to find out about my mother. My aunt told me my mother had been in and out of clinics, but nothing had worked, and then she'd left New York with some guy. They didn't know where she'd gone. Well, I believed that. And I moved to the coast. I took to LA right away. The climate and the laid-back feeling and the fact that everyone there seemed to have come from somewhere else, like me. First I got a job with a record company and then with a guy who managed rock stars. But I'm a restless person. I didn't like being stuck in an office and I started working on tours, freelance. As an assistant tour manager. Life on the road, really hectic – and then a rest in LA.' She raised her face to look into his. 'And I've always fallen for musicians. Are you a musician by any chance?'

James laughed. 'No. But I like music.'

'What type?'

'Well, Bach's my favourite.'

'Bach? Wow! I like some classical music – Mozart, a bit. But I've always found Bach . . . well, rather heavy.'

'You're thinking of the choral works and the organ music.'

'I am?'

'Yes. Not the keyboard stuff. The Inventions, the French Suites.'

'Right. The guy I married played keyboard – but not the kind you're talking about. Like I told you, it only lasted six months. After we broke up I bought my apartment. I love it. I took the money from my father. Do you think that was bad of me?'

'No – why should I?'

'Well . . . not liking him, or the family. But they certainly didn't miss it. And otherwise I live strictly on what I earn – which is quite a lot. Anyhow, three years ago, the strangest thing happened. This cousin of mine came to see me. I hadn't met her before, and I really liked her. And we started talking. And she told me she knew about my mother – the whole lot of them did, back in New York. But they'd told her not to tell me. And when we got friendly she decided she ought to, that I had a right to know. The family'd been supporting my mother all these years, and paying for clinics for her drinking, time after time – though my cousin said she hadn't been in treatment for nearly a year. And she was living in LA. In the San Fernando Valley. And I looked in the phone book and there she was – I couldn't believe it. Westwood, R – R for Rose . . . Anyhow, I called her, and said I wanted to see her. She sounded so nervous, but she said okay, and I went there – I hate the Valley – and she had this little apartment and a big white cat. She was sort of big and white, too. You could see she'd been good-looking but she was heavy and her face had sort of fallen apart. All that drinking. But she told me she'd been sober for nine months: "on the programme". "What programme?" I said. And she said, "AA". She said that, through AA, she'd finally got the message. Well, that sounded like born-again Christianity to me, so I switched off.'

'Was she pleased to see you?'

'I still can't decide that. She was so full of guilt and fear, and I think now all she could really concentrate on was keeping sober. She kept calling me "Dear". Right away I asked her

why she'd never written to me. And she said she had – for
years and years. And sent me presents on my birthday. Aunt
Lois told her I'd gone to live in Europe with my father, but
that she'd forward the letters and things. Later I found she had
– it was Maureen who hadn't let me see them. Anyway, my
mother admitted that, after a few years, she'd given up. She
said, "You've no idea what it's like to keep writing to someone
who never answers. Like on those desert islands. Putting a
paper in a bottle and dropping it in the sea." Well, that sort of
got through to me, and I tried to talk to her. I told her how I
hated Maureen – I thought that would please her. But she said
she just couldn't afford to harbour resentment. It was too
dangerous. I said, "How do you mean – *dangerous*?" and she
said, "To my sobriety." I thought that was sort of creepy.
Anyway I asked her if she'd come out to dinner with me that
night, and she said she couldn't. She was going to a meeting.
"AA, I suppose," I said in this sarcastic tone, and she said,
"Yes." Well, that really pissed me off. But we made an
arrangement I'd fetch her next day – she didn't drive – and
show her my apartment. And when she saw it she said, "Very
nice, dear." But she didn't sound too keen, and later she sort
of implied she thought it was a bit bare – her own apartment
was crammed with junk. Dolls of all nations and cut-glass and
stuff. And she didn't seem to like my neighbourhood. "All
these people, walking in the streets," she said. And I said,
"Well, it's not *suburbia*." And she said, "You sound just like
your Aunt Lois." I think that was the only bitchy thing she
ever said to me, though I don't even know if she really meant
it to be bitchy.'

Vee gulped. Then she went on. 'I wondered if I'd ever get
to know her better. Then I had this idea we might go away on
a trip together – sort of, to pin her down, so that she couldn't
get away from me. I'd never seen the Grand Canyon. I'd always
wanted to, and I thought we might go there. Just a short trip.

Stopping one night on the way and another on the way back. I thought perhaps we'd really be able to talk. In the car especially. Well, I suggested it to her a week or two later, and the first thing she said was, "But what about my meetings?" and I said, "You don't go to them every day, do you?" And she said, "Almost." And I said, "Surely you could miss just two nights?" I must have sounded so angry. And she said, "Well, what about Fluffy?" Fluffy was the cat, and I said surely a neighbour would feed him for that short time. I challenged her . . . sort of. I said, "Can't you spend three days with your only child?" And she said, "Of course I want to be with you, dear."'

Vee paused for a moment, then went on. 'Anyway, she came. She kept eating mints, all the time. I asked her about her family, and she told me all the business of her father saying *kaddish* – the prayers for the dead – and that she'd never heard a word from them or been in touch since. I didn't even know their name and she said it was Greenblatt – her stage name had been Rose Green. And she said she didn't know where they lived. She couldn't even remember their old address. We stopped in Sidona that night. At a motel. It's a little town with these strange red rock formations all round it, and she said what funny shapes they were. We had dinner in a pasta place. We both ate a lot – I felt that was all right for me but not for her because she was so heavy. She ate some kind of chocolate dessert. I wanted one too, but I didn't have one . . . sort of to show her up. And I started talking again about how awful Maureen had been – and she came out with that stuff again about not harbouring resentment. Well, this great wave of anger came over me, and I said, "That's certainly hard for *me*, after you *abandoned* me." I could see that got to her. She said, "I didn't. They took you away from me." And I said, "They couldn't have if you hadn't been a drunk." She said, "I couldn't help it." I said, "If you'd loved me, you could have. You abandoned me." And she said, "I did love you. I didn't abandon

you. Alcoholism is a disease. You should read the Big Book."
And I said, "You mean the Bible?" And she said, "No. I mean
the AA Big Book." And I said, "Fuck the AA Big Book." And
she looked at me and said, quite calmly, "Your eyes flashed
then. I've never seen anyone's eyes actually flash before." And
then she said, "I need a meeting. I wonder if there's a meeting
here tonight." And I said, "Tonight? You're crazy." And she
said, "I'm not," and she looked at her watch and said, "But it's
after nine. Probably too late." Then she said, "You know, AA
saved my life." And I said, "Oh yes? But what for?" After that
we went back to the motel. She wanted to pay for the meal but
I wouldn't let her.

'We had separate rooms at the motel. I don't think either of
us wanted to share. We were starting early in the morning,
and I went to her room to make sure she was awake. She was
half dressed, in a slip. Her shoulders were so white and soft-
looking. They made me feel sick. We hardly talked at all in
the car. She kept eating mints. In a way I wanted to say I was
sorry for the night before, but I couldn't. I felt it was she who
ought to apologize – for abandoning me. Well, we came to the
Canyon Park quite early. The weather was wonderful. Fresh
and clear. The Park wasn't crowded. It was early April. She
was reading the Guide, and she said, "They have AA meetings
here twice a week. Monday and Friday." And I said, "Well,
today's Saturday."

'We got out of the car at Maricopa Point. There was no one
else there except one couple going back to their car. We went
to the edge. There's no fence and it's not paved. You could
just gaze. I was . . . well, spellbound. Those great grey ridged
rocks, stretching to infinity, and down below the Colorado
River like a little dull-brown snake. Oh those rocks, though!
And I turned to my mother and I said, "Isn't it wonderful?" I
remember smiling. I was quite carried away. And she was
gazing, gazing. I felt we were sharing something at last. And

she turned to me, and she said, "I hate it." And I was so shocked. I said, "I hate *you*." And I just turned away and walked. Only a few steps because I felt this movement behind me. And I turned, and she was gone, and there was this dreadful echo. OH!'

She cried. He murmured endearments till at last she stopped, stretched out a hand, grabbed a handful of tissues from a box on the bedside table. 'I'm sorry,' she said.

'Don't be. I'm glad you talked about it. And to me.' Then he said, 'You mustn't blame yourself.'

'But I do.'

He said, 'She did abandon you.'

'But I should have tried to understand. Even after what happened, I didn't try at first. There was so much fuss. Luckily a young man walking along the trail saw it happen, or they might have thought I pushed her over the edge. In a way I did.'

'That's nonsense.'

'Mmm. Anyway, I called Aunt Lois – back to the family again! – and she arranged things. It wasn't difficult, with my mother's history of alcoholism. The lawyer suggested she might have been drunk, but I wouldn't have that. Mentally disturbed, they said.'

'And then?'

'Then? I went wild. I smoked dope. I did cocaine. I drank a lot. I picked up guys in bars. I even got involved with a thief.'

'A thief?'

'Yeah – a guy who used to burglarize apartments. I went with him a couple of times. He taught me how to pick a lock. I used to laugh while he collected the loot – we both did cocaine. We were reckless. It was incredible we didn't get caught. And then one night, after he'd collected the stuff, he pissed on the carpet and I looked round the room and there were these people's photographs of children and things. I didn't say anything. He was a dangerous sort of guy. But when I was back in my apartment alone I just couldn't stop crying. And when I did, I called Lucy. And she came and calmed me down. Luckily I was between tours, like now. She stayed three weeks and answered the phone, and when the burglar guy called she said I'd left town. He never called again. I haven't seen him since. And after Lucy left I started going to AA meetings – the open ones. Some of them are closed – for members only. And I read the Big Book. Well, it wasn't for me. But I could see what my mother found there. A serenity. Some of those recovered alcoholics are really amazing.'

'Recovered? They keep on going to meetings?'

'Oh yes. Some of them who've been sober for twenty years say they feel they'd get drunk if they didn't. It seems to be . . . kind of a support that never fails. I'm so glad she had that – my mother. If only . . .'

'Vee, don't. Sweet Vee.'

'Oh *you*'re so sweet,' she said after they had made love again. 'So sweet and gentle.' Then she looked at her watch. 'Help! Lucy could be back in half an hour.'

Dressing, he said, 'What happened to your father?'

'He married Maureen, of course. They live in Ireland now. And I don't visit them.'

'Families!' he said. 'Fathers, mothers – what hell they are!' He laughed.

'Yes. You and I have got a lot in common,' she said. 'We've both been abandoned. We both had alcoholic mothers.'

'And I don't see my mother's relations – they're awful. Rich. Rather like yours – except they're English.'

'Well, at least we're not weighed down by family, like Lucy is. By history. All those Rivens, stretching back.'

'History can weigh us down even if we don't know what it is.'

'In our genes you mean?'

'Something like that.' Then he said, 'I'll arrange for you to meet my mother. Would you mind coming down to Suffolk?'

'Not a bit. I'm hiring a car.'

'How about next weekend?' he said. 'It's the Bank Holiday.'

'That's when the Dumbles get back. I've got to find a place to stay before then. But that sounds fine. We'll talk on the phone.'

Vee had already told Lucy that she wanted to be out of the house by the Bank Holiday. 'I'm sure Mag would love you to stay on,' Lucy said.

'Yes. I realize how kind she is – and hospitable. Truly I do. But you know how she makes me feel. Just when I think you've pretty well cured me of being anti-Catholic, I spend two minutes with Mag and I want to picket Westminster Cathedral with a placard saying "No Popery".'

'Well, we must avoid *that*.' Lucy smiled, perhaps a little sadly.

Vee said, 'And you won't be alone in the house like you were.'

'Oh, don't worry about that. I'm not frightened any more. Since you came, and now Rupert's back, I've quite got over it. Of course I'm still sad about my hair, but Rupert's been so nice about it. He says he doesn't mind – though I know he does . . . a bit.' She put a hand up to her head: still a frequent gesture. 'He thinks it was some maniac who did it. Really, you know, I think that's the only possible explanation. And I could easily have imagined that figure on the Heath – I was under such strain, after the blood. The blood's the only thing I can't explain at all. But I've stopped bothering about it. I have this feeling that whatever was . . . against me . . . is – gone.' She laughed. 'My Guardian Angel has got rid of it.'

Today Lucy reached home about an hour after James left. Vee was sitting at the kitchen table. 'You're looking thoughtful,' Lucy said. 'Or do I mean dreamy? That's more like it. Anyway I've got news for you. There's this woman called Mary Collins – a protégée of Mag's. She works for a Catholic charity. I bumped into her today and we were talking about the trip to India she's making from the end of this week till the last week in September – four weeks. She was saying how much it cost, and I remembered she has this nice little flat in Islington and I asked her if she'd like to let it while she's away. To a friend of mine. I told her she wouldn't have to put away all her things – just make some space for your clothes. Well, she was thrilled by the idea. What do you think? There's a lovely view – and the tube's just down the road.'

'It sounds great. You don't have to sell it to me – and though I'll have a car, the subway is useful sometimes if one's in a hurry.'

'I said we'd ring her tonight – or rather you would, to arrange to see it – if you were interested.'

'I am.' Then Vee said, 'India! All those curries! But so much poverty.'

'Mary's fulfilling a dream . . . going to see Mother Teresa.'

Vee said, 'Perhaps it's her christian name that puts me off Mother Teresa.'

'Oh, Vee!' Lucy smiled, but then she said, 'It's the deathbed conversions that worry me. But Mary thinks she's a saint. Perhaps she is.' Lucy sighed. 'Mary thinks the present Pope is a saint.' She sighed again. Then she said, 'Oh don't let's talk about religion.'

'Suits me,' said Vee. Then she said, 'I met this guy I used to know. I may be seeing him next weekend.'

'Oh. Is he a musician?'

'Yeah.' Vee flinched as she lied to Lucy. But Lucy, who was laughing, did not notice.

The sash windows of the living-room faced the upper branches of big plane trees, their leaves not yet yellowed but dusty and a little tired. The living-room furniture was drab; there was an old television and a brand-new video which Mary Collins said she had won in a raffle and would probably sell when she came back. In the tiny kitchen with its double hotplate and small refrigerator, the cupboard held tins of baked beans and packets of herbal tea and bran. The bathroom had an air-extractor that roared and no window; the towels were small and thin. The bedroom, where a large, vivid crucifix hung over the bed – Vee put it in the wardrobe – overlooked a patchwork of London gardens and little sheds.

Today was Saturday. Vee had just moved in. James was coming up by train to share her first night in the flat; they were driving down to Suffolk next morning, when Lucy and Rupert were going to lunch with the Larches in Oxford. Lucy had asked Vee if she would like to come too, but Vee said she was meeting her musician.

She had bought a bottle of champagne and made smoked salmon sandwiches. 'What a feast!' James said, and then, 'How nice to have a drink without feeling guilty. I hope you won't mind not drinking tomorrow. My mother will offer it, but I always feel it's better not.'

'Fine,' Vee said. There was a slight shyness between them. He said, 'I like your view.'

She said, 'The flat's a bit stark, but I kind of like it. I bet no one's drunk champagne here before.' The cork popped loudly, and soared through the open window.

This was another narrow bed. He said, 'Your skin glows as if you had a fire inside you.'

'Yeah. I hardly ever sweat. I just burn. Better in winter.'

'I think it's okay in summer,' he said.

'You're so nice. And so gentle – I've never known anyone so gentle.'

'Are your lovers usually rough?'

'Not exactly. But I don't usually feel so safe.'

240

'That sounds dull.'

'It isn't . . . not at all.'

'Mmm. Really?'

'Oh . . . really.'

They set off after breakfast – coffee and toast. 'You drive,' he said. 'It'll give you practice.'

'Yes, I need it – on the wrong side of the road.'

'The right side.'

'Now I know you're crazy. It's the left. Having you next to me will give me confidence.'

'I think you've got plenty – enough for both of us.'

'You're not confident?'

'I'm just a bit edgy this morning. Oh, nothing to do with us. There's always this dread . . . that she might be drinking, though I don't think she will. When I left yesterday she was planning today's lunch, agog to meet you.'

'Agog! I love that. And she knows I'm a friend of Lucy's?'

'Yes. And that . . . *I* like you.'

'How does she feel about that?'

'Seemed thrilled.'

Vee laughed. 'You say she hated your last girlfriend?'

'Not quite *hated* – but she wasn't at all keen. Far from it.'

This was not just a weekend but a Bank Holiday: the last one of summer. Everyone who had deserted the city had gone on Friday or on Saturday morning and would not be returning till late on Monday. Now on Sunday, London and the roads out of it were quiet.

They left the motorway for winding lanes, tiny signposts, pinkwashed cottages, small but substantial churches with square towers. Everything charmed Vee, most of all the Deyntrees' village with its green and their big cottage with its overhanging tiled roof, the path leading through clumps of flowers and bushes.

Sarah opened the door as they came up the path. Afterwards both Sarah and Vee separately remarked to James on the instant currents of sympathy that flowed between them. Vee would say that Sarah's ravaged face brought a recollection of her mother and a piercing longing for some different outcome. Sarah would say that she was simply caught out of herself when she exclaimed, 'You're lovely.' Both would say that they almost – quite out of character – embraced: it was in the air; they compromised with a firm, eager handshake.

'A drink?' was Sarah's first question.

'Oh, something soft,' Vee said.

'You don't drink?'

'Hardly ever.'

'Mineral water? Or I have some Coca-Cola.'

'Mineral water, please.'

'The fizzy kind?'

'Yes, please.'

'I like that too. James prefers the still kind.'

Lunch was roast chicken: Sarah belonged to the last generation to consider this a treat. It had long been replaced as the favourite English meal by steak; today it was dished up proudly, with all its venerable trappings: real gravy, bread sauce redolent of cloves and onion, green peas flavoured with a sprig of fresh mint, roast potatoes crisp and brown but soft in the middle. Afterwards came an expensive kind of ice-cream: 'Blueberry cheesecake' chosen because, Sarah said, it sounded 'really American'.

Vee talked about her job – 'fascinating' to Sarah – and then about her friendship with Lucy. She said, 'You know, I think it was wonderful of you to call her, Mrs Deyntree.'

'Sarah – please.' She had flushed. Then she said, 'Really?'

'Yes. Kind . . . and brave, too.'

Sarah, glancing away, said, 'I suppose your friend will have told you I needed . . . Dutch courage to do it.'

242

'Yeah, well, I don't think I'd have had the courage to do it at all. In fact I haven't had the courage to tell Lucy I'm meeting you today – or even that James and I are friends. I'm so worried for her.'

'Because of Rupert?'

'Yes.'

'You've met him?'

'Oh yes.'

'Is he still so handsome and charming?'

'I guess so. Lucy thinks he is. But I don't trust him. I didn't like him from the moment we met.'

'That does surprise me. He was always so amusing. I remember when we first met he invented some wonderful characters he used to tell stories about. There was Colonel Al Dente—'

'And Sir Percy Flage and his wife Camou?'

Sarah gave a startled laugh. 'He's still talking about them?'

'Lucy thinks he invented them for her.'

'Oh!' Then she said, 'You've no idea how good-looking and charming and amusing he was when we met at Oxford. I never imagined he'd be interested in me. He used to go about with this . . . camp follower, as we used to call them – girls who took secretarial courses at Oxford to meet men. There were so many more male than female undergraduates in those days. But this one was stunning. Slanting green eyes and high cheekbones – quite Slavonic-looking, though actually she was English. A vet's daughter, I believe. Rupert was always rather a snob. I was a Huscott-Fenn. That won't mean a thing to you, but my family was known to be well off – it never occurred to me that Rupert might be interested in that.' Sarah laughed: a shrill hard sound. 'I was naïve. At home I was the ugly duckling – I wasn't actually ugly but my sister was much prettier and awfully popular. She was a wonderful rider, too – and I was always afraid of horses. I was the clever one. "Always got her

nose in a book," my father used to say in a disgusted voice.'
Sarah gave the shrill, hard laugh again: the laugh that is so
often a disguise for hurt. 'My parents thought that going to
Oxford was a really *outré* thing for a girl to want to do. But
they didn't care enough to object. And it was *something* for
me to do. They realized I'd never be a successful deb like my
sister. The ugly duckling – and then when I met Rupert, I felt
– oh ha, ha – like a swan. *What* a cliché! Too, too banal! But it
really was romantic when we eloped. It was just after his
schools – I had another year to go. I never took my degree . . .'

It was getting dark when Sarah finished the story she had
told throughout the afternoon.

'My family rather liked Rupert at first. They were really
amazed that I'd "caught" – that was the word my mother used
– someone so attractive, and a gentleman, too. He got this job
in Whitehall. He said he was a civil servant, but I could never
really believe that. I always thought he was some kind of spy
– rather glamorous! I really had quite a lot of money then, that
my grandfather had left me, but we lived very lavishly. He
was always extravagant. I remember when he insisted we buy
this Blake picture, even though the money was getting a bit
low . . .

'He was away a lot. After James was born, even when he
was in London, he usedn't to come home till late at night. I
hadn't any friends really. I'd made one or two at Oxford, but
when I went down before they did, I lost touch with them . . .

'He started telling me all the time how boring I was. And
then – it was just before James's second birthday – he told me
he wanted a divorce. He had met this Barbara.'

'And you agreed?' asked Vee.

'Yes. Well, it would have been so – undignified not to.'

'Did he pay you alimony?'

Sarah laughed. 'Oh no. We'd spent my grandfather's legacy,
but there was a trust as well. It paid for James's education and

I still live on it. It's not a lot, but it's just enough. And I was able to buy this cottage. I would have liked Rupert to contribute something for James. My family wanted me to insist. They really despised me when I wouldn't. But he and Barbara went to South Africa – some job connected with the High Commission – and I . . . well, I was ashamed to harry him and I was terribly depressed. Everything was such an effort . . .

'No, he never wanted to see James at all. It was as if he and I had never existed. I wondered if he'd get in touch after he came back from South Africa – but not a word. Well, by then I was really quite glad he was out of our lives entirely.' She paused. 'Though I don't suppose a day passes when I don't think of him. You know, sometimes I almost miss him – the fun!'

'Fun!' Vee exclaimed.

'Yes, he could be so charming, you know. At the beginning, he really lit up my life. Oh, but later, of course – oh, he wasn't kind. There are things I'd really rather not talk about. And the money side. He took the Blake, of course.'

'Of course?' said Vee.

'Well, it was he who loved it so much. It didn't really appeal to me. I thought it was a bit creepy. No, that was reasonable . . . but it really hurt me when he took back the ring.'

'The ring?'

'Yes, my engagement ring. I still wear the wedding ring, as you see. I don't know why. I think it was because of James. I thought people might think I was an unmarried mother. Don't laugh.'

'I'm not,' Vee said.

'Well, it sounds very old-fashioned, I know. Anyway, somehow I've gone on wearing it. It's just an ordinary gold band. But the engagement ring was so pretty. Not terribly valuable. Victorian. Two sapphire hearts—'

Vee broke in: 'With little flowers made of seed pearls and garnet chips and sprays of tiny diamonds.'

'Why, yes. Do you mean he's given it to *her*?'

'Yes. He said it was his mother's.'

'Yes. He told me that was why he wanted it back.'

Vee said, 'I wonder if he gave it to the other two as well.' She and Sarah burst into laughter. Even James, who had been looking from one to the other like a spectator at tennis, smiled. Suddenly Sarah started tugging at her wedding ring.

'Why do I wear it? It's stupid.' She had to struggle to get it off. When she did, she threw it out of the window. 'There!'

Now James was watching Sarah with an anxious look. Vee saw it and stood up. 'I've got to stop Lucy marrying him,' she said. 'But I don't know how. Anyway I really must go now. I'm not used to driving in England, in the dark.'

'Oh, but you must stay the night,' Sarah said.

'Oh no – you asked me to lunch.'

'Of course you must stay. You can leave early in the morning if you want to. Then you'll avoid the Bank Holiday rush. Please!'

Vee glanced at James. He was smiling now. She said, 'Well, thank you.'

Later, Vee insisted on helping Sarah to make up the single bed in one of the two spare rooms. Sarah said, 'I'm so pleased you're staying. And I'm sure James is too. You . . . like him, don't you?'

'Yes, I really do.'

'You must come again. What about next weekend?'

'I think that would be great.'

'Oh, good. It's so nice that you're trying to help your friend.'

'It's all so difficult. She's such a sensitive person.'

'Well then, she really shouldn't marry Rupert. I always suspected the other two were hard as nails. Especially Barbara. She used to be a well-known model. I've got pictures of her. I used to cut them from newspapers. A bit odd of me, I suppose.'

'Oh, I don't know . . .'

Vee

'Would you like to see them?'

'If it's no trouble.' They had finished the bed and went downstairs. Sarah fetched an envelope from the bottom drawer of a desk in the living-room. She said, 'I often used to take them out and look at them at one time. But I've got over that.'

'Wow,' Vee said. 'She was quite something. Those huge eyes. And those legs. That really is a mini-skirt!'

'Yes, it was the sixties. They were called birds . . . dolly rockers. I wonder what she looks like now. Jewish women often age badly.'

'I'm half Jewish.'

'Oh! Well . . . why not?'

'Why not, indeed!' But Vee laughed. Later – last thing – when she and James strolled round the green, she said, 'Your mother's kind of innocent.'

'Yes, I always have that impression. Whatever she does or says.'

'It's curious,' Vee said, 'this feeling I have about her. It's though, if I really like her, I'll be making up to my mother in some way.'

They were back at the gate. Vee sniffed. 'Such lovely scents,' she said.

'Yes, all carefully planned for you: pinks, nicotiana – that's tobacco plant – verbena, *lilium auratum*, the golden-rayed lily of Japan, honeysuckle . . .

> *"There has fallen a splendid tear*
> *From the passion-flower at the gate.*
> *She is coming, my dove, my dear;*
> *She is coming, my life, my fate;*
> *The red rose cries, 'She is near, she is near';*
> *And the white rose weeps, 'She is late';*
> *The larkspur listens, 'I hear, I hear';*
> *And the lily whispers, 'I wait.' "*

There was silence. Then quickly, lightly, he said, 'No passion-flowers here, I'm afraid.'

'Oh, I don't know,' Vee said. They kissed.

'Shall I . . .' He was a little breathless. He left the sentence unfinished.

'Not tonight,' she said. 'I feel sort of delicate about it.'

'Me too, actually,' he said, and then, 'Soon?'

'Oh yes.' Hand in hand they walked up the path. She said, 'When I get back to London I'm going to track down the other two. The other two Mrs Deyntrees.'

'Really?'

'Yes, I want to know it all. Of course Lucy might never forgive me.'

'If she finds out.'

'But she has to find out. If I find anything he just can't explain away. Of course you and I know how dreadful he is – everything your mother says adds to the picture.'

'*The Picture of Dorian Gray*,' he said.

'That was the guy whose face stayed perfect however vile he was, and only his portrait changed?'

'That's right. Doubles are always frightening. Dorian Gray and his picture. Frankenstein and his monster. Doctor Jekyll and Mr Hyde. Men who are werewolves and beautiful women who are vampires.'

'And charming Rupert Deyntree who's so horrible.' Then she said, 'But there's no way Lucy would believe that now. He's clever – he'd explain away everything I've heard here. And then . . . I feel Lucy wouldn't be my friend any more. I feel as if I'm walking on a tightrope.'

'Then you must walk carefully,' he said.

She was back in London before lunch. There had been a shower the night before. She could sense it in the air, and the leaves of the plane trees looked refreshed. But the sun was hot again; the scene in Highbury Fields was that of an English holiday. People were lying about, half undressed; dogs frisked and defecated; children played and fought. An ice-cream van gave its monotonous chime.

Upstairs, Vee drank a glass of wine and made herself a sandwich from the remains of Saturday's smoked salmon. Then she took the first volume of the telephone directory from the bottom shelf of the bookcase, and looked up Deyntree. There were three: Deyntree, B., Deyntree C., and Deyntree, Rupert. She dialled the number of Deyntree, B.

The telephone was answered, after the first ring, by a woman. 'Hullo?'

'Hullo. Is that Barbara Deyntree?'

'*Barbara* Deyntree? You've made a mistake.' The voice was peevish. 'This is Belinda Deyntree speaking.'

'Oh, I'm so sorry,' Vee said, and then, 'I think it's your mother I'm trying to contact.'

'*She* doesn't call herself Deyntree. She's gone back to her maiden name.' After a pause, Belinda added, 'That's . . . Korn.'

'Do you have her number?'

'Of course. I can give it to you.' Belinda sounded ungracious. 'After all, it's in the book.' She gave Vee the number, then said, 'All right?'

'Yes.' As Vee added, 'Thanks,' Belinda rang off. Vee raised her eyebrows. Then she dialled the number Belinda had given her. There was no answer. She went to the window and looked out for a minute or two. Then she went back to the telephone and dialled the Dumbles' number.

Mag's voice said, 'Hullo.'

'Oh . . . is Lucy there?'

'Why, that must be Vee, isn't it? I recognize the accent.'

'Yes, it is. Hi, Mag. Have you just got back from your holiday?'

'Yes – last night. We had a perfectly splendid time. The holiday did those poor children so much good. And the atmosphere was perfect – we had a wonderful spiritual director.'

'I'm so glad.'

There was a pause after which Mag said, 'You wanted Lucy. I'm afraid she's out. With the boyfriend. Or, I should say, fiancé.' There was another pause. 'You've met him?'

'Oh, yes.' Vee's tone was bright.

Mag said, 'Well what's your verdict?'

'Verdict?'

'On him. Do you approve?'

Vee said, 'I think he's charming.'

'Oh, yes. He is, isn't he? So you *do* like him? You don't think he's a bit old and experienced for our darling Lucy?'

Vee said, 'That's up to her, isn't it?'

'But of course! You're quite right. I was just interested to hear your opinion as you're such a close friend of Lucy's. By the way, we were so sorry you didn't stay on here, though of course your renting Mary's place will be a great help to her. *Such* a good person. But you will come and see us won't you – any time?'

'That's very kind of you.' Vee always sounded stilted when she talked to Mag who, as she had once said to Lucy, triggered some association with Maureen, even though Mag was quite different and much nicer. 'Will you tell Lucy I called?'

'Yes, of course.'

Vee looked in the bookcase for something to read. The collection was pious and chiefly non-fiction. But, as in every Catholic bookcase, there was an old Graham Greene. Lying down with *The Heart of the Matter*, Vee fell into a deep sleep from which she woke at five. She drank some mineral water and dialled Barbara Korn's number again. This time the telephone was answered: 'Michel Porter speaking.'

'Oh . . . I wanted to speak to Barbara Korn.'

'Hang on a minute.' The voice called loudly, 'Barbara, it's for you.'

After a moment, a softer voice said, 'Hullo. Barbara Korn here.'

'Oh, hullo. You don't know me. My name's Vee Westwood. I'm a friend of Lucy Riven's . . . Do you know who I mean?'

'Yes, I do.' Barbara sounded surprised. 'She's the unfortunate woman who's going to marry my ex-husband.'

Vee plunged on: 'Yes. Well, I want to ask you a favour. I'd like to talk with you. Would you mind?'

'What about exactly? You're American?'

'Yes. Lucy and I were at school together. She's my best friend. But she doesn't have any idea that I'm contacting you. You called her unfortunate. Well, that's just it. I think so too. I don't trust this guy, Rupert. I want to check up on him a bit.'

Barbara's tone was warmer when she said, 'Oh well, I don't see why I shouldn't talk to you. My friend Michel and I said that someone ought to warn her when my daughter told us about it.'

'Belinda? I rang her by mistake for you. She gave me your number.'

'Did you arrange to see her?'

'No.'

'I'm glad. I can't believe she could tell you anything useful. And it might upset her. What made you think of talking to me – has Rupert discussed me?'

'No. I saw Sarah Deyntree.'

'Sarah? Good heavens. Are you meeting every woman in Rupert's past? That should keep you busy.' Barbara laughed. Then she said, 'I'm willing to see you. Why don't you come round here? Would tomorrow evening suit you?'

'Yes. That would be great. Thank you.'

'Eight o'clock. For coffee. We're in Willesden. Will you be coming by tube?'

'No. By car. Just give me the address and I'll find it in the *A to Z*.'

A few moments after Vee rang off, the telephone rang. It was Lucy. 'Oh hi,' Vee said, 'How was your weekend?'

'Oh fine. We went to Oxford yesterday, as I told you. Francis's mother was a bit intimidating at first, but very kind. She adores Rupert. They both do.'

'That's nice.'

'Yes. And today we went out to lunch and saw a movie. I rang last night and this morning to see if you'd like to come too, but you were out.'

'Yeah. I was with this guy.'

'You like him?'

'Yeah.'

'Perhaps we could all go out together some time, you and him and Rupert and me.'

'Er . . . I don't think he's your style. Or Rupert's.'

'Sad, but when am I going to see *you*? How about tomorrow?'

'Well, not tomorrow. There's this gig this guy's playing, and I said I'd go. Wednesday?'

'Rupert's busy then. But I'm free.'

'Great! We'll go out and eat. I'll pick you up from work in my car.'

'The traffic's so awful.'

'I'll make it. Half past five?'

'Let's say six. I'll be waiting outside. You can't really stop there – let alone park.'

'No hassle. I'll be there.'

When they were drinking coffee and eating homemade cake, Barbara said, 'Michel and I think it's really nice that you should be so caring about your friend.'

Vee glanced from Michel with her Byronic hair and blue

jeans to Barbara, wearing an orange kaftan. Michel said, 'Perhaps I should clear off and leave you two to dissect the wrecker.'

Barbara said to Vee, 'That's one of Michel's names for Rupert.' Then she said to Michel, 'Oh no, love. Do stay.'

'I'm no authority on Deyntree,' Michel said. 'I've only seen him . . . well' – she hesitated – 'once or twice, years ago when he was with his third wife, Chris. He picked up Belinda. It must have been traumatic for him, visiting Willesden! *So* unsmart! Anyway he didn't do it often. And we always felt it was Chris who wanted to see Belinda, not the wrecker. Belinda liked Chris. I've always said it was a meeting of yuppie souls.'

'Oh, that's not fair,' Barbara said, but her look at Michel was fond. Then she said to Vee, 'Tell me about Sarah. I've never met her. I've sometimes wondered about her. Rupert said she was cold and snobbish and used to get drunk. He said she wanted the divorce as much as he did.'

Vee said, 'My impression was that she was very vulnerable. I think she was madly in love with him and has never really got over it.'

Barbara looked downcast. 'You amaze me. God, what pigs men are – such liars. Of course I was very young and foolish when I met Rupert. Would you believe it – I was a fashion model then?' With an unselfconscious gesture she pinched one ample hip.

Vee said, 'I saw pictures of you at Sarah's.'

'Sarah's got pictures of *me*?'

'Yes. Cut from old magazines. I think she used to brood over her beautiful rival.'

'Oh, God. How awful. Sad . . .'

'She is a bit sad. But I liked her. She's very fond of her son – James.'

'What's *he* like?'

'Nice.'

'What does *he* feel about his father?'

'Doesn't know him, but can't stand him.'

'Sounds sensible. How did you track them down?'

'Sarah called Lucy to warn her against Rupert.'

'That was good.'

'But Lucy didn't think so. She had a very bad time around then. She had this wonderful hair – and someone cut it off in the subway – the Underground.'

'Men are so sick. But Rupert must have been upset about the hair. He had a thing about hair. He wanted me to wear wigs in bed. I thought he was so kinky.'

'Kinky?'

'Perhaps I'm biased. I was a virgin when I married him. Still a nice Jewish girl, in spite of being a model. I was so confused about my sexuality. I realize now that I'd always absolutely dreaded the idea of going to bed with a man. But I couldn't face that then, and when I met Rupert, who was so handsome and smooth, I persuaded myself it would be all right.'

'Sarah says he's so amusing, such fun. Lucy thinks that too.'

'Amusing? Well, I think a lot of his jokes passed me by. There were all these puns he made. About people with names like Al Dente and Percy Flage. Well, I knew nothing about Italian food and I'd never heard the word "persiflage" so I hadn't a clue what he was talking about. And he was always quoting, though he talked so posh anyway that I never really knew what was a quote and what wasn't. And there was this Blake picture of two angels that he was mad about. *I* thought it was hideous, though I didn't say so. I was quite uneducated in those days. But I still don't like Blake. All those men with muscles.' She gave a small grimace.

Vee said, 'You went to South Africa?'

'That's right – Belinda was born there. Apartheid was another thing I was clueless about. Rupert had this job. Sort of

connected with the High Commission. Commercial something
– I don't remember. But it meant meeting all sorts of people.
Some Liberals and even left-wingers and others real Nats who
backed apartheid all the way. And Rupert would just listen,
and agree with whoever was there at the time. I used to tell
him he was a hypocrite, but actually I still haven't the faintest
idea what he really believed – if anything. *I* hated apartheid
from the moment I arrived. It made me think of the Nazis –
and I'm Jewish, you know.'

Vee said, 'So am I.'

'*Really*?'

'Well, my mother was, but her family cut her off completely
because my father was a Gentile.'

'Oh, that's terrible. My parents weren't pleased when I
married out, but they'd never have cut me off. And they were
wonderful to me and Belinda after the divorce. Anyway, in
Cape Town, I used to get into these huge arguments about
politics – at dinner parties and so on – it really used to make
Rupert angry. We were getting on worse and worse. I hated
the sex. I put on a lot of weight when I was pregnant, and went
on putting it on after Belinda was born. Of course, I couldn't
do any more modelling – I was sick of it, anyway. I wanted to
get educated. When I worked in London as a model I was
quite a success and I earned a lot. I still had a bit of that money
and I started taking courses at the university. I got to know
this group of Marxist students. At first they used to come to
our house. Rupert used to talk to them and ask them questions.
Then after a bit they stopped coming. One of them told me
they thought Rupert was a spy.'

'That's what Sarah says.'

'It fits. Of course the British and the Americans were hand
in glove with the South African government, but I'm sure they
both had their own spies, sniffing round and nosing out
Marxists. I fell in love with Marxism in Cape Town. It seemed

to explain everything.' Barbara sighed. 'It was a revelation to me.' Barbara paused. 'That was the first revelation I had in Cape Town. Then came the second.' She paused again.

Vee said, 'Yes?'

'Oh well . . . We had this big flat in Clifton – above the beach. I remember it was a Thursday, because it was the maid's day off. Belinda went to this sort of high-class crèche. I dropped her in the morning on my way to university and picked her up in the afternoon. That day, when I got to university, I learned that two of the students I knew best had been arrested – by the Special Branch. Well, I had a sort of panic attack, and drove back home.

'The sea was very loud at Clifton. Inside the flat, the waves were almost as loud as outside. I unlocked the door and went through into the bedroom. Rupert and this beautiful young girl were lying naked on the bed. It was the most extraordinary moment of my life. Because, seeing them there – a man and a woman together – *her* body made me breathless. I didn't feel angry – there just wasn't room for anger in my head, because it was full of this realization that I could only, ever, desire a woman. Never a man. I was stunned. Well, they saw me. No one moved. We all just stared at each other. And then – *I* left. I went down to the beach and just sat there. I thought about the arrests, but much more about the other thing, till I realized it was time to go and fetch Belinda. When I got back to the flat I knew there wouldn't be a trace of Rupert and that girl. There wasn't. But Rupert came home quite early that evening. Usually, unless we were going somewhere – we'd practically stopped entertaining – he was very late. That night he had this kind of ingratiating look. I saw he was dead nervous, and I understood why. He hadn't just been unfaithful – he'd been illegal. That girl wasn't white, you see. She must have been Cape Coloured. Her skin was this marvellous golden brown.

'I told Rupert that I wanted to go, I wanted to leave the country with Belinda and I was quite willing for him to divorce me for desertion. Of course I didn't tell him my reasons – he thought it was because of the girl. Actually, it was because those arrests had frightened me. I was terrified that the same thing might happen to me. I didn't think I'd be able to stand up to it. But I also had this hope that at last I might be able to fulfil myself, as a person, as a sexual being. I'd been totally confused until then.

'Actually, I think he was relieved. He did a bit of hectoring about custody – you see, I couldn't take Belinda out of the country without his consent. But that was just a kind of blackmail to stop me asking for child support. Well, it succeeded. He never paid me a penny. Once Belinda had some extra expenses and I wrote to him, but he never answered.

'He stayed on in South Africa for a few years. A friend of mine told me he seemed quite settled there. But then he suddenly came back to England. I couldn't help wondering if he was still involved with that girl and the police had found out and he'd had to make a dash for it. Who knows?

'Soon after he came back, he telephoned and said he'd like to see Belinda. By that time I'd met Michel. I remember feeling absolutely terrified that he'd find out and try to get Belinda away from me. But that was nonsense. I think he was just curious. And was disappointed. I remember him saying to me, "Belinda certainly hasn't inherited our looks, has she?" She wasn't in the room, but I remember thinking how awful it was of a father to talk about his child in that way.'

'And Belinda?'

'Oh, she adored him at first. I think that was why he went on seeing her sometimes. It flattered him.'

Vee said, 'Sarah says he never tried to see James at all.'

'Hmm. Perhaps a son would be different from an adoring daughter – even though she wasn't a raving beauty. And then, when he married Chris, she and Belinda seemed to sort of take to each other.'

'Yuppie soul-mates!' Michel said.

Barbara grimaced. 'Oh, nonsense!' But the connection between Chris and Belinda seemed distasteful to her. She said, 'Anyway I'm sure they haven't seen each other for ages. Belinda never mentions her.'

'Belinda's a cagey one,' said Michel.

'Oh no.' Barbara's tone was firmly dismissive. There was a silence.

Vee said, 'I really must go now.' Then she glanced at Barbara's hands on which Indian-silver rings, some with pale opaque stones, gave a knuckle-duster effect. Vee said, 'Did Rupert ever give you a ring?'

'A ring? Yes, a sort of Victorian thing. Two hearts. I didn't like it much – I thought it was fussy and old-fashioned. Well, it was. It had been his mother's. He asked for it back when we parted. I was only too glad. Why do you ask?'

Vee said, 'He gave it to Sarah. Now Lucy's wearing it – she loves it. I wonder if he gave it to Chris.'

'I wouldn't have thought it looked expensive enough for Chris,' Barbara said.

'I might get in touch with her. Is she the C. Deyntree in the telephone book? In N1?'

'That's right. Barnsbury. Very posh. But take my advice – don't appeal to her on the basis of sisterhood.'

Vee stood up. 'Thanks for talking to me so freely – and for the coffee and that great cake. I'll let myself out.'

They came to the top of the stairs and stood there, Michel with an arm round Barbara's waist. 'You've got our number,' Barbara said. 'If there's anything else you want to know.'

Vee was at the bottom of the stairs when Michel called out, 'Have *you* got a phone? In case Barbara thinks of anything else that might be useful to you.'

'Yes.' Vee called it out, and added, 'I'll probably be here till the last week in September.'

Michel repeated the number, and said, 'I'll write it down.'

When she was back at the flat, Vee telephoned James and told him about the evening. 'What a tangle,' he said. 'Do you wish you'd never got involved?'

'No ... The more I find out about Rupert, the more I want to. It's sort of like a series of rooms that open out of each other. You go deeper into the house, unlocking door after door.'

'Till you come to Bluebeard's chamber? The forbidden room.'

'No room's forbidden,' said Vee, and then, 'Lucy says her awful mother used to call Rupert "Bluebeard". It made Lucy furious. That woman's so stupid. The way she reacted to Rupert only made Lucy keener. Lucy's obstinate. If I'm going to get her to drop Rupert, I'll have to give her some really solid evidence.'

'Well, good luck. You've no idea how much I'm looking forward to seeing you again.'

'Me too.'

'Friday evening?'

'Yes – that will be great.'

At ten next morning, Vee was drinking coffee when the telephone rang.

'Is that Vee?'

'Yes.'

'Hullo. It's Michel Porter.'

'Oh, hi, Michel.'

'Actually ...' Michel hesitated. She sounded ill at ease. 'There's something I want to tell you in confidence.'

'Oh – sure.'

'I mean – well, I wouldn't want it mentioned to Barbara. If you should happen to meet again. I did something rather stupid.

Oh, not as stupid as it could have been. But, anyway, I'd prefer that Barbara didn't know about it.'

'Right.'

'I was visiting someone. Near Finsbury Park in North London. This person lives on the top floor of a house that's turned into three flats. Well, on the ground floor there's someone called November. Odd name. I noticed it by the door. And later the person I was visiting started talking about this November woman. Apparently she's Cape Coloured – it's a Cape Coloured name. My . . . friend said she was a terrible woman, terribly aggressive and appallingly rude. And sometimes she dresses like a prostitute and she has these numerous male visitors. Well, this person – my friend – is rather prim, and I didn't take much notice. But when I was leaving, on the way downstairs, I'd reached the first landing, and someone was coming out of this woman's flat. He didn't see me – and I only saw him for a moment. But you know – I could have sworn it was Rupert Deyntree.'

'*Really*?'

'Well . . . I say I "could have sworn", but I'm a lawyer so I know a lot about mistaken identity – and the fallibility of witnesses. And, if I were in court, I don't think I could "swear". I haven't seen him for so long – and then only a few times, as I said yesterday. But I really thought it was him. Anyway, I put it out of my mind. Then, last night, after we'd been talking, and Barbara had mentioned Rupert and that other Cape Coloured woman, I started thinking about it again, and about your friend Lucy and how if it was Deyntree and he was, well, visiting a prostitute when he's engaged to her . . .'

'This happened recently?'

'Oh yes – earlier this month.'

'Do you know the exact date?'

'Well, just a moment. I can check in my diary . . . Yes, here it is. It was the seventh.'

260

'The seventh of August?'

'Yes.'

'Oh, I don't think it can have been him. I remember Lucy telling me he went away that day . . . well, that's what she thought. You really believed you recognized him, though?'

'Yes.'

'Would you give me the address?'

'Well, if this woman's as ferocious as she sounds, I really wouldn't advise you to visit her.'

'I might telephone.'

Michel said, 'As a matter of fact, I just checked. She isn't in the book. If she's on the phone, she's ex-directory.'

'Do please give me the address.'

'Well . . . all right. It's 63 Tolland Road. That's N4. But I really . . .'

'Don't worry, Michel. I won't do anything stupid. And I'll respect your confidence. Bye.'

'Goodbye.'

Lucy was looking tired when Vee collected her from the office next day. She said, 'I wonder if we could go back to your flat instead of eating out. I just feel like being somewhere peaceful. Without people.'

'I've got some wine. But there's nothing to eat. Let's pick up some take-away. Fish and chips? There's this great place in Upper Street . . .'

Back in the flat they ate with enthusiasm. Lucy sighed. She said, 'I must be very insensitive – I never lose my appetite. Even when I'm unhappy.'

'You're unhappy now?'

'No, not exactly.' They were sitting by the window. It was dusk. The street lights had just come on, illuminating the thick masses of leaves on the plane trees.

'What, then?' Vee put her hand on Lucy's arm. She glanced

261

down at the pretty ring so many women had worn.

'Oh . . . I don't know. It's sort of, to do with . . . you know what happened that night we came back from Rivendale.'

'The sixth of August.'

'How on earth did you remember that?'

'You said you'd never forget. That it was like another birthday. At the time I thought I'd send you a card on the day next year.' They both laughed. Then Vee said, 'And Rupert went away the next day – the seventh.'

'That's right.'

'And while he was away you renewed your holy vows of chastity.'

'Oh, Vee, don't laugh at me. You've no idea how difficult it is.'

'I wasn't laughing, really. Actually I think you were right. You should stick to what you believe in.'

'You didn't say that when I first told you. You said I was crazy.'

'Well, I think that was gross of me. Really, I do.'

Lucy sighed. 'Oh dear. You know I was almost hoping you'd say I was crazy again, and persuade me. When we came back from Oxford on Sunday, and then again on Monday, he wanted me to come to his flat. And I wouldn't – because I knew what would happen. Oh, he wasn't angry. He just seemed . . . sad. Oh, Vee, you know I think he's still really upset about my hair.'

'Well, he should try not to show it.'

'That's unfair. He does try.' Lucy's tone was indignant. 'He really does.'

'Okay.'

'I'm sorry if I sounded cross. But he's so wonderful. I can't bear anyone to criticize him.'

'Rupert right or wrong?'

'But he isn't wrong. It's just . . . that he loves me . . . and he wasn't brought up the way I was . . . with the same ideals.

And . . . it's more difficult for men.'

'I think that's crap.'

Now Lucy laughed. 'Perhaps you're right. But really you can't object to my being loyal to him. You've always liked my being loyal. And you're loyal, too.'

Vee lightened her tone: 'Yes, we're the loyalty twins.'

Lucy said, 'I really want you to get to know Rupert better. Perhaps this weekend . . .'

Vee said, 'Well, actually, I sort of told this guy . . . this musician—'

'What's his *name*?'

'Er . . . Jim. I told him I might go away with him somewhere for this weekend.'

'Oh. But I do understand. Do you *really* like him?'

'Yes – quite a lot.'

'Rupert's got to go away again on Tuesday night. We're having dinner at the Firenze first.'

'So let's you and I meet on Wednesday.'

'Yes, let's.'

'When does Rupert get back?'

'Oh, very soon. On Saturday. But I'll miss him.'

'Oh well – only three days.'

'Yes. So you think I'm right . . . not to.'

'Well, that's what *you* believe, isn't it?'

'Yes.'

'Then I do.'

Lucy was tired, and Vee drove her home early, overruling her protests – weaker than usual – that she could go by tube. After dropping her at the Dumbles', where the open curtains revealed a group in earnest discussion, Vee stopped under a street lamp in East Heath Road, and mapped out her way to Tolland Road in the *A to Z*. Then, through Gospel Oak, Tufnell Park and Holloway – where she was quite near home – she drove there.

Number 63 was a long way down. She had to get out of the car to check the ugly metal numbers placed aslant on the door. A light glimmered behind curtains on the top floor, but the rest of the house was dark, and the utter darkness of the ground floor was unbroken. Behind the closed bay window, with the festoon blind night-drained of colour, this darkness seemed almost tangibly thick.

Vee did not mount the steps to check the labels by the door. She turned and moved, fast, to the car. She had planned a way home by continuing down Tolland Road and then turning right, but after she had started the car, the weight and blackness of a building looming on her left made her stop – the brakes gave a little shriek – and reverse quickly. She backed – with a single furtive glance at the house – onto the cement outside Number 63, then shot off the way she had come, towards the bright orange light of the Holloway Road and the short drive to Highbury Corner. Back at the house, she parked outside, hurried up the steps, keys in hand, and slammed the front door behind her. She went upstairs so fast that – fit as she was – she was breathless when she reached her flat.

Next morning, when she telephoned Suffolk, Sarah told her James had gone to the library. 'Is it anything urgent?' she asked.

'Oh no,' said Vee. 'It'll keep till tomorrow.' She added, 'I'm so looking forward to seeing you.'

Sarah prattled on for several minutes about the weather and about Vee's taste in food ('Is there anything you really dislike?' 'Only parsnips and barley'). As soon as they had said goodbye and rung off, Vee dialled the number of Deyntree, C. After four rings, a cool drawl on the answering machine repeated the number and told her to leave a message; she did not do so.

She was restless. She wandered down Upper Street to the Angel, drank an espresso and ate a croissant in a café, strolled round a bookshop and bought a paperback anthology of modern poems, walked home again, buying a few supplies on the way. Last night she had slept badly and now, after eating some fruit, she took off her jeans and, chilled by a poem of Philip Larkin's, huddled under the bedclothes and fell asleep. She woke at four. She washed and put on her jeans again, made up her face and drove to Tolland Road, this time approaching it from the other end.

She saw that the black-looking building she had flinched from last night was a church. She slowed down and stopped by Number 63: it rose, wan and misshapen, from its lake of cement. This time, as she walked to the steps she saw the thick curtains that were drawn behind the horribly pink festoon blind in the closed bay window. She went up the steps and studied the labels: Pringle, John Tessier, D. November. Her hand went slowly out towards D. November's bell, but then she snatched it back and hurried down the steps.

In the flat, she was restless again. She rang James's number and, when Sarah answered, rang off. She looked up Chris Deyntree's address in the telephone book, and then found the street in the *A to Z*, where she saw that it was only a short distance away. At six she set out to walk there.

She loitered on the pavement outside, examining the building's meticulous effect: clean brick, glossy black door, gate and railing, white woodwork. Only a heavy white metal blind over the basement window jarred. Through the huge drawing-room window, she could see a large black-and-white photograph on a wall and two facing white sofas, one with its back to the window. Everything was big; everything was black or white. Passing other houses in the street, Vee had seen right through the double drawing-rooms to the gardens behind: not here, where the back window was covered by another metal blind.

Vee started as a woman shut the door of a car just behind her and – with a cold glance at her – approached the black gate. She was dashingly dressed, perfectly painted and not quite haggard. She opened the gate – it creaked – and closed it behind her.

Vee called out, 'Ms Deyntree?'

The woman swung round on the path. Now, if not haggard, she looked hag-ridden and, for a moment, almost frantic. Then she blinked; her face set; she looked across the street to where a man was fiddling with the engine of a car, watched by two children. She came to the closed gate, saying, 'What do you want?'

'I wondered if you could spare me a few minutes. My name's Vee Westwood. I'm a friend of Lucy Riven's.' She paused, but the woman said nothing. She went on, 'I don't know if you know who I mean?'

Chris said, 'Oh yes, I know who you mean.'

Vee said, 'Could I talk with you briefly?'

' "Talk with me"?' Chris slightly mimicked Vee's American intonation. 'What about?'

'My friend—' Vee hesitated.

'Has your "friend" decided to make a few enquiries about her fascinating fiancé?'

'No.' Vee put a hand on the gate, but a movement of Chris's – a quelling gesture with outstretched palm – made her withdraw it, and even take a step back. She went on, 'Lucy doesn't know I'm here. It's just that she's a great friend—'

'Oh, you're one of *those* Americans. "Sisterhood is powerful" and all that garbage.' The contempt in Chris's tone was virulent.

Vee kept her temper. She even produced a small, forced smile as she said, 'Something like that.'

Chris said, 'What do you want to know? About whores? About stolen property?'

Vee said, 'I'd like to know whatever you care to tell me.'

'Well, actually, I don't *care* to tell you anything. I'm afraid

I haven't the time or the inclination to satisfy your *sisterly* curiosity. Let your friend find out for herself. The way I did. You say you haven't told her you were coming here?'

'No.'

'Well, if you pester me for one more minute, *I* shall.'

At the alarm on Vee's face, Chris smiled for the first time. 'Now please go.' As Chris went up the path again, Vee walked rapidly away.

Just after she got back to the flat, the telephone rang. It was James: 'Mum said you rang.'

'Oh, I so wanted to hear your voice. And I've got so much to tell you.' She told him about Michel's call and about her two visits to Tolland Road and how she had not been able to bring herself to ring D. November's bell.

'I'm glad to hear it,' James said. 'She sounds awful – and what ever would you have said if she'd answered?'

'I really just wanted to see her, I think – I would have said I'd made a mistake. But I just hadn't the courage. What a coward I am!' Then she told him about Chris.

'*She* sounds horrible,' James said.

'Yes. Weird.'

'My father's world is full of weird women.'

'Mmm. Oh, I do wonder about this November person. Lucy said he went away on the seventh. He's going away again next week.' Then she said, 'Perhaps I'll break into his flat while he's gone.'

'*What*?' James sounded horrified. 'You can't do that.'

'I might be able to. You remember I told you I learned how to pick a lock.'

'I didn't mean so much that you *can't* as that you mustn't.'

'We'll talk about it later. Tomorrow.'

'I'm longing to see you.'

'Me too. What time?'

'Get here before dark. Mum's really thrilled, too. The full

267

treatment. A tin of digestive biscuits by your bed.'

'Digestive biscuits?'

He laughed. 'An old English custom. And there'll be flowers in your room. And she's given you her best linen sheets. She's put you in the other spare room, this time. There's a double bed.'

'Oh.'

He said, 'We're going to have a wonderful weekend.'

But when Vee arrived early next evening, he was waiting by the gate and, seeing his face, Vee said, 'What's wrong?'

'Oh, Vee – she's drunk.'

They went up the path, through the scented bushes with, from underfoot, a puff of wild mint. At the door, James said, gesturing to the left. 'She's in the sitting-room. Perhaps you'd rather not—'

But, 'Oh yes – I must.' Vee hurried in. Sarah lolled half on, half off the sofa. Her flush was purple. She made an attempt to focus blurred eyes. 'Oh Vee,' she said, 'Vee.' Then she muttered, 'I'm sorry.' Then she wailed, 'Oh Vee – *help* me.'

It was Tuesday before Vee returned to London, though she had meant to leave early on Monday morning.

On Friday night she had been with Sarah till two in the morning. Vee had made her drink coffee and even, later, eat some of the beef casserole she had prepared before the mounting anticipation and tension of the day had been this time's reason for the only release she knew.

As Sarah sobered, Vee told her the story of her mother, and by the time – at two – Sarah fell asleep, she had agreed that, if Vee accompanied her, she would go to a meeting of AA.

On Saturday morning, Vee started telephoning; she found an open meeting that afternoon in a town forty miles away. 'An open meeting?' Sarah said. 'What does that mean?' She was sullen now.

'It means I can come with you,' Vee said. 'I went to lots of open meetings after my mother died.'

After a moment Sarah said, 'So it means anyone can go?'

'That's right. No one knows that anyone else is an alcoholic – unless they say so. And you don't have to say anything at all.'

'You're sure?'

'Completely.'

On the way Sarah said, 'I'm only coming because I promised. I hate the whole idea.'

Vee slowed down. 'Would you rather go back home?'

After a moment Sarah said irritably, 'No. I said I'd come. I might as well.' But when they found the building – a drab community centre – and went in, Sarah kept glancing nervously round her, and when a man passed them in the passage, she raised a hand to hide her face: grey under some gallant make-up. But the man was going to the meeting, at which a speaker and the chairman sat at a table, and about twenty other men and women faced them in chairs.

On the way home, Sarah said, 'It was odd. I expected them all to be down-and-outs, but there was only one man who looked a bit seedy.' A few minutes later she said, 'One or two of them said things that struck a chord with me. They seemed to understand. I've never felt that with anyone else. But that whole programme sounds so complicated.'

Vee said, 'Yet it says that the only requirement for AA membership is a desire to stop drinking.'

'Mmm. But what about the Higher Power they keep talking about. I've never been in the least religious.'

'People can think of that as anything . . . as the power of AA.'

'And I can't imagine talking about myself. It's all very well for Americans, that sort of thing.'

Vee laughed. She said, 'But no one at that meeting was American.'

'No.' Sarah sighed.

As they drew up outside the cottage, Sarah said, 'I don't know . . .' They got out of the car and James, who had been working in the garden, joined them.

Sarah went straight upstairs. James and Vee exchanged glances: his held terror and hers doubt. Several minutes passed. Then Sarah came downstairs with three bottles. She handed them to Vee. Then she said to James, 'Will you get rid of those bottles in the sideboard?' She went into the sitting-room and picked up the morning paper.

James said to Vee, 'What shall we do with them? Pour them down the kitchen sink?'

'No – what a waste! Let's put them in the trunk of my car. I'll give them to someone in London or leave them for Mary Collins. She'll be surprised. I feel she's probably teetotal.'

On Sunday morning Vee and James went for a walk. The night before they had made love in the double bed. James had said, 'I'm in love with you,' and Vee had answered, 'Yes. I think I am with you.' This morning, however, they did not talk about love; they argued about Vee's plan to break into Rupert's flat.

James said, 'It's impossible.'

'How do you know? I can *try*.'

He said, 'If you're doubtful about whether he went away last time, how do you know he's going this time?'

'Oh, I think he was away last time. I just don't know if he was on that day – the seventh. This time Lucy says he's leaving his car at Heathrow and she's going to meet his plane on Saturday. By tube – there's love for you! Then they're going to drive back to London together.'

James said, 'Has Lucy got a key?'

'No. Apparently there's this handicapped woman on the ground floor who has a spare key. But I'm sure she wouldn't give it to me.'

James said, 'But she might give it to *me*.'

'To you?'

'Yes. Everyone says how like him I am. If I said I was his son—' He broke off. 'Just tell me, darling Vee, what you think you might achieve by this.'

'I want to find some real evidence against him. Perhaps something connecting him with this D. November. But I don't want to involve you. Why should you get involved? I'm doing this for Lucy.'

'I'd be doing it for you.'

She said, 'But what would you say to this woman?'

'Oh, that my father telephoned from abroad . . . that he wants me to fetch something from the flat. The fact that I know she's got the spare key should add conviction.'

'But James – say she told him afterwards?'

James shrugged. 'What could he do? We'd have given her back the key. We aren't going to steal anything . . . I hope.'

'Lucy did say that this woman's a bit dotty. She talks a lot, and Rupert tries to avoid her.'

'You see . . .'

'I think I should try alone first.'

'No. Please let's do it together.'

'Well, okay.'

Vee did not leave till Tuesday because she wanted to take Sarah to a local AA meeting – in the nearby small town – on Monday evening.

'I can't go in,' Vee said, 'because it's a closed meeting.'

James said, 'I could take her.'

'No, I'd like to. Or why don't we take her together?'

When they reached the Methodist church-hall where the meeting was held, Sarah was trembling. 'Say I see someone I know?'

'It's a closed meeting,' Vee said. 'If you see someone you know, they'll be there for the same reason you are.'

James and Vee had a drink in a pub. When they collected Sarah, she said, 'It's quite extraordinary. Someone I know quite well was there.' She added, 'He said I could tell you, James. It was Paul. Our solicitor.'

'Really?'

'Yes. He says he's been in AA for fifteen years. He says he'll collect me for meetings every Monday and Thursday.'

'That's wonderful,' Vee said.

Before Vee left next morning, Sarah said to her, 'Do you know – I think this AA thing just might work for me.' They embraced. Sarah said, 'I'm so glad about you and James.'

Three

They had decided that James should come up to London on Thursday and spend that night at Vee's flat. On Wednesday morning, Lucy rang Vee.

'Oh hi,' Vee said. 'Did Rupert get off all right last night?'

'Yes.' They arranged for Vee to pick up Lucy at her office that evening, but at four Lucy telephoned again to say that she was feeling ill. Then she added, 'I'm going to see the doctor tomorrow – just for a check-up. I think I'd better not come out tonight.'

'What's the matter?' Vee asked.

'Oh, I don't know. I feel sick. I'm tired. Perhaps I'm a bit run down. I'm probably being a hypochondriac, but I usually feel so well.'

'Yes. I'm really sorry. Let me know what the doctor says, won't you? And take care.'

James came to the flat at lunchtime next day. Neither of them was hungry. They had a drink and a sandwich in a pub. They dawdled until three. They had decided that around four would be a good time to approach the old lady who, perhaps, slept after lunch.

They found a vacant parking-place round the corner from the house, and put money in the parking-meter. James was wearing a suit and a tie and carrying a briefcase, to look respectable.

'Brilliant!' Vee had said.

'Perhaps I should take after my father and become a spy.'

Vee waited by the steps to the basement while he rang the bell. Then she saw him speaking into the machine. Several moments passed. Then he came down the steps, but it was only to stand in view of the ground-floor window, at which an old lady now appeared in a wheelchair. He raised a hand. The old lady peered at him, gave Vee only a glance, then beckoned to him. She wheeled away from the window. He went up the steps, and pushed the door when the buzz sounded. He went inside, and the door closed behind him.

Nearly ten minutes passed – Vee kept glancing at her watch – before he reappeared, swinging the keys from his hand. He joined Vee, and they went down the steps to the basement. 'You took ages,' she said.

'Yes, she wouldn't stop talking. She kept saying how like him I was and that when I came to the window, she'd seen it at once. She said she was surprised she'd never seen me before. I said I'd been abroad. She said he was a great traveller, too. I thought I'd never get away – I can see why he avoids her.'

They were at the door. As he unfastened the locks, he said, 'You could never have picked these two – one of them's a mortice.'

Now they were inside the big room. It was rather dark, but neither of them switched on the light. 'There's my mother's picture,' he said. They crossed the room to stand in front of it. In this dim light, the gold brightness of the Good Angel seemed a glint: certain to be consumed by the Evil Angel's dark tongues of fire.

'He looks so powerful,' James said. 'I'm sure that fetter on

274

his foot's not strong enough to hold him.'

'But he's blind,' Vee said, and then, 'We can't waste time looking at pictures. Could you go through those papers on the table and have a look in that little cabinet?' She went to the computer, but whatever she tried, access was blocked: keyed to some password she had no hope of finding. She said, 'I'll have a look in the rest of the flat.'

The little cabinet held what seemed to be data relating to investments; so did the papers on the table. James saw an address book by the telephone and paged through it: there was no entry for 'November'. He stood staring at the two bookcases and at numerous stacked videos, some in illustrated covers, others in plain cardboard sleeves.

A sound made him turn. Vee stood at the back of the room. In one hand she held a cassette; from the other hung a long plait of pale blonde hair.

She said, 'It's Lucy's. There was this cardboard box at the back of the closet, behind his clothes. It was under a camcorder. It's Lucy's braid.' Then she cried out, 'I don't understand. He was shocked when he saw her, after it had been cut off. I know he was. His face . . . his voice.' Then she said, 'I'm going to put it back. But we'll take the cassette.'

'The cassette? Why?'

'It's not labelled. There must be some reason it was hidden there. With the braid and the camcorder. Lucy's never mentioned that he made home movies. We'll take one of the cassettes from here and put it where this one was, so that if he looks in the box he won't know it's gone. Now, let's get out of here.'

'You aren't going to take the plait? To show Lucy?'

'And we say we searched his flat? He'd make up some story. That he got it through the post and didn't show it to her because he thought it would upset her too much. And something like that could be *true*, you see. I *know* he didn't have any idea her braid was gone, when he saw her that time.'

'You're sure?'

'As sure as a person can be.'

He put the cassette in his briefcase, and Vee placed another unlabelled one in the box. After James had locked the front door, Vee glanced up. The woman was sitting at the ground-floor window.

James said, 'You go to the car. I'll take back the keys.' He added, 'I'll tell her I might have to come back tomorrow. Then we could replace the tape. You look pale. Why don't you go and wait in the car? She may keep me talking.'

'Okay.'

When Vee sat down in the car, she started to tremble. But by the time James rejoined her, she was calm again. He said, 'Goodness, what a talker. She said it would be all right if I came back tomorrow. She asked who you were. I said you were my fiancée.'

'Oh really?'

'Then she started talking about my father, and how *his* fiancée always reminded her of Debussy.'

'Debussy?'

'He wrote a piece called "The Girl with the Golden Hair".'

James and Vee sat on the living-room divan, side by side. Gradually, while the cassette unwound, they moved apart – each into a separate, huddled space – as they watched the varied rape and intricate abuse of a bound, gagged, blindfolded, naked woman.

The perpetrators were always partly clad: she – lean and brown – never took off her black boots, stockings and suspender belt, or he his blue polo-necked sweater. At times, when both of them were active, the camera was stationary; at others – when only one of them was busy on the screen – it shifted about; once – when the sound on the tape was the woman's laugh at what the man was doing – it jumped. No words were spoken: apart from that one shrill laugh, there were only grunts, gasps and panting breath. Muffled by her gag, the victim's groans were scarcely audible.

Near the beginning of the tape, James had muttered, 'Can that man be my father?' Vee nodded, but – staring at the screen, eyes wide with horror – said nothing till, with a last distance shot of the woman, still bound, gagged, blindfolded, naked, and now apparently unconscious between two large white sofas, with a black-and-white photograph on the wall, the screen went blank and silence fell.

After several moments it was James who switched off the machine. Vee said, 'That room, that woman – in spite of the gag and blindfold I recognized her. Chris Deyntree.' And then, 'Do you think the . . . other woman could be D. November?'

They did not sleep at all until after two when she lay down on her bed, and he sat holding her hand. At last she slept, and he went to lie on the living-room divan where he dozed but was woken at four by her crying out. He went and sat on the edge of her bed again; she did not want him to get in beside her.

A little later, exhaustion triumphed. Both slept, he on the divan again. When she woke, Vee groaned, then looked at her watch. It was nearly nine. As she came into the living-room, James started awake. Vee said, 'Chris will probably have left for work, but I'll see.' She dialled the number, heard the answering machine, and put down the receiver. 'No point leaving a message,' she said. 'I'm sure she wouldn't call back. I'll have to try again this evening. I'll make some coffee now.'

'Have you any tea?'

'I think there are some tea bags.' She went to look in the kitchen cupboard. 'Only herbal,' she called.

'I'll have coffee.' James sat on the edge of the bed, blinking. Neither of them had undressed.

They had agreed the night before that there was no question of returning the tape, and Vee was determined to show it to Chris before she showed it to Lucy: showing it to Lucy was something she wanted to postpone, something she flinched from the thought of doing.

Now she said to James, 'You should go back to Suffolk to be with your mother. I'm sure she'd like you to be there. She's been sober less than a week.'

'But – Chris?'

'*You* can't come with me. If I show her the tape, do you think she'd want a *man* there?'

'I suppose not.' Then he said, 'Vee, do remember, that woman was just as bad as he was.'

'Yes.'

'Please promise me you won't go to see . . . that November – to find out if it's her.'

'All right – not without telling you, anyway.'

'Promise.'

'Okay.'

Before he left, they embraced, but did not kiss. He said, 'Vee, I love you.'

'Yes. Yes, I know. Just give me a little time. After that tape.'

'Promise you'll be in touch.'

'Yes. Okay.'

The day dragged. When James left, she rewound the video, then put it away in a drawer, as she had done as a child with a book that frightened her. She bathed, and put on clean clothes. She drank too much coffee, then tried to counteract it with a glass of wine. She found it impossible to read. She went for a walk through Canonbury, but in the quiet pretty streets kept turning to look behind her. When she got home, she had another bath and changed again into fresh jeans and a white sweat shirt. At half past six, she telephoned Chris Deyntree.

The telephone was answered on the third ring. Into the

silence, Vee said, 'Ms Deyntree?'

'Who is that?'

'It's Vee Westwood. We . . . met outside your house last week. I have to see you.'

'I told you then – I've got nothing to say to you.'

'Please, Ms Deyntree—'

'Oh, stop calling me "Miz". I'm "Mrs".'

'Mrs Deyntree, do you have a VCR?'

'Of course I do.' Chris's tone was the same as if Vee had asked her if she owned a table or a bed.

'Mrs Deyntree – something awful happened to you. I don't know when. But it was terrible . . . I'm so sorry.'

After a moment's silence, Chris said, 'I don't know what you mean.'

'Yes you do. And I have a video tape of it.'

Chris made a gulping sound. Then, in a trembling voice, she said, 'I don't believe you.' After a brief pause, she tried – with limited success – to harden her tone. She said, 'What is this? Are you hoping to blackmail me?'

'Of course I'm not. How could I blackmail *you* with this? I have to show it to you. You know at least one of the people involved.'

'*What*?'

'May I come round?'

After another pause, Chris said, 'All right then. When?'

'How about now?'

'All right.' Chris's voice rose: 'I warn you – if this is some kind of trick—'

'It isn't. I'll be round as soon as I can.'

It was dark. Vee, with the cassette in her bag, started down the road on foot but, after walking only a few metres, turned back and got into her car. She should have walked. A traffic jam held her up for twenty minutes. When she reached Chris's street, she realized it was one-way. She had to drive round and round to find a parking place. It was three-quarters of an hour before she opened Chris's creaking gate.

All the lights in the house seemed to be on. The drawing-room shutters were open, and Chris stood at the window. She waited for Vee to reach the front door before she came quickly to unlock it. 'Please go upstairs. The video's in my bedroom. When you're up the stairs, I'll set the alarm for the ground floor. It's already set for the basement. If you try anything there's no way you'll be able to get away.'

'What would I try?' But Vee went upstairs. Chris pressed buttons on the alarm system. A beeping sound started, followed by a long low note. Chris joined Vee upstairs before it stopped.

Chris said, 'A friend of mine is phoning in half an hour. Just to check that I'm all right. And I've given her your name . . . if it is your name.'

'I have identification in my purse.'

'Oh, forget it.' Chris led the way into her bedroom which, though the early-September evening was warm, gave, with its pallor, a sense of chill.

'I'll put it on.' Vee turned on the television and video, and inserted the cassette. She said, 'I won't watch it again. It's so awful.' She switched it on, and went over to the window.

Vee turned when she heard Chris give a little moan. Later she cried out, and Vee made a hesitant movement towards her, but Chris thrust her back with a sweeping movement of her arm: 'Leave me alone!' Vee looked out of the window: across the road, a family was eating in a brightly lit room.

When the sounds on the tape ended, she looked at Chris again. Chris's face was buried in her hands. Vee came over to stop the tape and press the rewind button. Chris looked up. Her face was marked with tears. She said, 'And it was Rupert. Do you know, I never guessed. There was this ghastly reek of aftershave. I used to say he was capable of anything. But not that.'

'And her?' Vee said. 'Do you know her?'

Chris put her face in her hands again. A few moments passed before she looked up and said, 'I'd never seen her before that night.' The tears were gone now.

'Her face was made up pale, but she's – not white. Have you ever heard of someone called November?'

'No! No, never!' There was a shrillness in Chris's tone.

'You're sure?'

'Yes. Yes.'

'How did they get in?' Vee asked.

Briefly, Chris told her.

Vee said, 'Now I understand about your fortifications . . . your alarms . . . why you're so frightened.' Her tone was gentle.

Chris said, '*Frightened*? I'm not *frightened*. I'm just . . . sensible.'

'What did the police say?'

'The police?' The look Chris gave Vee was incredulous. 'Do you imagine I'd go to them? Do you imagine that I'd make something like this public?'

The tape had rewound. Now Vee pressed the eject button. The cassette emerged, and she put it in her bag.

Chris said, 'You can't take that away.'

'I can. I must.'

'To show to the police? I forbid you.' Vee was staring at her. 'Do you imagine I'd let them see it?'

Vee said, 'I'm baffled. I would have thought you'd want justice.'

'Justice. Oh, I want justice. But not *that* way. Give me the tape.'

Vee said, 'Perhaps later. But not now. I have to show it to Lucy.'

'No. No – she can't see it.'

'She needn't even know it's you. But I have to show it to her. To stop her marrying Rupert.'

In the silence that followed, the telephone rang. Chris picked up the receiver. 'Yes. Yes. Yes, I'm all right. But Belinda, please could you come round. Now. Yes, right away. I'd be so grateful.' She rang off.

Vee said, 'Belinda. Rupert's daughter?'

'Yes.'

'You don't propose to show it to *her*?'

'*No*! – what do you think I am?'

Vee said, 'I don't really know.'

'Whatever I am, I wouldn't be capable of *that* – her own father. No. I asked her round because I don't want to be alone.'

Vee said, 'I'm sorry.' Then she said, 'You must realize that I have to show this to Lucy.'

Chris said, 'Are there any other copies?'

'I doubt it. Though I can't be sure, of course.'

'Where did you get it?'

'I . . . broke into Rupert's flat.'

'*What*? When?'

'Yesterday. He's away.'

Chris was watching her, with a puzzled, measuring stare. 'I just can't understand why you're doing all this.'

'For Lucy.'

Chris grimaced. 'Can't she protect herself?'

'Against the man who's capable of what he did to you?'

Chris seemed not to hear this. She said, 'I know all about those Rivens. Pious snobs. Famous Catholics. And yet she's marrying a man who has been married three times before. Hypocritical bitch! Serve her right!'

'How can you talk like that? You don't even know her. Awful things have happened to her too.'

Chris shrugged and smiled.

Vee sighed. 'There's no point in our going on talking. I think I'll leave now.'

After a moment Chris said, 'All right. But would you just wait till Belinda comes?'

'You don't want to be alone?'

'No.'

'I can understand that. And I appreciate what an awful time you've had. Really. I just can't accept that you don't want to help Lucy. But of course I'll wait.'

'Thanks.' There was a silence. Chris still sat on the bed. Vee paced up and down. Then, from outside, came the unmistakable sound of a London taxi. Chris stood up and went to the window. Vee joined her. A young woman was getting out of the taxi, fast. She pushed money into the driver's hand.

Chris said, 'It's Belinda. Let's go down. I'll just dash ahead and turn off the alarm.' Down the stairs she ran, to press the buttons. She was opening the front door as Vee reached the bottom of the stairs.

There was the sound of the taxi driving off. Belinda said, 'I came as fast as I could,' as Chris pushed the door shut.

Chris said, 'Belinda – help me. This woman's trying to blackmail me. She's got something of mine in her bag. Hold her while I get it back.'

Belinda, nodding, looked eager. The two women closed in on Vee. But they had reckoned without her self-defence training. A chopping blow with her right hand sent Belinda sprawling; a thrust of her left made Chris reel into the drawing-room and fall. As Vee opened the front door, Chris screamed; it was the sound of pure rage. Vee slammed the door behind her. In seconds she was on the pavement, heading for her car at a run. She glanced behind her; she was not being followed.

As she entered the flat, the telephone was ringing. She picked up the receiver.

'Vee?'

'Oh, Lucy. I was going to call you.' She hesitated; then she said, 'How are you? What did the doctor say?'

'I've got some amazing news. Rupert will be back tomorrow—'

'You *told* me—'

'Don't sound so peevish. What I was going to say is that you'll be the first to hear – even before him. It's good news. Really it is. No one's going to be allowed to see it as anything else, though Mummy's going to be a problem.'

'Lucy, what *is* this? You sound sort of hysterical.'

'I'm not – not a bit. We're going to have to advance the wedding.'

'Advance it?'

'Yes – put it forward, have it sooner. Mummy will agree – she might even want to have it right away in the circumstances. But I should say in about a month's time. No white dress, but really that's only fair. Perhaps not even a Nuptial Mass, unless Rupert's received early.'

'Lucy!'

'Have you guessed? Don't sound so stricken. It's true – I'm pregnant.'

'*Pregnant*!'

'Vee, you sound quite shocked. You, of all people. I must say I never expected *you* to be shocked. *I* am, rather. I just didn't expect . . . But, well, it's God's will. I wonder how Rupert will feel. Oh, I do hope he'll be pleased. You're pleased, aren't you, Vee? Oh, I know you have to go back for your tour – is there any way you'd be able to slip away for the wedding?'

'No way,' Vee said.

'Oh Vee, I did so want you to be there.' Vee said nothing. Lucy went on, 'Are you bowled over? I suppose it is a bit startling. Especially as it was just that one time.'

'The sixth of August.'

'That's right. Even more of a red-letter day than I thought. I've been wondering for over a week – being always regular

284

as clockwork. So I had this test. Vee, aren't you going to congratulate me?'

Vee said, 'I'm dreadfully sorry, but can we talk later? *I'm feeling ill.*'

'Ill? Oh, I'm so sorry. What is it?'

'A . . . a sort of migraine . . . a blinding headache.'

'Oh . . . horrible. I didn't know you got those.'

'I don't . . . often.'

'Eva – at Rivers – gets them sometimes. She says the only thing to do is lie in a darkened room. Try that. And take some aspirin – though I don't think they help Eva much.'

'Lucy, I'll call you.'

'Are you sure there's nothing I can do?'

'Not a thing. And . . . thanks for telling me your news. I just can't talk any more now. Bye.'

When Vee put the receiver down, she sat in the dim room – only lit by the street lamps outside – for almost half an hour. Then she switched on the light, closed the curtains, poured herself a glass of wine, and telephoned James.

'Vee – I wanted to ring you . . . but I didn't want to disturb you, and you said you'd ring me. I thought you might be asleep.'

'I wish I were. Oh James, I went to Chris. She tried to get the tape away from me by force – she and your half-sister, Belinda.'

'What?'

'Anyway, they didn't succeed. But let's not go into all that now. I have the tape. I was going to show it to Lucy. But now I don't think I can.'

'Oh but Vee, you must. You've got to stop her marrying him.'

'Oh yes, I know that. But I don't think I can do it . . . with the tape. She's pregnant. How can I show it to her, when she's going to have his child? It's not as if anything in the world would make her have an abortion.'

285

'She's *pregnant*? By *him*?'

'Of course by him. And it only happened once. Oh James, when she told me – it was just now – I was stunned. I didn't know what to say. I even invented a migraine so that I wouldn't have to talk.'

'Poor Vee.'

'Poor Lucy!'

'You say she wouldn't consider an abortion? I thought you said she was a modern Catholic.'

'Oh, she is. In some ways. Women priests, married priests – she's open-minded about things like that. And, like a lot of her ancestors, she's often critical of the Pope. She's even in favour of birth control – oh, if only she'd *practised* it! But abortion – never. She believes it's murder. I don't think Lucy would have an abortion if she'd been raped by the devil himself. James . . .'

'Yes?'

'I've got to stop her marrying him.'

'Yes.'

'But I just can't show her that tape. There might be another way, though. I have to think.'

'Vee, shall I come up?'

'No, James. Just give me a bit of time. A bit of space. Please. I just have to think. Right?' Her tone changed. 'How's your mother?'

'A bit edgy. But . . . all right. She's going to those meetings.'

'Give her my love.'

Next evening – just before eleven – Vee dialled Rupert Deyntree's number. He answered the telephone after the third ring: 'Deyntree here.'

'Oh, it's Vee Westwood.'

'Why hullo. I wondered who it was – so late. I expect you want Lucy. She's just here. Hang on.'

'Oh!' Vee ran a distraught hand over her hair.

Lucy came on the line: 'Vee?'

'Hi, Lucy.'

'How's your migraine? I rang this afternoon, but you must have been out.'

'Yes . . . I went for a walk. It had gone by this morning – the headache.'

'I'm so glad. How did you know I'd be here? I didn't tell Mag. Actually I told her I'd be spending tonight at your place. Silly of me. Lying never pays. I expect you tried to get hold of me at Hampstead first. Did she sound surprised?'

'Actually I didn't call Hampstead . . . I just . . . guessed you'd be with Rupert.'

'Clairvoyant, huh? I just felt I had to be with him tonight to get up my courage to tell Mummy and Mag and everyone. None of the people I know seem to live in the modern world – I suppose I don't either. Anyway, I'm going to do all that tomorrow. I'll ring Mummy from here before I go back to Hampstead and chat to Mag.'

Vee said, 'And Rupert – is he pleased?'

'Well, it was a bit of a shock, I think. Poor darling! First my hair and now this. But he's bearing up wonderfully.' Lucy's laugh was happy. 'Let's talk on Monday. I'll tell you all about Mummy's reaction, and what we're going to do about the wedding. I think Rupert wants to be received right away – well, as soon as possible. It's all going to work out. I know it.'

'Yes, yes . . . well, bye for now.'

Vee dialled Rupert's number again next evening at ten. This time instead of 'Deyntree here,' he said, 'Hullo.'

'It's Vee Westwood.'

'Oh, I was certain it was going to be Francis – my old friend, Francis Larch. I expect you want Lucy – she went back to Hampstead this afternoon.'

'Actually, it's you I want to speak to. I have to see you – urgently.'

'Oh, really?'

'Tomorrow morning, in fact. And I'd advise you not to mention it to Lucy . . . for your own sake.'

'Goodness me. How intriguing. Tomorrow morning, you say? I expect you know I work from home when I'm in England. Would you like to come round here?'

'No, thanks. Isn't there somewhere near you where we could have coffee?'

'Coffee – where does one have coffee?'

'Surely you must have noticed some café in your neighbourhood?'

'Well, I think there's a place . . . Italian, perhaps – I don't mean the Firenze. This is just a café. In the Gloucester Road . . . practically opposite the tube station – a little further down towards the Brompton Road. Plastic ivy and formica tables. I've seen people having coffee in there, I think.'

'I'll find it. Half past ten?'

'Yes, that would be all right.'

'I'll see you.'

'Aren't you going to say "Take care"? So many Americans say that, and I'm never quite sure what it means. Not that you should look before you cross the road, as in the Highway Code, I think. Perhaps it's got something to do with "caring", which must be the most vulgar adjective ever invented. Probably American too.'

'I have to go now.'

'Goodbye.' He managed to ring off just before she did.

Francis exclaimed, 'Rupe! How very nice to hear you. Mother and I have been out. I telephoned a few minutes ago, but your number was engaged.'

'Yes. I'll tell you about that in a minute. Life's been extraordinarily hectic lately. I shall be a married man again within weeks.'

'Weeks?'

'Yes – Lucy's preggers. I can hardly believe I could have been so careless. Did you ever hear that slogan that was around when we were born, in the war? "Careless talk costs lives." Well, careless sex *makes* them. But what can one do? Lucy told Ma Riven today – you can imagine how unpleasant *that* was. And later she went to sob on the shoulder of that old bag, Mag. Well, not sob – she's not unhappy, but I think she's a bit sad about the wedding. Anyway she may as well have this Nuptial Mass she's so keen on. I'll leap straight into the arms of Rome. I know I can talk old Jessop into it. And we'll get married in that perfectly hideous parish church at Rivendale. You'll come up and be my best man, won't you, Francis? I shall need you, old friend.'

'Of course I shall.'

'Then that's settled. I suppose that ghastly Yank friend of Lucy's may be there. Though she's off on some rock tour soon – with luck she won't be able to get away. It's strange, you know. From the moment I met her, I couldn't stand her. And I'm absolutely convinced she feels the same about me. Loathing at first sight. But now something very odd has happened. Just before I telephoned you, she – this Vee – rang me up and demanded I meet her tomorrow morning. And she said I mustn't tell Lucy. I can't think what she's up to.'

Francis laughed. 'Not another victim of your fatal fascination?'

'Absolutely not. And she won't even cross my threshold. We're meeting for coffee in some appalling café. Francis, I must go now . . . but I'll let you know about this date with destiny. Meanwhile don't mention it to anyone – except your mother, of course. I know you tell her everything.'

'Well, *almost* everything.'

They both laughed.

The café – almost empty – was as he had described it. He was already there when Vee arrived. As she came towards the table he stood up. He was wearing a charcoal-grey sweater; it darkened his eyes. As they sat down, he glanced at a waitress, sallow and lumpy, in a black dress. She came to the table at once; her smile showed that she thought him delightful. 'What would you like?' he asked Vee. He was drinking cappuccino.

'Espresso, please.'

'*Un espresso, per favore*,' he said to the waitress, who smiled more and headed for the counter. 'And what can I do for you?' he said to Vee.

They were facing each other across the table. His slaty, beguiling eyes tried to establish contact. Vee picked up a little packet of sugar from a bowl on the table, and fiddled with it. She had given up smoking two years ago. She said, 'You've got to break it off.' She glanced up. His expression was puzzled and attentive. She went on, 'The engagement, I mean. I don't know how you're going to explain it, but you have to do it. A letter would be the easiest way, I should think and then . . . perhaps you could go away for a bit.'

'What are you talking about? Lucy and I are getting married – and very soon. I know she's told you she's pregnant.'

'Yes,' Vee said. 'That's why I'm not showing her the tape.'

'Tape?' The waitress came with Vee's espresso and a smile for Rupert which he did not see.

'Thanks,' Vee said to the waitress, who moved away. Vee said, 'The tape from the box at the back of your closet. The tape that was with Lucy's braid.'

Colour came – a dusky red – into his face. Then, just as suddenly, it ebbed; he was quite white: there were only the eyes. He said, 'What do you mean?'

'You know what I mean. When you get home, play the tape

290

I put in its place. One from your shelf. Then you'll believe me.'

'How did you get in?'

'I picked the lock.'

'I don't believe you.'

'Believe what you like. I have the tape. Or rather, it's in a place of safety. With a guy I know. After seeing it, I thought it would be wiser for me not to keep it around.'

Now their eyes met. It was she who looked away, taking a gulp of her espresso; perhaps it was its bitter heat that made her flinch. He said, 'Has anyone else seen it?'

'Only this friend of mine.'

He said, 'Of course there's nothing you could do with it. It's a bit pornographic, perhaps . . . but all just acting.'

'Oh yes? Then I can show it to Lucy?'

He said, 'You know she loves me. How can you do this to her?'

'How can I not?'

'I love her,' he said. 'And she's pregnant.'

'If she weren't pregnant I'd have shown it to her already.'

He said, 'It was years ago.'

'How odd that you haven't changed a bit!'

He said, 'Really, it was just amateur theatricals. Not at all what *you* think.'

'You expect me to believe that?'

He said, 'What are you going to do with it?'

'If you break off your engagement to Lucy and never see her again – nothing. I'll leave it with this friend of mine for safe-keeping. Just in case anything should happen to me.'

'Ah,' he said. 'The San Andreas fault.'

'That wasn't what I was thinking of. After seeing the tape. Anyhow, if ever you should try to get together with Lucy again, I promise *she*'ll see it.'

There was a silence. Glancing at his face, his eyes, she

almost flinched. She stiffened. She looked away. Then he said, 'You win.'

'Right. There's one thing I don't understand. Lucy's hair. Did you—'

He broke in. 'Lucy's hair – her wonderful hair? You think *I* did that. You're a fool.'

'I didn't say—' But he was standing up. By the window an elderly woman was sitting with a small dog on a lead. It started to bark. Then it lunged forward. The woman pulled it back. It was barking, straining. Vee stared. As she turned back Rupert was going out of the door.

Vee had never fainted in her life. At school – where fasting girls quite often fainted at early Mass – the nuns had told them to lower their heads to their knees to dispel giddiness. Now, as the dog barked and strained, and Rupert crossed the road outside the café, Vee lowered her head to the table top.

The barking had died away. Slowly Vee raised her head. The woman was scolding the dog. The waitress was coming towards Vee's table, with an inquisitive look: 'You all right?'

'Yes – I'm fine.'

'The gentleman has gone?'

'Yes. Yes. I'll pay for the coffee.'

On the gloomy platform of Gloucester Road Underground station – she had come by tube because of the Monday traffic and the difficulty of finding parking – Vee kept looking round. She did the same on the trains even after she had changed to the brightly-lit Victoria line. At Highbury station she slowed her pace to keep in sight of an elderly couple instead of striding ahead along the winding corridor. Out, at Highbury Corner, she glanced behind her before she crossed at the traffic lights, and several times as she walked along by the Fields; there was a frisson of autumn today, and one or two yellow leaves were drifting down. On the steps, she looked left and right before opening the front door; and upstairs in the flat, she locked the

292

Yale, something she had not done in the daytime.

That evening, when Sarah was at her meeting, Vee telephoned James: 'I saw your father alone this morning,' she told him. 'I arranged it yesterday. We met at a café. I told him I'd taken the tape and seen it, and that it was with a friend of mine. Oh, I didn't involve *you* – not in any way. I said I picked the lock of his flat, though I don't think he believed me.'

'You don't have to protect *me*.' James spoke hotly.

'Oh, don't be so macho. It's much better he shouldn't know. He tried to pretend it was all just acting. I didn't say anything about Chris. Or about November. Just that I'd show the tape to Lucy if he didn't break off the engagement.'

'And?'

'He agreed. He said "You win"!'

'Vee, he's dangerous.'

'Yes.'

'What have you done with the tape?'

'There's a sort of closet on the stairs here – not in the flat – with suitcases and things in it. I've put it there for the moment. But I'm convinced he believes I've given it to a friend to look after. Really. I put it in the closet more because I didn't want it in the flat than for any other reason. Oh, James.'

'Vee, sweet Vee. When am I going to see you?'

'I'm not quite sure. I don't know – since I saw that tape, I feel sort of numb. Oh, I do want to see you but . . . Anyhow, for the next few days, I've just got to be here. By myself. For Lucy. When he breaks it off.'

'But you'll be leaving soon.'

'On the twenty-second. That's another ten days.'

'Do you think you'll be able to come down here this weekend? It's your last.'

'Let's see how things go. With Lucy. I'll be in touch.'

'In touch. Oh Vee, I really love you.'

'Yes, James. We'll talk soon. Love to Sarah.'

Vee drank too much wine that night, and on the two that followed; it helped her sleep. When she tried to read, she put the book down after turning a couple of pages. She would switch on the radio or television, then switch off after a few minutes, head cocked as if listening for sounds in the building. She sat by the window for most of the day and, with her lights out, till late evening.

Lucy had said she would telephone on Monday; she did not do so, or on Tuesday or Wednesday. When James rang on Wednesday evening, Vee was monosyllabic and, after a few minutes, he said, 'I won't bother you. Ring me when you feel like it.' She sighed as she put down the receiver.

The door bell rang just before nine on Thursday morning. When Vee looked out of the window, she saw Lucy standing by the front door. She ran down to open it. Lucy plodded up the stairs, crying.

'Lucy, what's the matter?' Vee put her arms round her. For several minutes, Lucy was crying too much to talk. But at last, sitting next to Vee on the divan, she was able to. 'I didn't want to telephone you, with Mag there. So I just came round. I couldn't bear it any longer. Vee, Rupert's disappeared.'

'Disappeared?' Vee's voice sounded higher than usual.

'Yes. Completely. I'll tell you the whole thing.' Red-eyed and very pale, Lucy had stopped crying. 'I went back to Hampstead from Rupert's on Sunday, to tell Mag I was pregnant. She was really sweet – not like Mummy when I told her in the morning. *She* was horrible – she even said I'd behaved "like a shop-girl or a kitchen-maid". Can you believe it? In 1989?'

'Only of Mrs T,' Vee said.

'Anyway, Mag was really nice. She made me a cup of Ovaltine and treated me like an invalid. It was rather soothing, and I really slept well that night. I was very busy at the office. When I got home, I telephoned Rupert, but I only got the answering machine, and left a message. He didn't ring back, but I wasn't really worried. On Tuesday he had an appointment with Father Jessop in the afternoon and then he was going to take me out in the evening – picking me up at Mag's. Well, he never turned up. I rang him, but it was the answering machine again. After an hour or two, I telephoned Father Jessop – he said Rupert hadn't kept his appointment. Well, I thought he might have been involved in an accident or something. I didn't know what to do. But I waited till yesterday morning. Then I rang him once more. And this time I didn't get any answer at all. Just that high-pitched noise that usually means the telephone's out of order. So I rang enquiries, and they said it had been disconnected. I couldn't believe it. I went to work, but at about eleven I couldn't bear it any longer and I went round to the flat. The blind was drawn. I hammered away at the door and called out but there was no answer. And then that old lady on the ground floor who has his spare keys came to the window, so I made signs that I wanted to talk to her, and rang her bell, and she opened the door, and I asked her if she'd seen Rupert. She started asking me what I'd done to my lovely hair. I was almost hysterical. She said he'd been loading up his car with luggage and cardboard boxes: masses of stuff. It looked as if he was leaving. And she tapped on the window, but he just waved. And then he suddenly turned round and came to the door, and collected his spare keys. She said he seemed in a great hurry to get away. And I can understand that. I suppose she's lonely, poor woman and a bit dotty. She was burbling away about "his son". I don't know what she was talking about. Anyway apparently he'd told her he was going away. And I asked her if he'd said how long, and she said no. Well, I managed to get away – I was almost rude – and I went to the estate agent's, where he pays his rent. I know he has a three months' notice clause. And they said he'd been in and settled it up. I was really upset, almost crying and there was a young man there who was very nice. He said he'd been round to the flat with Rupert – you know, to check there wasn't any damage – and he said everything had gone, except the basic furniture – the flat was let furnished – and I made an awful fool of myself. I said I wanted to go round and see, and he took me. It was true. All his things – clothes, books, machines, videos, his picture – had gone. The young man told me he'd said he'd suddenly been transferred abroad. But, oh Vee, I can't believe that. He would have told me. It must have been because he didn't love me, because of my hair, because of the baby. Oh, Vee, what do you think?' Lucy gave one more shivering sob and was silent.

Vee spoke forcefully: 'I never liked him.'

'Oh, Vee, what do you mean?'

'It was instinctive. From the first. I disliked him – and I'm sure he disliked me. Didn't he?'

'Disliked you? Oh no, I don't think so. He used to make little jokes, sometimes. He always jokes about Americans. But that's just his way. I'm sure you're wrong. Oh, Vee I so much wanted you to like him.'

'Yes – but now haven't I been proved right not to?'

'Perhaps.'

'*Perhaps*?'

'Well, I still think there may be some other explanation. Vee, I *love* him.'

'Oh, Lucy!'

Lucy said, 'Could we have some coffee? And could I use your telephone? Before I go to the office.'

'You're going to work?'

'Oh yes, I have to keep on as usual. But I want to ring Oxford, and talk to Rupert's friend, Francis, now. I'll pay for the call.'

'Oh Lucy. For heaven's sake! I'll make the coffee.'

As Vee went into the kitchen, Lucy took an address book from her bag, and looked up Francis's number. He answered the telephone.

'Oh Francis, this is Lucy.'

'Oh hullo, Lucy.'

'You sound a bit harassed.'

'I was just on my way out, to give a lecture.'

'I won't keep you a minute. Francis, I really must see you. Could you possibly come up to London tomorrow, and have lunch with me? At that same place. It's really urgent. It's about Rupert.'

'Oh?' Then Francis said in an anxious tone, 'Is he all right?'

'He's not ill or anything. Could we talk tomorrow? One o'clock?'

'Yes. All right.'

'I'll see you then.' Lucy rang off.

When Vee brought in the coffee, Lucy said, 'I swept poor Francis off his feet. But I couldn't face going to Oxford. And I have to go up to Rivers tomorrow after work, I think, if Francis hasn't any news. He's Rupert's best friend. He loves him. So do I. Oh Vee, I wish you'd liked him. You can't understand how I feel.'

'I've been in love myself.'

'Yes . . . I know. But – we're different. You see, for me, Rupert's the only one. I must go now.'

The silence between them was a space. Vee said, 'I'll drive you.'

'No, no. It's all right.'

'Please.'

'No, really. I think I need to be alone. But thanks.'

'I'll call you tomorrow.'

'Well, tomorrow's going to be a bit of a rush. Of course I'll ring you if I have any news. But I've got work to catch up with, and then this lunch with Francis. And if he hasn't any news I'll got up to Rivers. To lick my wounds. And I suppose I'll have to tell Mummy.'

'Oh, Lucy!'

'Don't look so upset, Vee. We'll talk on Monday. Yes?'

'If that's what suits you.' Vee hugged her while Lucy stood, passive.

Lucy said, 'I'll see myself out.'

Vee went to the window, opened it, and leaned out. Lucy did not look up. Vee watched her walking, her back very straight, towards the tube. She slammed the window shut, and dialled James's number. Sarah answered: 'Oh, hullo, Vee. I'm afraid James is at the library.'

'Oh, Sarah, could I come down now? Right away. And stay for a couple of days. I promise not to be a nuisance.'

'A nuisance! My dear Vee, it will be wonderful to see you. And James will be thrilled.'

'Will he?'

'You know he will.'

'Sarah, please don't fuss about anything. Special cooking or anything. Please.'

'No, I promise. I'll be going to my meeting tonight. You don't mind?'

'Of course not.'

'James will look after you.'

Vee arrived at the cottage while James was still at work. She and Sarah had tea. She said, 'Sarah, you seem calmer.'

'Serenity's my goal these days,' Sarah said.

'Serenity!' Vee sighed. 'That's something I'll never achieve.'

'Why not?'

'Oh, I don't know. My feelings are all so confused. I'm so restless.'

'We have this prayer we say at AA. Oh goodness, I don't

298

know if I can quote a prayer . . . rather embarrassing.'

Vee laughed out loud. 'Oh Sarah, you're so British.'

'English. And I've never been religious. "Grant me the serenity to accept the things I cannot change, the courage to change the things I can, and the wisdom to know the difference." '

Vee said, 'I've heard it often. At AA meetings. But doesn't God come into it somewhere? "*God*, grant me" . . . and so on?'

Sarah said, 'Perhaps I'll get round to that in time.'

Vee said, ' "The things I cannot change" – what *are* they?'

'For me – my alcoholism. For you? I don't know – your history perhaps?'

'And how does a person know when it *is* wise to change something? Mightn't they be wrong?' But then a car stopped outside and Vee ran to the door: 'James!'

'Oh, Vee!' They embraced half way between the gate and the door.

When Sarah was picked up for her meeting, they were free to make love. But at first, for Vee, there were hesitations: 'I have these terrible pictures in my head.'

'The tape?'

'Yes.'

'It's over now. It's a disgusting old film. Chris is all right. Lucy's safe. He's gone.'

'And that woman?'

'Forget her. You took a decision to spare Lucy. You have.'

'And she's miserable. She's even sort of angry with me for criticizing him.'

'That'll wear off. When he doesn't come back. You know you had to save her.'

'Yes.'

'Now forget it all.'

Afterwards she said, 'The pictures went away. You were right.'

'Oh Vee, I love you so much. I so want us to be together.'

Vee said, 'Perhaps you could come to LA.'

'For a visit – perhaps. But I've got my work. Term's starting at the beginning of October. And I can't see UCLA wanting my thesis. Anyway, all my material's here. How about you getting a job in England?'

Moonlight came through the bedroom window, but she said, 'It's so dark.'

'Dark?'

'England, I mean. Oh I'm sure there's stuff like that tape in LA. And more crime of all kinds. But not that dark history, like you feel at Rivendale – and in London, too. It sort of presses in on you – it's claustrophobic. When I was a child, I always swore I'd get away from England as soon as possible. Oh, I don't know. We'll think it over.' Then she said, 'Sarah'll be back soon. Those meetings only last an hour. But I feel so much better . . . happier.'

Later, dressed and downstairs again, she said, 'It's strange – Rupert vanishing off the face of the earth like that. I thought he'd just break it off – perhaps go away for a bit – but not clear off completely. It's not as if Lucy would have pursued him, if he'd said it was over. She's too proud. As it is, she doesn't know what's happened . . . and she still loves him.'

'It's better this way – that he's gone for good.'

Next day, although Francis was ten minutes early, Lucy was already waiting in the restaurant. Now, in September, the tables and chairs were gone from the pavement, and Francis greeted her with the words, *'It is time for the destruction of error. The deck chairs are being brought in from the garden.'*

'What?'

Francis smiled at her blank expression. 'Just a quotation from Auden,' he said. 'I'm sorry. Rupe and I have this awful habit—' He broke off. 'You look exhausted. And I haven't even asked you what's the matter.' He said gently, 'A lovers' tiff?'

'Francis, he's gone. He's vanished.'

'What?' Then he said, 'I telephoned him yesterday evening, but it made this high-pitched sound. I thought he must have forgotten to pay the bill, and they'd cut it off.'

She told him what she had told Vee about Rupert's disappearance. Then she said, 'Francis, I can't understand it. But can you?'

He had looked amazed throughout her story. Now he said, 'No. I can't. I really can't.'

'When did you last speak to him? He told me you usually have a chat on Sunday evening.'

'Yes – we did this Sunday. He told me about . . . the marriage being put forward . . . and why. I hope you don't mind.'

'Of course not. Did he sound unhappy about it?'

'No. No. He asked me if I'd be best man. He said he was going to . . . convert to your Church right away. He was his usual exuberant self. No.' He paused for a moment. Then he said, 'No – there was nothing.'

'Oh, Francis. I keep wondering about so many things. He was so terribly upset when my hair was cut off.'

'Cut off? How do you mean?'

'Rupert didn't tell you?' He shook his head, and she said, 'How extraordinary . . . It was while he was away last month – just after you and I had lunch. All sorts of dreadful things happened. Apart from those telephone calls I told you about. Someone put a bag of blood through my letter-box.'

'*What*?'

'And then – just as I was getting onto the tube – someone cut off my plait.'

'Oh – no! Well, when you came to Oxford, I noticed it had gone. And I was rather sorry – it had been so wonderful, as I said to my mother afterwards. Though of course it still looks nice. But I had no idea—'

'That was when my friend Vee came over from LA to be with me – after my hair was gone. It was so sweet of her.' She paused. 'Now she says she didn't like Rupert and he didn't like her. Did he ever mention her to you?'

'Er . . . not that I can remember. Is she still here? In London?'

'Yes. Till the end of next week.' Lucy sighed. 'Oh Francis, what can have happened to him? Do you think he panicked at the idea of another marriage – after those three awful women who made his children hate him? And perhaps my being pregnant was just the last straw?'

'No. Oh, no. I told you how cheerful he was on the telephone.'

'And you don't think it was anything to do with . . . religious doubts? I would have understood.'

'No, I most certainly don't. As I say, on Sunday he was talking about converting early.'

'Yes, he had an appointment with Father Jessop on Tuesday. But you see, he never turned up.'

'I'm certain that wasn't it.'

'Then *what was it*? Oh Francis, I'm sorry to interrogate you like this. But I so want to know. It's not as if he had an accident or anything. He did all those things himself – moving, getting rid of the flat. Taking away all his things . . . his books, his Blake.'

'The Good and Evil Angels,' Francis said. 'That picture meant a lot to Rupert.'

'Yes, I couldn't quite see what.'

'I remember when he bought it – he was married to Sarah then – how excited he was . . .'

'But why?'

'Well, it's a remarkable work. But – oh, I don't know. I

302

remember once at Oxford he said his mother had been the good angel in his life, and his father the bad one. It was late at night. We'd been drinking. Next day I asked him what he'd meant, and he said that it was all nonsense, that he'd been drunk. I didn't think he'd been *that* drunk though. But Rupe's always been a bit cagey.'

'Cagey?' Lucy spoke the word uneasily. Then she said, 'I hardly know anything about his parents. I know they were divorced, and that his mother died at the time he left school, and he spent the year before he went up to Oxford with his father in Kenya, and his father died while he was there. Poor Rupert!'

'He didn't like his father much – he lived with a horrible woman, Rupe said.'

'Oh? I didn't know about her.' Lucy broke off. 'Oh, Francis, if only he'd written or something. You've no idea how awful it is just not knowing.' Then she said, 'You called him "cagey". Why?'

'Oh, well . . . I was really thinking about his work, I expect, when I said that.'

'His work?'

'Well, you know, his little missions for the government.'

'What missions?'

'Well, of course, he's a business consultant, but I think he did a little work for the government – on the side, you know.'

'Spying, you mean?'

'Well, not exactly. Helping the country.'

'He couldn't have *defected*?'

Francis's laugh was hearty and spontaneous. 'My dear Lucy, of course not. This is 1989. Anyway, I'm sure he's never had any connection with *Russia*. Africa, perhaps, at one time. And lately the Middle East.'

'So he could have disappeared for patriotic reasons?'

'Well . . .'

'Some dangerous mission that he just couldn't tell me about.'

'Lucy, my dear—'

She spoke with passion: 'I know it sounds far-fetched, but these things do happen. I'm sure they do. Don't they?'

'Well . . . I suppose.'

'Something very dangerous. And if it succeeds he could come back. And if it doesn't—' She paused. ' "We all owe God a death!" '

Francis's tone was dry when he said, 'I see you know your Shakespeare.'

'Oh, but I don't. I don't even know what play that comes from. My father used to quote it. He thought it was gallant, chivalrous. He always joked about chivalry but I think he did that to annoy my mother. Actually, I think he admired it. I think it was more real to him than it was to her. It's real to me too. Even when we were persecuted, we were always patriotic. I don't know much about the Middle East – those horrible Islamic fundamentalists and those ruthless Israelis. It all sounds so hateful and cruel and stupid, but I suppose there's room for a hero anywhere.'

Francis said, 'Lucy—' He glanced at her illuminated face, and stopped.

She said, 'Francis, please let's keep in touch. Whether we have news or not. You're Rupert's best friend, and you've helped me so much. Now I must go. I've a lot of work, and I'm going up to Yorkshire this evening to tell my mother that Rupert's gone. Oh, I won't say anything about this – don't worry.'

'I'm not – oh, please let me.' Lucy had snatched up the bill.

'*I* asked *you* this time.' She stood up. She smiled, raised a hand, headed for the cash desk by the door. Then she went to her office, and, at five, to King's Cross for the train to Darlington.

Francis went straight to Paddington, and as soon as he reached home, told his mother the whole story over China tea and a Victoria sponge. Then he said, 'Rupe seems to have behaved very badly.'

'Well, yes, I must say – with the girl pregnant.' There was a trace of disdain for the 'girl' in such a situation.

'But do you think I was right not to tell her about his meeting her American friend? I felt I'd be betraying his confidence.'

'Yes, of course. Your loyalty's to Rupert.' His mother's tone was soothing.

'You know, it even crossed my mind, knowing him – or perhaps never quite knowing him – that he might have run off with *her*. But Lucy says she's here. And I did believe him when he said he couldn't stand her or she him – Lucy confirmed that the woman didn't like him. Oh, dear! You know I can't help wondering – the hair and that bag of blood – if Jeanne Duval is involved. You remember all that business with Chris?'

'Of course.' Mrs Larch spoke with relish.

'If Jeanne Duval found out about Lucy, then . . . Oh, I begged him to tell her, and to tell Lucy about Jeanne Duval. But it was no use. Perhaps that's why he didn't tell me about those things that happened to Lucy.' Francis paused, then said, 'I wonder if he's gone off with Jeanne Duval.'

'Perhaps.' Mrs Larch shrugged. Then she smiled. 'He'll turn up again, like a bad penny.'

'But, Mother, really, he has gone a bit too far, this time. I feel so sorry for Lucy – the way she latched onto that idea of his being a hero. I'm sure Rupert's done Intelligence work most of his life, but nothing like what she imagines. The idea did seem to make her happier, though. Poor Lucy – deserted and pregnant.'

'Just like a Victorian novel! Well, she's old enough to know what she was doing.'

'You're such a very firm believer in the double standard,

aren't you, Mother?' Francis's tone was almost sharp. But then he sighed. He said, 'That very last time we spoke, Rupert said, "I shall need you, old friend." He was talking about the wedding. I was so touched.'

'He's very fond of you,' Mrs Larch said.

Francis sighed again. 'So I've always believed.'

On Friday and Saturday, Vee seemed gradually to unwind, though on the long walks she and James took, she often glanced behind her.

James said:

> *'Like one, that on a lonesome road*
> *Doth walk in fear and dread . . .*
> *Because he knows a frightful fiend*
> *Doth close behind him tread.'*

'Oh how horrible!' she exclaimed.

'But darling, there is no fiend. Look!' And indeed, over and around them, were only the vast Suffolk sky and huge unbroken wheatfields.

On Friday Sarah mentioned that she had always wanted a dog. 'Rupert hated dogs,' she said, 'and then later I just didn't think I could cope.' It was on Vee's suggestion, when she and James went shopping on Saturday morning, that they went to the RSPCA and bought a puppy with what Vee called 'bangs' and James called 'a fringe', from beneath which it gave timid but hopeful glances. A happy surprise to Sarah, it was fun for them all, and Vee laughed as they played with it.

At night she and James loved and slept in the double bed. But at two on Sunday morning she woke screaming from a nightmare; it was a long time before James soothed her back to sleep.

All along, Vee had been determined to leave on Sunday

morning. 'I have to be there for Lucy,' she told James.

'Can't I come with you?'

'No. It's impossible. Say Lucy turned up . . . and found out about you. I couldn't cope with that. But will you come on Thursday, for my last night?'

'Of course I will.' Then he said, 'I wish you'd brought the tape here with you. But you'll leave it with me when you go, won't you?'

'Yes.'

When they parted, Sarah said, 'You've saved my life, I think. Oh Vee, please come back. James will miss you so much. We both will.'

'Me too.' In the garden, there were dahlias, and the sharp smell of the first chrysanthemums had replaced the scents of summer flowers. James, Sarah and the puppy were at the gate as Vee set off.

She was in North London by early afternoon. The sky was grey. Although it was not cold, little gusts of wind, catching up dust and litter, gave the day a bleak feeling.

She drove straight to Tolland Road. She parked opposite Number 63, got out of the car, and crossed the road. She stood looking at the house. Behind the festoon blind, the curtains were still drawn. The closed windows were dull. She stood at the foot of the steps.

The front door opened. A young man carrying a musical instrument case came out, shut the door behind him, and came down the steps. He glanced at Vee, then headed for an old Volkswagen parked beside the house.

Vee said, 'Excuse me.'

He turned. He had a plump, pleasant face. Although still young, he was balding. 'Yes?' he said.

She came up to him and asked, gesturing towards the house, 'Do you live here?'

'Yes.' Then he frowned. He said, 'I suppose you're a journalist.'

'A journalist? No, I'm not.'

Evidently the surprise in her tone impressed him. 'Really?' he said, though he still looked doubtful.

'Really. Why should I be?'

'Well, I thought you might be. Though there haven't been all that many. One Sunday rag – and the local press of course.' Then he said, 'You don't know what I'm talking about, do you? But what *are* you doing here?'

She said, 'Do you know a woman called November?'

'You *are* a journalist.'

'*No.* I'm not.'

'Why are you asking about her then?'

'I wanted to see her. But – that place looks so closed up.'

'You're a *friend* of hers?' The look he gave her was astonished. 'You don't look like a friend of hers. I never saw her with a woman. Trish Pringle – she lives on the top floor – hated her like poison.' He was frowning again now. 'Are you a friend?'

'No – I've never met her. I'm – a friend of a friend.'

'Oh. Well, Dink's dead.'

'Dink?'

'She once told me her name was Dorcas, but she hated it. Everyone called her Dink. She was murdered.'

'What?'

'Yes.'

'When? Oh please tell me about it. Please.'

'All right. Well it was on the fifteenth of August – I'll never forget *that* date, after the police questioning. One night I was in the front room upstairs. Above the bay. And I heard this noise – banging about, and then a great thud. Well, there were often very odd noises from down there. If Trish had lived where I do – just above Dink – I can just imagine . . .' He left the

sentence unfinished. He was warming to the telling of his story.
'Goodness knows what she got up to down there . . . but I say
live and let live, and this place is cheap. Anyway, that night,
after the thud, there was silence. I didn't think any more about
it. I was practising the Mozart flute quintet. There's a very
tricky bit in the last movement, and I was going over and over
it. But there was this tom cat she used to feed, and I heard it
miaowing and miaowing, and I looked out, and it was on her
balcony. The balcony door was open – she always shut it when
she went out, of course – and I couldn't understand, if she was
in, how she could put up with all that miaowing. She was a
very irritable person. Well, two days passed, and her mail was
in the hall, and the balcony door stayed open, and this cat
kept on miaowing. And men came and rang her doorbell, and
then went away. Well I talked to Trish, and on the third day
we decided to ring the police, and they came round, and one
of them climbed in over the balcony, and she was dead in
the bedroom. Knocked out – apparently there was this great
bruise on her chin – and then suffocated with a pillow. It
broke . . . there were feathers everywhere. It was quite a story
in this Sunday tabloid – I think the police leak this stuff to the
press.'

He paused, at least partly for breath. Vee said, 'Go on.'

'Apparently she was a prostitute – well, I'd sort of guessed
that already. Sometimes she dressed like a real tart, though at
other times she looked quite ordinary. It was the way she
walked though . . . the way she looked at you. But apparently
it was sophisticated stuff. The wardrobe was full of fancy dress
and wigs and goodness knows what – whips and things. Even
a see-through mirror in the wardrobe door – and room for
someone to sit in there and watch what was going on. Well,
the police were busy for a few days, doing those things they
do, I suppose. Pics and finger-prints, though the paper said the
place had been ransacked and the bedroom had been wiped

clean. One of her clients did it – that's for sure. Well, the police watched the place for a few days. And, would you believe it, on Sunday, some old guy turned up with a live chicken. A present, he said. Funny present!'

Vee said, 'But they haven't arrested anyone?'

'Oh, no. I don't think they've got any idea . . . Probably they aren't too bothered. A prostitute, and Coloured, too. You know how they are. Anyway, I haven't seen sight or sound of them for the past week at least.' He paused. Then he said, 'So your friend – will he, or perhaps it's she, be upset?'

'Oh . . . I don't know. He hasn't seen her for a long time.'

'Would he be in South Africa – though you're from America, aren't you?' Vee nodded. 'She told me she came from South Africa – that she was a clergyman's daughter. You'd never have guessed it! But she and I got on all right. Oh, she was moody . . . but I quite liked her. She was . . . different. I really must go now. Got a rehearsal. Are you going to contact the police?'

'Oh no, I don't think I could help them at all. This friend of mine just asked me to give her his love.'

'Ah. Well, goodbye.' He got into the little car.

'Goodbye.' Vee hurried to her own car. Before John Tessier had even started his engine, she was gone, never glancing back.

In the flat, Vee lay on the divan in the sitting-room. She drank whisky from the confiscated supply brought from Suffolk. She was unused to spirits; she was drowsy when Lucy telephoned in the evening to say that she was staying on at Rivendale till Tuesday. 'I have to calm Mummy down. She's hysterical,' Lucy said. 'I've never known her like this.'

'When will I see you then? Tuesday evening?'

'You sound funny. Were you asleep?'

'No, no.'

'I don't know what time I'll be back on Tuesday. Let's

make it Wednesday. Or Thursday. Thursday's your last night, isn't it?'

'Thursday I'm seeing Jim. Lucy – you okay?'

'Wednesday then. Oh, I'm all right. You *do* sound odd.'

'No, no.'

'Well, I'll ring you on Wednesday to make arrangements. Goodbye, Vee.'

'Bye.' She fell asleep with her clothes on.

When she looked at herself in the mirror next morning, Vee slapped her own cheek: it was a vicious gesture. She bathed, scrubbing herself punitively; she washed her hair. She put on white clothes. Then she telephoned Michel Porter at her office.

'Good God!' Michel exclaimed when Vee told her what she had discovered at Tolland Road. 'How appalling. Most of these men who visit prostitutes are quite vile. And of course the police can't be bothered. They're so sexist, racist.'

Vee said, 'You hadn't heard anything about it – from your friend?'

'Oh, no – we're not in touch. Oh, what an awful story! But – there you are. And I think I must have been mistaken about Deyntree. He was away, you said. And really I had only a glimpse—'

'You said you could have sworn—'

'But then, remember, I said I *couldn't*. What's happened to your friend Lucy?'

'The engagement's off.'

'But that's splendid. Why did you go to Tolland Road?'

'Oh,' Vee said. 'Just curiosity.'

'Oh. Well, I'm so glad about the engagement being off. Why not ring Barbara and let her know? *Not* mentioning that *we've* spoken, of course. Then you could come round and tell us all about it.'

'Perhaps I'll do that.'

Vee did not ring Barbara, but that evening she rang Chris Deyntree, and kept getting the answering machine; she left no message. At half past eleven, the receiver was picked up.

'It's Vee Westwood here.' There was silence. Then she said, 'I've finished with that tape.'

'You mean' – Chris's voice rose – 'that you'll give it to me.'

'Mmm. There are just one or two questions I want to ask you. But if you'll answer them . . .'

'Oh, I will if I can.'

'I'm sure you can. I was going to suggest this evening, but it's too late now.'

'Oh,' Chris said, 'I'm wide awake – really. Why don't you come round right away?'

'No, let's make it tomorrow. And definitely not at your place. After my last experience there.'

Chris said, 'I'm sorry about that . . . I was upset. Now, it's quite different.'

'All the same, let's make it tomorrow. At the Rotonde. You know the Rotonde?'

'Yes. That café near the Angel. What time?'

'Let's say seven o'clock. All right?'

'Oh yes – fine. I'll be there.'

The café had a zinc counter, a sawdust floor, old French advertisements on the walls, uncomfortable wooden furniture and an expensive menu. Chris was sitting under a poster for Ricard. She stood up, smiling effusively, as Vee came in.

They sat down, and Chris said, 'You've got it?'

Vee opened her bag, to show the cassette in a cardboard sleeve. Smiling, Chris signalled to a waitress; they both ordered white wine. Vee said, 'Shall we talk now?' Chris nodded.

Vee said, 'I understand what you've been through. I know how that tape upset you. But you have to tell me . . . do you have any idea who the woman was?'

After a moment, Chris said, 'I thought it might be a woman called November. When I realized that it was Rupert – which I'd never imagined—'

'Why did you think that?'

'Well, Rupert and I were married a long time. We weren't happy, but we . . . got by. It was sort of convenient in lots of ways. And then one evening, the telephone rang. I answered, and this foreign woman's voice said, "Is Rupert Deyntree there?" And I said, "Who's speaking?" and she said, "Who the fuck are you?" And I said, "I beg your pardon – I'm his wife." And she shouted, "His fucking wife, you say? Tell that bastard Rupert, Dink's here – Dink November." Well, she was shouting, and Rupert was in the room, and he got up and came over, and took the receiver from me, and he said, "Hullo" and then "Dink, Dink," and he sort of gestured me away. Well, I was fuming and I stormed out into the hall, and paced up and down. And then a minute or two later, Rupert rang off, and then he came out into the hall and said, "I'm going out." And I said, "What the hell?" But he didn't take any notice. He went out and he didn't come back till six in the morning. Well, after that, it was over between us – really over. We hated each other. He was out most of the time, and then these funny things started happening. I nearly fell off a pavement – and I felt someone had pushed me. And when Rupert was away, abroad for a few days, on one of his trips, things came through the letter-box: shit once, and, next day, a bag of blood. And the phone kept ringing, and there was no one there. And when I told Rupert, he just shrugged. And that was when I finally decided I wanted a divorce. And we got one . . . though he really screwed me financially.'

'And Dink November?'

'I never saw her. But I got this private detective to track her down, following Rupert. He was always visiting her. In some squalid district. And she wasn't even white. But nowadays the law takes no account of how any filthy bastard behaves. He takes half the bloody money, even when most of it's yours.' Chris's voice and face were distorted with rage. 'And then he gets engaged to some young snob girl, and I thought "I bet he hasn't told Dink November about *that*"—' She broke off.

Vee said, 'So *you* told her. Yes, you did. I can see from your face.'

Chris said, 'Well, it was public knowledge, wasn't it? I just sent her the cutting.'

'Even after the things that had happened to you?' Vee stared at Chris. Then she said, 'You were lucky to have short hair.'

'Short hair?'

'Yes, Lucy's was cut off – she had beautiful hair.'

'And it was cut off – you don't say! That must have upset Rupert.' Chris laughed. 'He had this thing about hair. He was always trying to get me to grow mine. Once he brought home this ghastly wig he wanted me to wear. But I wouldn't do that kinky stuff.' Suddenly Chris's face became serious. She gave Vee a glance of alarm. 'You will give me the tape? I'm sorry about your friend, really . . . At the time, I thought . . . Well, I'd suffered – so why shouldn't she?'

'Yes, I'll give it to you. What are you going to do with it?'

'Destroy it, of course. Do you think I'd let anyone see it? But Christ, I'm going to find some way to make those two pay.'

Vee took the cassette from her bag; out came Chris's right hand to snatch it; there was a large solitaire diamond on the middle finger. Vee said, 'Did Rupert ever give you a ring?'

'A ring?' Chris who was putting the cassette in her pale Italian bag, glanced up.

'Two sapphire hearts?'

'Oh that thing? I thought it was tatty. I wanted a proper engagement ring.' She pointed to the solitaire. 'I paid for it. He took the other back.'

Vee stood up. She dropped money on the table. 'That should pay for my drink.' Then she said, 'You'll find it hard to "make them pay". Lucy's broken the engagement. Rupert has disappeared. And Dink November's dead.'

Chris gaped. When she stammered, 'B-but—' Vee had nearly reached the door.

Exhilaration seemed to charge Vee's rapid stride down brightly-lit Upper Street to Highbury Corner. But when she reached the darker terrace facing the Fields, she ran. She ran in the middle of the road, dodging aside for a single car that passed. As soon as she was in the flat she telephoned James; she told him of her visit to Tolland Road and then of her meeting with Chris.

'It's a maze,' he said. 'A maze of hell.' And then, 'I just can't understand your giving Chris the tape.'

Vee said, 'Oh, but I didn't. It was a blank cassette. I felt a bit guilty when I took it there. But not when I left. Anyway, her secret is safe with us!' Vee laughed; then she kept on laughing.

'Vee!'

She stopped. 'I'm sorry. I lost control for a moment.'

'I'd like to come to London now. To be with you till you leave.'

'No – I'm fine. I'm seeing Lucy tomorrow. Let's stick to Thursday. Like we arranged.'

Vee's and Lucy's last meal, like their first, was a curry. They ate in a different restaurant – the wallpaper in this one was purple – but the food was the same: chicken tikka, chicken masala, dahl, spinach bahji, rice, a paratha for Lucy and nan for Vee.

'Mummy was so awful,' Lucy said. 'I ought to have felt sorry for her – she was so upset. But I couldn't. She didn't seem to care about me at all. It was just the disgrace. I felt sure that, if we weren't Catholics, she would have wanted me to have an abortion. As it is, she wanted me to go to Switzerland – why Switzerland? – to have the baby in secret and then have it adopted. Of course I said no. I tried to make a joke at one point and I said, "Well I shan't be the last of the Rivens after all." And she said, "Oh yes, you will. This child won't be a Riven. It will be the bastard of a vile man." Then I was really angry. I said, "You must never ever call Rupert vile again." '

'You did?' Vee's eyebrows were raised.

'Yes, I did. You see, Vee, I'm quite sure that there's some good reason for what Rupert has done. Something he couldn't help, something he couldn't tell me, even though he loves me. And I know he loves me. I'm certain of it, Vee. Now I know I can trust *you*, so I'll just mention that when I saw Francis, he told me that Rupert does secret work. Work for the country. Dangerous work – perhaps so dangerous that I just can't be involved. I mustn't even know. Especially now I'm having a child.'

'Francis said that?'

'He implied it. And that's what I believe. Perhaps Rupert will come back. I hope he will. But if he doesn't, I'll know he's . . . well, a sort of hero. Like Peter Riven in the Pilgrimage of Grace. Like the Blessed Hugh.'

'You believe that?'

'Yes I do. Don't give me that blank stare, Vee. And *you're* not to criticize Rupert, either. You told me you didn't like him . . . but please don't mention it again. Dear Vee, you're my best friend. I love you. The only thing that could spoil that is you criticizing Rupert. Do you understand?'

Vee nodded. She said, 'I understand.'

'Then that's fine. And what about this musician of yours – this Jim that you haven't let me meet. Is it serious?'

Vee shrugged. 'You're the serious one, Lucy.' She laughed. 'Not me. Actually I don't know. He's a nice guy.'

'Is he going back to the States, too?'

'No, he works in England.'

'That's a pity.'

'Yeah . . . So, tell me what you plan – about having the baby, and so on.'

'I'll go on working as long as I can. And I'll have the baby at Rivers. If it's a boy, I'll call him Rupert Edward Hugh.'

'And if it's a girl? Not Veronica. I forbid it.' They both laughed.

Lucy said, 'No – I promise. Perhaps Teresa – for a second name . . . Teresa of Avila was an amazing woman. But not as a first name. Rupert's mother was called Angela. I rather like that – you know me and my Guardian Angel.'

Vee said, 'He seems to have been sleeping a lot lately.'

Lucy said, 'We don't know that.'

When they had driven back to Hampstead, Vee got out of the car to hug Lucy. There were tears on both their faces as they said goodbye. Intermittently, Vee kept on crying all the way back to Highbury.

Four

Vee was busy on Thursday. She returned the hired car: James was to drive her to the airport at eight next morning. She took washing to the launderette, and did some ironing. She cleaned the flat, bought flowers, and arranged them. She put Sarah's depleted bottles in the kitchen cupboard, and left extra money for the telephone. She packed her Haliburton. She re-hung the large crucifix over the bed.

James was due about six. At five, when she had bathed and changed, she fetched the cassette from the cupboard on the stairs. She put it in the VCR and turned it on. She sat down on the divan.

The effect on her was visibly worse this time. Perhaps she had become more vulnerable. Perhaps it was because she was alone that after a few minutes she started to gasp and gulp. Then a rise of uncontrollable nausea drove her to the bathroom where, kneeling on the floor by the lavatory, she vomited.

When she had finished, she washed her face and brushed her teeth. She rinsed her mouth with Listerine and re-applied her make-up. She went back into the living-room where the television screen was blank. She was crossing the room to turn it off when a new picture appeared on the screen.

A woman lay on a bed. The camera approached slowly; the

319

only sound was the deep breathing of whoever held it. The woman lay still – her eyes were shut – as the camera came closer. Now her head filled the whole screen. Her dark face was blanched and calm. The picture started to jiggle but she did not move. Her calm face, her closed eyes were drifted with feathers like a fall of snow. The screen went blank. Vee's doorbell rang.

After a moment or two, it rang again. Vee stood up, turned off the video and went to the window. James stood below. He was holding a bottle of champagne; Vee had put one in the refrigerator that morning. She went downstairs to open the door; a glance at her face banished his eager smile.

She had rewound the tape enough for him to watch what she had just seen. Then they talked in fits and starts; they drank, though James said, 'Champagne's an odd drink for a wake.'

She said: 'He must have just killed her. The bruise hadn't come up yet – the bruise from when he hit her before he suffocated her . . .'

She said: 'Now I understand why he disappeared like that – completely. He must have thought I'd seen the whole tape, seen the dead body . . .'

She said: 'Do you think this tape would be evidence?'

James said, 'The police must have taken photographs of her body. They'd see that this film was the same. Of course there's no proof that he made the film – though we found it in his flat.'

'And what a preposterous story *that* is.'

'The old lady saw us.'

'That dotty old lady . . .'

She said: 'I know when he did it. The fifteenth of August, that man at Tolland Road said. That was when Rupert came back, and when he saw Lucy's hair. You remember I told you he'd left early. He must have gone round to Tolland Road then.

After Chris – with the bag of blood and so on – he must have known that it was Dink November who'd cut off Lucy's hair.'

'And he killed her for *that*?'

'Just for that? No, I don't think so. Of course it would have made him furious. They would have quarrelled. Perhaps Dink said she'd tell Lucy everything about him. Surely *that* was why? He killed her. He filmed her. Then he took away the camera, the tape, the braid – and everything else that connected him with Dink.'

'Ugh.' James shuddered. 'How could he have *filmed* her?'

'Well, he's a voyeur. The mirror in the closet door, the cassette of Chris. He's kinky . . . beyond imagining. But perhaps he also wanted a sort of souvenir' – Vee winced – 'of Dink. I have this feeling he and she went back a long, long way. He knew her before he met Chris. It must have been in South Africa. That's back in the sixties. She could even have been the young girl Barbara saw him with in Cape Town.'

'Soon you'll be saying she was the only woman he ever loved.'

'No. Perhaps he "loved" Lucy too. The Good and Evil Angels.' There was silence.

She said: 'He's a murderer and a rapist. But we can't go to the police . . .'

Soon Lucy's friend and Rupert's son vied in giving reasons why they should not do this: reasons that ranged from Lucy's happiness and her child's future to Sarah's – perhaps still precarious – sobriety. They discussed Rupert's disappearance: the police might never find him; they had never found Lord Lucan. They stressed Dink's hateful role in the rape of Chris and her treatment of Lucy. As they talked, the evidence – what was there but the tape? – sounded less and less likely to impress the police or convince a jury. Vee and James were police, jury and judge; Vee and James at last pronounced the case dismissed.

321

James had a last demur: 'You could be in danger.' He paused. 'The terror by night . . . the frightful fiend . . .'

'James – stop it!' Vee emitted a laugh: not much of one. 'He's gone. He doesn't know I ever met Chris or heard of Dink. And he thinks I've given the tape to a friend.'

'You will. Tomorrow.'

'Yes, all right. I'll leave it with you.' She laughed – this one was better – and said, 'The San Andreas fault, you know.'

Death is known to arouse an opposing sexuality; towards dawn, they coupled desperately. Then tenderness came. 'I love you so much,' he said. 'Must you really leave me?'

'Now I must,' she said.

'But not for ever?'

'No – why for ever? Time will pass. I'll . . . recover. I shall miss you.'

'On the road?'

'So much noise,' she said. 'Noise on the road. Noise in the stadiums. Noise on the stage. Noise in the audience. Noise in bars, unwinding with the band after the show. Huge buses – sometimes you sleep in them if it's a one-night stop, and however tired you are, the noise seems to soak into your sleep. Perhaps the noise will drown you out, James.'

'Do you want it to?'

After a moment she said, 'No, I don't think so.' And then, 'There's bound to be a moment's silence somewhere. In the middle of the night perhaps, in a motel. Just a dog, barking in the distance maybe, and I'll wake and think of you. In the library with your Suffolk poet. Or in your garden.'

' "*The red rose cries, 'She is near, she is near'*;
And the white rose weeps, 'She is late';
The larkspur listens, 'I hear, I hear';
And the lily whispers, 'I wait.' " '

Then he added, 'Vee – I'll wait.'

For others, too, this was a time to wait. Belinda waited for her
heroine, Chris, to explain the truth behind their encounter with
Vee, and Barbara waited for Michel to confide whatever was
making her increasingly abstracted.

For some, it was also a time to plan. Sarah waited for a
future when the thought of a drink would never cross her mind;
meanwhile she planned her sobriety day by day. Chris often
studied her correspondence with the private detective she had
employed before her divorce. Several times she started to dial
his number, but halted half way and put the file back in her
cabinet; next day, however, she took it out again.

Lucy waited for her child's birth, and seemed to wait for
something else: she – like Francis, in Oxford – was first, each
morning, to pick up the post, first to answer a ringing telephone.
She planned – despite her mother's objections – to have her
child at home: at Rivendale.

A white, impersonal room gave particular intensity – an
awesome glow – to 'The Good and Evil Angels'. They hung
above the bed on which Rupert Deyntree lay for many hours
each day. Perhaps he waited; perhaps he planned. His
ceanothus-coloured eyes seemed to gaze at distant things while,
between his fingers, like a rosary, slid Lucy's golden rope of
hair.